Pseudo Callisthenes

# The History of Alexander the Great

being the Syriac version of the Pseudo-Callisthenes

Pseudo Callisthenes

**The History of Alexander the Great**
*being the Syriac version of the Pseudo-Callisthenes*

ISBN/EAN: 9783337247256

Printed in Europe, USA, Canada, Australia, Japan

Cover: Foto ©Andreas Hilbeck / pixelio.de

More available books at **www.hansebooks.com**

ܟܬܒܐ ܕܐܠܟܣܢܕܪܘܣ ܒܪ ܦܝܠܝܦܘܣ
ܡܠܟܐ ܕܡܩܕܘܢܝܐ ܀

# THE HISTORY

OF

# ALEXANDER THE GREAT,

BEING THE SYRIAC VERSION OF THE

## PSEUDO-CALLISTHENES.

EDITED FROM FIVE MANUSCRIPTS,

WITH AN

ENGLISH TRANSLATION AND NOTES,

BY

## ERNEST A. WALLIS BUDGE, M.A.,

FORMERLY SCHOLAR OF CHRIST'S COLLEGE, CAMBRIDGE, AND TYRWHITT SCHOLAR;
ASSISTANT IN THE DEPARTMENT OF EGYPTIAN AND ASSYRIAN ANTIQUITIES,
BRITISH MUSEUM.

EDITED FOR THE SYNDICS OF THE UNIVERSITY PRESS.

CAMBRIDGE:
AT THE UNIVERSITY PRESS.
1889

# THE HISTORY

## OF

# ALEXANDER THE GREAT.

The storie of Alisaundre is so comune
That every wyght that hath discrecioun
Hath herd somewhat or al of his fortune.

CHAUCER, *Canterbury Tales*, Group B, ll. 3821—3823,
or, Monkes Tale, ll. 640—642.

Seigneurs qui vivez à present,
Qui desirez ouyr cronicques,
Lisez Alixandre le Grant,
Qui dit chouses moult magnificques.
En luy chouses diverses orrez
Pour vous oster merencolye;
Car ses dits sont beaulx, bien narres
Par grans docteurs, je vous affya.
Ou romant les pourres vous veoir :
Chacun d'eulx y fait son devoir.

BERGER DE XIVREY, *Traditions Tératologiques*, p. XLVIII.

# PREFACE.

So far back as the year 1881 the late Professor W. Wright suggested to me that I should prepare an edition of the Syriac version of the Pseudo-Callisthenes and an English translation of it. I undertook this work in the hope that it would be useful not only to students of Syriac who will be glad of a new and amusing text to read, but also to the large and increasing number of enquirers into the folk-lore and legends connected with Alexander the Great who have not found time to learn Syriac, and to whom, necessarily, the contents of this ancient version are unknown. It may be argued that sufficient of the fabulous history of Alexander is known to us from the Greek text of the work which is attributed to Callisthenes, and from the Latin translations of it made by Julius Valerius and Leo the Archpresbyter. I am inclined to think, however, that a perusal of the Syriac version will reveal much of interest to the reader, and as it appears to represent a Greek text older than any known to us, that it will be of considerable help in determining one of the earliest forms of the Alexander story.

The Syriac text is edited from five manuscripts, the oldest of which was written about one hundred and eighty years ago: it has been divided into chapters which follow the order of the Greek text of Pseudo-Callisthenes published by Müller. The variant readings of the MSS. are printed at the foot of each page together with such emendations and corrections as it has been found possible to make. A few misprints have crept into the text and they are noted on pages 255, 256.

The English translation has been made as literal as possible, and only the most necessary notes have been added. Wherever I have been unable to translate a word the fact has been shown by dots.

The short Glossary which follows the English translation makes no pretence of being a complete dictionary to the book. In it, however, will be found such words as have been omitted in the Castle-Michaelis Lexicon and examples of words and forms which are given there without any references to places where they may be found; it is hoped that they will be useful to the beginner. In all cases the utmost brevity has been studied.

In the short introduction to this edition of the Syriac version of Pseudo-Callisthenes I have made a few remarks on some of the versions of the Alexander story based upon the careful works of Favre, Müller, Zacher, Berger de Xivrey, Spiegel and others. The Persian versions of the story I have not attempted to describe, for I have no knowledge of the language. Though late (A.D. 900—1300), they seem to me to be of considerable importance, for they in all probability represent Arabic originals which are no longer extant. Similarly I have not tried to discuss the story from the folk-lore point of view, for I possess neither the necessary knowledge nor the time.

The extracts from an unpublished Egyptian magical papyrus and the remarks on them have been inserted because they support the theory that the story of the magician Nectanebus being the father of Alexander the Great is one of Egyptian origin and composition. The chapter on Ethiopic versions of Pseudo-Callisthenes has been added, because, save for the short extract from the first chapter printed by the late

Prof. Wright in his *Catalogue of the Ethiopic MSS. in the British Museum*, p. 294, no part of it has, to my knowledge at least, been described or printed. It represents an Arabic original and is therefore of importance; besides this any new matter which helps to throw light on the history of the translations and age and travels of a book which has had more readers than any other, the Bible alone excepted, will be welcome. Zacher's observation with reference to the Syriac version of the Alexander story[1] applies equally to this.

My thanks are due to the German Oriental Society for the loan of the manuscript C, and to the American Oriental Society for their kindness in allowing me to have the manu-script B in my possession during the years in which this book was being prepared and was passing through the press. I am also much indebted to the Rev. Benjamin Labaree of Urmia, to Mr. Henry H. Lamb, British Vice-Consul at Scutari, and to Mr. Nimroud Rassam of Mosul, for the pains which they took in superintending the copying of manuscripts D and E, and for the numerous enquiries after ancient Syriac manuscripts of the Alexander story which they made at my request.

The Syndics of the Cambridge University Press have earned the gratitude of all Syriac scholars by their liberality in purchasing a fount of Nestorian Syriac type, which enabled the peculiar character and pointing of the Nestorian MSS. to be accurately reproduced; and my grateful thanks are due to Mr. C. J. Clay who has spared himself no trouble in the production of this, the first book printed in England in the Nestorian Syriac character.

---

[1] Diese Fragen erscheinen wol bedeutsam genug, nicht nur für die Alexan-dersage an sich, sondern auch für die orientalische Literaturgeschichte über-haupt, dass wir von den Kennern der syrischen und arabischen Literatur eine eingehende Würdigung und Erörterung derselben hoffen dürfen.

Zacher, *Pseudo-Callisthenes*, p. 108.

To the late Prof. William Wright I am most deeply indebted. He read through the whole of my copy of the Syriac
text and the English translation before it went to press, and I
had the great benefit of his unique experience and assistance in
correcting the proof sheets of the whole of the Syriac text of
the History of Alexander and of the English translation as far
as page 128. Throughout the preparation of this and other
works the ready helping hand, the judicious advice, and the
warm sympathy of my master were never wanting.

لَقَد جُدتَ لِي قَبلَ السُّوَالِ بِأنعَم    أتَتنِي بِلا مَطلٍ لَدَيكَ وَلا عُذرِ

فَمَا لِي لَا أعطِي ثَنَاءَكَ حَقَّهُ    وَأثنِي عَلَيَّ جَدوَاكَ فِي السِّرِ وَالجَهرِ

سَأذكُرُ مَا أولَيتَنِي مِن صَنَائِعٍ    يَخِفُّ بِهَا هَمِّي إنِ اثقَلتَ ظَهرِي

The acquaintance which began in March 1877 ripened, during
the five years in which I was his pupil, into a friendship
which grew stronger each year after, and was only broken
by his death on May 22nd, whereby the world lost one of its
few great Semitic scholars*, and I a true friend.

ܗܘܐ ܠܚܒܪܐ ܗܘܐ ܕܒܪܢܫܐ ܕܐܠܗܐ ܕܡܚܒܢܘܬܐ
ܘܕܚܟܝܡ̈ܝܢ ܐܝܟܪܐ ܘܐܟܠܦܘܗܝ̈ܐ ܠܐ ܚܪܝ
ܗܘܐ ܡܢ ܣܘ ܡܚܕܗ ܕܗܕܝܟܐ ܠܗܘܢ܀

E. A. WALLIS BUDGE.

LONDON,
    *November*, 1889.

* "Der bedeutendste englische Semitist und ein wahrhaft guter Mensch."
T. Nöldeke in *Deutsche Rundschau*, August, 1889, pp. 306—308. See also the
excellent accounts of his life and works by Prof. R. L. Bensly in the *Academy*,
June 1st, 1889, p. 378; by Dr. Neubauer in the *Athenaeum*, June 1st, 1889, p.
697; by M. J. de Goeje in the *Journal Asiatique*, 8ième Série, t. xiii. pp. 522—
529, and *Journal of the Royal Asiatic Society*, vol. xxi. N. S., pt. iii. pp. 708—713.

# CONTENTS.

# INTRODUCTION.

## DESCRIPTION OF THE SYRIAC MANUSCRIPTS CONTAINING THE HISTORY OF ALEXANDER THE GREAT.

THE text of the Syriac version of Pseudo-Callisthenes printed in this volume is edited from a manuscript in the British Museum (Add. 25, 875), and the variant readings printed at the foot of each page are taken from four MSS., of which the first and second belong to the American Oriental Society and to the German Oriental Society respectively ; the third and fourth are in my own possession. The British Museum MS. has been described by the late Prof. Wright in his *Catalogue of the Syriac Manuscripts in the British Museum*, London, 1872, Vol. iii. p. 1064, No. DCCCCXXII. It is of paper, about 8¼ in. by 6½ in., and consists of 362 leaves. The quires, signed with letters, are 36 in number. Each page is divided into two columns of 28 lines. This manuscript is written in a good Nestorian hand, with numerous vowel points, etc., and is dated A. Gr. 2020—21[1] = A.D. 1708—9. The History of Alexander the Great is the twelfth and last article in the MS., and its colophon runs as follows (Wright's *Cat.* p. 1069) :—

ܡܟܬܒ݂ܝܐ ܕ݂ܡܚܝܠܐ ܘܬܝܫܢܝܩܘܗ ܣܘܡܬܚܕ݂ ܘܙܡܬܚܩܘܐ ܘܟܓܒܗܝܕ݂ܘܗܐ

ܦܠܟܐ ܕ݂ܢܩܬ݂ܝܐ ܚܪ ܗܝܕ݂ܝܗܩܘܐ ܛܐܒ݂ܬ ܙܗܐ ܦܥܒ݂ܝܛܐ ܒ݂ܟܐ

---

[1] There are really two years ܐܝ̈ܠ and ܠܐܝ given in the manuscript.

ܕܫܩܠܐ ܐܘܢܐ ܐܢܐ. ܗܝܬ ܣܩܠܐ ܘܪܣܐܝܠ ܐܠܟܣܢܕܪ

"Here ends the history of the achievements and wars of Alexander the King of the Greeks, the son of Philip: [written] by the hands of the wretched priest Yaldâ and the priest Hômô[1], brothers, sons of the priest Daniel of Alkôsh[2], in the year two thousand and twenty-one of the blessed Greeks [A.D. 1709], on the third day of the month of the first Teshrî, on the fifth day of the week [Thursday]. Everlasting glory be to Him who makes times and seasons pass away; and may the com-

[1] Hômô was a contemporary of the Catholic patriarch, Mâr Elîyâ, and the Metropolitan Mâr Îshô'yabh (A. Gr. 2024 = A.D. 1712). See Hoffmann, *Opuscula Nestoriana*, pp. iii, iv.

[2] Alkôsh, القوش, is a village of a few hundred houses situated about six hours ride to the north of Mosul, الموصل, along the road which passes Tell Kôf تل كيف, Batnâyê or Tyinâyê, and Tell Uskuf تل أسقف. For a description of these villages see Sachau, *Reise in Syrien und Mesopotamien*, pp. 359—369; and Badger, *The Nestorians and their Rituals*, vol. i. p. 104, p. 174. In Alkôsh the grave of the prophet Nahum is shown, and on the sixth of Îyâr (May) many Jews make a pilgrimage to the synagogue which is supposed to mark the resting place of his body. Tell Kôf, Syr. ܟܐܦܐ or "Stone hill," is described by a modern writer as ... For a description of Tell Uskuf, or as the natives call it, Tell Skîpâ, see مراصد الاطلاع (ed. Juynboll) vol. i. p. ٢٠٩ and Yâkût معجم البلدان ed. Wüstenfeld, vol. i. p. ٨١٢.

...ssion and mercy of God be upon the writers and the man who ...ul this book written, the priest Joseph of Ḥôrdephnê'." This manuscript is indicated by "A" in the following pages; those belonging to the American Oriental Society and the German Oriental Society by "B" and "C" respectively, and those in my own possession by "D" and "E".

B is a paper manuscript, about 8½ in. by 6¾, consisting of 85 leaves. The quires signed with letters are 13 in number. One column of 20 lines occupies each page. This manuscript is written in a good Nestorian hand with numerous vowel points, etc., and is dated A. Gr. 2155, = A.D. 1844. It was given to the American Oriental Society by the Rev. J. Perkins, D.D., who had it copied from a manuscript found among the Nestorian Christians. Some pages of text from this manuscript, with a translation in English, were printed by Dr. Perkins and Dr. Woolsey in the *Transactions of the American Oriental Society*, vol. IV. pp. 359—440. Speaking generally, B and C agree closely in respect of omissions, etc.; I think, therefore, that these manuscripts were copied from the same original. They have, occasionally, better readings than A. On the margin of some of the pages of B are explanations in the modern Fellaḥî dialect of Urmia which I have given, as far as I was able, with the variant readings at the foot of the pages of printed text. It would be extremely interesting to have some particulars about the original manuscript or manuscripts from which these were copied, and with this object in view I wrote to my friend Dr. Benjamin Labaree of Urmia and asked him to make enquiries on this subject: he was, however, unable to trace the manuscript or manuscripts from which Dr. Perkins had caused his copies to be made. Wherever report said that a copy of the History of Alexander existed in Syriac he sent a messenger to make enquiries, but no satisfactory results followed these careful investigations.

The pointing of the proper names in this MS. usually

---

¹ حَرْدَنَّة and حَرْدْنَّين. See Yâḳût, vol. i. p. ٣٢٦; Badger, *The Nesto-rians and their Rituals*, vol. i. p. 254; Hoffmann, *Auszüge aus Syrischen Akten persischer Märtyrer*, p. 198, notes 1544, 5; Hoffmann, *Opuscula Nestoriana*, p. xiii; and Nachau, *Reise in Syrien und Mesopotamien*, p. 364.

agrees with that in A, and it also carefully marks *mârhḗṭând*
and *mĕhḏggĕyând*.  For example: ܘܗ p. 1. 4; ‫ܗܘܢ‬, ‫ܐܝܢܐ‬
p. 1. 10; ‫ܬܗܘܐ‬ p. 2. 3; ‫ܘܗܝ‬ p. 3. 12; ‫ܘܢܣܒܘܢ‬ p. 3. 15; ‫ܕܢܗܘܐ‬
p. 4. 1; ‫ܐܢܬ‬ p. 4. 5; ‫ܐܢܐ‬ p. 4. 7; ‫ܐܡܪܝܢ‬ p. 4. 17; ‫ܢܬܚܙܐ‬ p. 5. 12;
‫ܐܬܟܠܝ‬ ‫ܐܡܪܝܐ‬ p. 6. 9; ‫ܘܗܝ‬ p. 7. 16; ‫ܐܣܬܟܠܬܐ‬ p. 8. 15; ‫ܕܢܗܘܐ‬
p. 10. 4; ‫ܐܢܬ‬ p. 10. 11; ‫ܐܡܪܝܬܐ‬ p. 10. 20; ‫ܡܟܬܒܝܗܘܢ‬ p. 13. 4;
‫ܕܐܚܪܝ‬ p. 14. 5; ‫ܕܢܝܟܢܐ‬ p. 16. 3; ‫ܢܗܪܝܢܐ‬ p. 16. 11; ‫ܢܕܒܝܠܟܝ‬
p. 16. 12; ‫ܐܚܬܡܝ‬ p. 17. 4; ‫ܐܡܝܒܝܢܗ‬ p. 17. 10; ‫ܘܢܦܕܚܒܝܢܗ‬ p. 17.
18; ‫ܬܝܒܡܠܟܐ‬ p. 18. 20; ‫ܢܚܙܗܐ‬ p. 19. 15; ‫ܚܨܝܪܐ‬ p. 19. 20;
‫ܡܓܒܝܠܟܗܐ‬ p. 20. 4; ‫ܚܢܐ‬ p. 21. 6; ‫ܐܠܢܬܡܝܠ‬ p. 23. 4; ‫ܐܠܒܝܠܐ‬
p. 23. 7; ‫ܢܕܒܝܝܗ‬ p. 24. 15; ‫ܝܗܒܝܗ‬ p. 25. 1; ‫ܡܪܝܒܬܟܐ‬ p. 25. 12;
‫ܠܟܡܕܐܠܐ‬ p. 27. 3; ‫ܐܠܢܬܪܝܗ‬ p. 27. 9; ‫ܚܨܡܗ‬ ‫ܢܚܬܒ‬ p. 39. 9;
‫ܐܠܡܠܟܒ‬ p. 40. 11; ‫ܐܠܡܝܝܝ‬ p. 44. 10; ‫ܪܝܢܗܐ‬ p. 45. 3; ‫ܕܚܕܐܠ‬
p. 45. 13; ‫ܐܠܒܐܡ‬ p. 46. 4; ‫ܘܢܟܝܓܡܐ‬ p. 51. 15; ‫ܬܨܝܟܘܠ‬ p. 52. 2;
‫ܘܢܟܝܚܓܪܬ‬ p. 56. 11; ‫ܐܠܢܐ‬ p. 59. 18; ‫ܡܝܡܗܐܟܒܝܢ‬ p. 61. 12;
‫ܕܐܠܢܙܢܝ‬ p. 65. 11; ‫ܡܢܦܠܢܐܨܢ‬ p. 69. 13; ‫ܢܬܚܨܪܓܡܐ‬ p. 72. 10;
‫ܐܐܡܪܦ‬ p. 72. 13; ‫ܝܗܘܐܦܕ‬ p. 73. 17; ‫ܐܠܢܒܒ‬ p. 75. 16; ‫ܡܟܬܝܝܨ‬
p. 85. 7; ‫ܐܠܝܓܓܟ‬ p. 87. 3; ‫ܘܢܦܕܝܐܠ‬ p. 87. 17; ‫ܡܢܦܡܟܝܟܡܐܒܗ‬
p. 90. 1; ‫ܐܓܢܝܡ‬ p. 94. 3; ‫ܐܠܐܝܟܗ‬ p. 97. 20; ‫ܕܝܚܡܟܢܐ‬ p. 103. 10;
‫ܐܠܪܚܦ‬ p. 104. 7; ‫ܐܠܢܬܪܒ‬ p. 104. 8; ‫ܐܠܪܘܒ‬ p. 107. 2; ‫ܐܠܒܝܠ‬
p. 108. 2; ‫ܘܢܦܕܪܝܨܐ‬ p. 113. 4; ‫ܚܡܨܝܟܐ‬ p. 115. 2; ‫ܟܢܐܐܢܪ‬ p. 119.

 p. 264. 2;  p. 264. 8;  p. 266.
12;  p. 266. 16;  p. 266. 18;  p. 269.
12;  p. 269. 14;  p. 271. 11;  p. 273. 3;
 p. 273. 18.

In this manuscript  is usually written , with
 above; other words written with  above are  p. 11,
note 8;  p. 33. 21;  p. 165. 5;  p. 227.
7;  p. 230. 2; and  p. 239. 12. In this manuscript
words at the end of a line are frequently divided; Alexander's name is generally written in full, , while in
A it is most frequently contracted. The MS. is paged from  to
: the following is the colophon:—

 (sic) 
 p.) 

. (sic) 
 p.) 
(sic) 

 .p) 
. (sic) .
 .p) 
 (sic)
" Here ends the history of the achievements and wars of
Alexander the King of the Greeks, the son of Philip. To God
the Father who has aided, and the everlasting Son who has
assisted, and to the Holy Spirit the perfecter of all, be praise
and honour and dominion and exaltation and lasting gratitude,
now and ever, world without end.

" This book received conclusion and completion on the twelfth day of the blessed month of Tammôz, on the fourth day of the week (Wednesday), in the year two thousand one hundred and fifty-five of the Greeks (A.D. 1844). Glory be to Him who makes times pass away while He himself never passes away. Amen.

"It was written in the days of the admirable and energetic chief Shepherd, the wonderful and excellent director, pure and righteous and upright, the brilliant and illuminating star of the sky of the Church, rich and deeply versed in ecclesiastical doctrine, the wise sage and lawyer, thoroughly versed in the Holy Scriptures, and abundantly nurtured with their fruits, that is to say the understanding of them; the shepherd whose voice whistleth sweetly to his rational flock, and whose word driveth away the evening wolf like the smoke, Mâr Simeon the Catholic patriarch of the whole world. May his throne be established in justice and all righteousness, and may his arm be strong in victory which never . . . . . . . . . , that he may bind and loose in the height and in the depth, to the glory of his flock which is redeemed by the blood of the side (of our Lord), and to the pride of his people, who perpetually breathe the winds of his teaching. Amen.

"[This book was written] also in the days of the chosen shepherd and excellent governor and distinguished ruler, Mâr Gabriel the pious Metropolitan, the guardian of the throne of Addai[1] and Mârî. May he be strong and mighty in the victory that is without equal and without like, to the glory of the nation of Christ, and the pride of the congregation of Jesus, redeemed by the blood which flowed from the right side, poured out by the spear thrust in by the band of soldiers, through which there is for all who receive it life and everlasting pleasure. Amen.

"[This book] was written in the blessed and happy village of Sîr[2] near *Kula of the Sdhabe*[3] (i.e. the residence of the gen-

---

[1] See Assemâni, *Bibliotheca Orientalis*, t. iii, 1. pp. 229, 611, and Badger, *The Nestorians and their Rituals*, vol. i. p. 136.

[2] سير or سيرا . Dr. Perkins, der Senior der Urumia Mission, hat seinem bleibenden Aufenthalt in Seir, wo er auch das Seminar für die männliche Jugend leitet etc. See Sandreczki, *Reise nach Mosul und durch Kurdistan*, iii. p. 151.

[3] ܩܘܪ = Mr., صاحب . ܩܠܐ probably = قلعة *castle*, hence "the resi-

tlemen), which is founded and ordered and built by the side of
the most holy convent of Mâr Sargis and Mâr Bâkûs'; may our
Lord Christ make it to flourish, and guard its indwellers from all
secret and open injuries.   Amen.

"The deacon Aslan', the son of the deceased Muḥattas', the
son of Aslan, the son of Ḳârâ', the most wretched of all the
wretched, the most feeble of all the feeble, and most sinful of
all sinners, blackened, that is to say defiled and begrimed, these
pages.   Pr'ythee pray on his behalf that peradventure he may
obtain compassion from the Lord.   Amen.

"The priest Perkins, by race an Englishman, that is to say
from the country of America, the indefatigable and zealous
preacher and teacher and guide of the confession of Nestorian-
ism, took great pains and care to have a copy made of this book
of the History of Alexander the Macedonian King, that he might
read therein and profit thereby, and might benefit others.   He
has for a few years dwelt in a strange land in the country
of Urmi', with his American brethren in the spirit, Estâkan
Sâhab' [Mr. W. R. Stocking], Mr. Haldê [Mr. A. L. Holladay],
the doctor [Dr. Grant], Mr. Brayth [Mr. E. Breath], the printer,
Mr. Merik [Rev. J. L. Merrick], Mr. Estûdor [Lieut. Col. Stod-
dart], and Mr. Jûns [Mr. W. Jones]'.   These American brethren

---

dence of the missionaries."   Mr. Labaree says that the word لها is used in
modern Syriac for any dwelling surrounded by a high wall.

' Mr. Labaree tells me that the church of Mâr Sergius and Mâr Bacchus
is about one mile from the village of Sîr, سير

' Turk. ارسلان, "lion."   He died about the year 1877 being a very old
man.

' ܡܟܢܣ

' Turk. قرا or قره "black," but generally used with some other name.

' Urmi or Urmia is a district situated near the western shore of the lake of
that name in Kurdistân, and is the seat of the large and flourishing Mission
which was founded by Dr. Perkins and his companions, whose names are given
above.

' In Urmi Sâheb is used after the name, as in Hindustân.

' The names of the gentlemen inserted in my translation are obtained from
a perusal of A Residence of eight years in Persia, by the Rev. Justin Perkins,

forsook father and mother, brethren and sisters and kin, for the
love of our Lord Jesus Christ.  They came to this country
of Urmia, they opened schools, they opened a printing office[1],
they sowed spiritual seed in the field of the hearts of every one
who is in name a Christian; they forsook the earthly mammon
and loved heavenly riches; and the Lord God will give them a
recompense for their works, whether it be good or whether it be
bad.  Amen.

"Blessed be God, and His name be praised to all generations
world without end."

The manuscript C is dated A. Gr. 2162 (= A.D. 1851) and
belongs to the Deutsche Morgenländische Gesellschaft.  It is
of paper and consists of 196 leaves paginated from ܐ to ܩܨܘ;
a column of 18 lines occupies a page (page ܩܡܪ has only 15
lines and page ܩܠܗ has 19), and the leaves are 8⅛ in. by 6⅜.
Page ܐ has an illuminated heading, and through the pattern
endorsed on squares, the following letters are written around
the top and sides:

(1) ܠ ܐܬ ܘ ܡܟܬܒ ܢܐ ܗܕ ܣܒ ܠܐ ܘ ܢܒ ܗܘܐ ܘܡܢܐ ܙܢܐ ܐܝܟ ܚܛܦ ܡܝܟܕܐ.

".  .  . the feeble one, the sinner deserving of perfect wrath."

The quires, signed with letters, are twenty in number.  The
manuscript is carefully written, with points, etc., as far as
p. ܩܡܨ, but after this the writing is not so good, and some
of the pages appear to be by another hand.  It agrees generally
with B as to the text, but there are no glosses.  The pointing
has at times been carelessly executed, for example ܠܐܘ for ܠܐܘ;

ܘ̇ is used for ܘ in writing the same word in different places;
ܷ is confused with +; and the same proper name is often differ-
ently vowelled.  This manuscript was presented to the German
Oriental Society by the Rev. Justin Perkins in 1852.  It will be

Andover, 1813.  A very interesting life of Dr. Perkins was begun in ܙܗܪܝܪܐ
ܕܒܗܪܐ, p. 30, April, 1888.

[1] ܒܬܡܐ ܚܢܗ = ܕܦܘܬܟܢܬܐ

seen from the extracts given below[1] that he mentions having
made a translation of the History of Alexander the Great for
the American Oriental Society. This may exist in the Society's
Library, but I have never seen it. I only know of the translation of the extracts printed in the *Transactions of the American
Oriental Society*, Vol. iv. pp. 359—440. A description of this
manuscript was given in *Zeitschrift der Deutschen Morgenlän-
dischen Gesellschaft*, viii. ss. 835—837, by P. Zingerle. His
estimate of the relation of the Syriac text to those of the Greek
and Latin is very good, and is as follows: "Soweit ich es mit
dem Werke von Weismann verglichen habe, nämlich bis zum
13. Kapitel, welches die Geburt Alexander d. Gr. erzählt, ist
diese syrische Alexandergeschichte nichts andres als *eine Uebersetzung* des *Pseudo-Kallisthenes* und zwar nach der Bearbeitung
des Julius Valerius, soweit die von Weismann gelieferten
Auszüge in 2 Bande S. 227 ff. schliessen lassen; denn der syr.
Codex beginnt ebenfalls mit der Berühmtheit der Aegypter
in der Weisheit und den Wahrsagerkünsten .... Die Abweich-
ungen der syrischen Erzählung sind der *Hauptsache* nach (so
weit ich sie verglichen) wenig bedeutend: hie und da ein
verschiedener Name oder eine kleine Erweiterung, eine Abän-
derung von Nebenumständen."

The colophon is as follows:—

ܚܠܨܝ ܠܓܒܪܢ ܕܢܫܬܩܘܣ ܘܕܡܕܟܘܣ ܕܠܟܣܢܕܪܘܣ
ܗܠܟ ܢܘܢܐ ܕܩ ܦܝܠܝܦܘܣ : ܘܠܕܠܘܐ ܙܒ ܕܝܓܕܙ : ܘܠܚܕܪ
ܡܕܘܡܢ ܕܚܕ : ܘܠܕܘܡܠ ܕܡܘܪܟܐ ܠܦܢܕ ܚܠ. ܚܘܚܐ

---

[1] Aus zwei Briefen des Miss. Hrn. Perkins in Urmia, von 23. Mai und
1 Juni 1850. "Ich habe seit einigen Monaten *eine in syrischer Sprache abge-
fasste Geschichte Alexander's des Grossen* in Händen, von welcher ich in meinen
wenigen Mussestunden eine Uebersetzung für die American Oriental Society
ausarbeite. Wir fanden die Handschrift bei den Nestorianern, der Inhalt ist
ein Gemisch von spät-griechischen und muhammedanischen Erdichtungen."
*ZDMG* Vol. 4, S. 519. Aus einem Briefe des Mission. J. Perkins an Prof. Fleischer.
Orumia, d. 29. März 1851. — "Eine Abschrift der altsyrischen sogenannten
*Geschichte Alexanders* mit meiner nun fertigen Uebersetzung schicke ich an die
Amerikanische Morgenländische Gesellschaft. Eine andere Abschrift des Textes
für Ihre Gesellschaft will ich den Exemplaren unserer Druckschriften beilegen,
welche ich Ihnen statt der, wie es scheint, verloren gegangenen Sendung von
J. 1849 zu schicken gedenke." *ZDMG* Vol. 5, S. 398.

(ܥܟܡ p.) ܗܕܐܬ ܘܥܗܝܡ ܘܗܕܝܡ ܠܥܗܬܐܬ ܀

ܗܬܚܟܢܝܗ ܗܢܟܟܡܐ. (sic) ܕܗܕܡܐ ܕܬܕܗ ܥܟܐܗ ܟܬܢܐ ܟܠܒܟܠܕܐ
ܗܕܐ (ܥܟܗ. p.) ܝܚܬܢܟܟ ܗܝܚܕܚܟܩܗܟܟܒܝܗܕܐ ܣܥܚܐܬ. ܡܝܚܕ

ܠܝ ܚܕܬ݁ܝܪܘܿܦ.. ܐܡܝ ܀ ܬܕܝ ܐܠܗܐ ܐܒܐ ܡܥܿܕܪܢܐ ܠܘܕܘܕܝ.
ܣܕܡܐ ܠܠܠܡ ܚܠܡܝ. ܀ ܐܡܝ ܀

"Here ends the History of the achievements and wars of
Alexander the King of the Greeks, the son of Philip. To God
the Father who has aided, etc.

"This book received conclusion and completion on the ninth
day of the blessed month of Tammûz, on the second day of the
week (Monday), in the year two thousand one hundred and
sixty-two of the Greeks, *i.e.* A.D. 1851." From here to ܘܚܩܿܡܝ
the colophon is the same as in B.

From this point to ܐܚܕܐ ܒܝ ܚܝܿܚܕ, the colophon is the
same as in B; here however it continues: "The priest Aslan, the
son of the deceased Muhattas, the son of Aslan the son of Ḳârâ,
and the deacon Yûnân (Jonah) the son of Tamraz, the son of
Bâbônâ, the son of the deceased Muhattas, blackened, that is
to say defiled and begrimed, these pages, etc." A somewhat
longer list of names of the American brethren is given here,
viz., Mr. Stocking, Mr. Holladay, Mr. Wright, M.D., Mr. Breath,
Mr. Merrick, Lieut. Col. Stoddart, Mr. Jones, Mr. Kahran (Coch-
rane), Mr. Kavan (Coan)[1].

D is a paper manuscript, about 14 in. by 8½, consisting of
123 leaves paginated from ] to ܩܟܓ. The quires, signed with
letters, are 12 in number. One column of 22 lines occupies each
page. The manuscript is written in a fine, bold Nestorian
hand with numerous vowel-points, etc., and I owe the possession
of it to the kindness of the Rev. Benjamin Labaree, who spared
no pains in supervising the making of this copy from one in the
library of Dr. Shedd who was so kind as to allow it to be
made from that in his possession. The scribe, Ôsha'nâ, tells
us in the colophon that the copy from which he made it was
full of variant readings and mistakes, and that he corrected
these wherever he was able to do so. He gives, also, a copy of
the colophon of the manuscript from which D was made. The
colophon of D reads:—

---

[1] See Sandreczki, *Reise nach Mosul*, III. p. 142.

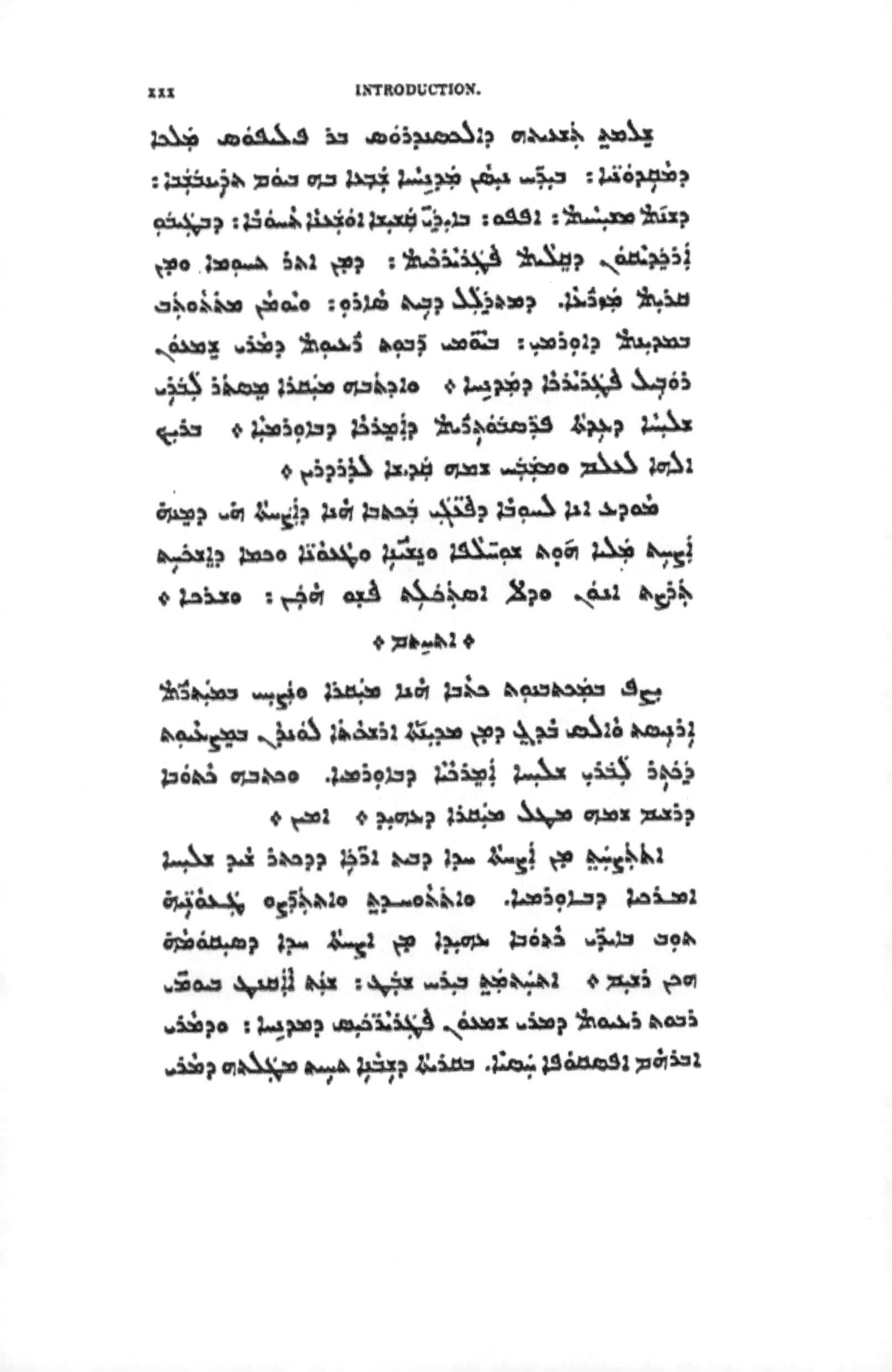

ܠܒܘܿܕܟܒܣ ܣܢܘܕܝ ܦܘܣܐ. ܚܕܬ ܟܬܒܬܝ̈ܗܘ ܘܠܡ ܐܬܒ
ܝܗܒܠܢ ܠܒܘܿܕܟܒܣ ܚܕ ܘܐܕܝ ܚܕ ܦܥܒܕ ܟܝܝ. ܘܚܝܠܝܗܘܣ
ܘܚܡ ܗܕܣ ܝܗܝܒܝ ܚܕܝܬܕܕܐ ܘܗܕܣ ܝܘܣܒܪܝܟ ܘܟܢܐ ܘܝܚܠ ܠܬܕ
ܘܕܝܢ. ܘܐܚܕܬܗ ܦܥܣܐ ܕܒ ܚܕܝܬܕܐ ܘܗܕܣ ܚܝܥܗܣܕ ܚܥܗܟܠܐ ٠

ܠܡܣ ٠

"Here endeth the History of Alexander, the son of Philip, King of the Macedonians. [It was finished] on the second day of the week (Monday), on the seventh day of the Eastern Nîsân[1] in the year of Christ 1886. [It was written] by the faulty Ôsha'nâ[2], who is by grace the archdeacon of the patriarchal chamber, and who comes from the land of Tĕḥûmâ[3] and from the village of Mazrâ'â, and is a kinsman of the house of Sârû, but who is to-day domiciled in the city of Urmî, in the days of the chief shepherdship of Mâr Shem'ûn Rôbîl[4], the patriarch of the East. Mr. Labaree, the honourable man, the missionary of the Presbyterian Church of America in Urmiâ had it written. Blessed be God for ever, and may His holy name be praised for ever and ever[5]!

"I hereby inform the kindness (lit. love) of those who come across this book that the codex from which I made this copy was full of variant readings and illegible passages and mistakes: these I have corrected as far as I was able, and those that I did not understand I left as they were.

"[This book] was copied from a codex in the library of Dr. Shedd the American missionary in Urmiâ which was taken,

[1] The scribe here uses the old style of calculation.
[2] He was a young priest from the mountains of Kurdistân and belonged to the family of Sârû. His native village was called ܡܲܙܪܲܐ݉ܟ݂ܐ Mazrâ'â.
[3] There are in this district, which is situated in the pashalik of Julamerk, four villages: Gûndiktâ, Mazrâ'â, Gâwâyâ and Birijai. When Sir Henry Layard visited this district Gâwâyâ was the largest village, and he says that it contained 160 houses. See *Nineveh and its Remains*, pp. 196, 200, 204; *Nineveh and Babylon*, p. 436.
[4] He was made patriarch in the year 1862.
[5] The next paragraph says that the copy was made for myself through the mediation of Dr. Labaree.

and the mistakes of which also were corrected by the scribe mentioned [below], from a codex the colophon of which was thus written :—' [This book] was finished in the month of Shĕbâṭ in the year [A. Gr.] 2159 [= A.D. 1848] in the days of the chief shepherdship of Mâr Shem'ûn, the patriarch of the East, and of the pious Bishop Mâr Abrâhâm, in the city of Shebânî[1] beneath the shadow of [the church] of Mâr Giwargis (George) the valiant martyr. The sinner Giwargis (George), the son of Zay'â, the son of Lâkîn, the elder, a kinsman of the house of Mâr Yôḥanân, the governor of Mâr Ḥazḳiail of Bânâ, which is near Dâryân, wrote these pages; and Rabban, the elder and governor of Mâr Bish'ô Kĕmôlâyâ[2], had the book written; Amen.'"

E is a paper manuscript, about 9¼ in. by 6¾, consisting of 160 leaves. The quires, signed with letters, are 15 in number. One column of 20 lines occupies each page. It was copied from an old Nestorian Syriac manuscript in a library at Alḳôsh and the work was "finished on the Sabbath (Saturday) of the 18th day of the blessed month of Tammôz, in the year of the birth of our Lord and Redeemer and King and Vivifier, Jesus Christ, one thousand eight hundred and eighty-six. Glory be to Him who makes times to pass away but who never passes away! Amen. It was written in the city of Alḳôsh, the city of Nâḥôm (Nahum) the prophet, which is founded and ordered and built by the side of the convent of Rabban Mâr Hôrmîzd[3], the Persian. It was written in the days of the pious fathers the distinguished rulers, the pure and excellent shepherds, Mâr Leo, the thirteenth of that name, the high-priest, the Pope of Rome, and Mâr Eliâ the Catholicus, the Patriarch of Bâbêl of the East, who is also the twelfth of that name. May Christ establish their thrones to the end of days in the prayer of the Apostles and

[1] Shebânî is in Tergawer, a Persian district on the border between Persia and Turkey; it is four hours' ride from Urmia.

[2] I.e., the man from Kamûlâ in Gezira. See Assemâni, *Bibliotheca Orientalis*, t. iii, i. p. 275; t. iii, ii. pp. 731, 732.

[3] For a description of sixteen monks who live in the convent of Rabban Hormizd and their convent; the destruction of the Patriarchal Library by the Kurds, ܐܠܟܪܕ; the grave of the saint, etc., see Sachau, *Reise in Syrien und Mesopotamien*, pp. 365, 366.

Fathers; Amen. The [above] mentioned Eliâ took pains to
have this book written. It was written by the wretched and
sinful deacon 'Îsâ the son of Êsha'yâ (Isaiah), son of the deacon
Ḳûryâḳôs (Cyriacus) from the city of Eḳrôr in the land of the
Sendâyâ. I entreat the distinguished readers [of this book] to
remember the scribe in their prayers, that compassion may be
shewn to him before the throne of Christ our Lord; Amen.
Blessed be God for ever, and may His holy name be praised for
ever and ever! Amen."

I obtained this manuscript through the kind offices of Mr.
Harry Lamb, formerly British Vice-Consul at Mosul, Mr. Hor-
muzd Rassam and Mr. Nimroud Rassam. The Chaldean
Patriarch took the greatest care to have the copy made by a
first-rate scribe, who was not only skilled in the mechanical part
of the work, but also possessed of a sound knowledge of Syriac.
When the copy was finished the Chaldean Patriarch collated it
with the original, and was, in this manner, able to make a few
corrections. Of the five MSS. A, B, C, D and E, E has the best
readings and agrees the most closely with A. I believe that
A and E were copied from the same manuscript. The colophon
of E is as follows:—

# THE EGYPTIAN ORIGIN OF THE ALEXANDER STORY.

FOR more than two thousand years the life and acts of Alexander the Great have been the subjects of numerous works and songs and poems, which have been written by many writers of many nationalities. The story of the deeds and of the events of his life has been eagerly received by every nation which it has reached, and the fame thereof has become so great that it has covered nearly the whole of the civilized world. It is not, however, the literal facts of the credible history of this king which have captivated the popular fancy of all nations, but the semi-mythical and fabulous legendary history which has sprung up round about them, and which has usurped the place of veritable history in the affection of the nations. While the careful work of Arrian[1] (written, it is true, nearly four hundred years after Alexander's death) has remained comparatively unknown by the side of the popular legends of Alexander which have found their way all over the world, the impossible history of Pseudo-Callisthenes has been translated into a large number of important languages and become known to all people.

Of the legendary history of Alexander, every version known to us is based upon the Greek history of him falsely attributed

[1] His Anabasis is based upon the lost works of the most trustworthy historians among the contemporaries of Alexander, such as Ptolemy, the son of Lagus, and Aristobulus, whose works he chiefly followed. See also Fraenkel, *Die Quellen der Alexander Historiker*, 1883; Petersdorff, *Beiträge zur Geschichte Alexanders des Grossen*; Droysen (J. G.), *Geschichte Alexanders des Grossen*; Sainte-Croix, *Examen Critique des Anciens Historiens d'Alexandre*, 1804; Petersdorff, R., *Eine neue Hauptquelle des Q. Curtius Rufus*, Beiträge zur Kritik der Quellen für die Geschichte Alexanders, 1884; Kaerst, *Forschungen zur Geschichte Alexanders des Grossen*, 1887; and Vogelstein, *Annotationes quaedam ex litteris orientalibus petitae ad fabulas quae de Alexandro Magno circumferuntur*, Vratislaviae, 1865.

to Callisthenes, his companion and friend. In translating this work the redactors of all nations have found opportunities for adding narratives of the marvellous, the fruits of their own imagination, and they, each and all, have helped to make the incredible history of Alexander by Pseudo-Callisthenes more incredible still. The Egyptians made him a hero and an Egyptian after their own fashion; the Persians asserted that he was a Persian; and the Christian writers from the sixth to the thirteenth century described him as a devout Christian, and as one worthy to be honoured by visions and commands from our Lord Himself.

The first book of the history of Alexander according to Pseudo-Callisthenes is certainly of Egyptian origin, and its birthplace was Alexandria. Colonel Yule places the composition of the work as far back as A.D. 200[1], but there is no doubt that the legends which are contained in it were current some hundreds of years before; indeed, some of them must have been known within a few years of Alexander's death. I am unable to say that it was originally written in Egyptian, but it is probable that it was. Even if it was actually written down for the first time in Greek, it must, nevertheless, have been the work of an Egyptian who wished to confirm and spread abroad in the minds of the people of Egypt the idea which a large number of the people of Alexandria believed, or at least wished others to believe, viz., that Alexander was the son of a former king of Egypt, and that for him to become king of their country was only what was right and proper. It would certainly never enter the head of Greeks to compose and promulgate a story which made the wife of one of their kings to commit adultery with a fugitive king of a foreign country, especially with the king of a nation which they themselves derided, nor is it likely that they would acknowledge the offspring of this adultery as their king. On the other hand, the improbability of the whole story and of the miraculous nature of its details makes it precisely the kind of fable which we should expect to receive from an Egyptian who wished to prove that Alexander was an Egyptian. In other words, the fable of

---

[1] *The Book of Ser Marco Polo the Venetian*, Vol. 1, Introduction, p. 110.

Nectanebus being the father of Alexander is a story quite in keeping with the other literary offspring of the lively Egyptian imagination which produced such stories as the *Tale of the Two Brothers*[1], *The Possessed Princess of Bechten*[2], *The Romance of Setna*[3], etc., and which, in the early times of the Coptic Church, imagined the marvellous events which we see described in the Life of Shenûti by Bêsa[4] and in the Encomium upon Pisentios, Bishop of Coptos, by Moses, Bishop of Keft[5]. Also the accurate description of Egyptian magical practices, the descriptions of the statues of kings and gods, the incidental allusions to the priests and gods of Egypt and to the customs of the Egyptians, make it certain that the man who composed the early part or the original book of the fabulous history of Alexander which was afterwards attributed to Callisthenes, was an Egyptian.

The story begins with the statement that the sages of Egypt were of divine origin and were masters of the powers of heaven and earth. They delivered their power over the elements to men by means of "invincible words" and by the powers of sorcery. The word "sages" naturally suggests the Egyptian name which was given to men who could read writing and who understood whatever science the Egyptians were acquainted with, viz., *reχi χet*[6], literally "knowers of things." These were the men who were called upon by the king in the *Tale of the Two Brothers* to explain to him the mystery of the lock of hair, and also by the king in

---

[1] For the Hieratic text see Birch, *Select Papyri*, ii, pl. ix—xix; for a hieroglyphic transcript see Budge, *Egyptian Reading Book*, pp. 1—27: and for an English translation see Renouf, *Records of the Past*, Vol. ii, p. 137 ff.

[2] De Rougé, *Étude sur une Stèle Égyptienne*, p. 97; for an English translation see *Records of the Past*, Vol. iv, pp. 53–60.

[3] Revillout, *Le Roman de Setna*, Paris, 1877.

[4] In *Monuments pour servir à l'histoire de L'Égypte Chrétienne aux iv<sup>e</sup> et v<sup>e</sup> Siècles*, ed. Amélineau, pp. 1–91.

[5] See Amélineau, *Étude sur le Christianisme en Égypte au Septième Siècle*, Paris, 1887.

[6] Brit. Mus. Papyrus Egypt. No. 10183, p. 11, l. 4. The form occurs in the stele of *The Possessed Princess*, l. 9.

the *Story of the Possessed Princess*, to decide what should be
done for the young woman who was afflicted by a disease
which was caused by an unclean spirit. *Rex χet* is a name
often given to scribes. In the Egyptian papyri which have
come down to us we find many specimens of the magical
names of demons and of the formulae which are referred
to by Pseudo-Callisthenes as forming the means by which
the powers of the Egyptian sages were handed on to mankind. In the 162nd chapter of the Book of the Dead[1]
various magical names such as

Uâurâuûaqersaânq and

Haqahaqahrà are quoted; and long
lists of such names are given both in Egyptian[2] and Greek[3]
magical papyri. In the Ethiopic version of the first chapter of
Pseudo-Callisthenes it is said that Nectanebus uttered the names
of the demons of the earth when he made use of his knowledge
of magic; the "fearful names" there alluded to remind us of
the abominable names of Āpepi the enemy of Rā[4].

Nectanebus, having acquired the knowledge[5] of magic, used
it in a remarkable way to preserve his country from invasion by
enemies. Whenever they came to make war against him he
used to go into his palace and overcome them from there by
means of magical practices. If they came by sea he took a
basin of water and set it in the middle of his room, and having

---

[1] Lepsius, *Das Todtenbuch der Aegypter*, pl. LXXVII.

[2] Chabas, *Le Papyrus Magique Harris*, p. 151.

[3] Leemans, *Papyri Graeci Musei Antiquarii Publici Lugduni-Batavi*, t. ii, pp.
123, 127, 145, 153. Many of the names of the demons and powers mentioned
in the Leyden papyri are found upon Gnostic gems in the British Museum
collection.

[4] See Brit. Mus. Egyptian papyrus No. 10188, page 16.

[5] It is difficult to discover how Nectanebus II., the last Egyptian king of
Egypt, obtained his reputation for working magic. There is nothing in
Egyptian history which, so far as I know, would explain the fact. Of the end
of this king we know absolutely nothing, but it is certain that at a very early
period he was considered to have been one of the most famous magicians.
Favre, *Mélanges d'Histoire Littéraire*, t. ii, p. 13, note 1. For the history of
Nectanebus according to the Egyptian monuments see Wiedemann, *Aegyptische
Geschichte*, p. 716.

made models of the soldiers of the enemy and of those of his own army, he placed them in models of ships which he set upon the water opposite to each other. He then took a rod of wood in his hand, and uttered magical formulae and the names of certain demons. Presently the ships would draw near to each other and the wax figures would begin to fight. If the figures which represented his own soldiers were victorious on the water in the basin his soldiers were victorious on the sea; but if they were beaten and the ships sunk, the same result would happen to his army if they attempted to fight. One day, by this means, Nectanebus discovered that the gods of Egypt had handed over the country to the invader, for his ships were scattered on the basin of water, and were driven hither and thither by those of the enemy; on seeing this he disguised himself and fled away.

The custom of performing acts of sorcery by means of wax figures was a very old one among the Egyptians. If a man burnt a wax figure of a demon in the fire and uttered certain prayers or formulae over it while it was burning, it was supposed to be efficacious in guarding him from the power of that demon. Frequently professional exorcists carried this practice to a farther extent and by substituting the figure of a person, upon which his name had been written, they were thought to be able to do serious bodily harm or even to cause death to the person whose effigy was burnt. This practice was not only very old but also very widespread, and we now know that it was regarded as a crime by the Egyptians themselves. The fragments of a papyrus discussed and partly translated by the late M. Chabas[1] tell us that a certain man, who was a superintendent of cattle, obtained a book of magic with which he was able to work dire effects upon his fellow-creatures. The book contained not only the formulae necessary for obtaining these results, but also directions how to proceed. His powers were supposed to be so harmful that finally he was brought before an Egyptian court of law, and accused of working harm to various people of the town. He was charged with having thrown spells ⟨hieroglyphs⟩ _sih_, upon men and

---

[1] Chabas, _Le Papyrus Magique Harris_, p. 170;

women; with having made figures of people in wax ⟨hieroglyphs⟩
⟨hieroglyphs⟩ *reθ en menḥ* and so causing paralysis of their limbs;
with writing love philtres ⟨hieroglyphs⟩ *nâu en
meri*; with having terrified ⟨hieroglyphs⟩ *seχennu*, men; and
with having generally applied himself to the working of sorcery
which Pharaoh did not allow any of his servants to do, and
which was "abominated by every god and goddess." It may
be asked why this man was prosecuted for carrying on magical
practices? We may perhaps find a satisfactory answer in the
148th chap. of the Book of the Dead, where it is expressly
stated that certain rites are not to be seen by anyone except the
king and the *χer ḥeb*, or precentor, and that no priest or
servant is to be allowed to see them in going and coming[1].
The fragmentary nature of the papyrus does not allow us to
see what the sentence passed upon the sorcerer was; but it shows
us quite clearly that we have in the person of the accused a
man of pursuits like unto those of Nectanebus.

In addition to his power of working magic by means of wax
figures and water this king knew how to cast nativities and to
send dreams and visions to men and women. In Book I. chap. 5,
we are told that when he wished to send Olympias a dream he
went out into the desert, and gathered roots of grass which, after
pressing and pounding, he used for sending a dream to her.
The Ethiopic version tells us that he made a fire of grasses,
that he melted into it a wax figure of Olympias, upon which
he had written her name, and that after he had muttered
certain incantations the god Ammon came to her in a dream,
and worked her will.

I have not been able to find in Egyptian papyri any instance
of working magic by means of wax or bitumen figures and water

---

[1] ⟨hieroglyphs⟩ . Lepsius, *Todtenbuch*, pl.
LIII, L 8.

analogous to that given above, but there are several passages
where magical effects are promised, if a figure made of wax is
burnt in the fire while certain formulae are recited. The following instances from an unpublished hieratic papyrus in the British
Museum (No. 10188) will explain the method of procedure in
such cases. The greater part of this papyrus is inscribed with
a composition entitled " The Book of the overthrowing of Āpepi
the enemy of Rā," which contains the following chapters :—

> Chapter of spitting at Āpepi.
> Chapter of defiling Āpepi.
> Chapter of taking a lance to smite Āpepi.
> Chapter of binding Āpepi.
> Chapter of setting fire to Āpepi.
> Book of overthrowing [Apepi] the enemy of Rā.
> Book of turning back Āpepi.
> Book of knowing the becomings of Rā.

In order to destroy the power of Āpepi, the demon of mist
and blackness, the enemy of Rā, it was necessary to say a
certain chapter of this composition "over an Āpepi written
upon new papyrus with green paint, and over a wax figure of
Apepi with his cursed name engraved and inscribed upon it with
green colour. Put it on the fire that the fire may burn the
enemy of Rā. Let a man put a figure on the fire at dawn, at
noon, and at night when Rā sets in the land of life. Put a
figure on the fire at the sixth hour of the night, at the eighth
hour of the day, at the arrival of evening until every hour of
the day and of the night, by the day of the festival and by day
and by month, by the sixth day of the festival, by the sixteenth day of the festival, and likewise every day. If this be
done Āpepi, the enemy of Rā, will be overthrown in the shower,
for Rā will shine and Āpepi will be destroyed in very truth.
The figure is to be burned in a flame of dried grass, and the
remains of it are to be mixed with dung and thrown into the
fire. A repetition of this is to be made at the sixth hour of the
night, at dawn on the eighth day. Āpepi is to be put on the fire,
and is to be spit upon many, many times at the beginning of

every hour of the day until the shadow comes round. After this must thou put Āpepi on the fire, spit upon him, kick him with thy left foot and then the roarings (thunders?) of the crocodile whose face is turned behind him will be repulsed. A repetition of this is to be made at dawn on the eighth day, for by it will Āpepi be slain at the *sekti* boat. A repetition of this is to be made when tempests boil in the east of the sky, when Rā sets in the land of life, in order that threatening clouds may not be allowed to arise in the east of the sky. A repetition of this is to be made many, many times in order that a shower and a rain-storm may not be allowed to arise in the sky. A repetition of this is to be made many, many times to keep away the shower, so that the sun's disk may shine and Āpepi be overthrown in very truth. It is good for a man to do this upon earth, and it is good for him in the underworld. Verily the man who does this shall attain to dignities which are above him, and he shall be delivered from every hateful and evil thing."

The following is the text with a literal translation :—

(Page 8, l. 6)

[This chapter is to be said over]

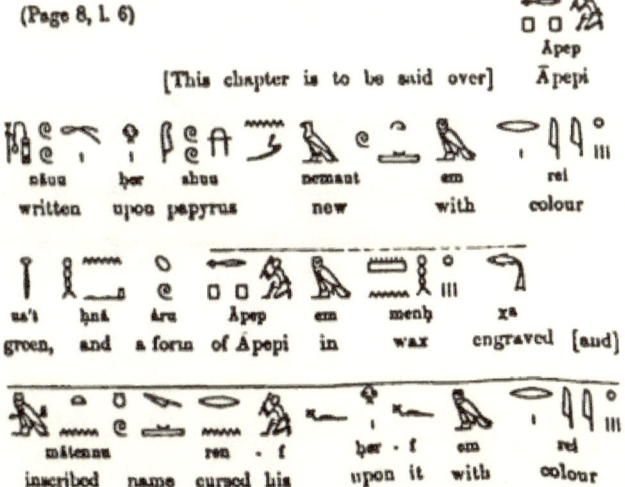

| nkua | her | shua | nemaut | em | rei |
|---|---|---|---|---|---|
| written | upon | papyrus | new | with | colour |

| ua't | hnā | āru | Āpep | em | menh | xa |
|---|---|---|---|---|---|---|
| green, | and | a form | of Āpepi | in | wax | engraved [and] |

| mitenna | | ren . f | her . f | em | rei |
|---|---|---|---|---|---|
| inscribed | name | cursed his | upon it | with | colour |

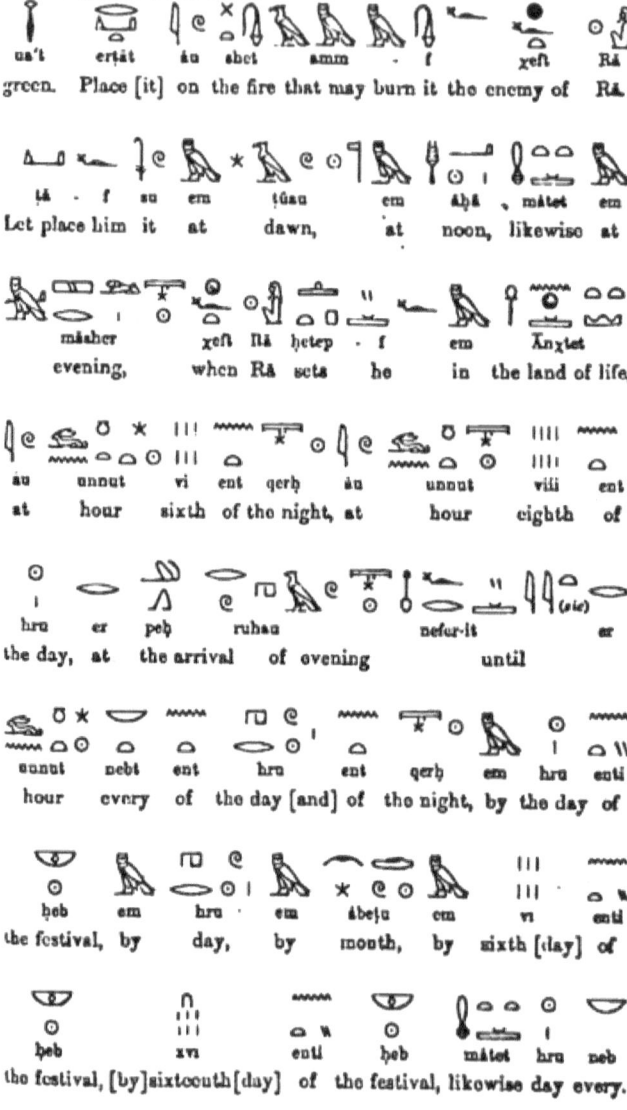

| ua't | ertât | âu | abet | amm | . | f | | xeft | Râ |
|---|---|---|---|---|---|---|---|---|---|
| green. | Place [it] | on | the fire | that may burn it | | the enemy of | | | Râ. |

| tâ | . | f | su | em | tûau | em | âbâ | . | mâtet | em |
|---|---|---|---|---|---|---|---|---|---|---|
| Let place him | | it | at | | dawn, | at | noon, | | likewise | at |

| mâsher | | xeft | Râ | hetep | . | f | em | Ânxtet |
|---|---|---|---|---|---|---|---|---|
| evening, | | when | Râ | sets | | he | in | the land of life, |

| âu | unnut | vi | ent | qerh | âu | unnut | viii | ent |
|---|---|---|---|---|---|---|---|---|
| at | hour | sixth | of the night, | | at | hour | eighth | of |

| hru | er | peh | ruhau | | nefer-it | | er |
|---|---|---|---|---|---|---|---|
| the day, | at | the arrival | of evening | | | until | |

| unnut | nebt | ent | hru | ent | qerh | em | hru | enti |
|---|---|---|---|---|---|---|---|---|
| hour | every | of | the day | [and] of | the night, | by | the day | of |

| heb | em | hru | em | âbetu | em | vi | enti |
|---|---|---|---|---|---|---|---|
| the festival, | by | day, | by | month, | by | sixth | [day] of |

| heb | xvi | enti | heb | mâtet | hru | neb |
|---|---|---|---|---|---|---|
| the festival, | [by] sixteenth [day] | of | the festival, | likewise | day | every. |

sexer     Apep         xeft       na   Râ   em
[Then] will be overthrown Apepi,   the enemy   of   Râ,   in

xapet  .   xer    pest   Râ   sexer   Apepi
the shower,   for   will shine   Râ   [and] be overthrown Apepi

em     an     mât   sennu   xet   pu    em     xet    ent
in     very   truth.   To be burned, to wit,   in   a flame   of

xemau          erṭât   sepu  .  f     er      xâa
dried grass.   Are to be given remains its   to   be mixed

xer    useah   amen   em   xet   ṇât   âru   xer - k
with   excrement [and] put   in   fire   one.   Is to be done by thee

mâtet    enen    âu    unnut   vi   ent   qerḥ   âu
the like   of this   at   hour   six   of the night,   at

ḥe't    vii   ent   hru     erṭât    Apep    er    shet
daylight   of the eighth   day.   Is to be given   Apepi   to   the fire,

pekaâs         ḥer . f     âaht   sep ii    em     ḥât
to be spit   upon [is] he   many, many times   at   the beginning

<hr>

¹ The words over which a line has been drawn are written in red ink on the papyrus.

| unnut | nebt | ent | hru | neferit | er | rer | xebit |
|---|---|---|---|---|---|---|---|
| of hour | every | of | the day | until | | comes round | the shadow. |

| ar | emxet | enen | heʻt | ri | ent | hru | erţát | xer-ek |
|---|---|---|---|---|---|---|---|---|
| After | this [at] day break | | | of the sixth day | | | is to be placed by thee |

| Ȧpep | ȧu | sbet | pekȧás | her·f | sȧnt | em |
|---|---|---|---|---|---|---|
| Ȧpepi | in the fire, | | to be spit | upon [is] he | and defiled | with |

| nemt·k | ȧb | xesef | hembemti | ent | hau |
|---|---|---|---|---|---|
| leg thy left, | | repulsed [are] | the roarings of the crocodile | | backward |

| ḥrá | | ȧrit | en | xer·ek | mȧtet | enen | ȧu |
|---|---|---|---|---|---|---|---|
| of face. | | Is to be done | by | thee | the like | of this | at |

| heʻt | vnu | ent | hru | xesef | Ȧpep | ȧm·f |
|---|---|---|---|---|---|---|
| daylight | of eighth day; | | | repulsed will be | Ȧpepi | by it [and] |

| ţebţeb | er | sekti | erţȧt | xer·k |
|---|---|---|---|---|
| slain | at | the *sekti* boat[2]. | Is to be made | by thee |

---

[1] Below the line, between ⟨hieroglyph⟩ and ⟨hieroglyph⟩, are the signs ⟨hieroglyph⟩.

[2] The *sekti* boat was the sacred boat in which the sun was supposed to sail across the sky in the morning; the boat in which he went to the place of his setting was called the ⟨hieroglyph⟩ *átet* boat.

| mátet | enen | xeft | pesáu | shenreá | em |
|---|---|---|---|---|---|
| the like | of this | when | boil | tempests | in |

| Àbtet | ent | pet | xeft | Rá | hetep·f | em | Ānxtet |
|---|---|---|---|---|---|---|---|
| the east | of the sky, | when | Rá | sets | he | in | the land of life, |

| er | tem | ertát | xeper | | teshert | em |
|---|---|---|---|---|---|---|

so that may not be allowed to become red threatening clouds in

| Àbtet | ent | pet | ári | xer·k | mátet | enen |
|---|---|---|---|---|---|---|
| the east | of the sky. | Is to be done by thee | the like | of this |

| áaht | sep ii | áu | tem | ertát | xeper |
|---|---|---|---|---|---|
| many, | many times | so that | not be | allowed | to become |

| xad | em | pet | temi | ertát |
|---|---|---|---|---|
| a shower | in the sky, and so that | not may be allowed |

| xeper | qerău | em | pet | ári | xer·ek |
|---|---|---|---|---|---|
| to become | a rainstorm | in the sky. | Is to be done by thee |

| mátet | enen | áaht | sep ii | er | xapet | er |
|---|---|---|---|---|---|---|
| the like | of this | many, many times | against | the shower, | so that |

peṣ | ȧtennu | seχer | Āpep | em | un
may shine | the disk | and be overthrown | Āpepi | in | very

mȧȧt | χut | en | ȧri · s | her ḥetep ta | χut | nef | em
truth. It is good for the doer of it upon earth, it is good for him in

neterχertet | erṭȧt | peḥti | en | se | pen. | er
the underworld. Is given | to attain | person | this | to

ȧȧut | ent | ḥer · f | neḥem · f
dignities | which [are] | above him, | delivered [is] he,

pu mȧ χet nebt bȧn | ta | em un mȧȧt.
to wit, from things all evil, | foul, | in very truth.

In order to overcome the fiends and companions of Āpepi it was necessary to recite a certain chapter of cursings "over an Āpepi with green paint painted upon new papyrus which is to be placed inside a case upon which his name is inscribed; tie up a case and put it in the fire every day. Kick it with thy left foot, spit upon it four times every day. When thou placest this form in the fire say, 'Rā triumphs over thee, O Āpepi; Horus triumphs over thee; and Pa-āa, life, strength and health! triumphs over his enemies' four times. Then must thou write the name of every devil male and female which thy heart fears, the name of every enemy of Pa-āa, life, strength, health! in life and in death, and the names of their fathers and mothers and children inside the cases; then put them in forms of wax and set them on the fire in addition to that with the name of Āpepi. Burn these when Rā rises, repeating the chapter the first time, at noon and at sunset while there is light at the foot of the mountain. Verily thou must recite this chapter over every wax figure; the doing of this is of great good (or of great power) upon earth and in the underworld."

The following is the text:—

(Page 13, l. 16)
| 'tetta | re | pen | her | Āpep | aiua |
|---|---|---|---|---|---|
| Is to be said | chapter | this | over an | Āpepi | written |

| her | ahau | nemaut | em | rei | ua't | ertā |
|---|---|---|---|---|---|---|
| upon | papyrus | new | with | colour | green | [and] placed |

| em | xenua | en | neset | āru | ren | - f | her | - f |
|---|---|---|---|---|---|---|---|
| inside | of | a case (?) being made | name | his | upon it, |

| senha | netat | tā | en | xet | hru | neb |
|---|---|---|---|---|---|---|
| bind, | tie | up [and] give [it] to | the fire | day | every. |

| aiu | em nemti - k | ābt | pekas | her - f | sep | ftu |
|---|---|---|---|---|---|
| Spurn | with leg thy left, | spit | upon it | times four |

| em | xerti | ent | hru | neb | 'kef | xer - k |
|---|---|---|---|---|---|
| in | the course | of | day | every. | Is to be said by thee |

| tā - k | sa | en | set | mātxeru | Rā | er - ek |
|---|---|---|---|---|---|
| [when] placest thou it | in the fire, | "Triumphs | Rā | over | thee. |

Āpep    sep    ftu    mâtχeru    Ḥeru    er    χeftı    .    f    sep

Āpepi, times four;    triumphs Horus    over    enemies    his, times

tu    mâtχeru    Pa-âa    ânχ    u'ta    senb    er    χeftı .

ur; triumphs    Pa-âa,    life, strength, health! over    enemies

f    sep    ftu    ȧs . k    nâut . nek    enen    ren

his, times four."    Now thou, writest thou    these    names of

seχeti    nebt    seχeti    nebt    senṭeti    āb . k

demons male    all and demons female all [which] fears heart thy

er    sen    em    χeft    neb    en    Pa-âa    ânχ    u'ta

at them,    enemy    every    of    Pa-âa,    life, strength,

senb    em    mit    em    ânχ    ren    sa    âtf . sen

health! in    death    in    life, the name of    father    their,

ren    en    mut . sen    ren    en    mesu

the name of    mother    their, [and] the name of [their] children

u-χenus    en    peset    erṭâi    en    āru    em    menḥ

inside    of    the cases    placed    in    work    of    wax;

R.

d

erȧt    ḥer    χet    ḥer-ṣa    ren    en    Āpep

place [them]  upon  the fire  by the side  of the  name of  Āpepi

am    χeft    Rā    ṭu·f    su    ka·k

and burn  when  Rā  gives he himself (*i.e.* rises). Repeatest thou

sep    ḥetepi    em    āḥā    en    Rā    χeft    Rā

[it] time  first,  at  standing  of  Rā (*i.e.* noon), when  Rā

ḥetep·f  em    ānχtet    āu    shun    ḥer

acts  he  in  the land of life,  whilst there is  light  at

uȧr    en    ṭu    āu    χut·nek    enen    āu

the foot  of the mountain. Is to be recited by thee this  over

semi    nebt    em    un    māt    χut

image  every  in  very  truth;  of great power [is]

ȧru·s    ḥer    ḥetep    ta    em    neterχertet

the doing of it upon  earth [and]  in  the under-world.

When Nectanebus wanted to send a dream to Philip he
adopted another method: he took a hawk, and having muttered
charms over it, sent it away with a small quantity of a drug,
and it showed Philip a dream. Here again I have not been
able to find any such custom noted in the Egyptian papyri;
but, judging from the minuteness of the description, there can
be no doubt this was one of the many practices resorted to by

he Egyptian sorcerer to shew people dreams. The design
ngraved on the ring which is described in Bk. I. Chap. VII.
vas, most probably, something like this;——

ach of these four signs is found engraved on gems and
carabaei.

Throughout the work Alexander is always spoken of as the
son of Åmen-Rā, and the accuracy of the references to him and
o this god is fully borne out by the hieroglyphic inscriptions.
His cartouches are ;——

and read *suten net setep Rā meri Åmen se Rā Aleksäntres se
Åmen*, "King of Upper and Lower Egypt, the chosen one of
Rā, the beloved of Åmen, son of the Sun, Alexander, son of
Åmen." Being the son of the god Åmen, who was frequently
represented on the sculptures[1] by a ram, it was only natural
that the two horns of this animal should be made attributes of
Alexander the Great, and that he should be called "two-horned."
In the Book of Daniel[2], though compared to a goat, he has only
one horn; the writer of the book must, however, have been
acquainted with the Egyptian notions concerning Alexander.
According to Arabic tradition he was called Two-Horned because of his having captured the two horns of the sun, that is,
the East and the West[3].

---

[1] 𓏏𓏏 and see Lanzone, *Dizionario di Mitologia Egizia*, tav. XX—XXV.

[2] Daniel, chap. viii.

[3] وسمي ذا القرنين لبلوغد قرني الشمس وهما المشرق والمغرب

ceck, *Hist. Dynastiarum*, text p. 96, Latin trans. p. 62. See also Korân,
surah XVIII, and Spiegel, *Die Alexandersage*, p. 57.

*d* 2

# THE VERSIONS OF THE FABULOUS HISTORY OF ALEXANDER.

## PSEUDO-CALLISTHENES.

THE work upon which all the legendary compositions relating to the history of Alexander are based is that of Pseudo-Callisthenes, which is thought to have been written in Greek about A.D. 200[1]. The Greek text of this work is extant in twenty manuscripts which have been enumerated and described by Zacher[2]. In the majority of them the name of no author is given, but some describe the narrative as the work of Καλλισθένης ἱστοριογράφος[3]. The text as printed by Müller[4] is edited from three MSS. in the Bibliothèque Nationale at Paris, which represent three different versions of the work, viz.:—No. 1711 (fonds grec) = A; No. 1685 = B; and No. 113 (suppl. grec) = C. The text in the first of these is very corrupt, but as a whole, it represents the original or Alexandrian form of the legend. In the second the differences between legend and history are made to be less marked, and the authorship of the composition is attributed to Pseudo-Callisthenes. In the third we have a modified and amplified redaction of the story which agrees oftener with B than A, in this respect resembling most of the other MSS. known to us[5]. The Greek text of a manuscript a

---

[1] Yule, *The Book of Ser Marco Polo*, vol. I. p. 110 (Introduction).

[2] Müller, op. cit., *Introductio*, p. viii. col. 2, No. 13.

[3] Pseudo-Callisthenes: *Forschungen zur Kritik und Geschichte der Aeltesten Aufzeichnung der Alexandersage*, Halle, 1867, pp. 7—25.

[4] *Pseudo-Callisthenes primum edidit* Carolus Müllerus, Parisiis, 1877.

[5] *Codex A* scribam arguit vel plane rudem et negligentissimum, vel cui oculis subjectum erat exemplar turpissimis vitiis ubique inquinatum. Ad pleraque corrupta et lacera sunt......Ipsa denique narratio uberior est de i rebus, unde quae prisca ejus forma fuerit intelligere liceat......Codices B et i

Leyden containing a version which follows A for the first nine chapters and B for the rest has been edited by Meusel[1]; it is of value for the study of the Syriac version. A German translation of the Greek codices A, B and C was published by Weismann[2].

It is improbable that any Greek text known to us represents the Alexander story as it was first written, but a study of the Syriac and Armenian versions and of the Latin translation of Pseudo-Callisthenes by Julius Valerius, which was made in the fourth century, will, in all probability, help us to restore it in many passages. M. Meyer thinks that, with the help of these versions, it can be restored to represent its form in the third century, for their variations represent Greek readings older than any that we have[3].

uti ætate non ita longe separati, sic oratione simillimi. Ubi res easdem eodem modo narrant, iisdem etiam verbis uti solent. Cetera indole valde differunt. Nimirum codex B narrationem habet quam cod. A breviorem. Alia omittit, alia contrahit, quædam mutavit et transposuit; nova præbet perpauca.—Contra codex C voluminis mole reliquos longe superat. Fundus narrationis ea est recensio quam sequitur cod. B. Nam quæ cod. B habet, eadem eodem ordine iisdemque verbis in C leguntur pæne omnia. At intercalata ille sunt alia multa, quæ ex diversis plane fontibus auctor corrasit. Pleraque ætatem redolent infimam, multa ineptissima; ac tanta est scriptoris negligentia, ut non modo pugnantia inter se proferat, sed cadem etiam bis vel ter repetat. Müller, Introductio, p. ix, col. 1, x. col. 2.

[1] *Pseudo-Callisthenes, nach der Leidener Handschrift herausgegeben,* Leipzig, 1871. Reprinted from *Jahrbücher für Classische Philologie,* t. v. suppl. iv.

[2] *Weismann, Alexander, Gedicht des zwölften Jahrhunderts, vom Pfaffen Lamprecht. Urtext und Uebersetzung, nebst geschichtlichen und sprachlichen Erläuterungen, so wie der vollständigen Uebersetzung des Pseudo-Kallisthenes und umfassenden Auszügen aus den lateinischen, französischen, englischen, persischen und türkischen Alexanderliedern.* 2 Bde, Frankfurt a. M. 1850. For other accounts of Pseudo-Callisthenes see Berger de Xivrey, *Notices sur la plupart des manuscrits grecs, latins, français, contenant l'histoire fabuleuse d'Alexandre le Grand connue sous le nom de Pseudo-Callisthenes,* in *Notices et Extraits des Manuscrits,* t. xiii., Paris, 1838, pp. 162—300; Frochetzr, *Histoire romanesque d'Alexandre le Grand, ou recherches sur les différentes versions du Pseudo-Callisthène* (in *Messager des sciences historiques et archives des Arts en Belgique,* 1847, pp. 303—486); Grässe, *Die grossen Sagenkreise des Mittelalters,* Leipzig, 1842; Favre, *Mélanges d'Histoire Littéraire,* t. ii. pp. 1—184; Fabricius, *Bibliotheca Graeca,* t. i. bk. 2, cap. 10, t. iii. bk. 3, cap. 2.

[3] *Alexandre le Grand dans la Littérature Française du Moyen Age,* Paris, 1860, t. ii. p. 1—7.

## THE LATIN TRANSLATIONS OF PSEUDO-CALLISTHENES BY JULIUS VALERIUS AND LEO THE ARCHPRESBYTER.

The history of Pseudo-Callisthenes has been translated into Latin by Julius Valerius[1] and Leo the Archpresbyter[2]. Julius Valerius is supposed to have lived about the third or fourth century A.D.[3] His work was one of the sources of the *Itinerarium Alexandri*[4], a work of unknown authorship, which was composed about 340—345 A.D., and it was through this version that the peoples of the north-west and west of Europe became acquainted with the fabulous history of Alexander. The oldest manuscript of the work is preserved at Turin, and was written about the end of the seventh or the beginning of the eighth century[5]. The Aesop mentioned in the titles of the work is generally thought to be the author of a very old recension of Pseudo-Callisthenes; Favre, however, considered his work to be quite distinct from that of Pseudo-Callisthenes, although many of the stories were common to both[6]. The Epitome of Julius Valerius was published for the first time by Zacher[7].

[1] The text has been published by Mai, *Julii Valerii res gestae Alexandri Macedonis translatae ex Aesopo Graeco.* In *Classicorum Auctorum e Vaticanis codd. editorum*, t. vii., Romae, 1835, pp. 61—215 and in *Bibliotheca Classica Latina*, ed. Lemaire, t. LXXIV. pp. 82—283; and by Müller at the foot of the Greek text of Pseudo-Callisthenes.

[2] The text has been published many times, but the most recent editions of it are Landgraf, *Die Vita Alexandri Magni des Archipresbyters Leo, Historia de Preliis......zum erstenmal herausgegeben*, 1885, 8vo; Zingerle, *Die Quellen zum Alexander des Rudolf von Ems*. In Anhange: Die Historia de preliis, 1882. 8vo. A work on the Historia de Preliis is being prepared by Dr. A. Ausfeld of Brüchsal.

[3] Mai, op. cit. p. xi.

[4] The text has been published by Mai, *Itinerarium Alexandri......edidit primus et notis illustravit A. Maius, nunc denuo publicat*, 1819 pp. 15—61. by Müller, at the end of Pseudo-Callisthenes, pp. 155—167; and by Volkmann Namburgi (no date) pp. 1—29. See also Kluge, *De Itinerario Alexandri Magni dissertatio*, Wratislaviae, 1861, 8vo.

[5] Meyer, *Alexandre*, t. II. p. 11.

[6] *Mélanges*, t. II. p. 22; Meyer, *Alexandre*, p. 18.

[7] *Julii Valerii Epitome zum erstenmal herausgegeben*, Halle, 1867.

The translation of Pseudo-Callisthenes by Leo the Arch-presbyter appeared for the first time in the xith century, entitled *Historia Alexandri Magni regis Macedoniae, de praeliis.* He had been sent on an embassy to Constantinople by John and Marinus, Dukes of Campania (914—965), and while there he spent his time in collecting books; among these was a Greek history of Alexander which the Duke John caused him to translate into Latin[1].

A Latin version of the History of Alexander, composed of a series of extracts from the works of Orosius, Josephus, Augustine, Bede and others, so arranged as to form a continuous narrative, was made in the twelfth century; it is usually attributed to Radulfus, Abbot of St Albans[2].

The Latin epic poem *Alexundreis* by Gaultier de Lille or de Châtillon is based upon the history of Alexander by Q. Curtius[3].

A small and late apocryphal Latin work which treats of Alexander's journey to Paradise is also known; the text was published by Zacher in 1859[4]. Some parts of the narrative, as, for example, the statement that Alexander was guided on his way through dark and unknown countries by a precious stone, remind us of the Ethiopic description of his journey in search of the water of life, in which we are told that a gem, which Adam brought out from Paradise, led him along the right path through the Land of Darkness (see p. cv.). M. Meyer admits[5] that the story may be of Hebrew origin, but he thinks that the traces of Christianity which are found in it do away with all chance of its being an exact translation of the Hebrew legend which makes

---

[1] The value of this translation has been discussed by Favre, *Mélanges,* t. II. pp. 67—77; by Meyer, *Alexandre,* t. II. p. 34 ff.; and by Zacher, *Pseudo-Callisthenes,* p. 108.

[2] See Meyer, *Alexandre,* t. II. pp. 52—63, and also his description of the *Compilation du MS. Douce,* p. 63 ff.

[3] See Ward, H. L. D., *Catalogue of Romances in the Dept. of MSS. in the British Museum,* Vol. I. p. 94. The poem has been published in Migne, *Patrologia Latina,* tom. ccix., 1855, coll. 463—572, and by Mueldener, entitled *M. Philippi Gualtheri ab insulis dicti de Castellione Alexandreis,* Leipzig, 1863.

[4] *Alexandri Magni Iter ad Paradisum,* Koenigsberg, 1859. This composition has been described by Favre, *Mélanges,* t. II. pp. 86, 87.

[5] *Alexandre,* t. II. p. 49.

Alexander attempt to enter Paradise[1]; he would place the date of its composition in the first half of the XIIIth century[2].

## THE ARMENIAN VERSION[3].

The text of the Armenian[4] version of the Alexander story was published at Venice in the year 1842 by the Mechitarist Fathers, who based their edition upon ten or twelve MSS. which were written during the sixteenth, seventeenth and eighteenth centuries. Among the undated MSS. was one which was illustrated with scenes in the life of Alexander, and which, from external evidence, was supposed to have been written during the twelfth or thirteenth century. This Armenian translation is considered to be a faithful equivalent of the Greek text from which it was translated, and to represent the oldest form of the work of Pseudo-Callisthenes; the Mechitarists place the date of this version in the fifth century and believe that it was made by Moses of Khorene[5]. Judging by the translations of parts of the contents given by Zacher it agrees closely with the Syriac version; and as it preserves in a fuller and better form many of the passages which are either given imperfectly or not at all in the Greek codex A and in the Latin translation of Julius Valerius, it is much to be desired that an Armenian scholar

---

[1] Eisenmenger, *Entdecktes Judenthums*, t. II. p. 331.

[2] See a discussion on the work by Israel Levi in *Revue des Études Juives*, t. II. p. 298; t. XII. p. 117.

[3] See Zacher, Pseudo-Callisthenes, pp. 85—101, and Favre, *Mélanges d'Histoire Littéraire*, t. II. pp. 34, 35. I am indebted to these works for the statements about the Armenian Pseudo-Callisthenes made above.

[4] *Padmuthiun Acheksandri Maketonazwui I Wenedig i dparani serbuin Chazaru.* Hami 1842 or "History of Alexander the Macedonian, Venice. At the printing press of Saint Lazarus, 1842." A notice of this work appeared in the *Hallischen Allgemeinen Literatur-Zeitung*, June, 1845, No. 129, ss. 1027—1029, and another by C. F. Neumann in *Gelehrten Anzeigen herausgegeben von Mitgliedern der k. Bayer. Akad. der Wissenschaften*, München, December, 1844, No. 250—252, coll. 961—965; 969—974; 977—968.

[5] The narrative of Pseudo-Callisthenes, or a similar history, was known to Moses of Chorene, for he says that Nectanebus was the last king of Egypt and that he was, according to some, the father of Alexander. See *Moise de Khorèn, histoire d'Arménie, texte Arménien et traduction Française*, par P. E. Le Vaillant de Florival, p. 178.

would undertake to make a translation of it into some European language. In a letter to Geier Dr. G. Petermann said, "Die Armenische Biographie ist, wie Sie ganz richtig vermuthet hatten, der *Pseudo-Callisthenes*, derselbe aber in der aeltesten Gestalt, oder wenigstens in derjenigen, welche der aeltesten zunaechst steht, ohne die vielen spaetern meist widersinnigen Zusaetze, ob er gleich auch wie alle andern Recensionen desselben des Wunderbaren Vieles enthaelt. Uebrigens ist diese Biographie, wie die armenischen Herausgeber ausdrücklich in der Vorrede bemerken—und wir mussen sie, die gelehrten Mechitaristen,...als die competentesten Richter in dieser Beziehung anerkennen—schon im 5ten Jahrhundert unserer Zeitrechnung uebersetzt worden ; auch hegen sie die Vermuthung, dass *Moses Chorenensis*, der berühmteste Armenische Geschichtsschreiber, der Uebersetzer derselben sei, so wie sie meinen, dass ebenderselbe auch die Chronik des Eusebius in das Armenische uebertragen haben moege." Müller, *Introductio*, p. x.

## THE SYRIAC VERSION.

The Syriac version of Pseudo-Callisthenes which has come down to us may be divided into three books or sections, which agree broadly with the three divisions which we find in the Greek codex A and with those of the Latin translation by Julius Valerius; these books or sections contain forty-seven, fourteen and twenty-four chapters respectively. The order of some of the chapters in Book I. is different from those in the Greek text, but the whole book substantially agrees with the Codex A.

In Book II. we have a lacuna of nearly eight chapters. The first sentence of Chap. VI. agrees with the first sentence of Chap. VI. of Müller's Greek text (p. 61, col. 1), but the Syriac then passes on immediately to Chap. XIV. of the Greek (Müller, p. 69, col. 1). This break can probably be accounted for by supposing that a couple of quires had fallen out of either the Greek or the Arabic translation of it from which the Syriac version was made.

Book III. corresponds generally with Book III. of the Greek text but omits the ten chapters which are interpolated into the Greek text of Codex A from the work of Palladius[1], Περὶ τῶν τῆς Ἰνδίας ἐθνῶν καὶ τῶν Βραγμάνων[2].

Although the Syriac work printed in the following pages agrees tolerably closely with the Greek text of codex A and the Latin translation of Julius Valerius, it will be seen on examining these versions that it cannot be considered a translation of either the Greek or the Latin or to represent any of the Greek and Latin texts known to us. Incidents which are extant in the Greek and are wanting in the Latin are found in the Syriac: similarly incidents which are extant in the Latin and are wanting in the Greek are preserved in the Syriac. For example the incident of the Egyptians enquiring of the oracle what had become of Nectanebus is given by the Greek and the Syriac, but it is wanting in the Latin of Julius Valerius. Also the augury of Nectanebus related in Chap. XII. of the Greek and Syriac texts is wanting in the Latin. Again the correspondence between Zintôs, Olympias and Philip, Alexander and Aristotle concerning the meagreness of the pocket money allowed to Alexander is given in the Latin and Syriac, but is wanting in the Greek text. The text of Aristotle's letter to Alexander in which he warns him not to undertake the building of so great a city as Alexandria, which is given in the Syriac, is wanting in both the Greek and the Latin texts. Other similar variations will be found in the second and third book of the Syriac version.

Of the Syrian translator of Pseudo-Callisthenes nothing is known. It seems most probable, however, that he was a Christian priest. Throughout his work he has used a number of rare words, and he appears, at times, not to have understood clearly the text before him[3]. Here and there he has turned a

[1] He is supposed to have been born in Galatia about A.D. 367; he was made Bishop of Helenopolis in 400, and died in the year 431.

[2] This work was first published by Joachimus Camerarius in *Liber Gnomologicus*, about the year 1571; it was afterwards printed under the name of Palladius together with S. Ambrosius, *De Moribus Brachmanorum*, and Anonymus, *De Bragmanibus*, by Sir Edward Bisse in 1665.

[3] See, for example, the description of an eclipse, Eng. trans. p. 95, and Müller, p. 121, col. 1.

passage in order to bring out a Christian sentiment. Thus
when Darius dies he makes him say, "In thy hands I leave
my spirit," a rendering which cannot have been made from the
Greek καὶ ταῦτα εἰπὼν Δαρεῖος ἐξέπνευσε τὸ πνεῦμα ἐν ταῖς
χερσὶν Ἀλεξάνδρου. (Müller, p. 78, col. 1.) It is clear that the
passage ܐܚܒ ܛܐܢܛܝ ܣܐܡܕ ܐܢܐ ܕܣܘܒ "My Father, in Thy
hands I lay my spirit" (S. Luke, ch. xxiii. 46), was running
in his mind. We have also "Shôshan, or Shûshan the fortress"
mentioned twice[1] where there is no original Greek from which
it could have been translated. Here the translator had in his
mind the הַבִּירָה שׁוּשַׁן, Chald. שׁוּשַׁן בִּירַנְתָּא, of Nehemiah i. 1;
and Esther i. 1; ii. 3, 5.

In Book I. chapter XXXI. we have a statement[2] regarding
the identity of Serapis and Joseph the son of Jacob. Now this
interpolation is clearly the work of the Syrian translator who
had obtained his information on this point from the works of
Christian writers. In the Oration of Meliton the Philosopher
addressed to Antoninus Caesar[3] we have it expressly stated
that "The Egyptians worshipped Joseph, a Hebrew, who was
called Serapis[4], because he supplied them with sustenance in
the years of famine," ܘܠܐܨܒ. ܚܒܝܢܐ ܐܢܐ ܡܝܢܐ ܘܐܪ
ܘܣܪܒܣ. and ܘܪܕܣܐ. ܚܣܬܝܐ ܚܟܚܣܘ܃ ܐܢܐ ܪܨܢܣܐ ܠܓܠܐ.
the same view is expressed by Tertullian[5], Maternus[6], Ruffinus[7]
and Suidas[8].

In the composition which I have called A Christian Legend

[1] Eng. trans. pp. 133 and 158.
[2] Eng. trans. p. 89.
[3] For the text see Cureton, Spicilegium Syriacum, p. ܒ
[4] The Egyptian form of this name is 𓏏𓇯𓊝 "Osiris was also worshipped under the form of Apis, the sacred bull of Memphis, or as a human
figure with a bull's head, accompanied by the name Apis-Osiris," Wilkinson,
Ancient Egyptians, ed. Birch, III. p. 86. "Apis was a fair and beautiful image
of the soul of Osiris," Plutarch, De Isid. 29, 80.
[5] "Nam Serapis iste quidem olim Joseph dictus fuit, de genere sanctorum,"
Ad Nationes, II. 8.
[6] De Errore Profan. Relig., cap. 9.
[7] In Auctores Hist. Eccl. Basil. p. 256.
[8] See in his Lexicon s.v. Σέραπις, ed. Gainsford, Oxford, 1834.

*concerning Alexander* the Christian translator betrays himself
by quoting a passage[1] from Jeremiah's prophecy concerning
the evil which shall come upon the land through the invasion
of the peoples from the north. Several other passages in the work
show that he was also acquainted with the prophecies which are
given in the Gospels, concerning the evils which should fall upon
the land of Judaea. Whether the writer of the metrical discourse upon Alexander and the gate which he built was Jacob
of Sĕrûgh or not is of little consequence here; it is so evidently
the work of a Christian translator that we need not discuss it
at all.

When the Syriac translation was made I am unable to say;
but I believe that we may assign it to some period between
the seventh and the ninth centuries. Professor Wright thought
that Syriac was not the native language of the translator, and
believed that he had only acquired it in the schools for the
purpose of studying the Bible and the Syriac translations of
Greek theological works; he believed that the Syriac version
of Pseudo-Callisthenes was made from an Arabic translation
of a Greek original, and placed the making of the work much
later than I have done, namely in the tenth century[2]. Zacher
placed the date of the making of our translation in the fifth
century[3]. An older Syriac translation may have appeared
in the sixth century, about the time when the first Syriac
translation of *Ḳalîlag wĕ-Damnag* was made; I do not, however, see any evidence in the Syriac translation of Pseudo-
Callisthenes which we have before us sufficient to justify us in
assigning the work to that early period. Whether we assign
the earlier or the later date to the translation it does not
appear that the value of the work as a means for helping to
restore the ancient form of the Alexander story will be im-

---

[1] English trans. p. 155.

[2] Wright, *Syriac Literature*, in the *Encyclopaedia Britannica*, vol. xxii. p.
850, col. 2.

[3] *Pseudo-Callisthenes*, p. 192. Wenn also die Abfassung des Julius Valerius
in den Anfang des vierten, die der armenischen Uebersetzung wahrscheinlich in
das fünfte Jahrhundert zu setzen ist, so würde die Abfassung dieser Syrischen
Uebersetzung vielleicht ebenfalls noch in das fünfte Jahrhundert fallen, in jene
Zeit, wo unter der Pflege der Nestorianer die Syrische Literatur in Edessa
blühte und durch Uebersetzungen aus dem Griechischen bereichert wurde.

paired. Also it is certain that the Syriac translation represents
one of the oldest forms of the story, older probably than any
other known to us.

The strongest evidence that the Syriac translation was
made from an Arabic translation of a Greek original is obtained from the Syriac forms of Greek proper names. The
Egyptian name Necht-neb-f (Nectanebus) is represented in
Greek by Νεκτανεβὼς and in Arabic by نقطنبوس [1]; the Syrian
translator reading by mistake نقطيبوس *i.e.* بـ for نـ arrived at
the Syriac form ܢܩܛܝܒܘܣ which we have throughout the
work. We have the correct transcription of this name
ܢܩܛܢܒܘܣ in Bruns, *Bar-Heb. Chron.*, Syr. text, p. 35, l. 19. On
page 20 (Syr. text), l. 8, we have the words ܪܡܚܐ ܩܪܢܐ ܡܚܒܐ
for the Greek κερασφόρος μηνί. The rendering of κερασφόρος
is sufficiently good, but what is ܡܚܒܐ? It seems that the
Arabic translator did not know what μηνί meant, and that he
transferred the word to his translation under some form like
مينا, which was taken over into the Syriac version under the
form of ܡܚܝܢܐ, which became corrupted into ܡܚܒܝܐ and ܡܚܒܐ. In
the next line we have the name ܐܢܕܝܡܝܢܐ for the Greek
Ἐνδυμίωνα. Now the Arabic form of this name would be
something like اندیمیونا, which the Syrian scribe probably read
ايدنمونا, and hence arrived at the Syriac form of the word
which we now have. On p. 52, l. 5, we have ܪܦܝܢܘܢ ܘܩܢܛܘܪܘܣ
for the Greek Λαπιθῶν καὶ Κενταύρων. The Arabic transcription of these names was probably رفینون نیلنطرون [2], the
translator not understanding the passage, which the Syriac
translator misread رفینون وتیلیطرون. On page 63, l. 5, the
total of Alexander's forces is given as two hundred and seventy
thousand: here clearly the Syriac translator read تسعین for سبعین.

---

[1] The form given by Bar-Hebraeus (*Historia Dynastiarum*, p. 89) is
نقطابیوس

[2] R for L as in the name Ḳandarôs = Candaules. Eng. trans. p. 121.

On page 70, l. 14, we have ܣܘܦܩܘܡܣ, for the Greek Σεσόγ-χωσις; the Arabic transcription of this word سيسنقوسيس was probably read by the Syriac translator as سيسيقوسس, hence the Syriac form which we now have. On p. 97, l. 4, we have ܠܐܒܕܐ for the Greek εἰς ᾿Αβδηρα. The Arabic transcription of the Greek would probably be بابدير, the whole of which the Syrian translator read as the name of the place and transcribed ܠܐܒܕܐ (with ܠ for ܪ). On p. 99, l. 3, the Syriac form of the name Croesus, Κροῖσος, is given as ܩܪܝܢܝܣ, which can only have arisen from the Syrian translator reading قرينيوس instead of قريسوس. The Syriac form of Κανδαύλης is ܟܢܕܐܪܣ, and as the Ethiopic form of this name is also Kandarôs, it seems certain that they are both transcribed from an Arabic original. It has been shewn that the Syrian translator, probably from the absence of points, misread ـج for ـخ and ـخ for ـج, ـز for ـر, ـس for ـش and ـس and ينية for ـس, and the following example of the confusion between ك and ن will be interesting. On page 242, line 5, we have ܦܪܝܣܩܣ, Prískôs, which is afterwards frequently written ܩܪܝܣܩܣ Krískos. An examination of the Index of Syriac forms of proper names will add considerably to the few examples given above of the confusion between the Arabic letters on the part of the Syrian scribe.

To sum up, then, the Syriac version seems to have been made from an Arabic translation of a Greek original by a Christian priest, whose native language was Arabic, some time between the seventh and the ninth centuries.

M. Jules Mohl believed[1] that Firdausi employed an Arabic translation of a Greek history of Alexander to complete the gap which he found in the traditions of his country. It is much to be wished that a manuscript of such an Arabic translation could be found, for there is little doubt that it would

---

[1] *Livre des Rois*, p. xlviii.

clear up many of the difficult passages which exist in the Syriac
version of Pseudo-Callisthenes.

To facilitate the comparison of the contents of the Syriac
version with the Greek texts of Pseudo-Callisthenes I have
added below a brief list of its contents. A short summary of
the Greek texts A, B and C[1] and of the Latin translation
of Julius Valerius has been printed by Müller in the introduction to his edition of Pseudo-Callisthenes, pp. x col. 2—
xv col. 1, and by Weismann[2] in the German translation of
Pseudo-Callisthenes at the head of each chapter. A complete
summary and scholarly analysis of each chapter of the oldest
Greek and Latin texts of the work, with remarks upon the
Armenian version (said to have been made in the fifth
century), has been given by Zacher in his *Pseudo-Callisthenes*,
pp. 113—176. The letters A, B and C refer to the three
principal Greek texts of Müller's edition; L to the Greek text
published by Meusel[3]; and V to the Latin translation made by
Julius Valerius, which is printed at the foot of the pages of the
Greek text in Müller's edition.


## BOOK I.

Chap. I. The sages of Egypt, of divine origin, ruled the
earth and sea by their power which they delivered to mankind
by means of magical words. Nectanebus the last king of Egypt
was a great magician. His sorcery with a bowl of water and
models of ships and men; conquers his enemies thereby[4].

Chap. II. A spy announces the coming of hosts of enemies. Nectanebus approves of the vigilance of the scout and
dismisses him[5].

[1] For Müller's description of the characteristics of these MSS. see his
*Introductio*, p. ix, col. 2; p. x, col. 1.

[2] *Alexander,......der vollständigen Uebersetzung des Pseudo-Kallisthenes*,
Band II, pp. 4—224.

[3] *Pseudo-Callisthenes nach der Leidener Handschrift, herausgegeben von*
H. Meusel. Besonderer Abdruck aus dem fünften Supplementband der Jahrbücher
für classische Philologie, Leipzig, 1871.

[4] AVL. So also the Armenian version. See Zacher, *Pseudo-Callisthenes*,
p. 88.

[5] ABCLV.

Chap. III. Nectanebus discovers by means of the basin of water and the bitumen figures that the gods of Egypt have forsaken and betrayed the land. He shaves his head and beard, changes his raiment, and flees from Egypt by way of Pelusium. He arrives at Pella and dresses like an Egyptian prophet[1]. After Nectanebus had fled the Egyptians asked Hephaestus the head of the race of the gods what had become of him. He sends them an oracle which they inscribe upon the base of the statue of Nectanebus[2].

Chap. IV. Nectanebus goes about in Macedonia. Olympias, the wife of Philip, king of Macedon, sends for him to consult him about a rumour which she has heard of Philip's intention to divorce her. He casts her nativity. Description of the table and horoscope. He tells her that Ammon the god of Libya will appear to her in a dream, and that he will afterwards come and sleep with her[3].

Chap. V. Nectanebus causes Olympias to dream that Ammon had come to her[4].

Chap. VI. Olympias sends for Nectanebus to come and explain the dream; he tells her that Ammon will come to her in three forms[5].

Chap. VII. A god, i.e., Nectanebus, visits Olympias under the forms of Ammon, of Hêraklês and of Dionysus. Nectanebus sends a dream to Philip in which he shews him the visit of Ammon to Olympias and her pregnancy[6].

Chap. VIII. Philip sends for the wise men to explain the dream, and they tell him that Olympias has become pregnant by Ammon the god of Libya[7].

Chap. IX. Philip returns home and finds Olympias ashamed to meet him. He comforts her and tells her that he has seen in a dream all that has happened[8].

Chap. X. Philip, suspecting the fidelity of his wife, upbraids her. Nectanebus in the form of a serpent glides into the room and embraces Olympias, and Philip is pacified[9].

---

[1] ABCLV.　　[2] ABCL.
[3] ABCLV.　　[4] ABCLV.　　　[5] ABCLV.
[6] ABCLV. See ܠܐܝ ܠܐܘܣܕܟܣܘܪ ܟܕܟ ed. Bruns, p. 35.
[7] ABCLV.　　　[8] ABCLV.　　　[9] ABCLV.

Chap. XI. A half-bred hen lays an egg in Philip's lap; and a serpent crawls therefrom and dies. Antiphon the chief augur interprets this as referring to the glory and death of the child which Olympias is about to bring forth[1].

Chap. XII. The time for Olympias to be delivered comes, and Nectanebus consults the stars in order that the child may not be born under an unlucky star[2]. At a favourable time Olympias gives birth to Alexander, and the earth quakes and lightnings flash forth from the sky[3].

Chap. XIII. Philip names the child Alexander after a son borne to him by a former wife. Description of Alexander's appearance and the names of his tutors[4]. Bucephalus is sent to Philip by the Cappadocians as a gift[5].

Chap. XIV. Alexander, being twelve years old, learns the arts of horsemanship and war. Nectanebus makes a good augury for Olympias. He shews Alexander the planets, and is pushed by him into a pit, where he dies after having told Alexander his history and relationship to him. Alexander buries his father[6].

Chap. XV. Philip sends to consult the oracle at Delphi about his successor: Pythia replies saying that the subduer of Bucephalus shall be lord of Macedonia[7].

Chap. XVI. Alexander makes Bucephalus run through Pella, and Philip, remembering the words of the oracle, rejoices[8].

Chap. XVII. Alexander returns wise answers to the questions of Aristotle[9]. His liberality. Correspondence between Zintis, Philip and Olympias, Aristotle and Alexander[10].

[1] ABCLV. See Zacher, *op. cit.*, p. 114.
[2] ABCLV. The description of the auguries of Nectanebus is shortened in LBCV. [3] ABCLV.
[4] ABCLV. The notice about the ancestors of Alexander given by J. Valerius only is from the fourth book of the Παντοδαπὴ ἱστορία of Favorinus. From the fact of this passage being found in the Armenian version, which was certainly translated from the Greek, Müller thinks that Valerius has here preserved a part of an older form of the Greek version than we at present possess. See *Pseudo-Call.*, p. 91.
[5] ABCLV. [6] ABCLV. [7] ABCLV.
[8] ABCLV. This is chap. xvii. of the Greek and Latin texts.
[9] ABCLV. This is chap. xvi. of the Greek and Latin texts.
[10] V. The Armenian version has preserved this correspondence between Alexander, his father and mother, Zeuxis and Aristotle. See Müller, p. 92.

---

[1] ABCLV.

[2] ABCLV. The Syriac text agrees with C only as far as it agrees with
and ᴮ.

[3] ABCLV.

[4] ABCLV. See Müller, op. cit., p. 116.

[5] ABCLV.

[6] ABCLV.

[7] ABLV. This incident forms part of chap. xxvi. in C, where it is narra
in a different manner.

[8] ABC.    [9] ABCLV.    [10] ABLV.

[11] ABLV.    [12] ABCLV.

[13] ABCLV. For the contents of chap. xxvi. in the Greek and Latin vers
see Zacher, p. 117.

Chap. XXVII. His troops put to sea[1].

Chap. XXVIII. Passing by Sicily he goes to Rome[2]. The Romans send him gifts and a crown[3].

Chap. XXIX. He goes to Carthage in Africa: the people of the city pay tribute to him[4].

Chap. XXX. He sacrifices to the god Ammon of Libya, who appears to him in a dream. He dedicates a brass statue to Ammon. The god appears to him a second time in a dream, and tells him where to found the city which he wishes to build[5].

Chap. XXXI. Alexander builds a sepulchral monument and offers sacrifices at Taphosiris. Origin of the name of the place[6].

Chap. XXXII. He sacrifices in the temples of Zeus and Hêra, and to the god Serapis who afterwards appears to him in a dream. He asks the god to shew him where he shall build his city; having received an answer from the god he lays the foundations of Alexandria[7].

Chap. XXXIII. Aristotle, hearing that Alexander has begun to build a great city, writes to him and advises him not to do so[8]; Alexander, encouraged by the augurs, continues to build the city.

Chap. XXXIV. He goes to Memphis and is crowned by the priests. He reads the oracle upon the statue of Nectanebus, and proclaims himself to be the son of Nectanebus and the young king referred to in the inscription[9]. He exhorts the Egyptians to deliver themselves from the Persians.

---

[1] This is chap. xxviii. of the Greek text.

[2] This is chap. xxix. of the Greek text.

[3] ADCLV.      [4] ABCLV.

[5] ABCLV. Chapters xxix. and xxx. of the Syriac = chap. xxx. of the Greek.

[6] ABCLV.

[7] ADCV. Chaps. xxxi. and xxxii. of the Syriac = chaps. xxxi—xxxiii. of the Greek. In the Syriac there is no mention of the comparison of the greatness of Antioch, Carthage, Babylon, Rome and Alexandria as given by AV; nor of the birds eating honey which had been strewn about, thereby pointing out where the beginning of the city (ABCLV) should be built; nor of the appearance of the snake (AV); nor of the indication of the parts of the town by the first five letters of the alphabet (ABCLV).

[8] There seems to be nothing like this chapter in the Greek and Latin texts.

[9] ABCLV.

*e* 2

Chap. XXXV. He goes to Syria and arrives at Tyre. The Tyrians do battle with him and repulse him[1]. Serapis appears to him in a dream and promises to him victory over the Tyrians. He attacks the Tyrians a second time and defeats them. Founds Tripolis[2].

Chap. XXXVI. The ambassadors of Darius tell him of the sagacity of Alexander and shew him his picture. Darius, having had the height of the picture of Alexander compared with that of his daughter Roxana, casts it away with scorn. It is carried off secretly by Roxana to her chamber where she honours it with spices and odours[3]. Darius, wishing to insult Alexander, writes an insolent letter to him and sends it to him with a whip, a ball and a box full of gold. In the letter Darius threatens to crucify Alexander[4].

Chap. XXXVII. Alexander encourages the minds of his soldiers who have been terrified at the words of Darius. He threatens to crucify the ambassadors of Darius, but does not do so in order that he may shew them how superior the customs of the Greeks are to those of the Persians[5].

Chap. XXXVIII. He sends an answer[6] to the letter of Darius with some mustard seed.

Chap. XXXIX. Darius eats the mustard seed. He writes to the satraps in the Taurus commanding them to beat Alexander with a whip for children and to take him to his mother. The satraps Gushtázaph and Sábántár write to Darius and tell him that they are awaiting his arrival. Darius answers this letter and upbraids them for their cowardice[7].

Chap. XL. Darius writes again to Alexander, and promises to forgive him all the offences which he has committed against him if he will go back to his own country[8].

Chap. XLI. Alexander receives Darius' letter and writes an answer to it, in which he says that he is obliged to return to Macedonia because his mother Olympias is grievously sick; he promises to return to Persia and to occupy the land. While

---

[1] ABCLV. The Syriac text makes no mention of the capture of Gaza.
[2] ABCLV.
[3] There is no mention of this in the Greek texts.
[4] ABCLV.　　　　　[5] ABCLV.　　　　　[6] ABCLV.
[7] ABCLV.　　　　　[8] ABCLV.

Alexander is on the road to his mother he engages in battle with one of the generals of Darius and defeats him[1].

Chap. XLII. Alexander goes to Achaia, Pieria and Phrygia; he makes offerings to Hector and Achilles. He saw the river Scamander which was five cubits wide[2].

Chap. XLIII. Alexander comes to Macedonia and finds his mother recovering from her sickness. He goes to Abdêra which city is shut against him[3].

Chap. XLIV. He goes to the region of the Euxine Sea[4]. The soldiers have no food to eat. He commands them to slay their horses, for they can be found in every place while Macedonian soldiers can not[5].

Chap. XLV. He comes to the Locri. At Akrantis he asks the priest of Apollo to consult the oracle for him. The priest refuses and Alexander attempts to carry away the tripod of divination. A voice from the temple rebukes Alexander and assures him that he shall be famous and his name renowned[6].

Chap. XLVI. He marches against Thebes. Description of the attack and defence of the city, the destruction of the houses and walls, and the slaughter of the people. A Theban bard turns aside the fierceness of Alexander's wrath and he orders the destruction of the city and the people to be stopped. The Thebans that remain are banished from their city, and Alexander forbids the name of Thebes to be mentioned again[7]. .

Chap. XLVII. The Thebans go to Apollo at Delphi to enquire when their city shall be rebuilt. Answer of the Pythia. Alexander goes to Corinth and is present at the Corinthian games; Clitomachus wins the three crowns and Alexander orders the city of Thebes to be rebuilt[8].

## BOOK II.

Chap. I. Alexander goes to Plataeae and receives a favourable augury from the priestess. She is removed from her office by the governor of the district. Alexander deposes that governor

---

[1] ABCLV.        [2] BCLV.        [3] BCLV.
    [4] ABCLV.        [5] ABCLV.        [6] AV.
[7] AV.  See Zacher, *op. cit.*, p. 126.        [8] AV.

and restores the priestess to her place, whereat the Athenians are displeased; he writes to them and orders them to pay a thousand talents of gold yearly as tribute[1].

Chap. II.  The ten orators in Athens write to Alexander. He returns answer to the Athenians and demands that the ten orators be delivered up to him.  The Athenians write to him and refuse both to deliver up the orators and to pay tribute.  The council of the Athenians.  Aeschines is in favour of going to Alexander, but Demades is not, and wishes to incite the Athenians to do battle with Alexander[2].

Chap. III.  The speech of Demosthenes the Athenian.  He approves of the conduct of Alexander in deposing the ruler[3].

Chap. IV.  The Athenians approve of the speech of Demosthenes.  He makes a second speech which convinces them of the futility of fighting with Alexander[4].

Chap. V.  The Athenians send a crown of gold with a letter of thanks to Alexander.  Alexander writes a letter to them in which he mentions many of their evil deeds[5].

Chap. VI.  Alexander marches against the Lacedemonians[6]. He encamps by the Tigris and goes on an embassy to Darius as far as Babylon.  He pretends to be an ambassador of Alexander[7], and is present at a feast of Darius and his generals.

Chap. VII.  Alexander hides the golden drinking goblets in his bosom.  He is recognised by Pasarges, quits the chamber and escapes on horseback.  The picture of Xerxes in the palace of Darius peels off from the wall and falls to the ground[8].

Chap. VIII.  Alexander counts his army and exhorts the soldiers to fight bravely[9].

Chap. IX.  Alexander comes to the river Strangas and fights the army of Darius.  Defeat of the Persians and flight of Darius[10].  He writes a letter to Alexander committing his mother, his wife and his daughter to his care.  Alexander sets

---

[1] AV.    [2] AV.    [3] AV.    [4] AV.    [5] AV.

[6] AV.  The other parts of chapter vi. in the Syriac belong to chapter xiv. of the Greek.  Perhaps a couple of quires had fallen out of the Greek MS. from which the translation was made.

[7] ABCLV.  See Zacher, op. cit., p. 129.

[8] ABCLV.  This is chap. xv. of the Greek.

[9] This is a part of chap. xvi. of the Greek.        [10] ABCLV.

the palace of Xerxes on fire, but afterwards he repents and orders the fire to be extinguished[1].

Chap. X. Alexander sees the grave of Pâkôr and the body of Cyrus in a golden coffin. He finds captive Greeks who had been mutilated and liberates them[2].

Chap. XI. Darius makes ready for a second war and writes to Porus, king of the Indians, asking help from him and promising to give him Alexander's horse Bucephalus. Alexander, hearing of this, arms his troops and sets out for the country of the Parthians. Darius then tries to escape but is pursued by Alexander[3].

Chap. XII. Bâgiz and Ânâbdêh stab Darius. Alexander finds him half dead and tries to comfort him. Darius commits his wife, his mother, and his daughter to Alexander's care and dies[4].

Chap. XIII. Alexander buries Darius with great ceremony. He makes a proclamation to the Persians, and crucifies the murderers of Darius[5].

Chap. XIV. He writes to the mother and wife of Darius; their reply. He writes to Roxana and takes her to wife[6].

## BOOK III.

Chap. I. Alexander, hearing that Porus had marched with troops to the assistance of Darius, and, finding that Darius was dead, had returned to his own land, sets out for India to overcome him. His soldiers complain that they have too much

[1] ABCLV. This is chap. xvii. of the Greek.
[2] ABCLV. This is chap. xviii. of the Greek.
[3] ABCLV. This is chap. xix. of the Greek. See Zacher, op. cit., p. 131.
[4] ABCLV. This is chap. xx. of the Greek.
[5] ABCLV. This is chap. xxi. of the Greek.
[6] ABCLV. This is chap. xxii. of the Greek. A and V end Book II. by adding the statement that Alexander sets out for India. B and C give the text of a letter from Alexander to Olympias and Aristotle in which he relates his adventures from the battle of Issus to the death of Darius and his own marriage. From this point onwards Müller has edited his Greek text from Codex C. Here the letter in C ends. B, however, adds in the first person, a description of the wonders which he saw in the far east, as a part of the letter, all of which C gives, in the third person, from Chapter xxxii. onwards. For a summary of the contents of BC and L see especially Zacher, op. cit., pp. 132—148.

fighting to do. He addresses them and eventually they ask his forgiveness[1].

Chap. II. He receives an insolent letter from Porus, which he reads before his troops and then answers[2].

Chap. III. The Persians and Macedonians draw near to the Indians to fight. Alexander and his troops are afraid when they see that wild beasts are employed by Porus to fight[3]. Alexander makes brazen images red-hot, and the wild beasts in the army of Porus seizing these in their mouths are terrified, and run back to their camp and begin to fight the Indians themselves. Bucephalus throws Alexander off his back and dies. The Greeks and Indians fight twenty days and Alexander's troops wish to surrender to the Indians[4].

Chap. IV. Seeing this, Alexander challenges Porus to single combat, and Porus is slain[5]; he buries Porus and then makes ready to go and see the naked sages[6].

Chap. V. The Brahmans send a letter to him. Description of their style of living[7].

Chap. VI. Alexander asks the Brahmans questions; their replies[8].

Chap. VII.[9] Writes a letter to Aristotle giving an account of his travels. I first came to a place called Prasinkê[10] where we saw men with faces like horses. I sent Philôn to land upon what was thought to be an island: it turned out, however, to be an animal, which, disappearing under the waves, caused Philôn to be drowned in the vortex of waters caused by its sinking[11]. I saw a beast like an elephant which escaped from our weapons. I saw an eclipse. We marched from the Caspian gates to the frontier of the Indians, and met all kinds of beasts and reptiles. We marched from the tenth hour of each day until the third hour of the next. After twelve days' march we

---

[1] ABCLV.　　[2] ABCLV.　　[3] ABCLV.
[4] ABCLV.　　[5] ABCLV.　　[6] ABLV.
[7] ABV.　　　　　　　　　　[8] ABLV.

[9] The work of Palladius entitled Περὶ τῶν τῆς Ἰνδίας ἐθνῶν καὶ τῶν βραγμάνων is here interpolated and forms chaps. VII.—XVI. of the Greek text. Chap. VII. of the Syriac text is chap. XVII. of the Greek.

[10] AV. Major Cunningham's *Ancient Geography of India*, London, 1871, should be studied for this and the following chapters.

[11] AV.

arrived at a city between rivers, where we saw reeds thirty
cubits high. Thirty-six of my soldiers swim in that river
and are devoured by alligators or crocodiles. We arrived
next at a lake of sweet waters where we found an inscribed
pillar of Sesonchosis. I lay down to sleep there and in the
night saw red scorpions, horned snakes, lions, rhinoceroses, wild
boars, wolves, leopards, panthers, beasts with scorpions' tails,
elephants, and men with twisted legs and teeth like dogs and
faces like women. I order the jungle to be set on fire and
many of these beasts perish in the flames. When the moon
had set the Mashkĕlath[1] came into the camp and killed twenty-
six men; when we had killed it three hundred men were
necessary to draw it out of the ditch. We saw night-foxes,
water crocodiles, bats as large as eagles, and night-ravens. We
came to a wood inhabited by wild men with faces like ravens.
We arrived at the country of the people whose feet are twisted,
and next we came to the land of lion-headed men. We came
to a river where we saw a tree which grew from dawn to the
sixth hour of the day, and which diminished from the sixth hour
until night. We marched through a wilderness and arrived at
the ocean. We saw what appeared to be an island and twenty
of my men tried to swim there, but beasts came up out of the
water and devoured them. We came to the land of the people
having their eyes and mouths in their breasts. We saw the
"palm bird" (phoenix). After a march of sixty-five days we
arrived at Obarkia and saw two birds, one of which spoke Greek.
We next came to a mountain on the top of which a temple was
built. In its windows were figures of Pan and the Satyrs;
within the temple dwelt a god who revealed himself to me as
Dionysus. I ordered our fifty Indian guides to be killed and
we turned to go to Prasiakê. On our road we encountered a
mighty wind, a black cloud full of fire and snow three cubits
deep. We arrived at Prasiakê where were shewn the two
talking trees which prophesied that I should die by the hands
of my troops in Babylon. Having received gifts from the

---

[1] See Palladius, *De Bragmanibus*, p. 10, and the description and notes on
*Bestia dens Tyrannus vocata* in Berger de Xivrey, *Traditions Tératologiques*,
p. 268, and Zacher, pp. 153—158.

Indians of Prasiakê we marched towards the east[1], and after ten days arrived at a high mountain where a dragon lived. I caused the dragon to be slain. We marched on and arrived at a river called Barsâtis and a high mountain. I left my troops, and with twenty of my friends marched to China in twenty-five days. Here I gave myself the name of Pîthâôs and pretended to be an ambassador of Alexander. Gundâphâr the general of the Chinese army asked me questions, and finally gave me gifts and sent me away. We marched thirteen days and did battle with the natives of the country in which we arrived. We set out from thence and came to Sêbâzâz and afterwards to Sogd, where I built a temple to Rhea. We set out and arrived at a river called Barţêsitôs over which I built a bridge of boats. Two days from here I built a city and a temple to Rhea. A body of men under the command of Paryôg seized a number of my horses and cattle; I pursued, overtook and slew him. We stayed there four months, and I founded the city of Merv there.

Chap. VIII. I marched from the land of Margiana to the country of the Samrâyê. Alexander's letter to Candace and her reply. Her gifts to him[2].

Chap. IX. Candace caused a portrait of Alexander to be painted secretly. Alexander gives orders to fight the chief of the Mârônîkâyê who had carried off the wife of her son, Candaules. He changes places with Antigonus the chief of the Greek host[3].

Chap. X. Alexander disguised as Antigonus goes and sets fire to the city of the Mârônîkâyê, and rescues the wife of Candaules[4].

Chap. XI. Alexander goes to the city of Candace and is welcomed cordially by her[5].

Chap. XII. Description of the palace of Candace. Candace leads him into her chamber and shows him his picture. She keeps the secret of his disguise[6].

---

[1] Here ends the epistle of Alexander to Aristotle in Müller's ed. p. 125, col. 2. What follows in the Syriac appears to be no longer extant in the Greek MSS.

[2] ABCLV. Chap. xviii. of the Greek text.

[3] ABCLV. Chap. xix. of the Greek text.

[4] ABCLV. Chap. xx. of the Greek text.

[5] ABCV. Chap. xxi. of the Greek text.

[6] ABCLV. Chap. xxii. of the Greek text.

Chap. XIII. Her son Kĕrâtôr, instigated by his wife, wishes to slay Alexander. He delivers himself by his own astuteness and is sent away in peace by Candace, laden with gifts[1].

Chap. XIV. He goes to a hill with Candaules, and sees and talks with Sesonchosis in a cave there. He sees Serapis who promises him that, living or dead, he shall return to the city which he has founded, and be honoured as a god[2].

Chap. XV. He sets out for the land of the Amazons, and sends a letter to them. They send an answer in which their customs are described[3].

Chap. XVI. He writes another letter to the Amazons, and they send back an answer to it[4].

Chap. XVII.[5] On the road to the Amazons' land he encounters great rains and a fierce heat[6]. He crossed over the river Zûtâ(?) and the people, attributing the rains and thunders and lightnings to his coming, bring him sixty elephants and one hundred thousand chariots, and entreat him to depart from their land. Departing from thence he is met by five hundred Amazon women who bring him gifts of gold. Continuing his march a letter from Aristotle meets him[7]. He returns to Babylon. He writes to Olympias[8] an account of what he did after he reached Asia, saying: "After a march of ninety-five days I arrived at the cave of Hêrakles[9]. From thence we arrived at a land of darkness where beautiful women lived.

Chap. XVIII. We came to a great sea where we sacrificed white horses to Poseidon. We set out in five ships, and in three days arrived at the city of the Sun[10]. We arrived at the river Sakhan which divides Asia and Europe, and afterwards came to the palace of Khusrau and Pâkôr.[11] Here follows a description of the wonderful things which he saw there[11].

---

[1] ABCLV. Chap. xxiii. of the Greek text.
[2] ABLV. Chap. xxiv. of the Greek text and chap. xxi. of G.
[3] ABCLV. Chap. xxv. of the Greek text.
[4] ABCLV. Chap. xxvi. of the Greek text.
[5] This is chaps. xxvii—xxix. of the Greek text.
[6] V.
[7] V. See Zacher, p. 167.
[8] V.
[9] V. See Zacher, p. 168.
[10] ABCLV.
[11] ABCLV. See Zacher, pp. 168—172.

Chap. XIX.[1] A woman brings forth a four-headed monster which she shews to the king. Alexander, having seen it, sends for the Chaldeans, who explain the sign as referring to himself and to his death[2].

Chap. XX. Olympias sends an accusation against Antipater to Alexander. Antipater determines to have Alexander poisoned, and having dissolved a deadly drug in a vessel, sends it by the hand of his son Cassander to Babylon. Cassander enters into a conspiracy with Iollas, the chief cup-bearer, who had been scourged by Alexander a few days previously. Cassander, watching his opportunity, administers the poison to Alexander while he is drinking wine with his friends. Alexander falls sick, and Cassander sends the news to his father that the king is poisoned[3]

Alexander tries to drown himself in the Euphrates, but is prevented by Roxana his wife. He dictates his will. Kriskòs (or Priskòs) and Ptolemy make a compact to share equally whatever is left to them by Alexander[4].

Chap. XXI. Tumult among the Macedonian soldiers who think that Alexander is dead. He orders them to go to the hippodrome and is himself carried there on his bed. He addresses the Macedonian soldiers who wish to stab themselves and to die with him[5].

Chap. XXII.[6] Text of Alexander's testament[7].

Chap. XXIII. Alexander dies. His body is brought to Memphis[8] and from thence to Alexandria, where Ptolemy buries it[9].

Chap. XXIV. The number of the years which Alexander lived and reigned[10]. List of the cities which he founded and the day of his death[11].

---

[1] Chap. xxx. of the Greek text.　　[2] ABCLV.

[3] ABCLV.　　[4] A. Chap. xxxii. of the Greek text.

[5] ABCL. Chap. xxin. of the Greek text.

[6] Chap. xii. of the Syriac contains parts of chap. xxxii. ABC and V, but neither follows nor agrees with either of them exactly. See Zacher, pp. 174, 175.

[7] A quaint work on this subject is the *Dissertatio historico-politica de testamento Alexandri Magni Macedonis*, 1709, by Wagner.

[8] BCLV.　　[9] V.

[10] ABCLV.　　[11] ABCLV.

## A Christian Legend concerning Alexander.

This composition appears to be an abbreviated form of a legend the most complete form of which known to us is that given in the metrical discourse on Alexander attributed to Jacob of Sĕrûgh; both these works, in turn, are based upon chapters XXXVII.—XXXIX. of the second book of Pseudo-Callisthenes according to Müller's Greek MS. C. The Christian legend has been burdened with many additions, evidently the work of the Christian redactor, which have no connexion whatever with the story. On the other hand many passages, as, for example, the account of his descent into the sea in a glass cage, have been entirely omitted. The names of places which are given us freely in this legend seem to indicate that it was drawn up at a very late period; that it is the work of Jacob of Sĕrûgh is improbable.

The short description of the manners of the Hûnâyê or Huns, and of the gate which Alexander built to keep them out, is based upon the twenty-ninth chapter of the third book of Pseudo-Callisthenes according to Müller's Greek MS. C, where it is stated that the door or gate was twenty cubits wide and sixty cubits high, and that it was covered inside and out with a substance (καὶ καταχρίσας...ἀσοκίτῳ[1]) which rendered it both iron and fire-proof. The description of the evils which Alexander is made to prophesy against mankind when the Huns break down this gate is clearly the work of a man who was acquainted with the popular traditions concerning the destruction wrought by Attila[2] when he overran Europe in the fifth century, and with the prophecies of the evil which should come upon mankind in the last days according to Jeremiah[3] and the writers of the Gospels[4]. The description of Paradise and its rivers is based upon the Bible account[5]. The following is a

---

[1] Müller, p. 143, col. 1.
[2] See Thierry, *Histoire d'Attila*, t. II, p. 221 ff.
[3] Jeremiah, chap. iv.
[4] S. Matt. chap. xxiv; Luke xix. 42—44; Mark xiii. 7—30.
[5] Sir John Mandeville's account of Paradise is based upon that of Pseudo-Callisthenes although he borrowed at second-hand. See the notes on Paradise

summary of the contents of the "Christian Legend" concerning Alexander.

In the second, or seventh year of his reign Alexander assembles the nobles of his kingdom and announces to them his intention to go and see the other countries of the world. His nobles describe to him the fœtid sea and the eleven bright seas. He sets out from Alexandria with three hundred and twenty thousand men. He prays to God. He comes to mount Sinai and passes over to Egypt, where he obtains from Samâkôs the king seven thousand smiths. He puts to sea, and after four months and twelve days arrives at the dry land beyond the eleven bright seas. He sends thirty-seven men to hammer in stakes for the ships by the side of the fœtid sea; they die instantly. He travels towards the east and looking westward sees mount Mûsâs. He goes to the source of the Euphrates and then towards the north; he enters Armenia. Three hundred old men go to him and give him information about Tûbârlâk the king of the country. Description of the Huns, the names of their kings, their manners and customs. Description of Paradise. Description of the gate or door which Alexander made to shut in the twenty-two nations. The inscription on the gate. Description of the troubles and evils which should come upon mankind when the Huns should go forth through the gate. Tûbârlâk and his allies, and eighty-two kings, and one million, one hundred and thirty thousand men make ready to fight with Alexander. The Lord appears to Alexander and promises victory to him. Alexander and his three hundred and sixteen thousand soldiers do battle with the forces of Tûbârlâk and overcome them; sixty-two kings are slain, their hosts are scattered, and Tûbârlâk is taken prisoner. Alexander thus subdues Persia. Tûbârlâk brings to him gifts of gold and silver and precious stones, and pledges Persia to pay tribute for fifteen years. Six thousand Greeks and six thousand Persians are to guard the iron gate. Tûbârlâk prophesies the destruction of Persia by the Greeks. Alexander leaves Persia, establishes the Egyptian smiths in Bêth-Dêma and Bêth-Dôshar, and goes

in the Roxburgh Club Edition of his *Travels*, by Mr. G. F. Warner, M.A., of the British Museum.

up to and worships in Jerusalem. He sails to Alexandria. He dies, leaving his silver throne to be placed in Jerusalem.

## A Brief Life of Alexander.

This excellent summary of the principal events in the Life of Alexander has been edited by Prof. Paul de Lagarde in his *Analecta Syriaca*, pp. 205—208, from Brit. Mus. Add. MS. 12,154 fol. 153 *b*—154 *b*. The manuscript was written at the end of the VIIIth or the beginning of the IXth century. See Wright, *Catalogue of the Syriac MSS. in the British Museum*, p. 984 col. 1.

## The Metrical Discourse on Alexander the Great attributed to Jacob of Sērūgh.

The English translation of this discourse printed on pp. 163—200 is made chiefly from the very faulty text published by Knös in his *Chrestomathia Syriaca*, pp. 66—107. Several of the passages are utterly corrupt, and when translated, make no sense; they have been generally corrected by the help of Brit. Mus. Add. MS. 14,624[1]. Most of the misprints in Knös' text have been corrected in the notes at the foot of the English translation, and all the important variant readings and additions have been added.

The Land of Darkness whither Alexander wishes to go calls to mind the passage in the Greek Codex C (Müller, p. 88, col. 2, chap. XXXVII.). According to Pseudo-Callisthenes (Müller, p. 89, col. 2), after his descent into the sea Alexander marched three days across a plain, and then arrived at the Land of the Blessed. Here he leaves all the old men and women that were with him, and with forty friends, one hundred boys, and twelve hundred soldiers sets out to explore the land. One curious old man, however, entreats his two sons, who are soldiers, to take him with them and they do so. After marching some time,

---

[1] This MS. was written in the ninth century. See Wright, *Catalogue of the Syriac MSS.*, p. 782.

Alexander and his company fall into difficulties, and he expresses a wish for an old man to be brought to shew them the way. The two sons, who had brought their father with them, confess to the king what they had done, and he is glad. The old man advises that she-asses which are suckling foals be obtained; that the foals be kept where the king and his troops now are; and that the king go forth with a few chosen troops to explore the land. If they lose their way the instinct of the she-asses will lead them back to their young ones, and the king will be saved. Alexander, following the old man's advice, sets out with three hundred and sixty warriors, and after marching some distance ($\sigma\chi o i \nu o v s$ $\delta\epsilon\kappa\alpha\pi\epsilon\nu\tau\epsilon$), they arrive at a well the water of which flashes like lightning. Alexander, being hungry, orders Andreas the cook to prepare some food for him. Andreas, taking a dried fish, goes to the water of this fountain to wash it; as soon as the fish is moved about in the water it comes to life and swims away.

In this discourse the writer gives a full description of the manners and appearance of the Hûnâyê or Huns, which agrees in every particular with the notices of this warlike people given by ancient writers[1]. He was well acquainted

[1] See Ammianus Marcellinus, xxxi. 2; and Thierry, *Histoire d'Attila*, t. i, pp. 7—9. Compare also the following: "Diese Hunjo des Ostens, welche ohne Zweifel die Hunnen des Westens sind, sowie die Peti (die Benennung für Hunnen, Türken und Mongolen) oder nördlichen Barbaren beschäftigen sich mit der Jagd wilder Thiere und der Viehzucht. Sie weiden ihre Pferde, Esel, Kamele, Rinder und Lämmer auf den längs der Flüsse sich hinziehenden fruchtreichen Auen, wandern hin und her, ohne sich bleibend anzusiedeln, und errichten weder Städte noch Festungswerke. Lassen sie sich irgendwo auf eine kurze Zeit nieder, so vertheilen sie das Land unter sich; jeder erhält eine bestimmte Strecke und macht sie urbar. Ihre vorzüglichste Nahrung erzielen sie aber immer aus wild wachsenden Gräsern, aus dem Ertrage der Jagden und ihrer Viehheerden. Sie fressen allerlei Thiere und widerliches Ungeziefer. Das Fleisch kochen und braten sie nicht, sondern machen es durch wiederholte Reibungen zwischen den Schenkeln ihrer Beine, oder indem sie sich, wenn sie zu Pferde sind, darauf setzen, mürbe und verschlucken es halbroh. Ihre Kleidung besteht aus den Häuten und Haaren wilder und zahmer Thiere und wird, da Niemand mehr als einen Anzug hat, so lange getragen, bis sie ihnen vom Leibe herabfault. Ein wunderlich schmutziger Aberglaube, den Göttern sei das Waschen und Trocknen besudelter Gegenstände unbehaglich; wenn diess geschehe, senden sie dem Menschengeschlechte zur Strafe Donner und Blitz; hat wohl die Hunnen, wie später die Mongolen, von dem Waschen ihrer Kleider

ith their physical characteristics, which he describes most
inutely, and also with the accounts of the troubles and evils
hich followed in the track of their conquests[1]. There seems
ɔ be no doubt that the description of the nation as given by
he Syriac writer is meant to apply to Attila who is described
s being " Forma brevis, lato pectore, capite grandiori, minutis
culis, rarus barba...simo naso, teter colore"...[2]. The statement that " where the wrath of God rises he sends the hosts of
iog and Magog " clearly has reference to the man who had
ive hundred thousand barbarians under his command, who
ried to invest himself in the eyes of Christendom with the
haracter and attributes of the predicted Antichrist[3], and who
ruly deserved the appellation of the "Scourge of God." The
l·feat of Tûbârlâk and his sixty-two kings by Alexander refers
robably to the defeat of Attila and his hosts by the Romans,
·u the plains of Chalons on the Marne, after his invasion of
the Western empire (A.D. 450—453); that Alexander happened
to live nearly eight hundred years before the defeat of Attila is
a matter which would trouble the Syriac writer very little. The
story of the appearance of Christ to Alexander before and after
the battle, as well as the prophecies put into his mouth, is of
Christian origin.

The following is a summary of the contents of the discourse
attributed to Jacob of Sĕrûgh.

Address to the Deity by the writer. Alexander gathers
together the chief men of his kingdom, and tells them that
he wishes to go and see the various countries of the world,
especially the Land of Darkness. Having taken possession of
Macedonia he goes to Egypt. His nobles point out the diffi-

abgehalten." Neumann, *Die Völker des Südischen Russlands*, p. 26. "Neben
der Jagd, der Viehzucht und dem Spiele, welchem die Hunnen sehr ergeben
waren, ist Kriegführen, Rauben, Plundern und Morden ihre Lieblingsbeschäfti-
rung." *Ibid.* p. 28. "In die Ferne schiessen sie mit Bogen, und bedienen sich
der sorgfältig zugespitzten Knochen anstatt der Pfeile; in der Nähe kämpfen sie
mit dem Schwerte." *Ibid.* pp. 28, 29.

[1] See Thierry, *Histoire d'Attila*, t. n. p. 231 ff.
[2] Jornandes, *Reb. Get.*, 11.
[3] Herbert, *Attila*, p. 360. For other works on the Huns see Howorth,
*History of the Mongols;* Lebeau, *Histoire du Bas-Empire* (ed. St. Martin), vols.
4–6, Paris, 1825—27; Des Guignes, *Hist. des Huns;* Gibbon, *Decline and Fall*,
chaps. 34, 35; and Müller, *Attila der Held des fünften Jahrhunderts.*

B.

culties of the road which he proposes to travel, and the impossibility of crossing the fœtid sea; nevertheless he determines to go. Ships are prepared for his army, which consists of thirteen hundred of the Âmôrîyâ, and twelve thousand cunning workmen whom he obtained from Sôrk the king of Egypt. He sets out, and after a voyage of four months arrives in India, where he begins to march in a northerly direction. After his proclamation of peace three hundred old men come to him and salute him as king. He asks them to shew him the way to the Land of Darkness. They tell him of the difficulties of the way, but as he persists in his intention to go there they promise to go with him. He sets out, and being questioned by the old men about his object in coming there, tells them that he is searching for the fountain of life. They advise him to go forward, and to take with him she-asses which are suckling young ones—these they propose to leave behind—so that if he loses the way, the maternal instinct of the she-asses will lead them back to their young ones. They also advise him to cause his cook to take with him a dried salt fish, and to command him to wash it wherever he sees a stream or fountain of water. The stream or fountain which causes the fish to come to life will contain the water of life.

The king and his company set out, and when the cook washes the fish in a fountain of water, which he sees by the road, it comes to life, and swims away and escapes. Alexander wishes to bathe in it and to live for ever; but he is not allowed to do so. He asks the old men whose territory is that which he sees beyond them. They tell him that it belongs to Tûbarlîki and that it is inhabited by the nations of Gog and Magog. Here follows a description of the peoples of Gog and Magog. Tûbarlîki is told of the arrival of Alexander, and he hires sixty-two kings to come and help him to fight him. Before the battle an angel appears to Alexander in a dream, and promises victory to him. Alexander encourages his troops to fight, and an engagement between them and the forces of Tûbarlîki takes place, in which the latter are defeated, and their king is taken prisoner. Alexander builds a brass and iron door, to shut in the nations of Gog and Magog, which was finished in the sixth month. A fiery watcher appears to

Alexander in a dream and brings to him the commands of
he Lord concerning the treatment which he is to mete out to
'übarliķ, and instructions concerning the division of his lands.
Description of the evils which shall happen in the seven thou-
andth year, when the gate which Alexander has made shall
be opened. Alexander, like Daniel, prophesies concerning the
end of times. The woes which shall come upon the earth
when the children of Gog and Magog break loose and over-
run the earth. Hymn of praise to God and to our Lord Jesus
Christ.

## HEBREW VERSIONS.

The legend of Alexander being the son of Nectanebus
appears to have been unknown to early Hebrew writers. In
the first book of Maccabees[1] we have a brief notice of his
conquest of Media and Persia, and the other countries of the
world, and a statement to the effect that he divided his kingdom
amongst those of his friends who had been brought up with
him, and that he reigned twelve years.

Flavius Josephus, who lived A.D. 37—103, gives a description of a part of his expedition against Darius, and of his visit
to Jerusalem[2]. According to him, Alexander first defeated the
generals of Darius at Granicum, and afterwards Darius himself
at Issus in Cilicia, when the wife and daughter of Darius fell
into his hands. He next captured Damascus and Sidon and
then began the siege of Tyre. Having taken Tyre and Gaza,
Alexander marched against Jerusalem to take vengeance upon
it, because, on a previous occasion, the Jewish high priest had
refused to send help to him. Jaddua the high priest feared
greatly, but when he heard that Alexander had drawn near to
the city he dressed himself in his finest garments, and putting
on his mitre, which was inscribed with the most holy name of
God, he went out to meet him at the head of a procession
of priests. Alexander did the priests and their city no harm,

[1] Chap. i. vv. 1—9.
[2] Josephus, *Antiquities*, Bk. xi. ch. viii, ed. Whiston, pp. 455—459.

and after they had shewn to him certain passages in the Book of Daniel[1] which referred, they said, to him and to his conquests, he promised to grant them any thing that they desired[2]. The remainder of the chapter on Alexander by Josephus is occupied by an account of his dealings with the Samaritans.

In the ninth or tenth century of our era, the Latin version of Pseudo-Callisthenes by Leo the Archpresbyter was turned into Hebrew by Pseudo-Josephus or Joseph ben-Gorion. Of this man very little is known. Gagnier thought[3] that he lived in the ninth century, as also did Zunz. Subsequently Zunz thought that he must have lived in the middle of the latter half of the tenth century[4], which is the date assigned to him by Steinschneider[5]. The History of Alexander by Joseph ben-Gorion begins in Bk. II. chap. 6, and occupies the remainder of the book. The value of the version and its variations from the *Historia de Præliis* have been discussed by Favre[6], and a summary of each chapter has been published by Weismann[7]. The Hebrew text has been published many times, and translations of it have been made in various languages[8].

Another fabulous history of Alexander was composed in the thirteenth century by Samuel ben-Judah ben-Tibbon of Granada.

---

[1] The passages shewn were Daniel viii. vv. 3—8, 20—22, where the "kid of the goats [is] Alexander the son of Philip" ܡ ܡܘܢ ܐܠܟܣܢܕܪ ܒܪ ܦܝܠܝܦܘܣ; see Ceriani, *Translatio Syra Pescitto Vet. Test. ex cod Ambrosiano*, Mediolani 1877, fol. 210 verso, col. 1.

[2] Good reasons for doubting this story have been given by Bishop Thirlwall, *History of Greece*, Vol. VI. p. 206.

[3] *Josippon sive Josephi Ben-Gorionis Historiae Judaicae libri sex*, Oxon. 1706, p. xxvi.

[4] See his notes on Benjamin of Tudela, ed. Asher, 1841, Vol. II. p. 246.

[5] *Jewish Literature*, p. 77.

[6] *Mélanges*, t. II. p. 89.

[7] *Alexander, Gedicht des zwölften Jahrhunderts, vom Pfaffen Lamprecht*, von H. Weismann, Band II. pp. 495—503.

[8] כספר בן גוריון Conath, Mantua, 1480 (?) fol.; *Josephus Hebraicus*, Heb. et Lat., Basle, 1541; יוסיפון בן גוריון *Latine versus......atque notis illustratus* a J. F. Breithaupto Heb. et Lat. Gotha, 1707. A German translation was published at Zurich by M. Adam in 1546; a Latin one by Gagnier at Oxford in 1706; an English one by P. Morwyng entitled *A Compendious History of the latter times of the Jews*, London, 1561; and another by J. Howell entitled *The wonderful......history of the later times of the Jews* in 1684.

Many rabbis regard it as a translation of a Greek work composed by Ptolemy the son of Lagus[1].

A Hebrew version, or original, of the *Iter ad Paradisum* has
recently been described by Israel Levi in the *Revue des Études
Juives*, t. II. p. 298, and t. XII. p. 117. For references to
passages in the Talmud and other Rabbinic literature where
notices of Alexander are given see Weismann, *Alexander*, t. II.
p. 503; the preface to Israel Levi's article in מקיצי נירדמים;
and Eisenmenger, *Entdeckten Judenthums*, t. II. pp. 321, 733,
734, 735.

## ARABIC VERSIONS.

In the tenth century Eutychius or Sa'ld ibn-Batrîk[2] (died
A.H. 328), the Patriarch of Alexandria, composed his universal
history, in which he says that the king of Egypt, fearing to fall
into the hands of Ochus, king of Persia, changed his garments,
and shaved his head and beard, and fled to Macedonia. The
name of this king is given as Pharaoh Shânâk فرعون شاناق[3].

Gregory abu-l-Farag or Bar Hebraeus (died A.H. 664), in
his History of Dynasties says that Artaxerxes the Third, sur-
named the "Black," and called Ochus by the Greeks, obtained
the mastery over Egypt; that its king, Nectanebus, fled away
to Macedonia, where he went about in the guise of an astrologer;
that by his flattery he succeeded in seducing Olympias, the wife
of Philip, the king of Macedon; and that she bore to him Alexander the "two-horned[4]."

---

[1] See Weismann, *Alexander*, B. 2, p. 503; and Favre, *Mélanges*, t. II., p. 90.
An anonymous Hebrew version of the history of Alexander has been published
by Levi in the *Sammelband*, II., of the Society מקיצי נירדמים. I owe this
reference to Dr. Ad. Neubauer, but I have not been able to see the publication.

[2] The work of Eutychius was edited with a Latin translation by Edward
Pocock under the title *Contextio Gemmarum, sive, Eutychii Patriarchae Alex-
andrini Annales*, Oxon. 1656.

[3] *Ibid.* p. 267.

[4] Pocock, *Historia Compendiosa Dynastiarum auctore Gregorio Abul-Pharajio*,
Oxon. 1663, p. 89. See also *Greg. Abulphar. Chron. Syriacum*, ed. Kirsch,
p. 36.

The histories of the reign of Alexander by the chief Arabic writers have comparatively little of the marvellous in them. Mas'ûdi' (died A.H. 346) merely describes the principal historical events of Alexander's life, giving only a few of the various traditions concerning him, together with a summary of the legendary account of his travels in India. Ja'kûbi', Ibn al-Athîr', and Tabari', have all of them brief accounts of Alexander's conquest of Darius, and the tradition that he was of Persian origin is mentioned. None of these accounts can in any way be considered as translations of a version of Pseudo-Callisthenes'.

## PERSIAN VERSIONS.

Between the tenth and fourteenth centuries a large number of works, based upon Arabic compositions, were written upon Alexander and his deeds by Persian writers. Of these the most important are the histories of Firdausi'

---

¹ See كتاب مروج الذهب *Les Prairies d'Or*, ed. Barbier de Meynard. Paris, 1861—1877, t. 11. pp. 125, 248, 249, 250, 260; t. 1x. p. 21. An edition of Mas'ûdi's work entitled الجزء الول (الثاني) من مروج الذهب ومعادن الجوهر في التاريخ was published at Bûlâk in the year 1867 بولاق ١٢٨٤ مصر القاهرة 4to.

² He lived A.H. 260. His work has been edited by T. Houtsma, *Ibn Wâdhih qui dicitur Al-Ja'qûbi Historiae*, Lugd. Bat. 1883. For his account of Alexander see pp. ٩٢ and ٩٧.

³ He died A.H. 630. For his notice of Alexander see *Ibn-el-Athiri, Chronicon* ed. C. J. Tornberg, t. 1. p. ١٩٧.

⁴ He died A.H. 411 or 416. See *Annales quos scripsit Ibn Djafar..... At-Tabari*, ed. I. Guidi, Prima series, 11. pp. ٦٩٢—٧٠٩.

⁵ For the summary of the travels of Dhu'lkarnein or Alexander the Macedonian by Muḥammad the Prophet see Kor'ân, Surah xviii.

⁶ See *Le Livre des Rois par Abou'lkasim Firdousi, publié, traduit et commenté par* J. Mohl, كتاب شاهنامه فردوسي Pers. and Fr. 7 tom. Paris 1838, fol.; *Le Livre des Rois par Abou'lkasim Firdousi, traduit et commenté par* J. Mohl, 7 tom. Paris 1876—1878; J. Atkinson, *The Shâh Nâmeh of the Persian poet Firdausi, translated and abridged in prose and verse, with notes and illustrations*, London, 1832; Turner Macan, *The Shah Namch containing the History of Persia from Kioomurs to Yezdejird*, Calcutta, 1829; Firdusii *Liber Regum, qui inscribitur Schahnamch*, ed. J. A. Vullers et S. Landauer

Niẓâmî[1] and Mirkhwând[2]. I have no knowledge of the Persian language and must therefore refer the reader to the works of Spiegel[3], Weismann[4], and Favre[5] for a description of the contents of the various Persian versions of the Alexander story. There seems to be some doubt as to whether Firdausî based his work upon older Persian or Arabic forms of the Alexander story. De Sacy thought[6] that the greater part of the ancient history of Persia was translated from Pehlevi into Arabic, and Malcolm believed[7] that Firdausî found the materials for his poem in the Arabic versions of the original documents. M. Jules Mohl[8], however, was of opinion that Firdausî employed an Arabic

Lugd. Bat. 1876; and for a native edition of the text see شاهنامهٔ فردوسی دهران ١٢٤٠—٦٧ [Teheran 1849—50]. Firdausî was born at Shâdâb near Tûs A.H. 320; he died A.H. 411 or 416. For a list of his works and editions of them see Rieu, *Catalogue of the Persian MSS. in the British Museum*, London, 1879—1883 pp. 533—539 and 1089.

[1] See Niẓâmî, Ganjavî, *The Sikandar Nâma e Dara, or Book of Alexander the Great,......translated for the first time out of the Persian into prose, with critical and explanatory remarks......by H. W. Clarke*, London, 1881; *Niẓâmî's Leben und Werke und der zweite Theil des Nizâmischen Alexanderbuches. Mit persischen Texten als Anhang. Beiträge zur Geschichte der Persischen Literatur und der Alexandersage* von Dr. W. Bacher, 2 pt. Leipzig, 1871, 8vo. [An English translation of this work was published in London, 1873]; for native editions of the text see سكندر نامه [بری], Lucknow, 1878, 9 [١٢٩٠] كانپور and سكندر نامه بحری [لكهنو] Cawnpore, 1878 [١٢٩٠—٦] An edition of the second part of the work, i.e., Sikandar-Nâmah Baḥry, was published in the *Bibliotheca Indica* by Sprenger, Calcutta, 1852—1869. An illustrated prose version of the *Sikandar Nâmah*, different from that of Niẓâmî, in seven books, was published in Persia A.H. 1274 (1857—8) fol. I owe the knowledge of the existence of this last book to Mr. A. G. Ellis of the British Museum. Niẓâmî died about A.H. 600.

[2] See Mîr Khwând (Muḥammad ibn Khâvand Shâh). *History of the Early Kings of Persia*, translated by D. Shea, London, 1832. An edition of the text entitled كتاب تاريخ روضة الصفا was published at Bombay in A.H. 1271 [١٢٧١ بمبئي]. Mîr Khwând died A.H. 903 aged 66 years.

[3] Spiegel, *Die Alexandersage bei den Orientalen*, pp. 13—60.
[4] Weismann, *Alexander*, Bd. II., p. 526 ff.
[5] *Mélanges*, t. II., pp. 5—18.
[6] *Mém. sur Calila et Dimna*, p. 18.
[7] *History of Persia*, I. p. 137.
[8] *Livre des Rois*, p. xlviii.

version[1] of a Greek original to complete the gap which he found
in the traditions of his country. His words are " Firdousi
parait n'avoir pas trouvé de matériaux persans pour le règne
d'Alexandre le Grand...mais au lieu de se livrer à son imagination dans un sujet qui y prêtait beaucoup, il aime mieux
emprunter les contes dont les soldats grecs, à leur retour en
Grèce, avaient rempli l'Occident. Ces contes avaient été re-
cueillis en plusieurs collections, dont quelques-unes existent
encore en grec et en latin et dont une avait été traduite du
grec en arabe. C'est à l'aide de cette dernière que Firdousi
a rempli la lacune qu'il avait trouvée dans les traditions de
son pays, en y adaptant le conte persan qui fait d'Alexandre un
chef de race persane, fils de Darab, roi de Perse et d'une fille de
Philippe de Macédoine, du même que les rédactions alexandrines
des fables grecques relatives à Alexandre lui donnaient pour
père l'Egyptien Nectanebo."

## TURKISH VERSIONS.

Upon the Iskender Nâmeh of Nizâmî, Aḥmedî[2] of Ker-
miyân (died A.H. 815) based his Turkish poem called *Iskender
Nâmeh*. "He adopted the main features of the Alexander legend
as shaped by his Persian predecessor ; but he tells the story in
his own way and adds much original matter. He weaves into
the narrative philosophical digressions on the origin and figure
of the world, on man, his bodily structure and mental faculties,
virtues and vices, etc. More than a quarter of the poem is
taken up with a review of Eastern history, placed in the mouth
of Aristotle, who tells Alexander of the kings who reigned before and who shall reign after him. The poem was composed
on the first day of Rebi' II, A.H. 792, corresponding to the
years 1700 of Alexander, 759 of Yezdegird, and 310 of
Melikshâb[3]."

---

[1] The author of the *Mugmil ut-tewârich* held a similar opinion (Favre,
*Mélanges*, t. II. p. 7). A chapter of this work was edited by Reinaud in his
*Fragments Arabes et Persans inédits relatifs à l'Inde*, Paris, 1845.

[2] His full name was Tâj ad-Din Aḥmed ben Ibrâhîm el-Aḥmedî.

[3] Rieu, *Catalogue of the Turkish MSS. in the British Museum*, London, 1888,
p. 162 b.

A Turkish translation of an Armenian life of Alexander was made in the seventeenth century by Jeremias Tschelebi (1635—1695)[1].

## ETHIOPIC VERSIONS.

The versions of the History of Alexander the Great in use among the Ethiopians are of two classes, viz., I. those which have in them a stratum of historical fact underlying large masses of fiction, and II. those which are works of pure imagination. The Ethiopians, in common with a large number of Oriental nations, have taken considerable pains to have translations of the History of Alexander the Great made into their language, but the translators seem to have allowed their fancy to run wild when they filled in the details of the historical events, which were described in the manuscript histories from which they made their translations. The Ethiopic translations were made from Arabic versions which had been made, I believe, from Greek originals. Ethiopic translations were sometimes made from Coptic[2], but an examination of the recently discovered fragments of the Coptic[3] version of the History of Alexander the Great shews that it has nothing in common with any of the Ethiopic versions known to me now. In respect of the age of the Ethiopic translations of the History of Alexander, in the absence of direct evidence it is only possible to assume that they came into existence some time between the XIVth and XVIth centuries, when so many Ethiopic translations from the Arabic were made[4].

A brief but favourite summary of the life and deeds of Alexander the Great among the Ethiopians is that which is

---

[1] Weismann, *Alexander*, Bd. II. p. 607. See J. von Hammer, *Geschichte der Türkischen Poesie*, p. 71 ff.; Favre, *Mélanges*, t. II. p. 14; and Neumann, *Geschichte der Armenischen Literatur*, p. 241.

[2] Wright, *Catalogue of the Ethiopic MSS. in the British Museum*, p. iv.

[3] *Journal Asiatique*, Série III. t. IX. pp. 5—38.

[4] Wright, *Catalogue of Ethiopic MSS.*, p. iv.

translated from 'Abû Shâkir, of which notices have been given by D'Abbadie[1], Wright[2] and Zotenberg[3]. The conquest of Persia and India by Alexander and the most important expeditions undertaken by him are concisely recorded, and the fabulous element which plays so large a part in all other Ethiopic accounts is here almost wanting[4].

Most important of all Ethiopic versions of the History of Alexander the Great for the study of the versions of Pseudo-Callisthenes is that which is, so far as I know, contained in a single manuscript only, viz. Brit. Mus. MS. Orient. No. 826 ff. 2a—147a[5]. This MS. is of vellum, measuring about 11⅔ in. by 7¼ in., and was written in the present century. It was one of the manuscripts which were destined by king Theodore of Magdala (ዎ፝ደላ *Makdalâ*) to form the library of the church which he intended to build there in honour of the Saviour of the World, and was brought to England by the British army in 1868. The version of the Alexander story given in this MS. has been translated from an Arabic work based upon Pseudo-Callisthenes. In places it runs almost word for word with the Syriac, and the forms of Greek proper names which occur in it agree often with the Syriac transcription of them. A large number of the proper names which are found in the Syriac version are not present here at all, and it seems to have been the custom of the Arabic or Ethiopic translator to omit the most difficult passages, as, for example, that which records the speech and computation of the stars by Nectanebus just before the birth of Alexander. Some passages of the Greek and Syriac are very much amplified, some are abridged, and some are translated twice over in different words. The Arabic or Ethiopic translator seems to have been a Christian priest. The legend which gives the account of Alexander's expedition against Gog and Magog is brought into the middle of the Ethiopic version, which seems to indicate that this is its proper place.

[1] *Catalogue Raisonné de MSS. Ethiopiens*, p. 61.
[2] *Catalogue of Ethiopic MSS.*, p. 310, col. 1.
[3] *Catalogue des MSS. Ethiopiens*, p. 215, col. 1.
[4] For the portion of the Ethiopic translation of Al-Makin's "Universal History" relating to Alexander, see *Brit. Mus. MS. Orient.* fol. 60 b, col. 3 ff.
[5] See Wright, *Catalogue of the Ethiopic MSS.*, p. 204.

The length of the Ethiopic version of Pseudo-Callisthenes renders it impossible to give a complete English translation of it here, but I give a free rendering of the first few chapters and a summary of the rest, that students of the Alexander story from the folk-lore point of view may know what the chief contents of this unique manuscript are. The Ethiopic title of the work is ዜና፡ እስክንድር፡ "The History of Alexander." After the usual beginning, "In the name of God, the Merciful, the Gracious," the scribe says that, by the help of God, he will write an account of Alexander according to the histories that have been written by the wise men who have described his rule over the seven parts of the earth; his expeditions from the east to the west; his rule over the whole earth; his sailing over the sea አሳንኔስ፡ e!-pantas; his flying through the air; and his journey into the darkness and into the places where God brought him. Necta-nebus በቅጣንስ Bektánts[1] is described as a very great magi-cian and as a man learned in all the knowledge of the Egyptians, ግብጽ፡ ግብጻውያን፡; he knew what was in the depths of the sea, he knew all the lore of the stars, and by their appearance he knew what would come to pass. By means of this knowledge he ruled over all the kings of the earth, and they were all subject to him through the greatness of his magical powers. When hos-tile forces came against him to slay him and to capture his land, it was not his custom to go out to meet them with soldiers set in array, but he used to go into a chamber and shut himself in, and he used to take a brass vessel ንዋይ፡ ኀብረት፡ and fill it with water, like a river (or sea), and say over it the words which he knew. Then he took wax and held it over the fire and made models of the ships of the enemy, and he set them on the water in the vessel like ships in the sea. And he said over them the names of demons of the earth and fearful and terrible words, and the ships of wax rode upon the water like the ships of the sea. When enemies came up against him from the sea he submerged the wax models of the ships by his magic, and this caused the ships of the enemies who wished to come and slay him to sink into the sea. If the enemy came against him by land (fol. 3 a, 1) he used to make wax models of

---

[1] See Zotenberg, *Chronique de Jean, Évêque de Nikiou*, p. 276.

men upon horses አመሳሰ፡ አፈራስ፡ ኸስመዐ፡ like unto the sol-
·diers of the enemy who were coming against him to kill him,
and he uttered over them fearful and terrible words, and the
enemy was overthrown before him, and submitted and became
subject unto him. And this and such like things he used to do
with every one whom he wished to slay. He never went forth
against his enemies with soldiers and instruments of death. He
used to make models of the soldiers of the two armies in wax,
then he set a space between them, and then he pronounced the
names of demons of the earth and invoked them and prayed
them to come to him and to help his army to overthrow the
enemy before him. In this manner he lived and acted for many
days, and he brought many men into misfortune through his
magical powers.

Chap. II. Now during the days of his rule over Egypt
ግብጽ፡, one of the scouts of his army came and told him that
nine kings with their armies, and innumerable multitudes of
people with them, were coming against him. The names of
these peoples are thus given on fol. 3 b: the Midianites,
መድናዊያን፡ Madanâwiyân, the Sargiyâwiyân ሰርጊያዊያን፡, the
Kimanâwiyân which are in Tarsôs አስተመናዊያን፡ ዘበ፡ ተርሴስ፡,
the Antâwiyân, አንታዊያን፡, the Halabâwiyân ሐለባዊያን፡, the
Sakâgâñwiyân ሰቃጋፈዊያን፡, the Emâhinâwiyân እማህናዊ[ያ]ን፡,
the Agamâwiyân which are in Kâdôs አጋማዊያን፡ ዘበቃዴስ፡,
the Gûergûe ጉርጌ፡, and the Sarakâwiyân: ሰረቃዊያን፡. Nectanebus praised the vigilance of the scout and told him that
armies and arms were alike useless to overcome these hosts, and
that only stoutness of heart and silence could do it. He added,
" as one lion overcomes many people and as one wolf scatters
many sheep, so likewise will I, with one word, destroy the peoples
who have come against me by sea and by land."

Chap. III. (fol. 3 b, 2). After this Nectanebus left the army,
and went into the chamber in his palace where he worked his
magic, and he looked into the water which was in the brass
basin ዓየ፡ መጽበ.ል፡ ዘብርት፡, and after he had said over it the
words which he was wont to say the gods of Egypt appeared to
him, and he asked them to help him when he made the models
of his army and those of the enemy to meet. . Now it came

to pass at this time that the gods took no notice of his request; although in days of old he was able to talk with them at all times. When he saw that his magical powers had no effect upon the gods and understood thereby that his rule over Egypt had come to an end, he was very sorrowful. And he rose up and took as much gold as he could carry and as much silver as he wished, and having shaved off his hair and beard and changed his raiment, he went out from his palace quickly, and crossed the sea in a ship and came to the city (sic) of Macedonia, in the gate of which he sat dressed like an astrologer and one of the prophets of Egypt. Meanwhile the Egyptians went to their god, and asked him to tell them what had become of their king. Now the god, who was hidden in a place called Sanôbl ሰኖቢ:, appeared to them and told them that their king had fled, that he would not return to Egypt, and that he had cast away everything for the salvation of his soul in peace[1]; and the Egyptians heard the oracle and believed it.

Chap. IV. (fol. 4 a, 2). Now the name of Nectanebus spread abroad in Macedonia, and the fame of his renown and of his learning came to the ears of Olympias, ሰሞበያስ Lêmbayda. And she wished to ask him questions and to talk with him about her husband Philip and the subject of her divorce. Nectanebus came and found her dressed in beautiful apparel; she was very beautiful to look upon, and she was playful, and his heart was drawn out of him to her. He saluted her by saying, "Peace be to thee, O Macedonian queen," but she neither spoke to him nor answered him nor returned his greeting. He said to her again, "O my lady, why dost thou not answer me?" Olympias then saluted him and asked him to sit down, and when he had sat down, she asked him if he was a prophet of Egypt and if his works were as marvellous as they were said to be. Having satisfied herself that he possessed the power of foretelling events she asked him to help her. Nectanebus then enumerated the different kinds of augurs that existed. Here the Ethiopic text

---

[1] The translator, either Arabic or Ethiopic, has utterly missed the point of the answer of the oracle. The Ethiopic runs እስመ: ንትሐሠሞ ፩: ገዖ: ወለረገበ: እንክ: ኅበ: ገብኇ: ወዐእተ: ጊዜ: ወፈዘ: ወእክ: አረፕ:: ወሞነነ: ከጐኈ: በእንተ: ይኅነተ: ፩ፈሊ: በሰላሞ::

becomes so confused that the sense given by the Greek is quite lost. Nectanebus then put his hand inside his garments አበአኅት:, and brought forth a tablet, ስኔይ: *salédá*, of gold studded with stars in precious stones, and upon it were inscribed pictures of the seven planets which were arranged according to the hours of the day and night. The stars or planets which are mentioned are the Sun[1], Moon[2], Jupiter[3], Venus[4], Mars[5], and Mercury[6]; the scribe has omitted the seventh planet or Saturn[7] (fol. 5 a, col. 2). Each planet was represented by a precious stone. After examining the stars carefully Nectanebus tells her that he will help her, and that the gods who come forth from the depths of the earth shall come to her, and that she shall bear a son to them who shall avenge her upon Philip, because he has treated her badly. He adds that the god is noble in appearance, that he will wear a ram's horns, and that he will sleep with her. Olympias then declares that if this comes to pass she will consider Nectanebus to be a god and not a man.

Chap. V. (fol. 6 a, 1). Then Nectanebus went out to the field and pounded and crushed drugs, and he made a model of a woman, and wrote upon it the letters of the name of Olympias, and threw it in the fire, and he repeated words and names over it; and Olympias dreamed a dream in which the god Ammon was united with her.

Chap. VI. (fol. 6 a, col. 2). In the Ethiopic version the description of the god is wanting.

Chap. VII. (fol. 6 b, col. 2). Nectanebus disguises himself with ram's wool and horns, and takes the form of a serpent and goes into the chamber of Olympias. Afterwards she sends for him and prepares a chamber for him (fol. 7 b, col. 1). When

---

[1] ጸሕይ:   [2] ወርኅ:   [3] አልመስተሬ: Arab. المشتري

[4] አዝሁራ: Arab. زهرة   [5] አልመርኅ: Arab. مريخ

[6] ዐጥርይ: Arab. عطارد

[7] ዛሕል: Arab. زحل   For Ethiopic lists of the names of the stars, see *Brit. Mus.* MSS. Add. 16211, fol. 55 and Add. 16217, fol. 64. According to a native historian names were given to the planets by Seth, the son of Adam. See Zotenberg, *Chronique de Jean, Évêque de Nikiou*, pp. 26, 239.

Olympias is troubled about her pregnancy Nectanebus promises that Ammon አመኅ፡ will help her.  Then Nectanebus took a bird ፈዖጸ፡ (fol. 8 a, 1) and muttered words over it, and it flew through the sky over lands and cities and seas, and came to Philip by night, and that same night he had a wonderful dream in which he saw a terrestrial divinity of great stature, wearing ram's horns and having his head and beard shaved, sleeping with Olympias.  In it he saw also the queen's womb sealed with a gold ring, upon which were engraved the head of a lion and a spear.

Chap. VIII. (fol. 8 a, col. 2).  The interpretation of the dream is substantially the same as in the Syriac.

Chap. IX. (fol. 8 b, col. 2, l. 15).  This chapter is almost identical in sense with that of the Syriac.  Olympias sends, however, for Nectanebus after Philip has talked with her.

Chap. X. (fol. 9 a, col. 1, l. 19).  Philip upbraids Olympias, and says that she is with child by Ammon.  Nectanebus, in the guise of a serpent, glides into the chamber where they are sitting, and hisses fearfully.  Philip is terrified when he sees the serpent, and Olympias says that its voice was thus when he came to her and said that he was the god of all the world; when Philip heard this he was glad that he was to have a son.

Chap. XI. (fol. 9 b, col. 2, l. 14) is the same as in the Syriac.

Chap. XII. (fol. 10 a, col. 2, l. 23).  Nectanebus stands and calculates the stars, and advises the queen not to give birth to her child.  He prevents her by force from so doing until a fortunate hour arrives, and then he allows her to bring forth.  Here the Ethiopic text is much confused, and all allusions to incidents in Greek mythology are omitted.

Chap. XIII. (fol. 11 a, col. 1, l. 2).  Macedonia and Abrâkâ አብራክ፡ are mentioned.  In appearance Alexander was like (sic) his parents Philip and Olympias, and when he was six years old he went to school to learn Greek learning, war and astronomy.  The incident of the Cappadocians sending a gift of horses to Philip is omitted.

Chap. XIV. (fol. 11 b, col. 1, l. 14).  The incident of the departure of Philip to another city and the sending for Nectanebus by Olympias is omitted.  Alexander goes to the top of the mountains to see the stars, and Nectanebus says, "Verily

thou art my son, and the god knows that thou art my son;
I slept with thy mother in the temple and she conceived thee;
do not despise my word, for I am a great king, and I am the
king of Egypt." When Alexander heard this he threw Nectanebus down from the top of the mountain and he died. When
Alexander met Philip his father he said, "I have killed the
priest of idols," and when Philip asked him what he had
done he told him. After this Alexander is sent to Aristotle
ኣርስ ጥጠሳስ፦.

Up to this point the Ethiopic version runs fairly closely
with the Syriac, but from here onwards the sequence of events
as given in the Syriac and Greek is much disturbed.

Chap. XXIII. (fol. 12 a, col. 1, l. 19). Now Philip used to
give tribute to the king of Persia who ruled over the empire of
Nimrod, the mighty man who worshipped fire and established
priests thereto, who spread the Magian belief ሃይማኖት፡
ማጎሳፒት፡, and who had intercourse with his mother and sister
and daughter. One day when the ambassadors of the Persian
king Darius came to ask for tribute Alexander saw them, and
came down and talked with them. His scoffing message to
Darius is not given in the Ethiopic, but he promises to go to
Persia riding upon Bucephalus, whom he describes as "my horse
which was born with me" ፈረስ፡ እኁ፡ ተወልደት፡ ምስሌይ፡.
The chief ambassador instead of admiring Alexander's discourse
says that "the boy knows not what he says." Then Darius
sent two greater messengers with a golden box ሀበ-ኍ፡ filled
with sesame seed ፈረ፡ ስሊፕ፡, among which was a precious
stone. When the ambassadors came to Alexander they gave
him their letters, and he opened them and read them; then he
went and sat upon his father's throne, and took the golden box,
and found therein sesame seed and a jewel. And he said to his
friends, "Interpret these things for me," but they refused, saying,
"Thou knowest these things better than we do." Alexander
said, "Sesame seed is food, and food is to be eaten; the Persian
army is like sesame seed, and we will devour it as we devour
sesame seed. As for the gem, it is like the head of a king and
the Persian king has God given into my hand." Alexander
then sent back an insolent message to Darius, but Philip wanted

to send him to Persia so that Darius might do what he liked to
him. Chap. ends fol. 13 *b*, col. 1, l. 9.

Chap. XVI. (fol. 13 *b*, col. 1, l. 10). Now there was in the
house a horse that was born with Alexander, and no one could
go near him or mount him, and he was kept chained with six
chains day and night. Alexander however went up to him and
mounted him, and then his father gave orders that the horse
was to be well looked after, for he was very fleet and could go a
distance of 300 መሕፖር: in one hour. The chapter ends fol.
14 *a*, col. 1, l. 9.

After this Alexander mounts this horse, and taking his army
with him, he goes to the East. Next we have a prayer in
which Alexander acknowledges his submission to God; he took
for his teacher Aristotle, whose belief was the belief of the
philosophers who say "'The heavens declare the glory of the
Creator, the Maker of all and King of all, who killeth and
maketh alive, in whom and from whom are all things" (fol.
14 *b*, col. 1). Alexander prays to God, and advises his friends
and nobles not to commit sin. He says that he is king (fol.
15 *a*, col. 1); and speaks of the redemption of man's soul; his
friends promise to do what he wishes (fol. 15 *b*, col. 1), and
crown him and present an address to him (fol. 16 *a*, 1), to which
he replies (fol. 16 *a*, col. 2). He then writes an address to the
people of his palace which begins on fol. 18 *a*, col. 1 and ends
fol. 19 *b*, col. 2, l. 11. His title "two-horned" ዘክልኤ: አቅርንቲሁ:
occurs for the first time in this manuscript in this address. The
Ethiopic writers explain this title by saying that he was so
called because he "ruled in the two horns of the Sun, the east
and the west[1]." He next writes to his army (fol. 19 *b*, col. 2, l.
11,—fol. 21 *b*, col. 2, l. 8), and then to all the kings of the earth,
saying that God has given him the world, and that he will help
them to know Him as he knows Him (fol. 19 *b*, col. 2, l. 12—fol.
23 *a*, col. 2, l. 16). A copy of this proclamation is sent to Darius

---

[1] ወበ: ዘይበ: ተስ መዖP: ዘᎦ ለቅርንቲሁ: እስመ: ነገሠ: ዘᎦ ለቅርንተ:
0ሐፀ: እመሥራቅ: እስከ: መዕራብ:: Brit. Mus. MS. Orient. 818, fol.
125 *b*, col. 1, ll. 23—27. See also D'Abbadie, *Catalogue de MSS. Éthiop.*, p. 81;
and the Ethiopic translation of Al-Makin's "Universal History" in Brit. Mus.
MS. Orient. 814, fol. 69 *b*, col. 3.

ደፊ: king of Persia, who read it before all the army. Darius, "king of kings," next writes a letter to the men of Tiberius Cæsar ሰብእ: ፕብይኗክ: ቀሰር: the Roman, in which he abuses and curses Alexander, and begs them not to allow him to come into their country (fol. 23 b, col. 1, l. 5—col. 2, l. 11). Presently Darius heard that Alexander had arrived at the great river called Kôparôs ፆጸኗክ:, and he wrote him a letter beginning, "To Alexander, the king of the Greeks, son of Philip, the two-horned, my servant." He reminds him in it that Philip paid tribute, and insists on his doing likewise (fol. 24 b, col. 1, l. 8). Alexander orders that the ambassadors who have brought this letter to him shall be slain, but he spares them eventually to shew the superiority of the manners of the Greeks to those of the Persians. Darius imagines that Alexander has slain his ambassadors, he therefore sends others with another letter (fol. 25 b, col. 2, l. 9—fol. 26 a, col. 1, l. 13). Alexander sends a reply to this last letter which begins "From the servant of God, the two-horned" (fol. 26 b, col. 1, l. 4), and determines that all his letters shall begin in this manner (fol. 26 b, col. 2, l. 12). In it Alexander tells Darius that if he kills him he will only be killing a thief, and he says that the sesame seed represents Darius' army which he will overthrow because his trust is in God; in return, however, he sends a little mustard seed ፈፈ: ሰፕፕ: that Darius may know what the Macedonian army is like. The letter ends fol. 27 b, col. 1. In a second letter to Darius Alexander threatens to come against him (fol. 27 b, col. 2, l. 8). The ambassadors who bring his letters to Darius praise him greatly, and tell Darius that he ate some of the sesame seed : Darius then orders one of his soldiers to eat some of the mustard seeds; the soldier, not knowing how pungent they are, throws a handful into his mouth, but he cannot swallow them and so spits them out. On the report reaching him that Alexander has set out to come against him Darius writes to the satraps under his rule demanding their help; but meanwhile Alexander returns to Egypt (fol. 28 b, col. 1), and founds a city after his name. All Egypt submits to him except Tâkâtelô, Nôbâ and Ethiopia; the people of Africa come to do homage to him. He passed through Syria and came with his army to Palestine. While there he wrote to the chief priests of the sanctuary of Jerusalem calling

upon them to submit to him; this they declined to do, saying
that they were under the dominion of the king of Persia
(fol. 29 a, col. 2, ll. 9—16). When Alexander marched into
Jerusalem with his army all the Jews and the governor of the
town, who had been appointed by Darius, submitted to him.
The priests went out to meet him carrying a book of the Law
(fol. 29 a, col. 1, l. 24) and the prophecy of Daniel the prophet
concerning Alexander spread out on the top of a spear. Alexander said, "What is this that I see with you?" and they
replied, "It is the writing of God which came down by the prophets, and the prophecy of Daniel who prophesied concerning
thy kingdom." When Alexander saw this he wept, and came
down from his horse, and went near to the writing of the Law
and the Prophets and worshipped God; then he went into the
Temple and asked God to direct his paths. He admired greatly
the beauty of the Temple, for it was morning. When the
soldiers ask Alexander why he honours the Jews who slew
the prophets he says that he only honours the name of God
which they carry upon their persons[1]. The chief priest gives
Alexander a copy of the prophecy of Daniel and then, after a
little talk, he leaves the Temple (fol. 30 b, col. 1).

Going eastward Alexander crossed the Euphrates, and built
a city there which he called Baratâ በረታ፣, he next came to a
country called ደሴት: Dasêt. He fought with Darius at a place
called በዚ፣ for forty days, and after a further five days' fight
with Ardeshir, Darius' general, nearly all Darius' army was
killed. Alexander then marched against the royal city of
Darius, but before he attacked it, he addressed his army with
words of encouragement (fol. 31 a, coll. 1, 2); the battle was
obstinate, and Darius gained some advantage over Alexander,
who wrote to Darius and said that he was going back to his own
country (fol. 32 a, col. 1, l. 21), and asked for a truce. Darius
refused to allow this, whereupon Alexander made a very fierce
attack upon him and utterly routed him. Darius escapes by
crossing over a river (fol. 32 b, col. 2) and takes refuge in the
temple of his god (lit. the house of the idol), where he laments

[1] See the *History of the holy men in the days of Jerusalem*, in Wright,
*Catalogue of the Ethiopic MSS.*, p. 309.

his fate (fol. 33 *a*, col. 2). When Darius heard that Alexander
had captured his wife and daughter he wrote commending them
to his clemency, and sent to him gold and silver and jewels and
clothing. Alexander reads this letter to his friend Salonós who
asked why Darius had not done this before (fol. 34 *a*, col. 1).
When he had slain all Darius' nobles, Darius wrote to Porus
ፎሕ: *Puz*) king of India asking for help; Porus replies (fol.
34 *b*, col. 1, L 18—35 *a*, col. 1, L 17). Alexander then asked his
soldiers to find out men who will give him information about
Darius; two men called Ḥashish ኃሀሏሐ: and Arsalās ኣርስሰስ:
offered to do this, but they stabbed Darius thinking to gain
a reward (fol. 35 *b*, coll. 1, 2). Alexander came up and finding
Darius stabbed, dismounted and put his head upon his knees,
and exhorted him to rise up and to become king of Persia once
more (fol. 36 *a*, col. 2). Before his death Darius asked Alexander to do three things for him; Alexander promised to carry
out his wishes and asked to be allowed to marry his daughter
(fol. 37 *b*, col. 1). Darius dies and is buried by Alexander (fol.
38 *a*, col. 1). Alexander issues a proclamation to the Persians
(fol. 38 *a*, col. 2—38 *b*, col. 2, L 23). Alexander promises to reward
the murderers of Darius (fol. 39 *a*, col. 1), and crucifies (fol. 39 *b*.
col. 2) them. He writes to the mother of Darius (fol. 40 *a*, col.
2—40 *b*, col. 2, L 19), and Roxana (ሮስቅ *Rasik*) writes to him
applauding his kindness to them (fol. 41 *b*, col. 2, L 19). Alexander writes to her (fol. 42 *a*, col. 1, L 19), and goes to see her;
and next writes to the mother of Darius ስረ: Saragó (fol. 42 *b*,
col. 1).

About this time Alexander heard that Porus had come
to fight with him and he set out to meet him; his troops
grumble on the way (fol. 42 *a*, col. 2—44 *a*, col. 2). Alexander
writes to Porus (fol. 44 *a*, col. 2, L 14), and Porus replies (fol.
45 *a*, col. 1, L 9); on the receipt of this letter Alexander marches
against him (fol. 46 *a*, col. 1, l. 7). Porus writes again (fol. 46 *a*.
col. 1, L 21), and Alexander sends a reply (fol. 47 *a*, col. 2, L 14),
which Porus reads to his nobles (fol. 48 *a*, col. 1, l. 14). Porus
collects rhinoceroses and lions to fight against Alexander. Alexander also makes 24,000 metal rhinoceroses, which his soldiers
make red-hot by lighting fires inside them (fol. 48 *b*, col. 1). The
hostile forces meet and Porus' beasts run away, but Porus throws

Alexander's horse upon the ground by sorcery, and prevents Alexander from pursuing him by keeping him there while he makes good his escape (fol. 49 *a*, col. 1). Alexander then challenges him to single combat (fol. 49 *b*, col. 1); Porus accepts the challenge and is killed (fol. 50 *a*, col. 1). Alexander addresses the Indian army and afterwards buries Porus (fol. 50 *b*, col. 2).

The defeat of Porus accomplished Alexander set out to go to see the Brahmans, አልበርግናውያን፡ *al-Baragândwĕyân*, who, hearing of his arrival in their country, write to him (fol. 51 *a*, col. 1, l. 22) and mention Baal Peor ፌጎር፡ (fol. 51 *b*, col. 1, l. 2); Alexander reads their letter and goes to them (fol. 52 *a*, col. 1), and asks one of them:—

"How do you live, and how do you die?" fol. 52 *a*, col. 2, l. 12.

"Have you no graves in which to bury your dead?" fol. 53 *a*, col. 2, l. 3.

"Are the dead more in number than the living?" fol. 53 *b*, col. 1.

"Is death mightier than life?" fol. 53 *b*, col. 1, l. 22.

"What is the wickedest thing in creation?" fol. 54 *a*, col. 1, l. 1.

"Is night older than day or day older than night?" fol. 54 *a*, col. 2.

"Who is He that has never been born?" fol. 54 *b*, col. 1.

"Which is man's strongest limb, his right hand or his left?" fol. 54 *b*, col. 1.

After Alexander had asked these questions the Brahman asks him to give them immortality; he says that he is unable to do this because everything depends upon the will of God. He writes to Aristotle (fol. 56 *b*, col. 2, l. 11), and then wishes to go and see the grave of a king on an island, but eventually sends one of his friends there with 800 men (fol. 57 *b*, col. 2). After a march of twelve nights they come to a city situated between two rivers (fol. 58 *b*, col. 1), and see the pillar upon which is inscribed "I am Sesonchosis (ሶስ፡ *sic*) king of the world" (fol. 59 *a*, col. 1). The *Mashkĕlath* is described as being "greater than a rhinoceros" (fol. 59 *b*, col. 2, l. 14), and as having required forty men to kill it (fol. 60 *a*, col. 1) and three hundred men to cut it open. Alexander then came to a country where the men were like ravens ቋዓት፡ (fol. 60 *b*, col. 1); and the

Macedonians stayed there seven days and slew six thousand of
them.  They met creatures half men half beast (fol. 60 b, col. 2,
ll. 3—6); they saw the people who had "legs like a camel" (fol.
61 a, col. 2, l. 15); the men with lions' heads (fol. 61 a, col. 2,
l. 25); the tree which grew and diminished (fol. 61 b, col. 1);
and the river which was full of birds (fol. 61 b, col. 2, l. 21).
They came to the sea called Pontus, where twenty of Alexander's
men were devoured by beasts (fol. 62 a, col. 2).  After a march
of 65 nights he comes to a place where there were two birds,
one of which said, "O two-horned one, behold, thou marchest
through a land in which no man has ever before walked; it is
not good for thee.  Why dost thou not go back?  Behold, thou
hast slain Darius the king of all the kings of the world (fol.
62 b, col. 1), and also Porus the king of the Indians who was lord
over demons and devils, and who had captured all the ends
of the world.  Now, therefore, turn back from this place, for
what thou hast done is sufficient for thee."  In this place Alexander goes into a temple where there is a chain weighing 300
ⲛ̅ⲑ̅ⲡ̅ⲅ̅: according to the weight of Constantinople (?) (fol. 63 a,
col. 1, l. 8), and sees there a throne with 2500 steps (fol. 63 a,
col. 2, l. 3) and two candlesticks, each of which is 40 cubits
in height.  In the temple is a nameless god who tells Alexander
that he will bring him to the place where Enoch, Elijah, Abraham, Isaac, Jacob and those like unto them dwell (fol. 64 a, col.
1, line 11).

From this place Alexander goes to "a city of India" (Pra-
siakē), and is obliged to stay there thirty nights on account
of the snow (fol. 64 b, col. 2).  He asks the Indians if there
is any thing wonderful to be seen in that country and they tell
him of two talking trees (fol. 65 a, col. 2) which "speak in all
tongues."  After a journey of ten days they reach a place where
there is a garden, and in it are two figures of the sun and moon
and a great altar called "the rising of the sun and moon,"
because the sun and moon rise here (fol. 65 b, col. 2, l. 20).
Taking fifty men he goes into the temple, and the trees speak
(fol. 66 b, col. 1).  One of them prophesies his death in the land
of Babylon, and says that it will be caused by poison being
administered to him by friends (fol. 67 a, col. 1).  After a march
of fifteen nights they come to a city called Sapin (fol. 67 a, col.

2, L 7), the people of which tell him about a god in the form of
a serpent which lives in the mountains at a distance of three
days (fol. 67 b, col. 1); Alexander kills the serpent by stratagem
(fol. 69 a, col. 1, L 8). He next arrives at a river called Bar-
sâṭis (?) near which he builds a city which he called Maskâmâ
(fol. 69 b, col. 2, L 22) or "Alexandria the second" (fol. 70 a, col.
1, L 13). From here he marches to a place called Ḳasmâḳâtîn,
and then, after a march of fifteen nights through marshes and
fifteen nights through deserts, he arrives in China, ሲን፡ Sîn
(fol. 70 b, col. 1, L 8), the king of which country presents him
with many beautiful things (fol. 73 b, col. 2—74 a, col. 1).
Leaving China Alexander comes to a land where the people
have heads of wolves (fol. 74 b, col. 1, L 20), and next to a place
called Dârâ where he sacrifices to the "great god." He comes to
Sôd (Sughd) and founds the city of Samarḳand (fol. 76 a, col. 2,
l. 12); and having built five hundred boats to cross a river (fol.
76 b, col. 1) he goes to Persia to see the city called Sâmera (fol.
77 a, col. 1, L 4), which is governed by a queen called Candace.
He writes to her (fol. 77 a, col. 2), and she replies (fol. 77 b, col. 1).
The list of the gifts which, according to the Syriac, she gives to
him is omitted, but she sends a painter to paint his portrait
(fol. 78 a, col. 1). Candaules ቀንደርስ፡ Ḳandarôs (fol. 78 a, col.
2, L 1) her son goes to the land of Ḳarûmân, and his wife is
stolen from him (fol. 78 a, col. 2). Alexander changes places
with Ptolemy and, calling himself Antigonus, goes off with 3000
horsemen to rescue the wife of Candaules (fol. 79 b, col. 1): he
succeeds in bringing back the wife (fol. 80 a, col. 2). Alexander
then journeys on to see Candace in her city (fol. 81 a, col. 1), and
when he sees her and finds that she is like his mother Olympias, he weeps (fol. 81 b, col. 1). The narrative is now told by
Alexander in the first person; he describes the chamber in
which he first saw her (fol. 82 a, col. 1) and the second chamber
and her bed room (fol. 83 a, col. 1); afterwards Alexander
marries her ሰበበ፡ መሳሀ፡ ወአት፡ ዐስት፡ ወ.ደአት፡ ሰሳ.ት፡ (fol.
84 a, col. 2, l. 14). The Ethiopic form of the name of her eldest
son is Ḳanira, Syr. Ḳărûṭôr (fol. 85 a, col. 2, l. 18). After Alexander has been dismissed by Candace, her son Candaules takes
him to see the temple of a god, built on a hill (fol. 86 b, col. 2),
with whom he holds a conversation and asks questions. He

next writes to the Amazons, *Mertâs* (sic) and their queen replies (fol. 87 *b*, coll. 1, 2); he then makes his way back to Persia (fol. 88 *a*, col. 1, l. 22). At this period Aristotle writes to him (fol. 88 *a*, col. 2), advising him to do some good act before he dies, and reminding him that he has done a very great work for a young man of thirty years, for which he should thank God.

On fol. 88 *b*, col. 2, l. 2 begins the Ethiopic version of Alexander's expedition against the Huns, which, according to it, took place in the seventh year of his reign. Priskôs is not mentioned at all, but the "eleven bright seas" (fol. 89 *b*, col. 1) and the eleven lands situated in a land ten miles away and the great sea are all described as in the Syriac version. The waters of the foetid sea are like pus መግሳ: (fol. 89 *b*, col. 2, l. 14), and when Alexander asks some of the people if they have seen it they say that they have (fol. 90 *a*, col. 1). He then assembles 32,000 men (fol. 90 *b*, col. 1, l. 17), prays to God (fol. 90 *b*, col. 2), and goes to Egypt where he obtains 7000 skilled workmen (fol. 91 *b*, col. 1); he sets out with all his forces, and after a journey of four months and twelve days they arrive at a land "behind" the twelve great seas (fol. 91 *b*, col. 2). At the foetid sea thirty-seven men bring his ships to anchor, and he sees a pillar with an inscription (fol. 92 *a*, col. 2). He passes through lands called Tárakes, Martakut, Rûkĕl, Dafûr, Tarmât, Kânem, Hûr and Marak, through the mountain of Mûsâs (fol. 93 *b*, col. 1, l. 13), and arrives at a place called Nalhemyâ, where three hundred sages come to him (fol. 93 *b*, col. 2) and tell him that this place is in the territory of Persia, and that they are subject to Akseyûs አክሰዩስ: the Persian (fol. 94 *a*, col. 1, l. 11). They also tell him that the mountain which he sees extends to the Ocean (በንቶስ: *Bôntôs*), that it comes to an end near the land of Persia and that roads go from it to Adorbaigân (fol. 94 *a*, col. 2, l. 5). Alexander enquires what are the names of the kingdoms in this land, and they tell him Mâgûg (Magog), Yâgûg (Gog), Nûli, Aguna'a, Amribân, Namû, Burgis, Samrak, Hûsiĕ, 'Asfû, Salgû, Katlûbî, Amrûk, Kawâbir and Hanâ (fol. 94 *b*, col. 1). The Ethiopic translator says that he has seen in another book a description of these kingdoms, and he gives their twenty-two names as follows: Mâgûg, Yâgûg, Nûyâl, Yûal, Aknûk, Asâkâbir, Ḳaryâwîyân, Kerba, Lakan, Dabo'ân, Ḳarṭân, Rabaan, Zauâbén, Dûlî, Marḳû, Ṭarḳî, Mâyâwîyân, Kalbâtâs, Manzö'a, Yûmân, Kaslöwî and Malkî (fol. 94 b, col. 2). Their manners and customs are described (fol. 94 a, col. 1—fol. 95 b, col. 2, l. 15); the people called Nagâshâwîyân have faces like dogs (fol. 96 a, col. 2, l. 12).

The old men are next questioned by Alexander about Paradise and its four rivers Sêḥun, Gihon, Euphrates and Tigris (fol. 96 a, col. 2), and they tell him that God drew them into the earth.

Alexander then gathers together 3000 men and they make a gate twelve cubits in height (fol. 97 b, col. 2) to shut in Gog and Magog. He writes a prophecy on the gate that these nations shall go forth in the eight hundred and sixty-fourth year (fol. 98 a, col. 2, l. 10), and that when they have gone forth twenty thousand Greeks and Persians and Arabs shall be gathered together under four thousand kings (fol. 98 b, col. 2, l. 8), and that multitudes of men shall be slain.

The iron gate being finished Alexander sets out to go to the land of darkness (fol. 99 a, col. 1). When he arrives there a god of the country describes to him the land and the sea that is in it (fol. 101 a, col. 1), and tells him that the throne of God is set in this land, and that it is supported by an angel having the faces of a bull, a lion, an eagle and a man; beneath it flows the river of the water of life (fol. 101 a, col. 1). Beyond this land of darkness are seventy other lands, and beyond there are other seventy lands (fol. 101 b, col. 1), and a mountain eighty thousand measures high which rests upon water (fol. 104 b, col. 2, l. 15). In this land there is no distinction between day and night (fol. 106 a, col. 1), but Alexander prays to God, and He makes his paths straight so that he is able to proceed (fol. 108 b, col. 1). He travels in the dark land for two years (fol. 110 a, col. 1, l. 11), and finally comes to a place beyond which the people tell him that there is nothing. He insists on advancing, and leaving ten thousand of his troops (fol. 110 b, col. 1) to live and to wait for him there for ten years, he sets out with some of the natives for guides; the king of the land also gives him a precious stone, which was one of those brought out of Paradise by our father Adam, to shew him the way (fol. 111 a, col. 1, l. 20). The stone

pointed out the right road and led him to the fountain of life;
Alexander had a dried fish with him which he put into the water
to see if it would live and swim, and as soon as the fish touched
the water it came to life, and darted away and escaped (fol.
111 b, col. 1). When Mâtûn, that is El-Khidr or the "Ever-
green" (Elijah), saw that the fish came to life he took off his
clothes and bathed in the water of life, and dipped himself
therein three times, saying, "In the name of the Father, and of
the Son, and of the Holy Ghost" (fol. 111 b, col. 1). The sixty
thousand kings that live in that land contend with El-Khidr
(fol. 111 b, col. 2), who asks their permission for Alexander's
army to go through the land because he is doing God's will (fol.
112 a, col. 2). Alexander passes through the land, and comes
to a place where the water was so clear that he thought it
was the water of life. He saw there emeralds and jacinths and
other precious stones and a bird with a ring in its nose with
which he talked (fol. 113 a, col. 2). At a place near here he
finds much gold, and he makes for himself a crown of it, in
which he sets the stone which came from Paradise (fol. 115 a,
col. 1). From there he travels east and west and flies through
the air, higher than the eagle, and sees all the stars of heaven:
he writes a book about all these things (fol. 115 b, col. 1). He
next sets up a great furnace and casts a door and walls of iron to
keep out Gog and Magog (fol. 116 a, col. 1), the children of Adam,
who are like wild beasts (fol. 116 a, col. 2, l. 14). He prays to
God (fol. 116 a, col. 2, l. 14), and then sets out for the sea which
is behind the heavens and the land which has never been
trodden before by man (fol. 116 b, col. 2). He flies through the
air by the help of three eagles (fol. 116 b, col. 2), and when on
the sea he sends out these eagles one after the other to look for
land (fol. 117 a, col. 1). Having crossed the sea Alexander sets
out for Babylon (fol. 118 b, col. 2), where he seeks for the seven
wonderful things which Solomon made (fol. 118 b, col. 2—fol.
120 b, col. 1). He is twice attacked by fever; he writes to his
mother (fol. 121 a, col. 1 and fol. 121 b, col. 1), and he receives a
second letter from Aristotle (fol. 127 b, col. 2). Ten whole folios
(129—139) are filled with a discourse in which the names of
Pharaoh and Job occur, and which points out the benefits which
accrue to those who do not commit sin.

On fol. 139 a, col. 1 his second letter to Olympias is begun, in it he tells her that having left Babylon he came to the Pillars of Hercules ʾ〉ፐ፥〇: ሐርቀላ.ክ:, where he stayed ninety-five days. He found there a door of gold and one of silver: each one of them was twelve cubits in height. He saw there twenty thousand five hundred crowns of gold which he took, and left the country (fol. 139 b, col. 1), and journeying on he came to the country of beautiful women (fol. 139 b, col. 2). After another march he came to a river or sea called Dalị̄ṭûn, where it is very dark (fol. 140 a, col. 1), and after five days more he arrived at the city of the sun where there is a palace of gold. Near this place there was a very great darkness (fol. 140 a, col. 2), and eventually he came to the river Yôrdânôs, on the confines of Asia and Armenia (fol. 140 b, col. 1). Here he saw a golden bird, like a dove, in a cage of gold, which he wanted to send to his mother; but the people of the place begged him not to do it, and he did not. He also saw there the golden objects which were in the city of Dios and which were brought thither when the Persians ruled Egypt (fol. 140 b, col. 2), and the golden throne with eight steps, etc. The letter to Olympias ends fol. 141 a, col. 2.

Meanwhile the day of Alexander's death was drawing nigh. He had made a feast (fol. 141 b, col. 1), when Iollas (Eth. Yôlyôs) came and proposed to him that he should invite his friends to drink with him, and twenty-one of Alexander's friends were straightway invited. Watching his opportunity Iollas gives Alexander the cup of poisoned wine, and he drinks, and knows that he is poisoned (fol. 142 a, col. 1, l. 11); the news of the success of the plot is sent by Iollas to Antipater at once. Alexander leaves the feast chamber and tries to drown himself by night in the Euphrates, but is stopped by Roxana his wife (fol. 142 b, col. 2). On the following day Bardaksa (Perdiccas), Kâbâs (Lysias?), Abaṭlemîs (Ptolemy) and Lїsimikos (Lysimachus) write his testament, and he addresses the Macedonian soldiers who think that he has been poisoned (fol. 143 a, col. 1). One of them called Bûkelâs (Phainoclês?) addresses Alexander, and seventy of them wish to die with him (fol. 143 b, col. 1). Alexander's testament begins (fol. 143 b, col. 2). He bequeaths twenty thousand dinârs to the Christian temples of

Egypt (fol. 144 a, col. 2, l. 4) and to the temple of Ammon. If Ahrûksênâ (Roxana) bears a son he is to be called Alexander (fol. 145 a, col. 1). The names of the provinces of Alexander's empire and of the rulers whom he appoints over them are horribly corrupt in the Ethiopic version, and can only in a few places be identified. He orders a gold coffin to be made (fol. 145 b, col. 1), and commands that gifts be made to the temple of Hercules (fol. 145 b, col. 2); and having given directions concerning his coffin and the filling of it with myrrh and other spices (fol. 146 a, col. 1), he dies. His body is brought to Babylon in Egypt, and many of the nobles of the city of Memphis come out to meet it, but they refuse to allow it to be buried there; they advise Ptolemy to bury it in the city of Alexandria, and he does so (fol. 146 b, col. 1). He lived thirty-eight years and began to reign when he was fifteen years old. Twenty-two nations were subject to him among the barbarians and thirteen others; he founded twelve cities which are enumerated (fol. 146 b, col. 2). He was born on the first day of the month Ter[1] at sunrise and he finished his days on the first day of the month Miyâzyâ[2] ᎀᎃᎅᎅ: at sunset[1]; on account of his death taking place on this day it was called ᎀᎃᎅᎅ: ᎀᎃᎅᎅ:.

It will be seen from the foregoing pages that the Ethiopic version of the Alexander story reproduces in one form or another most of the principal incidents of the life of Alexander the Great according to Pseudo-Callisthenes. Whether the Ethiopic or the Arabic translator is responsible for the chapters which are omitted I cannot say. The proper names are much corrupted, and it is clear that the Ethiopic translator has helped to make the confusion greater. For example we have Pûz for Porus which shews that he read ; instead of ر; and we have Mêrtâs ᎀᎃᎅᎅ: for Amazons. The Arabic transcription of the Greek form of the name would be something like امزانس or

---

[1] The fifth month of the Abyssinian year, corresponding roughly to Dec. 27—Jan. 25.

[2] The eighth month of the Abyssinian year, corresponding roughly to Mar. 27—April 25. See also the Ethiopic version of Joseph ben-Gorion, Brit. Mus. MS. Orient. 822, fol. 20 a, col. 1, ll. 6—9.

مزناس, which the Ethiopic translator has clearly misread رئاسا
*Mertas*; many instances of the confusion between the letters
ك and ل, ف and ج and ;, ز, ح, ج and ر, could be given.

In the fabulous histories of Alexander the Great which are
commonly found among the Ethiopians the work of the imagination plays so large a part that it is difficult to discover the
grain of fact which has given rise to the fantastic stories which
have come down to us. In them Alexander is made to hold in-
terviews with Christ, Who tells him that He will take upon
Himself flesh in the fulness of time; he is made to preach
sermons on the advantages of living in chastity and continence
like Elijah and St. John; and he is made to abolish the worship
of idols throughout his dominions. The accounts of his travels
which are given in these stories are based upon the incidents of
his Indian journey according to Pseudo-Callisthenes, but the
hand of the Christian redactor or scribe has ever been active in
adding details which savour of the marvellous and the impossible.
In the desert he meets Elijah and Enoch, who leave him in
a chariot of fire; he is instructed by the Holy Ghost concerning
virtue and the six doors of the heart; and he learns the mystery
of the Holy Trinity. Philip his father having learned by means
of the astrolabe of the incarnation and death of Jesus Christ
throws himself into the sea; the Holy Spirit tells Alexander
that his father will be counted as one of the martyrs[1]. When
Alexander returns home he gives all his goods to the poor, and
then exhorts men and women to lead good and holy lives. The
above are specimens of the contents of these fabulous histories
of Alexander; it will be seen that they are of little value for
any other purpose than that of amusement.

[1] See the full summary of the contents of such a history in Zotenberg's
*Catalogue des MSS. Éthiopiens*, pp. 243—245, and D'Abbadie, *Catalogue raisonné
de MSS. Éthiopiens*, p. 81.

## THE COPTIC VERSION.

The existence of a Coptic version of the history of Alexander was first pointed out by Bouriant[1], who published the text from three mutilated leaves of a manuscript of the work found at Aḥmîm[2], the ancient Panopolis, in Upper Egypt, which are now in the Bibliothèque Nationale at Paris. The composition is in Sahidic, the dialect of Upper Egypt, and M. Bouriant thinks that it was written in the xvth century of our era; the contents do not agree with those of any other version known to me and I am not able to say from what language the work was translated. The first fragment refers to an expedition of Alexander in Judaea, and the second and third give some details of an expedition into Gedrosia.

### MISCELLANEOUS EUROPEAN VERSIONS.

Translations of the Alexander story were made into French[3] by Alberic de Besançon, Lambert li Tors and Alexandre de Bernay[4], Thomas of Kent and many others. It was also rendered into German by Lamprecht or Lambert[5], into Italian[6],

---

[1] *Fragments d'un Roman d'Alexandre en dialecte Thébain*, in *Journal Asiatique*, Série 8, t. IX., 1887. See especially the remarks by M. Maspero on pp. 37, 38.

[2] The ancient Panopolis, a town situated on the east bank of the Nile not far from This. See Champollion, *L'Égypte sous les Pharaons*, t. I. p. 257.

[3] In his scholarly monograph *Alexandre le Grand dans la Littérature Française du Moyen Age*, M. Meyer has given the history of all the French versions of the Alexander story. See also Favre, *Mélanges*, t. II. pp. 97—114, and Talbot, *Essai sur la légende d'Alexandre le Grand dans les Romans Français du XII⁰ siècle*, 1850.

[4] The text is published by Michelant in the *Bibliothek des Literarischen Vereins* in Stuttgart, t. XIII., entitled *Li Romans d'Alexandre*, par Lambert li Tors et Alexandre Bernay.

[5] See Weismann, *Alexander, Gedicht des zwölften Jahrhunderts, vom Pfaffen Lamprecht*, Frankfort, 1850; and the authorities on this version quoted by Meyer, *Alexandre*, t. II. p. 71, and Favre, *Mélanges*, t. II. p. 127.

[6] Favre, *Mélanges*, t. II. p. 119; Commenza el libro del nascimento. De la vita. Con grandissimi fatti. Et della morte infortunata de Alexandro Magno, Veneoia, 1477.

Spanish[1], Norwegian[2], Swedish[3], Dutch[4], and English[5]. In 1880 the facsimile of an ancient Slavonic manuscript, belonging to P. P. Vyazemsky, containing a history of Alexander was published[6]. Malay and Siamese[7] histories of Alexander are also known.

[1] Favre, *op. cit.* p. 115.

[2] Favre, *ibid.* p. 143.

[3] Favre, *ibid.* p. 143. The Swedish work was printed at Wijsingzborg in 1672, edited by J. Hadorphius. See also *Konung Alexander; en Medeltids dikt, från hatinet vänd i Svenska rim omkring år 1380...Efter den enda kända handskriften utgifven af* G. E. Klemming, Stockholm, 1844.

[4] Moltzer, H. E., *Roman van Cassamus in Bibliothek van Middelnederlandsche Letterkunde*, Afl. 2, 1868.

[5] See Weber, *King Alisaunder in Metrical Romances*, Vol. I. pp. xxxi, lxxiv, and 3—327, 1810; *The Romaunce of Alexander*, Edinburgh, 1850; Ward, *Catalogue of Romances*, p. 180; *The gestes of the worthie king and emperour, Alisaunder of Macedoine*, and Favre, *Mélanges*, t. II. pp. 139—142.

[6] Issued by the Early Russian Text Society at St. Petersburg. *An account of Alexander the Great in ancient Serbian Literature* was published in the *Messenger* of the Society of Serbian Literature, 2nd Series, Vol. IX. at Belgrade in 1868. I owe this information to Mr. J. T. Naaké of the British Museum.

[7] Yule, *The Book of Ser Marco Polo*, Vol. I. Intro. p. 110.

# THE HISTORY OF ALEXANDER THE SON OF PHILIP KING OF THE MACEDONIANS.

## BOOK I.

I. Now there used to be Egyptian sages, who were sprung from the families of the gods. They measured the earth, and stood thereon; they put in commotion the waves of the sea; and laid hold of the great Nile by its measure. They calculated the ordering of the stars of heaven. They delivered all these things to the world by the might of invincible words and by the powers of sorcery. Men say then of Naḳṭlbôs (Nectanebus)[1] who was the last king of Egypt and was famed for great discoveries, that he was through his perfect knowledge the glory of Egypt, and to him were the creatures of the world subservient by reason of his magic. This king was a marvel, for when suddenly the hosts of the enemy were standing ready at his gate[2], and wished to come to battle, he used not to trouble his camp, neither did he bring weapons of war for the use of the men, nor polished iron that glittered, nor was it his wont to contrive the stratagems or plans which are necessary for war; but he used to go into his palace and to set a brazen basin in the middle of the hall and to fill it with rain water. He then made small

---

[1] The (⬚⬚⬚⬚⬚) *Necht-neb-f,* or Nectanebus II of the hieroglyphics. Egyptian history is silent as to the end of this king. An *ushabti* figure bearing his name was found at Memphis (Marietta, *Mon. Div.,* p. 82) and hence it has been supposed that he was buried there. Diodorus says (XVI. 49—51) that he fled to Ethiopia. A statue of this king is in the British Museum.

[2] Or rather, *getting ready against his land.*

B. A. 1

models of ships and men in asphalt[1] and placed them in the
basin. And he took in his hand a rod of plane wood[2], and then
uttered those words which he knew, and invoked the angels and
Ammon the god of Lybia[3]. Now by this form of sorcery which
took place in the basin, he was wont to contrive plans, until
those models of ships and men which were in the basin went
forth against the enemy and turned them back. In this manner
he held constantly by his skill for a great length of time the
kingdom of Egypt.

II. After a while, a certain man, a spy from among the
guards who were there, came to him and answered and said, "O
Nectanebus, while as yet thou hast peace, seek deliverance for
thyself, for behold innumerable multitudes of hosts of enemies
are making ready and coming against thee, to wit the Tûrâyê
(or mountaineers), the Alâni, the Gûbarbĕdâyê, the Armenians, the Medes, the Arabs, the Midianites, the people of
Adôrbâigân, the Bulsâyê, the Álôsâyê, the Shabrônkâyê, the
Alinîkâyê, the Galatians, the Ṭĕbarînîkâyê[4], the people of Gurgân,
the Chaldeans, the eaters of fish and of beasts of prey, multitudes
without end of the nations from the regions of the East, mighty
men, with a vast host, hastening to come to this land of Egypt
which is thine. Consider now what is expedient and useful [to
be done]." When the spy had spoken after this manner, Nectanebus laughed and said to the scout, "Thou hast done well, and
hast acted properly as regards the watch which was entrusted to
thee, in that thou hast spied out these things for me; but thou
hast spoken timidly and not courageously. For I have observed
that host of men which is coming, and they have no strength,
although their will is very ready. One little word of wisdom
however is able to turn back many, and a man who does good
things can overwhelm a multitude of armies in the waves of the

---

[1] Or *bitumen*, ܟܘܦܪܐ, in Arabic قَفَر and قِير. The Greek text has "of
wax", ἐκ κηροῦ (see Müller, p. 2, col. 1). The Ethiopic version has also
"wax".

[2] Or rather, *teakwood*, ܣܐܓܐ, Ar. ساج. The Greek text has "ebony"
(see Müller, loc. cit.).

[3] ܠܒܘܐܣ, transcription of the Greek genitive Λιβύης.

[4] Or people of Ṭabaristân?

sea." And when he had spoken these things to the spy, he called him and said to him, "One dog is able to turn back many deer, and one wolf is able to destroy a whole flock of she-goats. Do thou, then, with those numerous horsemen that are under thy orders, go and keep thy watch carefully; for by one word I am able to overwhelm and drown in the waves of the sea this innumerable band of enemies."

III. And Nectanebus went into his palace, and put out all the people, and remained by himself. Then he filled the brazen basin with rain water, made those ships of asphalt spring up[1] in the middle of the house, took the rod of plane wood in his hand, and began to speak those words which were full of terror. And when he had spoken them, he looked into the basin, and saw all the gods of Egypt leading the ships and guarding them. When he saw that Egypt was betrayed by her gods, he left his kingdom and fled. He shaved the hair of his head and his beard, and put on other apparel; then he took as much gold as he was able [to carry] and departed from Egypt, and went by way of Pelusium. Now when he had travelled through a multitude of countries and a number of nations, he came to Pella of the Macedonians. And he put on linen clothing like the Egyptian prophets and astrologers (lit., those who shew the signs of the zodiac), and sat in the midst of the highways, and the people of the land came to ask him questions. In those times he was renowned. And after Nectanebus had gone away from the land of Egypt, all the Egyptians drew near to Hephaestus, the head of the race of the gods, and besought him with entreaty to shew them what had happened to Nectanebus the king of Egypt, and at what place he had arrived. Then Hephaestus promptly sent to them an oracle concerning him by the hands of the priests, saying, "The king of Egypt who has fled, a mighty man and a warrior, but an old man, will after a time bring a new lord, a young man, mightier and more powerful than he, who will kill him and seize his land; and he shall traverse the world, and shall subjugate all the enemies of Egypt to your service." And when the Egyptians had heard this oracle, they forthwith inscribed it with letters (lit., carvings) under the tablet of brass on the stone

---

[1] The word ܐܣ̈ܩ], he made to grow, or spring up, does not suit the context well, and is probably corrupt.

1—2

pedestal upon which [the statue of] king Nectanebus stood, that they might see what would be the issue of the oracle.

IV. And Nectanebus was going to and fro openly in Macedonia, and many people came to see him and to ask him questions. He was so renowned that even Olympias[1] the queen desired to enquire of him as to what was about to happen. Now Philip, the husband of Olympias, had gone to war, and she commanded that Nectanebus should come to her. And when he had come and had entered the royal palace, he saw the beautiful countenance of the queen, whose countenance was more beautiful than the moon. He was a man innocent of women, but at the sight of Olympias his mind was excited and his heart burned with love for her. He stretched out his hand, and saluted Olympias, and answered and said to her, " Peace be with thee, O queen of the Macedonians." Now he could not persuade himself to call her " lady," for as yet the royal manner of speech was in his mouth. Olympias answered and said to him, " Peace be with thee, O doer of good things, and knower of everything ; come, seat thyself." And when he had sat down, Olympias said to him, " Art thou really an Egyptian ? for in thy speech there is no lying." Nectanebus answered and said to her, " Those who have had experience of me speak well [of me]." Olympias said to him, " By what wisdom and knowledge, or by what power, knowest thou to speak correctly what is going to happen ?" Nectanebus answered and said to her, " O queen, well dost thou know how to put a question ; for the interpreters of dreams are of many kinds, and the knowers of signs, those who understand divination, Chaldeans [or] augurs, and casters of nativities ; the Greeks call the signs of the Zodiac ' sorcerers'[2]; and others are counters of the stars. As for me, all these are in my hands, and I myself am an Egyptian prophet, a magus, and a counter of the stars." And while he was saying these and other such like things to her, he was scrutinising her with great earnestness and intentness. Now when she saw in what manner he was looking at and scrutinising her, she answered and said to him, " O sage, whilst thou wert enumerating thy wisdom and skill in these things, why didst thou gaze on me lustfully ?"

[1] In the Syriac *Olympidi*, from the acc. 'Ολυμπιάδα.
[2] This clause seems to have been mistranslated, or to be corrupt.

Nectanebus answered and said to her, "I looked at thee carefully
for the sake of becoming well acquainted with thee; for there
is something which I heard a long time ago, and which I now
remember.   It was revealed to me of old by my god, who said
to me ' In the future thou wilt give augury to a queen, and
everything that thou shalt say to her shall really come to pass.'"
And when he had thus spoken to her with such like words,
she straightway brought out into the midst a beautiful and
magnificent table of ivory which belonged to the palace, set
with splendid stones and of great value, the qualities of which
the mouth of man knows not how to describe, for it was made
of acacia wood and gold and silver.   Three circles were fitted
to it after the manner of belts.   Upon the outer belt there was
a representation of Zeus with the thirty-six *decani*[1] surrounding
him; upon the second the twelve signs of the Zodiac were
represented; and upon the third the sun and moon.   Then he
set the table upon a tripod, and he emptied a small box which
was set [with stones] after the manner of the table upon the
table, and there were in it [models of] those seven stars that
were in the belts, and in that one which was in the middle,
which they call in Greek ' the watcher of the hours' ($\tau\grave{o}\nu$ $\dot{\omega}\rho o$-
$\sigma\kappa\acute{o}\pi o\nu$), were set by the crafts of art eight kinds of precious
stones; and he arranged them upon the table with the other
gems.   Thus he completed his representation of the great
heavens upon so small a table.   He arranged a sun of
crystal and a moon of adamant; and Arès, whom they call in

Persian *Vahrâm* (ﺑﻬﺮﺍﻡ), of a red stone, the colour of blood;
Nâbô the scribe, who is called in Persian *Tîr* (ﺗﻴﺮ), of an

emerald; Bêl, who is called in Persian *Hormazd* (ﻫﺮﻣﺰﺩ), of a

white stone; Baltî, who is called in Persian *Andhîd* (ﺍﻧﺎﻫﻴﺪ), of

---

[1] On the top of the table were represented in the inner circle the sun and
moon; in the middle circle the twelve signs of the zodiac; and in the outer
circle the thirty-six *decani*, three to each sign of the zodiac.   Lepsius in his
*Chronologie der Aegypter*, p. 71, gives a list of them, and shews which three
belong to which sign.   He also gives a list of them at pp. 68, 69, from five
different sources, with the list of Salmasius and an emended text.   See also
Brugsch, *Astronomische und astrologische Inschriften*, pp. 137 foll.; and *Description de l'Égypte*, t. IV. pl. 20.

a sapphire stone of a dark colour, and the horoscope of copper (?),
which is called in Persian *Farnój* (فرنوج)[1]. And after he
had set these in order, he said to Olympias, "Tell me, O queen,
the year, the month, the day and the hour of thy birth;" and
she told him. Then Nectanebus calculated his own nativity
and that of Olympias, that he might know if the stars of both
of them coincided exactly. And when he saw that they were
precisely the same, he said to her, "It is fitting that thou
shouldest tell me thy mind, and what thou wishest to ask, and
what it is that thou desirest?" She said to him, "[I wish to
ask] concerning my husband Philip, for I have heard a rumour
that, after he returns from the war, he will divorce me, and will
take another wife." Then Nectanebus answered and said to
her, "This report about thyself which thou hast mentioned, O
queen, is false, in so far as that it will happen now shortly; after
a time, however, it will actually be done. But I, being an
Egyptian prophet and a magus, am able to help thee in many
things, when thou hast need of it in any such matter as this.
Now, however, it is granted unto thee—according to what thy
nativity which is before me reveals—that a god of the land shall
sleep with thee; thou shalt be pregnant by him, and thou shalt
bear a son to him, who shall avenge thee upon Philip thy husband for the offence which he has committed against thee."
Olympias answered and said to him, "Who is this god who thou
sayest will sleep with me?" Nectanebus answered and said to
her, "He will have horns on his head, and will be clothed in the
rich apparel of Ammon the god of Libya." Olympias said to
him, "What is the age of this god, and what is his appearance,
and the form of his figure?" Then Nectanebus answered, "He
is of middle age, and his form and appearance are thus; upon

---

[1] Possibly the modern Persian برنج, *burinj*, or برنگ, *piring*. The
Persian word برنج is used in modern Syriac under the form of ܒܪܝܢܓ,
and the American missionaries use it to translate ܢܚܫܐ, Heb. נְחֹשֶׁת, in
their version of the Bible (e.g. Gen. iv. 22; Ps. cvii. 16; Dan. x. 6), and the History of the Jews published by them in their monthly journal, ܙܗܪܝܪܐ ܕܒܗܪܐ.
See the number for ܚܙܝܪܢ 1887, p. 44, col. 2, line 54.

each side of his head he has the like of ram's horns. Do thou, however, O queen, prepare thyself to sleep with him; but first of all in a dream thou wilt see this god who is going to sleep with thee." Olympias answered and said to him, "When?" Nectanebus said to her, "It will not be far off, but to-day; therefore I counsel thee to prepare thyself magnificently like a queen, for in this very night he will unite with thee in thy dream." Olympias said to him, "If it be that I see any such thing, I will not only hold thee to be a prophet, but I will worship thee as if thou wert a god."

V. Now when they had spoken these words with one another and conversed, Nectanebus went forth from the royal palace, and went out swiftly and speedily to the plain. Then he hastened to the desert, and gathered those roots which men use for dreams, and he pounded and pressed them all; and in a dream of the night Nectanebus by his magic sent to Olympias what she desired, so that in her dream she thought that she was actually sleeping with the god Ammon, and that he was embracing her, and that of his own free will he abode with her, and that when he had done with her he said to her, "O woman, behold, thy womb will avenge thee."

VI. And when Olympias awoke from her sleep, great terror laid hold of her because of this dream; and she sent and called Nectanebus to her. And when he had come into her presence, she commanded that everyone should go forth from her. Then Olympias answered and said to Nectanebus, "Behold I have this day seen a dream according to what thou didst say unto me, and the god Ammon sleeping with me; but I wish that when I am awake, he should sleep with me continually. This I require of thee, and thou art able to supply this need. I wonder now if I shall obtain this through thee." Nectanebus answered, "Nothing is more feeble than I, but inasmuch as thou desirest this, that thou mightest see him when thou art waking, it is right for me to consider, because a dream is one thing, but the thing that thou requirest is another. Now, I have thought that since thou hast this desire, bid them construct a place for me close by thy bedchamber, that, if thou art terrified when the god comes to thee, I who know thee may strengthen thee; for this god when he comes to thee will be in

the form of a serpent and will creep and crawl on the ground,
sending forth loud hisses. Then he will return, and his horns
will be in the form of those of a ram; thus will he be. Then
he will return again, and will appear in the form of the hero
Hêraklês; and he will return a third time, and appear in the
form of Dionysus, decorated and ornamented with ringlets; and
he will return yet again, coming back and appearing in my own
form." When Olympias heard these things, she said to him,
"O prophet, thou hast spoken well; abide now in one of the
bedchambers within the palace where I sleep, and if it happens
that, being awake, I see such things and know that I am
pregnant by the race of the gods, I will honour thee and will
hold thee to be the father of the child." Then Nectanebus
answered and said to her, "Behold, I have told thee beforehand
concerning the snake; now therefore fear him not, but trust
thyself the more to him, and be fearless."

VII. When therefore all these things happened as Nectanebus had said, the queen was not terrified at all at the change
of the forms of the gods, but she feared when she slept with the
form of the serpent. Now when he had done with her, he
again stood over her, and set his mouth upon her mouth, and
said to her, "An unconquerable seed, and one which shall not
be subject to any man, flows into this womb." And when
Nectanebus had said these words, he went to his own bedchamber; and afterwards at this time he slept with her in
the form of Ammon and of Hêraklês and of Dionysus. And
when she was great with child, she lifted up her eyes and
saw Nectanebus, and she answered and said to him, "O prophet,
what shall I do when Philip my husband returns from
war and finds me pregnant?" Nectanebus answered and said
to her, "Fear not, O queen, this Ammon of the three-fold form
is able to help thee in every way, and can shew Philip in a
dream [what has happened], that thou mayest be without blame
and without care." So for a long time Olympias was beguiled
by these words and played the harlot with a man, thinking he
was a god. Then Nectanebus the Egyptian king brought a
hawk and muttered over it his charms, and made it fly away
with a small quantity of a drug, and that night it shewed
Philip a dream. In his dream it shewed him a god, whose

form was fair, of middle age, with horns upon his head like the god Ammon, who was sleeping with Olympias. And when he had done with her, he said to her, "Behold thou hast in thy womb my seed, and thou shalt bear me a child who will avenge thee and Philip his father." And in the same dream he saw as if a river like the Nile flowed and went forth from the couch on which they were lying; and [he saw] the figure of a man sewing linen. He saw too the womb of Olympias sealed with a gold ring, with a gem on which was engraved the head of a lion holding the sun in his claws, or in his paws, and there was a whip beside him, and a hawk which overshadowed him with its wings[1].

VIII. Now when Philip had seen these appearances in his dream, he rose up early in the morning, and sent and brought into his presence the wise men the interpreters of dreams, and related before them the dream which he had seen. Then they answered and said to him, "O king Philip, as thou hast seen in the dream, so shall it be; behold, Olympias is pregnant, but she is pregnant by a god. Forasmuch as thou hast seen her womb sealed, surely it is pregnant; for an empty vessel is not sealed, but only one that is full. And whereas thou hast seen the form of a man sewing linen, this seed is Egyptian; for they do not sew linen in any other place but Egypt. And his fortune is not little, but great and mighty and glorious and renowned, because [the womb] was sealed with a seal of gold, and there is nothing more valued than gold, for even the gods are worshipped for the sake of gold. And the lion which held the sun in his claws, and the whip which was [engraved] on the ring, [shew that] he will go to the east, and will walk like a lion in his might; and he will subdue all countries and cities with his whip. And as for the god whom thou didst see, of middle age and with horns on his head, this is Ammon the god of Libya, and the seed is his." Now when the learned in dreams had given the explanation in this manner, Philip believed of a certainty that Olympias was pregnant by a god.

IX. And when [Philip] had conquered, he returned from the war, and came to his own house and greeted Olympias.

---

[1] Plutarch, *Life of Alexander*, ch. 2, says that Philip dreamt that he sealed up the queen's womb with a seal, the impression of which was a lion.

Then she was ashamed; and when he saw that she was agitated through fear of him, he answered and said to her, "To whom didst thou deliver thyself to be defiled, O Olympias? He has not, however, defiled thee, for thou shalt bear a son by him, and shalt name him the son of Philip; for I have seen in a dream everything that has happened to thee, and therefore I leave thee in peace. Kings are able to contend with everything, but to contend with the gods they are not able." And when he had said these things to her, he heartened her and Olympias regained her selfpossession.

X. Now it fell out one day, because Nectanebus was within the royal palace, that he heard Philip say to Olympias, "Thou art an erring woman, for thou art not with child by a god, but by one of the human race." And while they were thus speaking together, Nectanebus by his sorcery changed his own form and assumed that of a huge serpent, and he hissed with a loud voice in the midst of the hall where Philip was standing, gliding in a terrible manner, and hissing as he went, so that all who heard quaked and trembled at his voice. And when Olympias saw her lover, she lay down upon her couch, while the monster reared himself up over her, and suddenly he straightened himself out. Then Olympias spread out her hands and embraced his neck, whereupon the serpent opened his mouth and placed his lips upon her lips, kissing her repeatedly just as a man kisses his friend out of love. And while it was doing thus, every one in the palace and Philip too saw it. Philip answered and said to Olympias, "O great queen Olympias, and all the rest of you who stand before me, I saw such a serpent as this when I was fighting with my enemies at yon time, and also the mind of many of the enemy was humbled and made weak thereby. But as for me, from this time forward I will glorify and praise myself because men will call me father of one sprung from a god."

XI. Now after some days, when Philip was sitting in his summerhouse by the side of the royal reservoir of water, and all kinds of birds were pecking grain before and around him, he was reading in the book of the philosophers. Suddenly a halfbred hen which was being reared in the house happened to sit in Philip's lap. Now she was but a small [bird], and when she had sat in his lap, she laid an egg thereon. When Philip saw this

egg, he put it upon the ground; but the egg rolled about and
broke, and immediately a small serpent sprang from within the
egg and crawled round about it. Then it turned back and began
to enter the egg again, and when it had put its head within the
egg, it died immediately. Now when Philip saw such a wonder,
he was sore afraid and was much troubled; and straightway he
commanded, and they called the chief of the Chaldeans at that
time, whose name was Antiphon, into his presence. And when
he arrived, Philip related to him the matter just as it had
occurred. And when he had told it to him, Antiphon answered
and said, "O king Philip, the child that is to be born to thee
will be a son, and he will be a king; he will traverse the whole
world and subjugate all men by his power, and he will not be
conquered by man; but when this [son of thine] shall retrace
his steps and return to his own place, within a few days he shall
die. For the serpent is a sign of royalty, and the egg is the
whole world; and the serpent which went forth from thence and
went round about it, when it returned and put its head into it,
died immediately: even so in this manner, when he has traversed the whole world and returns to enter his own land, he
will die." And when he had spoken according to this augury,
Philip gave him many gifts and he went home.

XII[1]. Now when the time for the delivery of Olympias had
arrived, she sat upon the childbed, and the birthpangs began to
pain her. Nectanebus was standing before her and calculating
the stars of heaven. When he had made his calculation, he said
to Olympias, "Rise up for a little, O queen, from the seat until
an hour pass, for the sign of the Scorpion holds this hour, and
Saturn and the Sun and the Balance are opposed to it, and a
vast host of wild beasts devour him who is born in this hour.
In this hour the signs of the heaven revolve swiftly; but be
strong and restrain thyself, and pass by this hour, for in this
hour Cancer [predominates], and Saturn was plotted against by
his children, and he was born in Gemini; and he bound him and
cast him into the ocean and he was deprived[1] of his superiority,

[1] With this chapter compare in particular the Greek of Cod. A, as given by
Müller, p. 11, in the note. The text is very corrupt in both Greek and Syriac.
[1] Literally, "emptied of". The Syriac text is obviously somewhat confused,
and I am therefore not sure of its rendering.

and Bèl obtained the throne of heaven in his place. In this
hour Leopos (?) was born, who taught wandering[1]. In this
hour the horned Moon[2] forsook the Balance[3], and descended from
her height to the earth, and was united with the simple Endymion[4];
and she gave birth to a beautiful son by him, but he died by the
flame of fire, therefore whosoever is born in this hour dies by fire.
In this hour home-loving Baltin (Venus) was with her husband,
and she was slain by the hand of Arès without sword and without
wound. In this hour the women who worship Baltin (Venus) set up
mourning and weep for her husband. Let this hour pass, because
the god Arès stands in it wrathfully and threatens. In this
hour Arès the lover of weapons and the warrior, naked and
unarmed, placed his trust in the men of (?) Electryône the daughter
of the Sun, and he stands put to shame; therefore everyone
born in this hour will be despised and of no account among men.
Restrain thyself in this hour too, O queen, for the star of Nâbo
the scribe holds the sign of the zodiac, and he was born in [the
sign of] the horned Goat, and afterwards his children rid themselves of him, and were estranged [from him], and went to the
desert. In this hour Rhea was born; do thou then sit upon the
childbed, and bear bravely thy pains as best thou mayest, because
Bèl is the lover of virgins. In this hour Dionysus was born, the
gentle and humble, who makes to dwell in peace, who taught
gentleness. And under this sign of the zodiac, Ammon with
the ram's horns was born over Aquarius and Pisces of Egypt (?). In
this hour Bel was born, the father of men, and the king of the
gods, and the ruler of the world, who establishes royalty. In
this hour give birth, O queen." And when Nectanebus had
finished speaking, the queen brought forth. And when the child
fell upon the ground, suddenly there was the noise of thunders
and lightnings, and mighty earthquakes, so that the whole world
trembled.

[1] Or mendicity, begging.       [2] Reading Selêne, as proposed p. 20, note 8.
[3] The word ܠܡܣܐܬܐ in the Syriac text is evidently a gloss upon
ܩܘܣ ܛܠܐ. On the names of the signs of the Zodiac in Syriac see
Sachau, Inedita Syr., p. ܩܘܣ, and Noeldeke in the Zeitschrift der Deutschen
Morgenl. Gesellschaft, xxv, pp. 256—8. Compare Maimonides ספר המורה פרק נ
[4] The Syriac name seems to be a corruption of the Greek accus. 'Ενδυμίωνα,
which might be written ܐܢܕܘܡܝܘܢܐ.

XIII. And when Philip saw these things, he said, "I had determined that thou shouldst not rear him, O woman, because he was not begotten by me; but since the several parts of the world have given such signs as these concerning him, he must be of the seed of the gods. Let the gods now rear him; let the name Alexander be given him in remembrance of the son who was borne to me by a former wife." And when Philip had spoken thus, he gave orders that they should surely rear the boy with watchfulness, solicitude, and care; and he commanded all the towns of Thrace and Macedonia to bring crowns to him. And the child grew, and was weaned; and he became strong, and increased in stature and wisdom; but as regards his form and appearance, he was neither like Philip, nor Olympias his mother, nor the god by whom he was begotten, but his features and looks differed from theirs, for his hair resembled the mane of a lion, and one eye was different from the other, one being white (light) and the other black (dark); and his teeth were sharp like a razor, and his steps were firm like those of a lion. From his person then it was evident what he was destined to become afterwards. He had for his tutor in his boyhood a great man whose name was Lekrânîkos (?) the Pellaean; and his master in letters was Âpos (?) the Lemnian; and his teacher in geometry, which is [used] for measuring lands, was Philip; and his master in the art of speaking with brevity was Ârespimôn (?); and his teacher in philosophy was Aristotle the Milesian; and his instructor in war was Ardippos the Dmatskian (?). And after a long time, when the child had reached boyhood and youth, he began to accustom himself to the manners and customs of royalty, for one of the gods had shewn him in a vision [that he was to be a king]. When then he was with the boys at school, he used to hold contests with the rest of the boys, and he strove and did not stir from his place, until he had gained the victory over all of them.

Now at that time the princes of the Cappadocians brought as an offering to Philip from their herds of horses a foal of great size, bound with fetters of iron, for, said they, he devours men. And when Philip observed his appearance and beauty, he said to his friends, "True it is what is said in the proverb, for they

say, 'something bad springs up by the side of anything good';
but now since the chiefs of the Cappadocians, my friends, have
brought me a present, accept it from them, and let him be kept
in restraint and guarded in an iron-barred enclosure, and let the
dead bodies of evildoers, by whom crimes worthy of death have
been committed, and who are appointed to be slain by the
decrees of the judges, be thrown to this [beast]." And when
Philip had thus spoken, they executed his orders with all speed.

XIV.   And after these things, when Alexander was twelve
years old, he went with Philip his father to war, and he
practised horsemanship, and exercised himself along with skilful and brave horsemen.   And his training was so good, that
Philip himself applauded, and answered and said to him, " I love
thee, my son, because thou art right well trained in the art of
gaining the victory in war; but it grieves me that thy appearance does not resemble mine."   Now it fell out that Philip
went to a certain city on some business, and certain thoughts
were stirring in Olympias after the manner of women, and she
commanded to call Nectanebus to her presence.   And she
answered and said to him, " Look by thy wisdom concerning me,
and see what Philip meditates in his mind about me."   Then
Nectanebus set a small table before her in the midst, and
placed in order upon it the gems of the signs of the zodiac;
and Alexander was sitting in that place.   And he began to
compute the signs of the zodiac, and answered and said to her,
" O queen, the guidance of the will of the gods suffers not by
anything which takes place by chance.   The place of thy con-
stellation is now exceedingly great beyond all expectation; so
do not abandon thyself to care and doubt.   For I have observed
and seen, and just now the Sun stands against the sign of the
Baltîn (Venus) of Philip, and quenches his desire and longing
and turns him away from the love of women."   And Olympias
answered and said to him, " Is the sign thus, O Nectanebus?"
He answered and said, "It is thus; would that thou wert
able to understand, that I might shew thee this sign in the
heavens, and thou mightest understand that it is even as I
have said to thee."   When these words had been spoken,
Alexander answered and said to Nectanebus his father, "My
father, are all the signs of the zodiac to be recognised in the

heavens as thou hast said?" And Nectanebus said, "Yea,
my son." Alexander says to him, "I wish to see them."
Nectanebus said to him, "This shall be this very night, if
the sky be clear. Come with me to the open plain, and
thou shalt see them, provided the sky be clear." Alexander
said, "My master, since thou knowest [the heavens] so accurately, it befits thee to know also thine own nativity."
Nectanebus said, "Yes, my son, I know also my own nativity."
Alexander said, "I desire to ask thee this [question], though
thou knowest that it is not of a matter which concerns me that
I ask, but it is necessary to learn what I have seen; now tell
me of thy death, in what manner it will be." Nectanebus said,
"This is [the manner of] my death; I shall perish by the hands
of my son." And while they had talked of these things together,
the day had passed and the night was come, and the moon had
risen in the heavens, and the signs of the zodiac were visible.
Then Alexander walked behind his father, whom he knew not,
and they went outside the city. Then Nectanebus lifted up
his eyes, and said to the boy, "Observe how gloomy this sign of
Saturn is, how much this [sign of] Arês resembles blood, how
this [sign of] Baltî (Venus) stands in joyfulness, how favourable
is this [sign] of Nâbo the scribe, and how bright is the sign of
Bêl." And while the eyes of Nectanebus were fixed upon the
signs, and both of them were walking along together, and there
was a pit very near them, the boy Alexander pushed Nectanebus
and pitilessly cast him into the pit. And when he had fallen,
he answered and said to Alexander, "What wast thou thinking
of in thy mind, O my son Alexander, that thou hast stretched
out thy hand against me and hast cast me into this pit?" Alexander answered and said to him, "O teacher, what is upon earth
thou dost not know, [and yet] thou dost investigate that which
is in the heavens; it did not become thee, seeing that thou
knewest not what is upon earth, to dare to investigate and
examine and vex thyself with what is in the heavens." Then
Nectanebus lifted up his voice and said to him, "I know, O my
son, that some such thing as this would befall me, but I was
unable to help my life in any way, for no man is able to flee
from what is decreed." Alexander answered and said to him, "I
blame also thy lack of knowledge, in that thou didst say that

thy death would happen by the hands of thy son, and thou didst not know that thou shouldest die by my hands." Then Nectanebus said, "I did indeed say that I should die through my son, and I have not lied in what I said, for thou thyself art my son." Alexander said, "Am I thy son?" Then Nectanebus answered, "Hear, my son, what I say regarding thee, that thou mayest know about thyself." So Nectanebus went on to speak from the beginning, of his being king when he was in Egypt, and of the rumour which was reported to him by the spy; of the divination in the bowl, and of his foreknowledge of the betrayal of Egypt by the hands of its gods; of his flight from Egypt, of his arrival in Pella, and of his teaching the ordering of the signs of the zodiac; of his thoughts concerning Olympias, of his desire for her love, and of his sorcery; of Ammon, and Hèraclès, and Dionysus, and of his union with Olympias, and of her pregnancy; of Philip's dream, of the serpent, and of the heaven of constellations. And when he had spoken these words, his soul departed from him and he died.

Now when Alexander knew that Philip was not his father, but that he was begotten of the seed of Nectanebus, he was afraid to leave the body of Nectanebus in the pit lest wild beasts should devour it. Then love of his father entered into his mind, and he took up the body upon his shoulders, and came back to the royal palace. When Olympias saw Alexander carrying the body of Nectanebus, she said to him, "A second Telamonian Ajax! what is this that thou art carrying, my son?" Alexander answered and said to her, "Æneas carried his father upon his shoulders affectionately and lovingly, because [Anchises] was an old man and decrepit; but I carry this body cruelly and as a parricide." Olympias said to him, "Hast thou slain thy father Philip?" Alexander said, "I have not slain Philip, but Nectanebus have I slain." Olympias said to him, "Was Nectanebus then thy father?" Alexander said, "Yes; the gods sent him to thee according to the will which they had." And he forthwith laid down the body from his shoulder and began to speak of the time of the night at which he went forth, and of the pointing out [by Nectanebus] of the constellations, and of the pit, and of his pushing [him in], and of what he said, and of his replies.

When Olympias heard all these things, she blamed herself, and [wondered] how Alexander was able to carry so great a body upon his shoulders; and in the midst of her affliction she derived consolation from the strength of the youth, [thinking] that, although she had fallen and had been led astray, it was no mean man that had seduced her, but a king of Egypt, and that her pregnancy had taken place by the fate of the gods. And when the boy had said these words, he turned to the corpse of Nectanebus, and buried his father as a son should do, and like an Egyptian in the burial place of his caste; and he said to him, "Who will be master of the constellations after thee, and will know who shall be king?"

XV. Then Philip returned from whence he had gone, and sent his servants to Polias the diviner at Delphi to ask of the diviner, that he might know who would be king after him. When they drew near, and came to the fountain of Castalia, they asked an augury. And the virgin Pythia answered them saying, "Say ye to Philip, the father and lord of Macedonia, 'He that shall receive the kingdom, being sent by the gods, the rulers of the world, to this kingdom of the Macedonians, this is the sign that I have seen concerning him; he shall make the mighty steed which is called Bucephalus (the interpretation of which is Bull-head) run through Pella.'" And when those who had been sent to bring the augury returned to Philip, they told this sign to him, and he, after he had received this augury, used to watch when he might see this sign; and he used to enquire of every one who made a horse run through Pella what its name was and how it was called.

XVI[1]. Now when Alexander was nearly old enough to reign[2], he went to a distance to the place [where Bucephalus was kept]; and he looked and saw from the door, and went out and saw the horse guarded by an iron grating, with its whole body bound with chains; and he saw that the horse was very excited and furious. By reason of the smell of the human bones and skulls which he devoured, the place itself was foul, and the

---

[1] This is ch. xvii. of the Greek text (Müller, p. 16).

[2] After the words "to reign" the Syriac text has the unintelligible word ܠܡܚܫ. A clause has also fallen out after "to the place".

horse emitted a foetid odour from his mouth. When Alexander
saw the many human bones lying under him near his feet, he
questioned those who had the care of him, saying, "I want to
know what is the reason that this horse is bound in this
manner?" And they said to him, "This horse is a man-eater."
Now when Alexander heard this speech, he marvelled and drew
near to the iron grating, and admired the strength and size and
beauty of the horse. He was especially struck with wonder at
his being so terrible and at his fierce appearance. And after
the horse took no notice of him, he put his hands gently
through the railings, and put a bit into his mouth; and the
horse licked the hand of Alexander with his tongue. Then
Alexander began to rub his side and legs, and he was quiet.
And when he saw that the horse was gratified, he commanded
and they took away the railings from him. And he led the
horse out, holding the bridle with his right hand, while with
the left he stroked the horse's body, and the horse wagged his
tail like a dog. And when Alexander saw that he was so gentle,
he led him by the bridle and brought him out into the street,
and he saw upon the right side of the horse a birthmark in the
form of a wolf, a sign that was born with him, and this wolf
held a bull in its mouth. Then [Alexander] mounted and rode
upon him, and made him run through the city [of Pella]. Now
it happened that Philip was sitting upon the wall of the city,
making the horsemen pass before him by number, and he
enquired of them the names of their horses, if peradventure
there might be one who had a horse called Bull-head, for he had
learned the augury from the diviner. And while Philip was
sitting upon the wall, Alexander came up to him at a gallop;
and when Philip saw Alexander guiding the horse with his
hand and standing upon his feet, he said, "My son Alexander,
the whole oracle refers to thee; I believe that after my death
thou wilt reign, and that thou wilt rule the whole world."

XVII[1]. Then Alexander, after he had made the horse
gallop, took him away and put him in his own stable; and
he drew near to Aristotle the sage and saluted him, and
answered and said, "Peace be with thee, my teacher." And

[1] Chap. xvi. in the Greek (Müller, p. 15, col. 2).

Aristotle answered and said to him, "Peace be with thee,
Alexander; come and stand by the side of thy companions in
order." And when he had taken his place by the side of his
fellows, Aristotle answered and said to him[1], "Be thou rich, O son
of a king! O excellent youth, filled with wealth, if the kingdom
comes to thee after thy father, what wilt thou give me or
wherewith wilt thou enrich me?" He replied, "O teacher, if the
dominion comes to me, I will make thee a ruler." And he said
to another, "And thou, what sayest thou to me Kalkalva?"
Kalkalva[2] answered and said to him, "I will make thee my
secret counsellor." And he said to another, "And thou, what
wouldst thou give me, Partion?" And he said, "I will make
thee a companion and associate." And he said to Alexander,
"And thou, what wouldst thou give me, Alexander?" Alexander answered and said to him, "Ask not now concerning that
which is future, and take not a pledge of me for the morrow:
wait and see if I live until the morrow; and if I live, I will
do that something, and times and seasons are commanded
for me." And Aristotle said, "Peace be with thee, O Alexander,
ruler of the world! From thy nature thou art known to be
the future ruler of the world." Now Philip heard all these
things concerning Alexander, and when he heard them he rejoiced greatly; he was however a little grieved in his mind that
the looks of Alexander did not resemble his own.

[3]Now Alexander was exceedingly liberal in everything;
accordingly, that which his father and mother were wont to
send him for expenses, he divided among his friends. Then
Zintôs (Zethus? Zeuxis?)[4], Alexander's tutor, sent a letter to
Philip and Olympias, and in it there was written thus: "To my
lords Philip and Olympias from your servant Zintôs greeting.
Know ye that what ye send to Alexander for his expenses is not
sufficient for him, because he distributes it all in gifts; and now

---

[1] This is a mistake. The Greek has "to one of them".

[2] This name is corrupt. Partiôn may be Παρίων or Πρωτίων.

[3] The following paragraph does not appear in the Greek, but Müller gives a
Latin version (Pseudo-Call. p. 16).

[4] In some places the MSS. write ܩܘܠܝܛ Zintôs, in others ܩܘܠܝܛ
Zîgintôs.

2—2

see and look into this matter, and do according to what appears right unto you."

When Philip had read this letter, he wrote a letter to Aristotle, Alexander's teacher [as follows]: "From Philip and Olympias to Aristotle, greeting. Our servant Zintôs, whom we have sent for the purpose of educating and training Alexander, has made known to us by letter that what we send him for expenses is not sufficient for him, because he gives many presents; now he thus informs us as if blaming and murmuring against thee, and it is of thee he complains."

When Aristotle had heard this, he wrote a letter to Philip and to Olympias his wife and made answer [saying]: "In every way it beseems us [to acknowledge] that this giving of presents by Alexander proceeds from us and is the result of our teaching[1]. Ye also yourselves have examined and seen that he is wise and superior in everything, and in knowledge and understanding he is not at all like [other] youths, but he is well fitted by his wisdom for the business of life; neither does he do anything unseemly or improper, but everything whatsoever ye command him that he does."

Then Philip sent this letter to Zintôs the tutor, and he himself wrote to him thus and said: "From Philip and Olympias to our servant Zintôs greeting. We wrote and informed Aristotle, Alexander's teacher, concerning his affairs, according to what thou didst write to us, and we desire that the answer which he sent to us should be conveyed to thee. Do thou therefore take it and read it, and do thou what is right and proper."

After Aristotle knew that Alexander's father complained of him, he wrote a letter to Alexander, and in it thus informed him: "From me to my son Alexander greeting. Philip thy father and Olympias thy mother have written and informed me, saying, 'That which we sent for expenses is not sufficient for him, because he distributes it all in gifts.' Now I know that thou wilt not do what is not right, and I know not from whom thou hast learned this practice, which thy father and thy mother disapprove of, and I too; but if thou hast done anything which

---

[1] The context seems to require "giving of presents", but the Syriac more literally has "that Alexander's training has been by us, and that he will go forth from our teaching."

befits not thy skilled knowledge, in thy wisdom correct it, O wise and beloved son. Be thou well.*

When Alexander had read this letter, he immediately made answer to Aristotle: "From thy son Alexander to Aristotle, my master and chief and teacher, greeting. What my father and mother send me for expenses is not sufficient, nor is it adequate for me; and instead of doing that which was right when they heard that the amount was too small for my expenses, that is, to blame themselves, they now complain bitterly [of others]."

And Alexander also wrote a letter to Philip his father and Olympias his mother, in which was as follows: "From Alexander to Philip and Olympias greeting. That which ye have sent to me for my expenses by the hands of Zintôs is not sufficient, for I am Alexander; and, moreover, I have not spent it in an improper manner. I have also seen Aristotle's letter, and I will never blame Aristotle, because from him I have received knowledge and instruction in good things: but I do blame you, because ye have shown such parsimony to me, who am your son, while ye also blame me and cease not, and think nothing good of me.*

XVIII. So the youth Alexander returned from school, being fifteen years of age, and came home with honour. And when Philip saw him, he embraced him and kissed him. Then Alexander said to his father, "Bid me, O my father, to embark in a ship and go to Pisa, for I would enter and see the horse and chariot races." Philip says to him, "Dost thou desire to see the contest?" Alexander says, "Nay, my father, but I will go thither myself to the contest, and will contend with them with horses and chariots, and I will moreover bring back the crown of victory." When Philip heard these words, he rejoiced, and said to Alexander, "Go, my son, and good luck go with thee. I know, my son, that thou wilt not contend like a king's son, but like a king himself; and I will entreat the gods that thou mayest return with victory, my son. Go now into the stables, and [take] forty colts and sixty wheels and chariots, together with harness and bridles and everything which thou mayest require, that thou mayest not lack horses in the contest. Take too ten thousand daries for thy expenses, and go, my son, and good luck go with thee; and keep thyself in good training, for this contest is great and renowned." And Alexander said, "Do thou but give me the command, and I will go without taking aught; for I have trained horses and exercised colts, which I myself have trained." Then Philip kissed Alexander, and admired him for his will and purpose, and said to him, "My son, everything shall be according to thy wish." And Philip went with him to the harbour, and commanded to bring a ship. Then he commanded to bring the horses, the chariots, and the baggage, and they brought them and placed them in the ship. And Alexander and his friend Hephaestion embarked in the ship. And they loosed the ship and departed from their kinsfolk. And when they had disembarked from the ship, they received many gifts from their friends[1]; and Alexander commanded his servants to feed the horses regularly and to anoint them with oil; and he and his friend Hephaestion went to the place where the nobles were wont to walk.

And while he was walking in this place in the costume of an athlete, Nicolaus the king of Ârêtâ[2], who had brought a large retinue to the contest and combat, saw that Alexander was small in stature (now Nicolaus was huge in stature, rich in property, great in strength, and fair in appearance), and he answered and said, "Who is this? and from what country does he come?" And when he had learnt that he was the son of king Philip, and had come on account of the contest, he answered and said to him, "Peace be with thee;" and Alexander answered him, "Peace be with thee; and who art thou?" Nicolaus said, "As whom dost thou greet me? I am Nicolaus of Hâlûâ, and the son of Karyânâ[3]." And Alexander said, "Do not boast of this, and be not insolent(?) on account of such things, and do not be out of thy senses because of thy royalty, because thou knowest not the manner of thy death; for thy fortune and fate, O Nicolaus, remain not in one place; for this fickle fortune[4] has the habit of

---

[1] An inaccurate rendering of καὶ λαβὼν ξενία (Müller, p. 18, col. 1).

[2] The Greek text has ὁ υἱὸς Ἀρείου (var. Ἀρδίου) βασιλέως Ἀκαρνάνων (Müller, loc. cit.).

[3] It is possible that ‏ܐܪܛܐ‏ may stand for ‏ܐܪܛܐ ܒܪ‏, ὁ υἱὸς Ἀρείου, and that ‏ܩܪܝܢܐ‏ ‏ܕܚܠܘܐ‏ may be a mistake for ‏ܕܐܩܪܢܘ ܡܠܟܐ‏, βασιλέως Ἀκαρνάνων.

[4] Syr. fate of Kêwân (Saturn).

departing even from him that is great, and of going to him
that is little." Nicolaus said to him, "Thou hast spoken rightly
as regards one that is weak, and hast made known that thy fate
is thus; but my fate does not change in this manner, neither
does it depart. Now, therefore, inform me of thy business, and
for what reason thou hast now come hither, whether to see the
contest, or to take part in it; for thy stature and thy appearance
are not like those of an athlete." Alexander said, "Get thee gone
from my presence, for it is not to be seen that thou art in any
way like me." Nicolaus said, "I asked thee this question, for
what thou hadst come hither, whether to see this contest or to
take part in it, because thou art the son of Philip the Macedonian." Alexander said, "If thou desirest to hear and to know,
give me thine ear and I will tell thee. I am not one of those
who will look on at the struggle, but I am one of those who will
perform valiant deeds at the contest; and though I be little and
short in stature, yet I am mighty in chariot races, and I will
defeat the proud." When Nicolaus heard this speech, his gall
was stirred up within him, and he answered and said, "Look and
see to what a pass this strife of Zeus has come, that even a mere
boy, the son of Olympias, has come to take part in it, and so we
think that it is the sport of children. By the life of my father,
if they should make only a sprinkling of drops of water come to
his mouth upon his chariot, his soul would depart from his body."
Then he looked at him from head to foot, and despised him
greatly, and spat, saying, "Go, get thyself a rag, and wipe away
thy sweat with it, because thou art famished, and thy sweat is
abundant." And he shot out his lip at him, thinking him to be
already dead and not alive. Then Alexander said to him,
"Nicolaus, I swear this oath by the race of my gods and ancestors, and by my conception from the divine seed in the womb of
my mother, that in this contest I will defeat thee in the strife of
horses and chariots; and I will come to thy country, and will
subdue thee and all the people therein with the point of my
spear." And when he had spoken these words, they separated
one from the other.

XIX. And on the third day all the athletes went prepared
to the race-course and to the place of the contest with horses
and chariots. Now the athletes were nine in number, and four

of them were king's sons; the fifth was Nicolaus, the son of
Hêlâ and king Ḳeryânâ[1]; the sixth, Kestios, the king of the
Philippians (?); the seventh, Ksosios (?), the king of Bithynia;
the eighth, Alexander the son of Philip, the king of the Macedonians; and the ninth, Aristoteles of Pisa (?); with the rest of
the ...... and the chariots from various places. Callimachus from
Aḳimtarnêtos (?), Anistippos (Aristippus) from Corinth, Ṭridiṭ (?)
from Ârôntir (?), Sephilâ (?) from Lêbâria (?), Elḳârôn (?) from
Phocis, Armîtos (?) from Lôdâ (?), Nikinâmos (?) from Ḳrîmîtos (?),
Pardânis (?) from Klôphiôn (?), all these were assembled together
in one place. And they placed a boat of silver in the midst of
the race-course, and this boat was of pure silver. And they
proclaimed the names of the horses that were yoked to the
chariots, and they made the horses stand beside the gates. The
first gate fell by lot to Nicolaus, the second to Kestos, the third
to Bantirâ Eustaniḳâ (?), the fourth to Ḳlitmaos (Cleitomachus),
the fifth to Adasṭâos (?), the sixth to Ksômios (?), the seventh to
Ḳôrantidos (?), the eighth to Alexander, the ninth to Nîḳômos (?).
Now these athletes were clothed in garments of various colours;
the first had put on sky-blue apparel, the second and third
scarlet robes, the fourth green vestments, the fifth and sixth
yellow apparel, the seventh dark blue clothing, and the eighth
and ninth purple raiment.

So they mounted the chariots, and the war trumpets were
sounded; and the athletes punished the horses with bit and
whipcord, and suddenly the horses started and went forth with a
rush, each contending as to who should get first; and they urged
on their horses with lashes. Now Ksîtos (?) got foremost, Nicolaus second, Timotheus third, Eliḳiôr (?) fourth, Ḳlinathmâchos
(Cleitomachus) fifth, Philacus (Piêris) sixth, Aristoteles seventh,
Nicolaus eighth, and Alexander ninth. [They kept this order]
in the first, second and third rounds; but in the fourth round
the chariot of Kestios (?) was overturned, and the horses and
chariot and rider fell head over heels. Then Nicodemus turned
his horses to the left, and wished to pass through them all and
get first in the race, but he too stumbled over the chariot of
Kestios. Then Ḳimrênôos (?), when he wished to turn his

[1] See page 22, note 3. The Syriac translator has blundered sadly here-
abouts, and the scribes have made confusion worse confounded.

horses to the right, was unable to pass because of those that were overthrown. Then Eliķiôr too stumbled over the chariot of Ķimotheus[1], and fell. And Klinathmâchos (Cleito-machus) wished to turn back his horses and chariot from the midst [of the strife], but was unable to do so on account of the horses and chariots which were overthrown before and behind him; and he too fell. When Nicolaus saw that Alexander was behind all these, he wished that Alexander would pass on to the front, and that he might be behind him, in order to throw him down and kill him; and Nicolaus began to turn his horses aside from before those of Alexander. Now Alexander under-stood this artifice of Nicolaus who was wishing to kill him. When Nicolaus had turned his horses to the left, Alexander saw an empty space between two chariots which had been upset and overthrown, and he guided his horses before Nicolaus, and passed through that spot to the front. When Nicolaus saw that he had passed him, he guided his horses after him; but when he reached the spot through which Alexander had passed to t'.e front, he was upset by the struggling of the horses which were down, and fell. Then Alexander began to urge on his horses alone; [but Nicolaus], in order to save himself, leaped out of his chariot, and stood upon his feet, and began to call out, saying, " O thou that art not able to conquer lawfully, there thou runnest by thyself! Every one knows that the foremost was overturned and fell, until the arena was full; and now thou runnest by thyself, and thinkest to receive the crown of victory!" Now, inasmuch as the people of Pisa were spectators and judges at this contest, they commanded all the tumult to cease, and made a proclamation by their heralds to all the people who were sitting in that place, saying, " O men of Pisa, dwellers in the city and its suburbs, and ye too, O Athenians, and ye people who have come from a multitude of places, we declare that we all have seen that, when Ksîţos (?) was first in the race, he was tripped up among the horses and fell, and the other six charioteers stumbled over him. Moreover Alexander drove on contrary to the rules of the contest. Let them therefore return, and bring back their horses."

[1] This name should clearly be *Timotheus*.

Then in accordance with this command, they brought Alexander back and ordered that other horses should be yoked to the chariots in the place of the eight on the left side, because that horse of Ksiṭos (?) had been injured. And when they had spoken in this manner, and each charioteer had changed one of his horses and had put another in his place, then Alexander too changed one horse and yoked Bucephalus in his stead. So they all returned to the gate of the race-course; and when they were ready, the trumpet sounded again, and they all started together, and urged on their horses with severe lashing, all [running] furiously until they reached the farthest[1] turn together. Now when they had reached the turn, Nikimos (Nicodemus) passed first, Elikiôr second, Philaeus third, Alexander fourth, Nicolaus fifth, Aristippus sixth, Kriṭomachos (Cleitomachus) seventh, Timotheus eighth, Kasṭis (?) ninth. They went the first, second and third rounds, and at the fourth round the horses of Aristippus lagged behind the horses of Kriṭomachus (Cleitomachus), and Kimis (Nicodemus) restrained his horses, and turned and went to one side. Then Alexander, who had been fourth, became first; and after him Nicolaus was foremost. He wished to let Alexander pass a little ahead that he might come up with him and kill him, on account of the enmity which existed between Philip, Alexander's father, and himself, for Philip had taken by force a number of villages and their inhabitants from Nicolaus. Then Alexander, being full of wisdom, gave Nicolaus room to pass before him. Now after he had passed Alexander in this way, he was meditating some means whereby he might gain the crown of victory, so he stopped his chariot before Alexander, and beckoned with his hand to Nicanor (Elikiôr ?) and Pithâos (Philaeus ?), as much as to say, " Do ye who are behind me keep to the left side," to the intent that they might get Alexander between them and might lay hold of him and kill him. Then Elikiôr (?) and Pithâos (Philaeus) turned their horses to the left behind Alexander; and when they had come close to Alexander's chariot in this manner, so that Alexander was already contending with these two, then Nicolaus looked behind him from his chariot, and stooped down to lay

---

[1] Literally, *the lowest turn*, or *bend*, the farthest point of the course where they turned homewards.

hold of the thongs of the bridles of Alexander's horses that his
two allies might come up with him. Then Alexander turned
his whip upon his horse Bucephalus, and smote him without
sparing upon his back, until the horse was beside himself with
rage and fury, and raised his fore feet in the air, and struck at
Nicolaus, who died immediately with his hand upon the bridle
of the horses. And again Alexander smote Bucephalus with
the lash mercilessly and pitilessly, until the horse, from the
pain of the blows, stretched forward his mouth and seized
the right hand of Nicolaus between his teeth and lifted him
from his chariot. Now Nicodemus, wishing to come to the
assistance of Nicolaus, drove his horses with care, and when he
had come alongside of Alexander's chariot, he smote Bucephalus
violently upon his head with a stick. Then Bucephalus let go
Nicolaus, who was already dead, and seized Nicodemus by his
left hand, and dragged him from his chariot. Nicodemus, crying out and shrieking with pain, begged Eliķiôr to come to
his assistance. Then Alexander guided his horses to the left,
and when he (Eliķiôr) had come up alongside of Nicodemus, he
(Alexander) turned again from the left [to the right], and
Eliķiôr was tripped up by the axle of Alexander's chariot
wheels, and fell head foremost, he and the horses and the
chariot; and he died together with his horses.

Then Alexander obtained the victory mightily and gloriously,
and gained the four crowns of victory. And a herald proclaimed
in the race-course, "These four crowns of victory belong to
Alexander the son of Olympias and of Philip the king of the
Macedonians; [the judges] have awarded them to him for his
strength and his might and his victory." Now the names of
the horses that were yoked to Alexander's chariot were these:
the first Ksithidos (Xanthus?), the second Îdâdô (?); the third
Achlios (or Ulios?); the fourth Bucephalus; and by the might
and strength of these four horses he obtained the victory
over four athletes, Nicolaus, Nicodemus, Eliķiôr and Philâdâos
(Philacus). Thus by good fortune Alexander won the crown,
and with his horses obtained the victory; and he turned to
go to his mother Olympias. Now when he had come to
Iûnûsia (?) the priest, [he said to him], "Receive this crown
which Zeus has given to thee;" and he answered and said to

him, "Now thou hast vanquished Nicolaus; so also wilt thou vanquish all nations and peoples which dwell upon the earth and {all} thine enemies."

XX. After Alexander had received this augury, he went to Pella. And when he had arrived there, he asked for his father; and he found his mother Olympias divorced by Philip and put away from being his wife. Now on that very day Philip was going to take a certain woman whose name was Cleopatra, the daughter of king Athlis (Attalus), to be his wife. And when all the guests were seated before Philip, Alexander came in amongst those that sat at meat. And when he saw his father Philip reclining like a bridegroom at the head of the table, he went straight in with his horses, and said to his father, "Receive from me these crowns of victory, the fruits of this my first labour. I will give my mother Olympias to another king to wife, but I will not invite thee to the feast, even as thou hast not waited for me until I returned." And when he had spoken these words, he drew near just as he was, in the dress of an athlete, and sat down by his father, with his garments unwashed from the mud and stains of the contest. At these words Philip was filled with anger.

XXI. Now there was a certain man called Lysias, Philip's jester, who was sitting with him on the same couch. This Lysias answered and said to Philip, "O Philip, thou possessest a number of countries; if from thy youth until now thou hadst had a wife like Cleopatra, thou wouldst now have had a son, and him not from adultery, and his look and face would have been exactly like thine." When Alexander heard this speech, he was at once greatly enraged, and he overturned the table which stood by the couch, and took a dish, and hurled it suddenly at the head of Lysias, whose soul immediately departed from him and he died. When Philip saw these things, he seized a carver's knife, and leaped among the guests, and wished to stab Alexander; but when he got near to him, he stumbled and fell heavily. When Alexander saw this, he answered and said to him, "He who wishes to seize and enslave the land of Asia, is unable to go a single step among his guests, and cannot save himself from stumbling!" And having said this, he drew near and went and took the knife from the hands of Philip and smote the guests and left them half dead, Rphîthôn and Kîliṭârôn with the rest of their companions; and the house was filled with the slain as at yon time [when Ulysses slew] those who were......because of Pkîṭîrpos (Penelope)[1].

XXII. Now after Alexander had acted in this manner, and had taken vengeance upon the guests and gone forth, the servants took Philip who was sick and laid him upon a bed, and carried him into a bed chamber, and his sickness was very sore. After a few days, Alexander went to Philip, and sat by his side, and said to him, "O Philip (for now I call thee by thy name, and perhaps it might not be pleasing to thee were I to call thee father, nor from this time will I call thee by the name of father), I have not come to thee of my own will,—[for] thou art not my father, nor I thy son,—but I have come as a friend and an associate, that I may be a mediator between thee and thy wife in respect of that which thou hast violently done unto her. But since I stood up at the beginning, I will not make [many] words[2]. Tell me this: did Alexander act in an unbecoming manner when he slew Lysias, who spoke that disgraceful speech mockingly? and didst thou thyself act well when thou didst rise up and lift a knife upon thy son? And thou wishest to take another woman to wife, and wantest to forsake the wife who has not done thee any wrong! Rise now and heal thyself, for thy disease is not bodily but mental; for a man becomes more ill through a mental than through a bodily ailment. Now therefore I Alexander will go and beg of my mother and persuade her to make peace with thee again. My father,—I have again

---

[1] The last sentence of this chapter is so corrupt in the Syriac as to be untranslateable. The Greek text (Müller, p. 21) contains references to the battle of the Lapithae and the Centaurs, and the slaughter of the suitors of Penelope by Ulysses.

[2] This clause is somewhat obscure and may be corrupt. The Syriac seems to agree with the Latin translation rather than with the Greek text (Müller, p. 21). If we follow the Greek, we should read : ܐܢܝܒܨܡ ܬܡܪܩ ܢܘܗ

done wrong in that I have called thee father, but although I
do not wish to call thee by this name, yet nature acknowledges
that which is the truth." And when he had thus spoken, tears
were flowing from Philip's eyes. When Alexander saw Philip
weeping, he went to his mother, and said to her, "O my mother,
be not angry any longer at that wrong which my father has
done, for he has not forgotten the offence which thou thyself
didst commit against him, and the more so since I am the
mediator, whom they call a Macedonian, though I am in truth
an Egyptian. Now therefore, O my mother, go in and first
of all entreat thy husband that he may be reconciled to thee,
for it is right that thou shouldest be subservient to thy husband
inasmuch as thou art a woman." And when he had spoken
these things to his mother, holding her by her hand, he went to
his father. Philip was lying on his bed, and had turned his face
to the wall. Alexander answered and said to Philip, "O my
father—for henceforward I will call thee father, and I do not
shun what is right,—turn thy face hither, for behold I have
brought my mother, and have set her before thee, having
implored her with many prayers and much entreaty until she
gave her consent. I have moreover persuaded and begged of
her to forget the offence which thou didst commit against her
and to put it away from her mind. And now do ye embrace one
another before me who am your son, and be ye now reconciled,
that I too may be happy in reconciling and re-uniting you who
begat me, and in urging you to make peace with one another."
By this speech he reconciled his father and mother, and on
account of this all who dwelt in Macedonia applauded Alexander,
and every one held his wife in honour, and because of the
death of Lysias, every one guarded his mouth from speaking
calumny.

XXIII. Whilst these things were taking place, a certain
city called Methônê had rebelled against the sovereignty of
Philip, and he sent Alexander thither to make an end of the
inhabitants by war. When Alexander had gone thither, he
persuaded the people of the city by his words to return to the
service of Philip; and the people of that city did so through
Alexander's words and admonition, and went back to the service
of Philip.

When Alexander had returned from thence and come back, he found men in the garb of foreigners sitting at the gate of Philip. Alexander asked them, "Who are ye?" They said to him, "We are satraps, servants of Darius the king." Alexander says to them, "For what purpose have ye come?" They say to him, "To receive the customary tribute from Philip thy father." Alexander said to them, "By whom have ye been sent?" The satraps say, "We have been sent by Darius the king of the Persians." Alexander said to them, "And for what is the tribute ye receive?" They say to him, "In lieu of lands and waters." He says to them, "Why does your master lay tribute upon what God has appointed and given for food? It is not right for Philip, being a Greek, to give tribute to the Persians. By the good fortune of Zeus, this is a matter of greed and not of royalty; now therefore turn and go, and say to your lord Darius, 'When Philip had no children, his hens used to lay golden eggs, but from the time that his son Alexander has been born, they have become barren, and do not lay eggs any longer. Now I will go thither in person, and will take the tribute from thee which until now thou hast received from my father.'" And when he had spoken these words to them, they departed from the gate of Philip, and he deigned not to give them a written answer. Now when those ambassadors perceived the pride, the greatness, and the understanding of Alexander, they wondered, and when they heard his wisdom and his well trained words, they marvelled. And they hired and brought a very skilful painter, and said to him, "Paint Alexander accurately upon linen just as he is," that they might take it to their own country. And when he had painted him, they took the picture and went to their own land; and Philip rejoiced, when he saw the wittiness of Alexander's speech and the might of his deeds. Again the country of the Armenians was disturbed, and Philip sent Alexander thither with a large army of soldiers, that he might either bring them to peace or contend with them in battle.

XXIV. And when Alexander had departed from his father, a certain man named Theosídos[1]—a small man and slight in

[1] The name is evidently corrupt, but cannot be emended with certainty at present. Possibly *Theodosius*, the Greek and Latin texts have *Pausanias* (Müller, p. 24).

body, purseproud and honoured because of his money, who had
come from the land of the Thessalonians and had a multitude
of slaves, and whose mind and heart were inflamed with love
for Olympias, and because of his love for her he gave goods and
gifts to many people of the city, and communicated his secret
to them—this man sought to slay Philip by some means, for
he saw that Alexander was not in the country. Now in those
days there was in the city an amphitheatre which was called
the Olympic, and certain people, partisans of Theosidos, by his
instruction and advice, begged Philip with tumult and clamour
to go with them and see the contest of the athletes. And
Philip, because he was unacquainted with the craft of Theosidos,
was persuaded to look on with them. Now in the middle of
the spectacle the partisans of Theosidos made a disturbance and
an uproar in the theatre by his advice and command. Theosidos himself was outside the theatre, and when he heard the
uproar and disturbance, he rejoiced, and together with his
partisans armed himself and went into the theatre, and gave
people to understand that he had come in to assist Philip.
Then he brandished the spear that was in his hand, and
pretending that he was going to smite another, cast it and
pierced the heart of Philip, whilst feigning to be a helper of the
king. Philip straightway fell to the ground, and Theosidos
with his companions went out at once from the theatre, because
they thought that Philip was already dead, but his life yet
remained in him. Then Theosidos went swiftly to the royal
palace, and going to Philip's apartment, he seized Olympias
unexpectedly and carried her off to another apartment in the
palace, for he thought that Philip was dead, and he said to himself, "Alexander is still a boy, and Philip is dead; therefore, if
I take Olympias to wife, I myself will become king."

Now on that day Alexander returned with victory from the
war with the Armenians, and came to the city of Pella; and
when he saw that the whole city was in an uproar, he asked,
"What is the reason that the city is thus disturbed?" And when
he had learned what had happened, he was furiously angry,
and went on horseback to the palace, and found Theosidos and
Olympias there, and at once raising up his whip[1], he smote Theo-

<hr>

[1] The Greek text has λόγχη, *spear*, and the Latin translation *jaculum*.
See Müller, p. 24, col. 2, at the foot, and p. 25, col. 1, first line.

sidos as Heracles smote Arminos (?), because he held Olympias
in his embrace, for Theosîdos wished to escape and save himself.
Now Alexander was very near slaying his mother too. And
when Theosîdos had fallen, and Olympias saw her son Alexander, she lifted up her voice and wept at the change her
fortune and lot had undergone. And when Alexander heard
that Philip was still alive, he gave orders to carry Theosîdos
tied to poles, and he went to his father. And when he saw that
Philip was near death, he wept bitterly and bade them raise
him up from the couch; and when they had lifted him up, he
put a sword in his hand, and made Theosîdos stand before him,
while his life was still in him, and he said to Philip, "This is he
that slew thee." And Philip said, "Is this he?" And Alexander said to him, "Yea, it is he." Then Philip stabbed Theosîdos with the sword and slew him. And he said, "O my son
Alexander, my soul will not depart in sorrow, since I with my
own hands have slain him that slew me. My son, mighty and
great shalt thou be, for I call to mind the day of thy conception,
when the god Ammon spake to Olympias thy mother, saying,
'Behold in thy womb is one who shall avenge the cause of his
father and his mother;' and thus my son has avenged the
cause of both of us." And immediately Philip died. And
Alexander with his nobles and the princes of the Macedonians
buried him honourably, and Olympias too went to the grave on
foot.

XXV. And when Alexander had returned from the grave,
he gave orders to inform the Macedonians that they should assemble on the morrow in the midst of the city by the pedestal of
the statue of Philip his father; and he himself came there, and
all the Macedonians gathered together unto him. Then Alexander went up and stood by the statue of his father, and lifted
up his voice, and said to the Macedonians, "To you I speak, ye
inhabitants of the land, Macedonians, Thracians[1], Greeks,
Thessalonians, and peoples of every race; to you too, O Amphictyons and the rest of all the peoples of the Greeks, and you
Athenians and Corinthians; hear my speech and the counsel
with which I counsel you, and trust yourselves to me, and form

---

[1] In the Syriac Tarmîkâyê or Tharmîkâyê.

a league with me, that we may go against the barbarians our
enemies, and may free ourselves from the bondage of the
Persians, and bring them into bondage to us, and subjugate
them to ourselves." And when he had said this, many applauded him; and he came down from the statue and gave
orders to write letters to every country and city under his
rule, as follows: " Let every one who approves of my advice
come to the city of Pella." Then many troops of men came
with good and ready will, as if a god were urging them on[1].

Then Alexander opened the door of his father's treasury, and
clothed every man with all kinds of armour. But when he
commanded those who had carried arms in the bodyguard of
Philip his father to take them up again, they answered and
said to him, " O good king Alexander, we are greyhaired and aged
men, and we have been with thy father Philip in a number of
wars during the whole time he was in the world, and we have
become wearied and exhausted by many battles, and we speak
truly before thee when we say that we have not sufficient
strength in our bodies to bear arms; therefore we now ask to
be excused from military duty and service." When they had
spoken these words, Alexander looked on them with a gloomy
face and said to them in anger, "I desire particularly that ye
should go with me to war. It is true that ye are greyhaired
and aged, but all kinds of warfare have been experienced and
seen by you more than by these young men, for the aged by
their experience and knowledge are stronger than those who
are in the vigour of youth. Many a time, therefore, when
young men neglect the safety of their lives, and do something
which it was not their intention to do, they come into difficulties and distresses thereby; but as for you, ye greyheaded
and aged men, I know that ye first of all consider carefully, so
that, when ye are about to do something, no mistake or [cause
for] repentance may arise thereby. Now therefore go ye with me
to the war, and be ye with me as ye were with my father; for I
desire that ye go with me in this capacity, not that ye should
make war, but go with me as persons of tried knowledge and
experience. Ye will be a shield to the young men, and the

---

[1] Or, as if there were some one sent from God to urge them on.

knowledge of the aged will be thus mingled willingly with the strength of the young; and so we shall obtain a great victory, and the aged shall serve for knowledge to the youth, and shall rescue and deliver [them] from troubles like a shield. And this too I wish you to know, that the victory of the young is the life of the old, while the defeat of the young is affliction and trouble to the old. Therefore, ye veterans, rejoice and exult in the victory, and divide the crowns of victory with them, for by your knowledge and experience and understanding, ye veterans, the young men will become conquerors."

With these words then Alexander encouraged Philip's body-guard, and persuaded them to go to the war; and they consented, and drew near and received arms from Alexander.

XXVI.[1] The horsemen also gathered together to Alexander in countless numbers, as did the foot soldiers who served willingly, and the troops of Philip his father, 50,000; Thessalonians, 30,000; Greeks of every tribe, together with the Pokoṭolanians [Paph-lagonians?][2] and Lacedaemonians, 80,000; Skophians [Scy-thians?][3], 60,000; Corinthians, 70,000 [besides the former 70,000 which he had sent][4]; in all 270,000[5]. He armed these out of the armoury of Philip his father.

XXVII.[6] And he made them embark in triremes and in large transport ships, and put to sea, and he made the Macedonians dwell by the sea Dithâos (?) and Thrace, which was under his dominion[7].

XXVIII.[8] And [from thence] by Lucania and Sicily he came to Rome[9]. And as soon as the inhabitants of Rome heard [of his arrival], they sent him six hundred talents of gold by the hands of their chiefs, together with the golden crown of Zeus which

---

[1] Compare Müller, p. 27, col. 2, and the Latin version.

[2] See Müller, p. 28, line 6 of the note.

[3] See Müller, loc. cit.

[4] This clause is incorrect or misplaced. It is not taken into account in summing up the total.

[5] The total ought to be 290,000.

[6] Corresponding to ch. xxviii. of the Greek text (see Müller, p. 30).

[7] Very unintelligible. But compare the Latin version in Müller, p. 28, at the foot. "The sea Dithâos (?)" seems not to be named in any of our Greek texts.

[8] Corresponding to ch. xxix. of the Greek text (Müller, p. 30).

[9] See Müller's note 8 on ch. xxix. (p. 30).

was in the Capitol, one hundred pounds of gold [in weight], and
they brought it as a gift before Alexander. They also sent one
thousand horsemen as auxiliaries to Alexander's army, and they
entreated him to take vengeance for them upon the Chalķidonians[1], who had rebelled against them. Then Alexander said to
them, "I will do you this favour because of this honour which
ye have done me; and I will recompense you for this honour by
subduing your enemies in war, while the victory in the war I
will give to you."

XXIX.[2] Then Alexander set out from Italy, and came by
sea to Africa. And when the generals of the Africans had
heard the fame of him, they came to him and entreated him,
saying, "Free our city from the Romans." Then Alexander was
angry at this speech, and said to them, "O Carthaginians, either
be yourselves brave[3], or give tribute to the brave." When they
heard this speech, they set their faces to war, and they all went
and armed themselves, and they could not be persuaded to come
to Alexander. Then Alexander made war upon them; and when
they fought, they were unable to stand before the army of
Alexander. Then they returned and entreated him, saying,
"Permit not the Romans to rule over us." Again Alexander
said to them, "Ye Carthaginians, I have [already] said to you,
'Either be yourselves brave or give tribute to the brave.' Now
therefore go, and whatever tribute is right for you to give, of that
give justly; for henceforward [the Romans] shall receive tribute
from you." When the Carthaginians saw that they had no
remedy, they made a statue of brass to Alexander and set it in
the midst of the city: and they made a box of wood and fastened
it upon a stone in front of the feet of the statue. They then
collected the tribute of their country for four years, and placed
it in the box; and the Romans waited for four years, and then
they came and took that tribute and carried it to Rome.

XXX.[4] And Alexander departed from the Carthaginians,

---

[1] i.e. the Karchedonians or Carthaginians. Χαλχηδὼν = Καλχηδὼν = Carthage
(חדשה קריה, Neapolis).

[2] Corresponding to ch. xxx. of the Greek text (Müller, p. 81).

[3] Literally good.

[4] Corresponding to the remainder of ch. xxx. in the Greek text (Müller, p. 81).

and made some of the troops put to sea in ships and vessels,
and commanded them to remain opposite the islands of the
Pláthâyê¹, while he went parallel to them on the land with a few
troops to the country of Libya. From thence he dismissed all
the troops of the Álômôḥdâyê (?)², because he offered sacrifices
there to the god Ammon, especially because he remembered the
words of Olympias his mother, which she spake to him, saying,
"Thou wert begotten by Ammon, the god of Libya." And Alexander answered and said to the god, "If the words be true which
my mother Olympias spake to me saying, 'I bore thee to the
god Ammon of Libya,' shew it me to-day in a dream." Now
when Alexander was asleep, he saw in a dream the god Ammon
speaking with him and saying, "Thou art of my race, and thou
hast in thee parts of the characteristics of four gods; and if
thou dost not believe that it is possible for a mortal and corruptible man to be born of the race of an immortal and incorruptible god, I tell thee that they are able, as men, to be of the
race of the gods, not in respect of the nature of the body,
but in respect of wisdom, intelligence and fore-knowledge.
Therefore by the union of the race of the gods with men, they
are able both to know and to do everything that is marvellous
and difficult in the world. Now thou hast in thee somewhat of
the race of the serpent, and of Hêraclês, and of Dionysus, and of
Ammon. Through the serpent thou wilt encircle the whole
world like a dragon; through Hêraclês thou wilt be strong like
Hêraclês, and thou wilt shew forth in thy person the finding of
power and might; through Dionysus thou wilt be continually in
pleasure, and merriment, and joy; and through Ammon who is
like myself, thou wilt hold a rich sceptre, and thou wilt be lord
of the world in royalty and wealth. As regards these words,
have then no doubt." When Alexander had seen all these things
in his dream, he awoke from his sleep, and commanded that a
statue of brass should be made to Ammon in the midst of the
temple of Ammon, and he set it up on a pillar, and upon the base

---

¹ In the Greek εἰς τὴν Φαρίτιδα [var. Πρωτηίδα] νῆσον.
² There is nothing like this clause in our Greek texts, so that the word
Ḷᵫ̈ˈａ̈ṡꙩä̈ˉꙅ̣ remains a puzzle.

of the pillar he wrote thus: "This statue Alexander his son
made to his father Ammon, and set it up in this temple."

And again, when he was dreaming, he made supplication to the
god Ammon, and said, "O my father, shew me the place where
to build a great city which shall be named after me, and from
which my memory shall not pass away." And again the god
Ammon appeared to him in a dream, saying, "Alexander, king
of the Macedonians, I grant thee to build a city in.........[1] in the
fields where they plough the furrows, and it shall be famous and
renowned, and possessions and wealth shall abound in it, and the
supreme god shall dwell therein. Around it shall be the river
Nile, and it shall water its fields with abundant moisture, and
many shall be nourished by its produce, for this river without
any [human] labour will lay the hamlets and arable lands beneath its irrigation, and no damage shall arise therefrom."

XXXI. And when he had seen this vision in his dream, and
had quitted the land of the Âmôndîķâyê (?), a stag came towards
him. When he saw that stag, he turned round and said to his
nobles, "If it be granted me to build a city in this land of Egypt,
when I command and shoot an arrow at this stag, it shall strike
it." And having taken the weapon, he shot an arrow at the
stag, but the arrow glanced off the stag in its rapid flight, and
having run a long distance it stumbled and fell by reason of the
wound, and died on the spot. Then Alexander cried out and said,
"O thou that didst die without feeling, thou hast shewn me the
place which I require;" therefore to this very day they call the
spot upon which the stag died, "He that died without feeling."
So Alexander ran and came to that spot, and on this side of the
stag a sepulchral monument was built, and they call it, "The
tomb of the god Âsîîs (Osiris)[2]." In this place too he commanded to offer sacrifices; and from thence he returned and came to
the stag[3], and he found a large mound, and fifteen (twelve) towns
lay around it, the names of which were: Şţîlîmos, Paḥḥârâ,
Imthâos, Aķlios, Înôķpîlas, Pithônos, Lindos, Ķiphrîn, Espâʃd,
Mîmisţîrâ, Phîlâos, and Hanķlţos in the centre of the mound,

---

[1] In the Syriac *in Ain Wâls*, which looks somewhat like a corruption of
*Héliopolis*.

[2] Ταφόσιρις or Ταφοσίρισ.

[3] The Syrian translator confounded *the god* with *the stag* (Müller, p. 82, col. 3).

which they called "the great city." And when Alexander saw
this, astonishment laid hold of him at the waters which were
encircling the villages; and he wondered at the greatness of the
waves how marvellous they were, for although they entered the
sea, they did not mingle [therewith]. And he found there also
a place which they called Melââ, and its waters used to enter the
sea one cubit and make a great commotion. Then Alexander
asked, "What is this place? and who built it?" And they said
to him, "First of all Dios, whom they call Zeus, and next
Irthâos (?)." And from these towns twelve rivers went forth
and mingled with the sea. And Alexander saw that the greater
number of these rivers, as well as the springs of the city, had
been stopped up, and that all the streets and squares were
destroyed; and there only remained two rivers which were
not obstructed, and whose place of outlet was not destroyed, and
whose mouth mingled with the sea: the name of the one was
Lûkthesnêdos, which great river they call that of the god
Serapis (this Serapis is Joseph the son of Jacob, whom the
Egyptians used to hold as a god[1]), and from it there went forth
another which they call Ôk̤ôrida (or Euk̤ôrida), and yet another
large stream which they call Klîdnâva; and the name of the
other great river was Nûphîrt̤îr[2]. When Alexander saw that spot
around which mighty rivers and large streams ran, he remembered the dream which the god Ammon shewed him, and he
saw that there were fifteen (twelve) towns upon that one
spot.

XXXII.[3] And he heard that there was a temple of Zeus
there, and one of Hêra[4], whom they call 'the mother of the gods.'
And when he had entered the temple, he bowed down there and
sacrificed. And while he was examining the temple, he saw
there two tablets[5] of red marble, which were very beautiful,
fixed under a statue, and upon them was engraved a legend in

---

[1] This statement regarding the identity of Serapis and Joseph is probably an
interpolation by the Syrian translator or by a later hand.

[2] For the Greek text corresponding to this passage see Müller, p. 32, note 14.

[3] See ch. xxxiii. of the Greek text (Müller, p. 36, col. 2).

[4] The Syriac text has Ahlâ, ܗܠܐ, a corruption of ܐܝܠܐ

[5] The Greek text has *obelisks*.

hieroglyphs[1], which ran thus: "After that I Sesonchôsis[2], the ruler of the earth (or world), was first recognised as lord upon earth, I erected this statue in honour of the great god the Sun, the equal of Serapis, in gratitude for the benefits which I have received from him." And when Alexander had read this legend, he considered Serapis to be the first god. He went also to the spot where he was told that the temple of this god existed, and in the temple he found a golden cup of the god's upon the ground, and on the cup there was written as follows: "I Ahlâ[3], the son of the mighty Prométheus[4], made this cup for the great god Serapis before mankind were brought forth." And when Alexander had read this legend he said, "It is evident from this that Serapis is the first god, for this cup was fabricated when as yet Prometheus had not made men; and thus also did Ammon shew me in a dream, saying, 'I will grant thee to build a city where the first god dwells.' And now I will supplicate this [god] and will entreat a favour from him, because Sesonchôsis[5] too has shewn me by his inscription that he appeared [as] the first god in this world." Then Alexander offered sacrifices to Serapis, and made supplication to him saying, "If indeed thou art he who has governed the world from olden time until now, and hast revealed thyself at the first as god, instruct me, O Serapis, how to build the city which I have in my mind, and I will give it the name of Alexandria; and inform me also whether they will make my name to pass away from it and will call it by the name of another king." And when he had spoken these words, he slept; and he saw in his dream that the [god] took him by the hand and brought him up into a high mountain, and said to him, "Alexander, art thou able to lift up this mountain and to remove [it] to another place?" Alexander answered and said, "How can I, my lord?" Then

---

[1] Literally, "in letters of the priests."

[2] In the Syriac ܣܣܘܢܟܘܣܣ, Sisikîsas, for ܣܣܘܢܟܘܣܣ Sîsonkôsis.

[3] There must be some error here. A little above we had ܗܘܐ for Ἥρα.

[4] In the Syriac Parmithos.

[5] In the Syriac ܣܣܘܢܟܘܣ, Sisikôsos, for ܣܣܘܢܟܘܣ.

the god said to him, "Even as thou art not able to remove this mountain, so another king will not be able to remove thy name from this city, nor to set his own name upon it." And again Alexander said, "My lord Serapis, what might and strength shall there be in Alexandria that [men] shall carry its name into the world?" Serapis said, "In the same manner, when the city is built, [people] will call it 'the great city,' and the fame of its greatness shall be spoken of in the whole world, and men innumerable shall dwell therein, who shall be famous through thee. Gentle winds too shall minister unto it with the favourable temperature, and the knowledge and craft of its inhabitants shall be renowned throughout the world, for I will build it with cunning, and I will be a helper to it. Storms shall not disturb the sea, neither shall drought nor heat be therein; winter and cold shall not remain therein, neither shall there be in it the mischief and destruction of demons, and there shall be but few earthquakes in it, and they shall not cause much damage therein, for these are caused by the envy of wicked devils. If the armies of all the kings of the earth were to encamp round about it, they would not be able to injure it in any way. It has been decreed that it shall be renowned in the world, and alive or dead, hither shalt thou come, and in the city which thou hast made to be inhabited, thou shalt have thy grave." And again Alexander said to him, "My lord Serapis, I desire to know what thy real name is." And again Serapis said to him, "First of all consider in thy mind, for if thou art able to comprehend one of a hundred of the powers of heaven, or to speak twenty of their two hundred names, thou art able to understand my name[1]." And when the god had spoken these words to him, Alexander said to him, "My lord Serapis, tell me this also, where, and when, and by what death I shall die." And the god said to him in a dream, "Man that is born is without anxiety, and honourable, and comely, when the time of his death and the manner thereof are concealed from him; for mankind, though mortal, are wont to think in their minds that they are immortal, and that this world will not be dissolved. But if thou desirest to know by what death

---

[1] This passage seems to be quite corrupt. The Greek text (Müller, p. 38, col. 1, lines 6—9) is simple enough, turning upon the numerical value of the letters in the name of Σάραπις.

thou shalt die, know that thy death will be fair and peaceful;
thy sickness will be like that of one who drinketh poison; fear
not then, for thy death will not be caused by any bodily sickness,
and shouldst thou die in thy youth, thou wilt be innocent of a
multitude of evil."

And when Alexander had seen all these oracular responses
in his dream, he commanded them to call the architects,—that
is the chief carpenters,—three skilful and cunning men[1];
one was Sinkarṭis of Ârontios[2], another Aryânâos the Egyptian,
and another Ḳrirmâtîn of Ḳôḳellîn. And he set them over the
building of the city, Sinkarṭis to lay the foundations, and
Aryânâos to measure and plan the streets and squares, and
Baryâthmîn (sic) to build houses in the city; and Alexander gave
them five hundred thousand talents of gold, each talent consisting
of four hundred pounds. The length[3] of the city was from the
grave of Asîlls (Osiris) to Barṭînâ, and its breadth from Dânôd
to Îkarsṭra which they call ' by Hermopolis.'

XXXIII.[4] When Aristotle, the teacher of Alexander, heard
of the building of the city, he sent to him saying thus, " Nay my
lord, do not begin to build so great and mighty a city, nor to
make people of various countries and tongues to dwell therein;
peradventure they may rebel against thy service, and take the city
from thee; and again, if [the people of] the city should hold a
festival and games, the herald would not be able to make the
proclamation in many days; and if all the winged fowl in creation
were to be gathered together, and if thou didst store up all the
barley meal in thy dominions in one spot, it would not suffice for
the nourishment of the people that are in it." And after this
message had come to Alexander, great grief took hold of him,
and he was anxious and perplexed; and he commanded them to
call the Egyptian soothsayers who were skilled in augury, and
related to them this message. And when the augurs had heard
this message, and had seen that the king was in grief and trouble,

---

[1] See Müller, p. 33, col. 2, last paragraph.

[2] As Ârontios is almost certainly 'Ολόνβιοι, Sinkarṭin must represent Κρόντϊ
or Κρόντρωι. If so, then Aryânâos, or Arinâos, the Egyptian, is probably =
"Ηρων Αιβυκὶι, and Ḳrirmâtîn of Ḳôḳellîn = Κλεομίνηι Ναυκρατίτηι.

[3] Compare Müller, p. 32, col. 2; and see also p. 33, col. 2, at the top.

[4] There is nothing like this chapter in the Greek save a few passages in the
first paragraph of ch. xxxii.

they said to him, "O king, begin the building of the city, for it will be great, and renowned, and abounding in revenues, and all the ends of the earth will bring articles of trade to it. Many countries will be fed by it, but it will not be dependent on any country for sustenance; and everything manufactured in it will be esteemed by the rest of the world, and they will carry it to remote lands." And when Alexander had heard this speech from the soothsayers, he gave orders to build the city from Dedaknâtos as far as Ḳaiôphâ.

XXXIV. From thence he went into the middle of the country of Egypt, and commanded his troops to await him in Eslôna[1]. And when he had come to Egypt, all the Egyptians, with the priests and prophets of their gods came to him, and glorified him with a loud voice, saying, "Welcome, O Sesonchôsis[2], the youthful god and ruler of the world;" for he went to the city of Memphis, and they seated him upon the throne of Hephaestus[3], and clothed him after the manner of the Egyptians. Then he saw there a statue of a king, which was made of black stone, and he read the letters which were engraved beneath its feet, and the legend ran thus: "The king of Egypt who fled, a mighty man and astute and aged, after a time died, [and] there became king[4] a young man and strong, who shall surpass him in bravery, and shall go round the whole world by his might, and shall bring all mankind into subjection to the Egyptians, and shall give you might and power." Then Alexander asked, "Whose statue is this?" And the prophets said, "Of the last king of Egypt, Nectanebus." Alexander said, "And why are these letters inscribed beneath?" The prophets said, "It is an augury which the great god gave at the time when the Egyptians drew near to seek their king." When he heard this, he went up to the pillar on which the statue stood, and embraced the image with his arms, and kissed it, and answered and said to the Egyptians, "Ye men of Egypt, this is he that begat me,

---

[1] In the Greek *Tripolis* (see Müller, p. 88, note 1 on ch. xxxiv.).

[2] In the Syriac *Slenipos*.

[3] In the Syriac *Eslphasjos*.

[4] There is evidently some error in the Syriac translation at this place. The Greek text runs (Müller, p. 38, col. 2), Ὁ φυγὼν βασιλεὺς ἥξει πάλιν εἰς Αἴγυπτον, οὐ γηράσκων ἀλλὰ νεάζων, καὶ τοὺς ἐχθροὺς ἡμῶν Πέρσας ὑποτάξει.

and this is my father. I am the youth whose father is Nectanebus; and he is concealed, but I am revealed to avenge your
cause on your enemies. I am however astonished, how ye have
remained and stayed in this country and have not utterly perished by the hands of your enemies, since the wall of your city
is so weak, and ye have no fortified place for treasure houses;
but I think that your preservation is chiefly due to the many
rivers which encompass your territory. Now that tribute
which ye were wont to give to Darius, give to me; not that
I may put it in my treasury for my own use, but that I may
use it for expenses for my city Alexandria, so that ye [really]
give it to your protectors." Then they brought him much
gold, and a crown of gold, and [other] presents and large gifts,
and they took [them] before Alexander, and they went with him
as far as Pelusium.

XXXV. Then he commanded his troops to get ready, and
he took them and they went to the country of Syria. Then all
the country of Syria gave the right hand to him, and came
under his rule. And they drew near and came to Tyre. Because
the Tyrians had heard from Apollo the augur, " When a mighty
king shall march through the plain of Tyre, Tyre shall be taken
away from its deep place," the Tyrians of their own accord
promptly drew up in battle array against Alexander, and fought
with him, and slew many men of Alexander's host, and would
not allow them to enter the city. And Alexander was fiercely
enraged, and his anger rose, and he lifted up his eyes to heaven,
and said, " O my lord Serapis, thou art a god and hast made me
a king; shew me now if I shall be able to take Tyre." And
when he fell asleep, he saw in his dream the ranks of the singers
(or satyrs), who were standing before Dionysus and singing and
dancing, and they had garlands of young vine branches with their
clusters on their heads; and Dionysus was standing and holding
a Tyrian daric in his hand, and he gave it to Alexander; and a
cluster of grapes from the garland on the head of Dionysus fell
to the ground, and Alexander trod upon it and squeezed out the
wine from it. When Alexander awoke, he gave orders to call
those skilled in dreams; and when they came and heard the dream
from him, they answered and said to him, " O king, it is granted
to thee to take the land of Tyre; for the daric which Dionysus

gave thee represents the country which is going to be delivered
over to thee; and those grapes which thou sawest fall from the
garland of Dionysus are the people of the city who are to fall
and be crushed beneath the feet of thy hosts; and the wine
which thou didst see is the blood of the slain which will be shed."
Then Alexander commanded to give gifts to those men skilled
in dreams, and to assemble the troops, and to fight with the
Tyrians.  And the Tyrians were conquered, and surrendered[1] to
Alexander; and Alexander made a war in Tyre, the fame of
which has gone forth into the whole world.  And the city and
three noble and famous men from three towns were destroyed
by Alexander in this contest[2].  The towns were by the side
of the city, and according to the name of the three towns he
built a city and called its name Tripolis.  And Alexander
appointed the satrap of Phœnicia to take charge of and guard
the country.

XXXVI.  Now when the ambassadors of Darius, who had
been sent by their lord to Alexander[3], had departed, they spoke
of the sagacity and wisdom and astuteness of Alexander.  Then
Darius asked them, "What manner of person is Alexander?"
Then the ambassadors brought forth and shewed him the likeness of Alexander the Macedonian which they had had painted,
and when Darius saw the likeness, he gave orders to carry it to
Roxana[4] his daughter, and he bade them compare her height
with that of the picture.  And when he had measured the
picture, he took it up and cast it with his hands to a distance,
and he thrust out his lips in scorn as one mocks at a young
child.  But Roxana, the daughter of Darius, took the likeness
in secret, and carried it to her bed chamber, and kept it there,
and honoured it continually with sweet spices and odours, for
from the time that Roxana saw it her love went forth to
Alexander.

Now Darius was meditating in what way he could avenge
himself on Alexander, first of all, because of his contempt for his
ambassadors; and secondly, because, after his father Philip's

---

[1] Literally, "gave the hand."
[2] This passage is obviously defective and corrupt.  See Müller, p. 40, col. 2.
[3] See chap. xxiii.
[4] In the Syriac *Rūshnāk* or *Rūshnāk*.

death, Alexander assumed the royal crown of his own will and
became king; [and thirdly, because] Alexander had taken his
troops and had come to the country of Darius and seized his
lands. Then Darius sent to Alexander a whip and a ball and
a box full of gold, and wrote him a letter, and gave it to his
ambassadors to deliver to Alexander. And while Alexander
was marching through the country [of Syria], the ambassadors
of Darius met him, and gave him Darius's letter. Then
Alexander ordered the letter to be read, and found that there
was written therein as follows: "From the king of kings and
the kinsman of the gods, who is enthroned with the god
Mithras, the son of the stars, Darius the Persian, to Alexander
my servant, greeting. I have heard of thee that thou by thy
evil destiny hast set thyself to come from thy land to mine
and to do mischief. Now we command thee, withdraw and
return, and go to thy mother, and sleep in the bosom of thy
mother Olympias, for as yet thou art a child, and art in fact not
educated; therefore I send thee a whip, wherewith thou mayest
train thy youth; and a ball, wherewith thou mayest play with
the boys of thine own age, and not meddle with the business of
men; and a box full of gold for thy expenses, that thou mayest
be able to retire and go back to thine own country, for I have
heard of thee that thou art poor and mean and feeble; and
therefore I have given orders that the tribute of Philip thy
father shall be left with thee. Do thou therefore restrain
thyself from worry and folly, and [check] this crowd of robbers
which thou hast gathered together and brought with thee, for
as the chief of a band of robbers dost thou go round about and
disturb our cities. Art thou able to comprehend the number
of the stars of heaven? If all the people in the world were to
come as allies to thy army, thou wouldst not be able to make
an end of and destroy the kingdom of the Persians, for I have
tens of thousands of horses and warriors, even as the number of
the sand which is upon the shore of the sea. And I have sent
thee ten measures of sesame seed, that thou mayest know that I
have myriads of troops even as these grains of sesame. I have
also gold as [abundant as] the sunlight in the world; therefore I
have sent thee a box [full of it], that if thou hast no money for
expenses, thou mayest expend this on thyself, and, together with

the robbers thy companions, mayest be able to return to thy country. Now therefore repent of the things thou hast done, and count thyself an offender; for if thou art not persuaded to do what thou art commanded by me, and in thy disobedience still persistest in this thy contention, we will give orders to send the police after thee to take thee and bring thee to us, for thou art not one of those after whom it is fitting to send [armed] men, but we will send the police against thee and they will fetch thee, not as the son of Philip but as a leader of robbers, and we will crucify thee upon a tree."

XXXVII. And when they had read the letter before Alexander, great terror fell upon all Alexander's troops. And when he saw that the face of his troops was sad because of the words of Darius's letter, he answered and said to his troops, " Ye men of Macedon, ye who are my fellow soldiers, wherefore are your minds troubled by the letter of Darius as if his words were true, or as if he had any power at all ? Now this boasting and arrogance that is written in his letter is a mere pretence, and there is no truth in it ; for among dogs there are some which are small and feeble, and yet they bark with a loud voice, thinking they may be able to effect something by their loud barks : and in the same manner does Darius act, for in reality he is unable to do anything ; therefore he has written these words, that we might imagine them to be true. Do ye however prepare yourselves and be ready, and fight with all your strength, that we may be victorious; and do not do your duty sluggishly and feebly, that we may not be conquered : and now fight bravely, that we may receive the crowns of victory." And when he had spoken these words, Alexander stretched out his hand, and took a handful of the sesame seeds which Darius had sent, and put them into his mouth, and ate some of them, and said, " They are numerous, but they have no taste." And when he had said this, he gave orders to tie the arms of the ambassadors who had brought Darius's letter behind their backs and to crucify them. Then those men were afraid, and by reason of their fear they said to Alexander, " My lord, what offence have we committed ? for we whom thou desirest to slay are ambassadors." Alexander said to them, " Blame Darius your master and not me, for he who sent this letter did not send it as to a

fellow king, but as to a man who is the chief of [a gang of]
robbers. Now therefore I am going to slay you as if ye had
really come to a robber chief." They said, "My lord, Darius
wrote such a letter as this because he did not know who thou
wert; but now we see that thou art a prince and hast a mighty
army, and that thou art a warrior and a king, and rich in knowledge, and the son of Philip. Show then this act of grace to
us, that thy compassion may appear in our persons, so that
when we return to Darius, we may there bear witness as to everything that we have seen here." He said to them, "Do not
imagine that I have mercy upon you because of the fear
through which ye have made supplication to me, and so set you
free from death; for I had not originally intended to slay
you, but only to let you know the difference between the
knowledge of the Greeks and that of the barbarians, how much
that of the former is superior to that of the latter. A king
does not kill ambassadors."

When Alexander had spoken in this manner, he gave
orders to release the ambassadors, and at the time of sitting
down to meat he commanded to make them sit down before
him. And when they had come in and sat down in his
presence, they began to speak before him of the ambushes
which he ought to make in his war against Darius, and how it
behoved him to make war craftily and to take Darius prisoner.
Then Alexander said to them, "Be silent and say nothing to
me. Had it not been your purpose to return and go to
Darius, I would have listened to your advice; but since ye are
going to return to Darius, I do not wish to listen to you, lest, if
any contention should arise between one of you and his fellow,
and this matter be carried to Darius, he may take away on my
account these lives which ye have obtained to-day from me by
grace." Then these ambassadors made obeisance to him and
applauded him for this speech.

XXXVIII. On the following day Alexander sat down and
wrote an answer to Darius as follows: "From Alexander, the
son of Philip and of his mother Olympias, to the king of kings,
who moves the heavenly hosts, and who is enthroned with the
god Mithras, the kinsman of the gods, the son of light, Darius
the sun, the god of the Persians. It [must appear] disgraceful

and bitter to him that hath such greatness and excellence and superiority, who is the counterpart of the gods, and who together with the sun lights and warms the whole world, whose throne is in the firmament with the god Mithras, when he feels that he may be defeated by his servant Alexander, a despicable and contemptible man, and still have to walk in the world beneath the sun and the moon. But do not imagine that any one of the gods is pleased to share his name or his fellowship, or the likeness of his glory, with mortals, or that they will give victory to the mortal man who assumes to himself the name 'divine;' but they will be angry and wroth with him who takes the immortal and incorruptible and unchangeable name, and applies it to one who is mortal and corruptible. And now I regard thee thus, since, because thou art not able to perform the deeds of brave men, thou desirest to call thyself by the name of the gods, and to draw down their heavenly power upon earth by words, and to set it upon thyself. But now I am coming against thee and will enter into war with thee; and I come against thee as against a mortal king, even as I myself am mortal. Now fortune and opportunity and victory are given by the power and command of the heavenly One; I have therefore committed myself to the immortal gods, and entrusted myself to them, and I shall be victorious over thee. Why didst thou then inform us in thy letter of the vast amount of thy gold and silver? For the sake of thy wealth will we fight the more against thee, until all thy possessions become ours. As for thee..........[1] among all nations and peoples, saying, 'So great a king and warrior as this Darius died by the hands of a little Greek boy;' whereas if thou slayest me, it will not be accounted as bravery and as a great triumph, because thou wilt have slain merely a 'robber chief,' according to what thou didst send in writing to me. Thou hast also sent me a whip and a ball and a box of gold. Now though I know that thou hast sent them to me in mockery, yet I have accepted them as a good omen, an augury of victory, and a prophecy of the gods. I have received the whip, and as a chief and the head of kings I will smite and subdue with my weapons all my enemies. As for the round ball, it is a sign that I shall hold the whole world; for the

---

[1] The Syriac text is corrupt and untranslateable. See Müller, p. 43, col. 1.

world is round and resembles a sphere exactly. And the box
[of gold] which thou hast sent me is a great portent and
signifies my subjugation of thee in war, and makes known that
thou wilt pay me tribute. And as for the sesame seeds which
thou hast sent me, the signification thereof is that thy troops
are numerous, but I have seen and tasted them; they are
numerous, but they are tasteless, and good for nothing:
therefore I have sent thee a <u>bushel of mustard</u> seed, that
thou mayest know how the troops of the Macedonians are
in comparison with the Persians."

XXXIX. Thus Alexander wrote, and he gave the letter to
the ambassadors and sent them away; and likewise the gold
which Darius had sent him he gave to the servants of Darius,
when they made obeisance before him that they might depart.
And when these [ambassadors] had seen the learning and
knowledge of Alexander, they turned to go to their lord. And
when they had come to Darius their lord, and had given him
the letter containing Alexander's reply, Darius commanded it to
be read, and he heard also that Alexander had put a handful of
the sesame seeds into his mouth and had eaten them. At this
Darius was exceedingly angry, and wishing to act in the same
manner, he straightway stretched out his hand, and took a
handful of the mustard seed, and put it into his mouth and ate
some thereof, and said, " They are small, but pungent." And he
forthwith gave orders and wrote letters to the satraps of the
land, saying thus: "From Darius the king of kings of the
Persians to the satraps who dwell in the Taurus, greeting. We
have heard a report that that rebel Alexander the son of Philip,
an impudent and shameless boy, in his madness and ignorance
has come forth from his own land, and is trying to come to our
land of Asia and to do mischief. Do ye therefore seize him and
bind him, and bring him bound to our gate, but do him no harm.
But I command that they beat him with a whip for children,
and dress him in purple vestment, and send Persian slaves with
him as guardians to take him and carry him to his mother, that
she may keep him in training there; and I will give him
castanets and dice[1], that he may amuse himself with them after

---

[1] Or rather, to use an old English word, *tables and dice*, something like our
modern draughts.

the manner of Macedonian children. It is not seemly to make war with him, but it is right to frighten him as a child. Now therefore be ye diligent to seize and bind those robbers that are marching with him, and to throw them into the sea; and take ye their armour and their horses and the possessions which are with them for yourselves, and be ye strong to take [them] and to give to your friends. Farewell."

Now when the satraps had received this letter, they made known their answer to him in writing thus: "From the satraps Gushtâzaph and Sâbânṭâr[1] to Darius, the king of kings and the great god, greeting. Know, O ye gods, that the youth Alexander has come to your country, and is marching through your land exactly like a prince. Now we are making preparations to flee before him, but together with all the other satraps who are in this country we are awaiting your coming. Ye will therefore do well, O ye gods, if ye come hither quickly and take heed unto your country. It is necessary that ye should come with a strong force, and by our joining together, what ye have written to us concerning Alexander will be really accomplished. Know this also, that if ye do not make safe (?) your country, he will take it by force like other countries, and will enslave us."

When Darius had received this answer, he straightway ordered another letter to be written, saying thus: "From the mighty, the king of kings, Darius the god, to Gushtâzaph and Scôṭnâr, and all the other satraps that are in the Taurus, and in the districts beyond the Taurus, and to those who dwell in its vicinity, greeting. Do not think that any good hope [of escape] exists for you or your wives or your children [in flight]; for if ye abandon the country and go to [another] place, your enemies will spoil part of the land. But bethink ye that when Ṭir[2] came to spoil and to take captive, he brought with him mighty men and warriors, who by their power were able to defeat and conquer fearful lightning flashes, which men ye, being skilful and experienced in war, defeated at that time and

---

[1] In the Greek Ύδάσπης καὶ Σπιγχθηρ, in the Latin translation *Hystaspes et Spinther* (Müller, p. 44).

[2] The Syriac translator has missed the meaning of the Greek, having taken ήν for a proper name, which he has transcribed ܛܝܪ. See Müller, p. 44, col. 2.

4—2

overcame, and took no disgrace to yourselves. And shall ye
now be worsted before a little boy, and disgrace yourselves?
And if ye do this, what excuse will ye have to offer to us?
since none of you will be wounded in the fight, nor smitten in
the war, nor pierced by a spear; and what answer [for your
conduct] will ye make to us, having disgraced the rule of
the Persians? or do ye think, pray, that you will be found of
any use?"

XL. After these things Darius heard that Alexander had
come to the river which is called Estalraglos[1], and he wrote a
letter to Alexander, in which was thus written: "From the
great king Darius to Alexander the great and mighty, whose
name God has set upon the earth,.........[2] And thou hearest
that even the gods hold me in honour, and yet thou hast dared to
cross over rivers and mountains and the sea and to come to me;
and it was not enough for thee to assume the crown of royalty
without my permission, and to acquire a kingdom and dominion
in Macedonia, but thou hast also taken men inexperienced in
war from every country, and with a mob like a swarm of
ants hast thou come to our country to do mischief. It would
have been but right for thee before doing these things to have
informed us that it was planned by thy evil mind to do them,
and then thou mightest have done them; and we, having learnt
these things, would have prepared what was requisite for us.
Even now however, turn and go, and return to thy country. I
have sent thee sesame seeds, that if thou art able to number
them, thou mayest know also how many are my troops. Turn
back from where thou art and go to thy country, and I will no
longer remember against thee this damage which thou hast
done."

XLI. Then the ambassadors of Darius took this letter,
together with the sesame seeds, and carried it to Alexander.
And as soon as he had read the letter of Darius, he again filled
his hand with the sesame seeds and put them into his mouth
and said, "They are many but tasteless." At that time a report

---

[1] This name seems to be corrupted from the words προς τω τιναγρω.
according to the reading of the Cod. A (see Müller, p. 44).

[2] There is some corruption here in our text. The Syriac words mean "of
Darius like this."

reached Alexander that Olympias his mother was seized with a great and sore sickness. Then he wrote a letter to Darius as follows: "From Alexander to Darius the king. Thou writest many new and artful words to me, and thinkest in thy pride that thou wilt glorify thyself by words, [which is] more than is right and beyond thy capacity. This is a sign of inferiority, and thy shame and disgrace will increase and become more in the world than that of other kings thy equals. Neither imagine this, that I now return because of the words of the letter which thou hast sent me; but the sickness of my mother Olympias compels me to return and to go to Macedonia. But I will make ready to come again against thee. So I retire from thy country in good order and in strength and might, like the blossoms of a tree glorious in its bloom; and I will become firm in thy land, like a vine branch which is cut off from the tree and planted in another spot. But as for these sesame seeds, which thou hast sent me to inform me of the number of thy army, I send thee a little mustard seed that thou mayest know that a little mustard is more pungent than a great deal of sesame."

Then Alexander wrote this letter and gave it, with the mustard, to the ambassadors, and sent them away; and he himself turned to go to Olympias his mother. While he was on the way, a report reached him, that one of Darius's generals was encamped in Arabia, and forthwith he marched against him, and they engaged in battle one with the other, and many men perished on both sides. So great was the number of slain there that even the sun was saddened by the sight of the multitude of dead and of the blood which was shed on the ground, and he shrouded his light as in a cloud, because he too was ashamed of this sight of pitilessness and want of mercy, and was grieved and desired not to look upon such impurity as this[1]. And when they had fought together thus violently for three days, Darius's general was defeated and gave way before Alexander, and fled with his troops and went back to Persia.

Before Darius took in his hand the letter which Alexander had sent, he questioned the ambassadors, saying, "What did Alexander do with the sesame seed which I sent him?" The

---

[1] Compare Meusel, p. 737, lines 1 and 2; Müller, p. 46, col. 2.

ambassadors said to him, "He took a handful of it and put it into his mouth; and when he had eaten it, he said, 'They are many but tasteless!'" Then Darius took a handful of the mustard seed and put it into his mouth, and when he had eaten it, he said, "They are small but very pungent." When Eumenes the general heard this speech he said to him, "Thou hast spoken rightly, my lord the king, for although the army of Alexander is small, yet it is fierce and warlike, for of my army they have slain a multitude, both horse and foot."

Then Alexander gave orders to bury the corpses of the numbers of Macedonians and Persians who had died in this battle, for he did not neglect such a thing as this.

XLII. And when Alexander was ready, with the spoil which he had taken, to go to Achaia[1], there too he captured a number of cities, and others of them he made horsemen and footsoldiers. And he departed from thence and went to the city of Picria[2], which is in Bebrukia, of which city people say that the Nine Muses (that is, the Sciences) went forth from it. And from thence he came to Phrygia, that is Ilion, and in that place he offered sacrifices to Hector, whom in the Persian tongue they call Sòti; and he made offerings to Achilles, and to the river Alis, which they call Pòlis[3], and to the rest of the warriors. He saw the river which they call Eskamlis (Skamander), into which Achilles leaped, the breadth of which was five cubits. He saw also the river Òltis (?), which was not very large, even as Homer wrote of it. And he answered and said to the rivers, "Happy are ye in that ye have found heralds (to proclaim your merits), even Homer himself who has named you in his poem great and glorious! Your deeds however, and the sight of your works, are not so worthy of admiration as the words of him who wrote of you." And when Alexander had made this speech, Krintimos (?) drew near to Alexander the king of the Athenians and said, "O king Alexander, I too can put in writing this thy bravery and all thy actions in a better manner

---

[1] This name is evidently corrupt.

[2] In the Syriac *Pikra*.

[3] This clause seems to be corrupt. The Latin translation (Muller, p. 48, col. 1) merely has "atque illic Hectora Achillemque unaque alios heroes divum honore participat."

than Homer wrote concerning these (rivers), because the might of thy deeds and thy wars is greater than these." Then Alexander said to him, " Would that thy deeds were better than the words which Homer spake concerning them."

XLIII. And Alexander departed thence and came to Macedonia, and when he had entered there he found his mother Olympias recovering from her sickness; and he remained there with her a few days, and departed thence. And after these things he came to Abdêra[1]; and when the people of Abdêra heard it, they shut the gates of their city that Alexander might not enter it. And when Alexander saw this, he was exceedingly angry, and gave orders to set fire to it. And when the inhabitants of the city saw that they were setting their city on fire, they cried out with a loud voice and said to Alexander, "O king Alexander, we have not closed the gates of the city on this account, as if we wished to fight against thee, but we have shut them for this reason, lest when Darius hears of it, he may think we have delivered up the city into thy hands of our own will, and may utterly destroy us out of the world." Then Alexander said to them, "Open the gates according to your former custom; for I am not going to enter your city at present, but at the time when I shall have conquered Darius."

XLIV. And he departed thence, and came to Ķûsíṭîres and to Nûṭîrí, to the shore of the river Usṭîn[2], and he saw the lake which they call ' the second death', and the country was a place of cannibals; and a scarcity of food overtook them in that place, and they had nothing to eat and were distressed in their souls therein. Alexander bade them slay the horses which were in the camp, that the horsemen and footsoldiers might eat; and they ate and were satisfied; but they were all grieved about the horses, and were all without horses. Then Alexander said to them, " O my comrades, ye are alive instead of the horses, and in very deed ye are more needed than they. I know that horses are also necessary, but God forbid that ye should die, for of what use would the horses be then ? But now our horses being dead and we alive, we shall be able by our strength to

---

[1] In the Syriac Dâbedlâ or Bâbeldâ.

[2] Probably the Euxine Sea, ὁ Εΰξεινος πόντος. The other names are also obviously corrupt.

find a land of food, where we shall also find horses. Horses may be found in many places, but Macedonians cannot be found everywhere." And by these words he persuaded his forces.

XLV. And he departed thence and came to the Locri, whence they obtained food and horses; and they remained there one day. And from thence he came to Akrantis[1]; and thence he went to the temple of Apollo, and there he begged and entreated of the priest to ask an oracle from Apollo for him. And the priest said to him, "Thou art not permitted to ask an oracle from here." When Alexander heard these words, he was angered and said to the priest, "If thou dost not ask an oracle for me, I will take this tripod of divination and carry it away from here, even as Heracles did to his gods when they did not wish to give him an oracle." Having spoken these words, he straightway took the tripod of divination, which king Krithithos [Croesus] of Lydia had made, from its place, and put it upon his shoulders. And when he had taken it, he heard a voice from within the temple which said, "Alexander, if Heracles did any such deed as this, he did it to the gods his equals; but thou art a mortal man. Strive not with the immortal gods, that the gods may be thy helpers and may tell thy power in the world." And when he had heard a voice like this, again another voice from within the temple answered and said: "O Alexander, listen to the oracle of Apollo which I have heard, and hearken and I will speak to thee. Men shall tell of thy power and thy name in the world, and thy name shall last for ever, because thy might and thy deeds will be great and glorious." When Alexander had heard these words, he said, "O Apollo, henceforward I will believe this augury, as I likewise so believed thy father at yon time."

XLVI. And he departed thence and began to march towards Thebes. And when he had drawn nigh and arrived at Thebes, he demanded of them four thousand men to recruit his army. But when they heard this request, they closed the gates of the city, and answered him never a word, but straightway armed themselves and mounted the wall. And four hundred men said from the wall to Alexander, "Come and

---

[1] 'Επὶ τοῦ 'Ακραγαντίνου (Müller, p. 49, col. 2).

fight, or else depart from our city." When he heard this speech, he laughed, and answered and said, "Men of Thebes, who of your freewill have shut yourselves up, and who now command me saying, 'Either fight or depart from our city,' I am therefore going to fight with you, and by the fortune of Zeus, I will not make war with you as with brave and tried men, but I will fight with you as I would with weak and despicable fellows who are fit for nothing. Therefore shall ye be smitten with the point of the spear, because ye have of your own free will shut yourselves up in a cage. It is fitting to fight with valiant men and warriors in a plain or in a level place; but for effeminate men who live in cages it is good that they should be shut up in chambers and die like young girls." And when he had said this, he commanded a thousand horsemen to ride round the wall, and to shoot arrows at those who stood upon the wall. He likewise commanded two thousand footmen to destroy the foundations of the wall with picks and spades, and the upper part of it with long hooks and iron crowbars[1]. He also commanded four hundred other foot-soldiers to set fire to the gates of the city with burning torches, and other foot-soldiers to let go the battering rams[2] with violence against the wall and to shatter the wall. Now the battering ram is a warlike instrument used for the assault of cities, made of a huge log, the head of which is bound with iron, and fashioned in the shape of a ram's head; and it is fitted and fixed upon a revolving wheel, and men urge it forward with force from a distance, and grasp it and let it go with great violence, and it goes with impetus and strikes the wall or the gate, and wherever it strikes it makes a breach. Meanwhile Alexander with ten thousand men, slingers and casters of javelins[3] was fighting against one of the gates of the city. And when the fire had taken hold of the wall on all sides, and the arrows and missiles from the slings were shaking the wall everywhere, and were shot over the wall into the midst of the city, and fell like

---

[1] In the Greek καὶ μακροπόρους ὀρυγῇ τε [καὶ] σιδηρίοις μοχλοῖς. The Syriac words are unknown to me.

[2] Literally "ram's heads."

[3] The Syriac has *casters with the right hand*, but the Greek word is λογχοβόλων (Müller, p. 50, col. 2).

lightnings when they flash from heaven to earth, the people
who were wounded with the stones from the slings were many,
and within the city and in the houses they were smitten by the
arrows and missiles, and died. The city of the Thebans was
burning three days and three nights; and on the fourth day,
the gate of the city, at which Alexander was fighting, fell down
all at once, and Alexander entered the city with a number of
men; and when he had entered he commanded to throw open
the other gates. And the four thousand horsemen with their
horses[1] entered the city, and Alexander commanded them and
said to them, "Slay all the people of the city." Now the walls
of the city and the houses were broken up by the fire and were
falling down. Then the army of the Macedonians made haste
to slay the people, as the king had commanded them; and on a
sudden much blood was shed in the city. When Alexander
saw the great bloodshed and the destruction of the Thebans,
he rejoiced in his mind and was glad. As the Macedonians
desisted not from slaughter, neither were the blades of their
swords sated with blood, and the Thebans, since they had no
deliverance nor place of refuge, were perishing [before them], a
certain singer who was a Theban by race, a man well trained
and wise and of understanding, and who knew the Macedonian
language,—this man, when he saw that the whole city of
Thebes was on fire, and that every class of people in it were
perishing, groaned bitterly like a man who was mourning for
his country. Then he took his pipe in his hand and chanted
skilfully and cunningly in the Macedonian tongue in strains
doleful and sad and full of lamentation, and came before
Alexander. Now by that mournful song and lugubrious strain
Alexander's anger was a little pacified, and he spake with a
loud voice to his forces saying, "Fellow soldiers, this singer
knows how to work ill, for that implacable anger [of mine]
against the Thebans, behold, he has extinguished."

And when the singer came into the presence of Alexander,
he said, "Mighty king, great in power, and rich in knowledge,
listen with compassionate heart to the voice of the Thebans thy

[1] The Syriac text has "with their heads" or "chiefs." Considering the
Greek text (Müller, p. 51, col. 1), we must read either "with their horses,"
or "with their arms." The former seems better.

servants who have rightly received their chastisement, who
have not understood that thy power is like unto that of the
gods. Now therefore we worship thee as a god, and take thee
as a lord, the greatest of the gods. All we Thebans are in thy
victorious hands that never yield : let thy mind be pacified and
spare us. Know also that the destruction of the Thebans will
be an injury to thyself in the first place, because thou too art
a Theban and a son of our divine race, and thy serpent's head,
which [thou dost inherit] from thy father, is from here; for the
country belongs to Zeus. Dionysus, glorious in his being, and
beautiful and splendid in his appearance, was born here; and
Heracles, the hero of the twelve labours, the son of Zeus and
Alcmene, appeared here; and Ammon, clothed with pride and
......his horns[1], was born in Thebes. All these gods are thy
fathers and thy progenitors; and when they were born, they
were born for the rest and the peace and the joy of men, and
their aid and protection were extended over all mankind. Do
thou too, therefore, rest from thine anger, and turn again to
thy compassion ; put away wrath, and draw nigh to gentleness;
for thou too art of the race of the gods. Turn not away thy
face from this beautiful gate which they call after Dionysus,
which is now burning with flames of fire and ready to fall ; and
do not uproot this place built with oxen (?), for a temple like this
[has never been] made in all [the world]. With a kind heart
turn thy face [toward us], and look upon thy servants; for
behold, small and great are perishing by one blow ! Spare this
great temple, thou that art of the race of the three gods ; despise
not the strength of the mighty Heracles, nor the pride of the
glorious Ammon, nor the watchfulness of the beloved Dionysus.
That these walls are thus rent asunder and falling is a great
disgrace to the Macedonians. Knowest thou not, king Alexander, that thou thyself art a Theban, and that Philip was not
thy father ? Look and spare and compassionate the Thebans
thy countrymen, for behold they all entreat thee with supplication, with the gods upon their hands, and they are seized with
weeping on account of thee. Look at this Heracles, who for

---

[1] In the Syriac text the name of "Darius" has taken the place of an
adjective referring to the god Ammon and his horns.

the sake of the peace of mankind wrought twelve wondrous
deeds in the world. Do thou also be like him, and turn thy
wrath to mercy; and as the rain that waters the ground, do
thou too in thy mercy rain down goodness upon them. Please
all the gods, and do not ignorantly uproot the city of thy
ancestors. Look, O king, and see, for this wall Zēthus the
shepherd made, and Amphion who sang to the lyre[1], and they
dwelt therein; and in this place Cadmus took Harmonia to
wife; and in this place Aphrodite committed adultery with the
Thracian. Do not then stupidly and without counsel uproot
and destroy this place, founded by all the gods. For Zeus the
first (of the gods) slept in this place three nights and begat
children here, and then ascended to heaven. This high altar
which thou seest is that of Hera, the mother of the gods, and
this tripod of divination belonged to Teiresias; and all augury
went forth from here. In this place Ardipos perished by the
hands of Phôkos[2], and this river which thou seest is......[3] and
this is the fountain the pipes of which are silver, which the
gods gave[4]. This place dense with foliage belongs to Artemis;
she came to bathe therein, and the lustful Actaeon appeared to
her naked, but he was severely punished by her, because he
desired to see what was not lawful. And in this mountain
which thou commandest to be destroyed, Artemis followed the
chase. Why then dost thou despise in this manner the gods
whose offspring thou art? for thou art of the race of Heracles."

While the singer was chanting these verses to Alexander in
a lugubrious voice, anger seized on Alexander and he gnashed
his teeth, saying, "O thou of evil race, fellow-counsellor and
plotter with devils, thou stringest words together to the sound
of the pipes, and thinkest that thou wilt be able to lead Alex-

---

[1] In the Syriac "and Alôros and Olympios."

[2] Both names in this clause are obviously corrupt. The Greek text has
Αίαρχος and 'Αθάμας (see Müller, p. 52, col. 1, line 20).

[3] Too corrupt to admit of translation. The corresponding Greek is, οὖτος
ἀνέρρουν ἐκ μέσου Κιθαιρῶνος Ἰσμηνὸς ἐστι βασχείαν φέρων ὕδωρ (Müller, loc. cit.,
l. 26, 27).

[4] Or according to another reading, "and this is the fountain in which
the gods placed pipes of silver." The corresponding Greek words (Müller,
p. 52, col. 2, line 2) are αὕτη ἐστὶν πηγή καὶ ἱερὰ ἐρήτη, ἐξ ἧς ἀναβλύζουσιν ἀργυραῖ
νύμφαι.

ander astray with words strung together and learned by heart,
and knowest not that thou art leading thyself astray and not
me. Even if this city be really, as thou sayest it is, the
dwellingplace of the gods, thou knowest now that it has been
destroyed on account of the baseness of the Thebans. Its
temples too have been polluted and defiled, and therefore it is
right that I should purify them by fire, because, according to
what thou thyself hast said, the city belongs to my ancestors.
This too I desire to know; since ye know, as ye yourselves say,
who I am and by whom I was begotten, and that I am the
offspring of the gods whose temples are here, why did ye come
forth with battle and war against your own countryman? It
would have been far more fitting, had ye given horsemen and
foot-soldiers to aid me, and had ye thought within yourselves
saying, 'Alexander is our countryman, and now that he is in
difficulties it is good for us that we be his helpers;' it would
also have been right for you to have received the Macedonians
with kisses and affection as if they were your brethren. But
now that ye have contended in war with Alexander, and have
made trial of his arms, and have seen that ye are not able to
stand before him, ye string words together, saying, 'Alexander
is a Theban and our own countryman.' Now therefore I make
known to you that ye should not have contended with nor
opposed in war one that is your countryman, more especially
one who is of the race of the gods, as ye yourselves have said;
and on account of this deed ye are all guilty of death; but
everyone who up to the present has escaped death I will let live
for the sake of the skill of this singer. Go whithersoever ye
please, for ye shall no longer have a home in Thebes, and no one
shall be allowed to make mention again of the name of
Thebes, and whoever shall name its name shall die; for
henceforth this name shall no longer be a name, and this
city shall be no city." Then he straightway expelled from the
country those Thebans who remained alive, and he himself
departed with his troops.

XLVII. Those Thebans whom Alexander had expelled
from their country went to Apollo at Delphi to divine and to
ask an oracle, if a time would come to their country when their
city should be rebuilt. Then the Pythia drank of the water of

the fountain of Castalia, that she might receive an oracle therefrom : and straightway she answered and said to them, " When
the three athletes Polynicus, Antimachus [Clitomachus] and
Ţarķâŭs (?) hold contest with one another, then will Thebes
be rebuilt." When they heard this oracle, they turned and
came from thence, and were continually awaiting [the fulfilment
of] this augury.

Alexander went to Corinth, and arrived there while the
Olympic games of the Corinthians were going on. Then the
people of Corinth asked Alexander to become a spectator of the
Olympic games with them; and Alexander consented, and went
to the place of the contest, and sat with the Corinthians, and
distributed crowns and gifts to the athletes who were victorious
in the contest. On that same day a man from the city of the
Thebans was present at the Olympic games, and he contested
bravely in the athletic exercises, and his name was Antimachus
[Clitomachus]. Now this man had written down his name and
held himself ready to contest with three athletes. And when
the man came into the arena, he threw two of them dexterously
and skilfully to the ground, at which even Alexander marvelled
and applauded him greatly. And when he came to Alexander
to receive the crown, Alexander said to him, " If thou art able
to throw this third man also, go, first of all take up the contest
with him, and then return, and thou shalt receive the three
crowns at one time and gifts, and whatsoever favour thou shalt
ask of me I will give thee." Now when this athlete took up
the third contest, he exhibited in it many tricks of skill in
wrestling, and then he threw his adversary to the ground.
And when he rose up from off him, and came to receive the
crowns, the herald said to him, " What is thy name, and from
what city art thou, that I may proclaim concerning thee and
may make known thy deeds?" He said to the herald, " My name
is Antimachus [Clitomachus] but I have no city." Alexander
said to him, " How is it that so brave and expert and trained
and skilful a man as thou art, who in one contest hast thrown
three athletes, and who art now about to receive from me the
crowns of victory, hast no city?" The athlete said, "O illustrious
king and doer of good things, formerly, when Alexander was
not king, I had a city; but after Alexander became king, he

destroyed my city and made its name no name." Then
Alexander recognised him by his speech to be a Theban,
and handed to him the three crowns of victory, and bade the
herald proclaim him to be of the city of Thebes, " but ", said he,
" I command the city to be built anew, because of these three
gods who aided him in this contest."

# BOOK II.

I. AGAIN Alexander set out from Corinth and came to Plataeae, a city of the Athenians, where they worship Proserpine[1]; and when he entered the temple of the god he found a priestess weaving purple. And as soon as she saw Alexander she said to him, "King Alexander, it is granted to thee to be renowned and chief among all men." When Alexander heard this speech, he commanded gifts to be given to her. A few days after, he who was ruler in the land went into the temple; and when the priestess saw the ruler, she said to him, "They will now speedily remove thee from this thy rule." The ruler however did not believe her, but he laughed in his anger and said to the priestess, "O woman unworthy of the office of divination, when Alexander entered this place, thou saidst to him, 'Thou wilt be chief and famous among all mankind'; and now when I come thou sayest to me, 'They will remove thee from thy rule.' Now I will make an interpretation of this augury of thine on thyself." So he gave orders and expelled her from her office of priestess, and set another in her place. Then the priestess said to the ruler, "Be not angry at this, for the gods determine beforehand everything that is to be, and indicate it to men in various countries, especially concerning the affairs of governors and rulers and distinguished men. When Alexander entered this place, it fell out that I had just thrown purple upon the garment which I was weaving and had begun to weave; now purple is a well known sign of royalty: but now, when thou didst enter, I was cutting off the garment from the loom, and this is a sign that the end is come to thy work, and that they will remove thee from the rule."

When Alexander heard that the ruler had removed that

---

[1] The Syriac text has "worship fire," but the word ܟܘܡܐ seems to be an error for ܟܘܡܐ, i.e. ἡ Κόρη (see Müller, p. 54, col. 1).

priestess from her office, he commanded that she should be
reinstated therein, and he made another ruler in his place.
And it was straightway done as Alexander had commanded.
But the ruler who was dismissed went to the Athenians, and
related to them everything which Alexander had done to him.
When the Athenians heard this, they considered it, and it
displeased them much, and they reproached Alexander. When
Alexander heard this, he wrote a letter to the Athenians, and
put in it as follows. " From king Alexander to the Athenians.
Since my father died, I have by destiny received the kingdom,
and I have subdued most of the nations of the regions of the
west, and all of them have received me with good will as king.
I have also taken from them troops as auxiliaries to my army,
and by their strength I have subdued the country of Europe,
and have destroyed from its very foundations the city of the
Thebans who of their own will did wickedness. And now I am
come to this region of Asia, because I desire to know how ye
will receive me. Therefore I have not written a letter of many
words to you, but I speak briefly. Ye Athenians, either be brave,
or surrender to the brave, and give a thousand talents of gold
every year (as tribute)."

II. And when the Athenians had read this letter, they
returned answer: " We the ten orators that are in Athens
write thus to Alexander. During the time that thy father
was alive, we were much afflicted by his living; and when he
died, we were very glad at the death of Philip thy father (whose
bones ought to be dug up), whom all the Greeks too hated.
And now in the same manner we are incensed against thee,
that a foolish boy and impudent, wicked and audacious, should
demand a thousand talents every year, and under such a pretext
should stir up war with us. Now however, if it be that thou
really seekest war, come against us thus in battle array, and we
shall be ready." When Alexander had read this letter, he
wrote another letter to them. " From Alexander to the Athenians. I have sent Prôdis[1] thither to cut out your tongues
and to seize those ten orators who are in your city, and to bring
them to me as they deserve; and ye who have not known

---

[1] Or *Phriatis*. The Greek and Latin texts have *Leontas* (Müller, p. 65, col. 2).

μ. A.                                                        5

how to be persuaded by words will then be persuaded by the blaze of fire and the conflagration, at the time when ye see the demolition and destruction of your city. Now therefore send to us those ten orators, that perchance our thought may be for good and our pity be upon the land."

Again they wrote in reply to him: " We will not send them to thee, neither will we do that thing on account of which thou desirest to make war, namely to give tribute." Now when they were gathered together, Aeschines the orator stood upon his feet, and said to the people of the land: " Men of Athens, what is this delay that ye meditate so upon a thing like this? If ye desire to send us to Alexander, send us; and if not, we ourselves will go to Alexander trustfully. Now Philip was a lover of war, and his star was given to battles and contests; but Alexander was trained by the hands of Aristotle, and he was at school with us. And we are confident that when we go to Alexander, he will be ashamed before us who are his teachers and fellow-learners, and his furious disposition will turn to love."

And when Aeschines had spoken thus, Dêmâtheos [Demades], a young orator stood upon his feet and said: " How long, O Aeschines, wilt thou send forth from thy mouth such timid and alarming words, (saying,) 'Let us not fight with Alexander.' What is this demon of timidity that has power over thee, that thou speakest such words to the people of Athens, and givest them such counsel? Dost thou desire by such counsel as this to make enmity between us and the king of the Persians on account of this silly and proud boy, who has adopted the impudence and insolence of his father, and now wishes to intimidate the Athenians? and even thou wishest to cast terror upon them now. Why pray should we fear to fight with Alexander? We who have chased away the Persians, we who have conquered the Lacedaemonians and the Corinthians, we who in battle have put to flight the Phocians, we who have routed the Zacynthians, shall we be concerned because of this boy Alexander? As to what Aeschines has said, that when Alexander sees his teachers, he will be ashamed before them, and will turn away his wrath, and his disposition will become loving towards us as towards his friends,—he has disgraced us all; he has turned out and removed one who was a ruler in our land

and has put in his place another who is our enemy." And the youthful orator went on: "Aeschines has said, 'When he sees us, he will be ashamed before us,' but he wishes in this way to deliver us naked into his hands. Let us fight," said he to them, "with that headstrong Alexander, for the disposition of the young is ever set upon pride, and their strength loves battle. Some will say, 'Alexander destroyed the Tyrians'; but they do not know that the Tyrians were fit for naught. Others will say, 'Alexander rased the city of the Thebans'; but they do not know that the Thebans were worn out and exhausted by continual battles and wars, wherefore Alexander prevailed over them. Others again will say, 'He led captive the Peloponnesians'; but this was not because of bravery, but owing to a scarcity of food and a famine in their land. Now I remember the mighty Xerxes[1] who essayed the sea with boats and ships and galleys, and covered the dry land with his horsemen, and darkened the brightness of the atmosphere with the sheen of his weapons, and filled the land of the Persians with Greek [slaves]. If then we turned back from here so great a prince and warrior as Xerxes, and broke his boats and ships on the sea, and drove away his horsemen from the land,—I do not mean we who are here present, but Kûdkânôr and Antiphon and Misichis and Keryâdklis[2] and the rest of the mighty Athenian warriors who were among us at that time,—shall we now be afraid to make war with this impudent boy Alexander? If however ye wish to send us to Alexander, we are willing to go and die. But we tell you that words are our weapons, and that we are not different from dogs which have merely voice; and ye know that very often the sound of the barking of ten dogs is sufficient to deliver a flock of timid sheep from the claws of the wolves."

III. And when Demades had spoken all these words in the assembly, the Athenians rose and begged of Demosthenes that he would stand up and give counsel beneficial to the commonwealth. Then Demosthenes stood upon his feet and made a sign with his hand to the assembly to be silent. And when

---

[1] In the Syriac K'husrô or Chosroes.

[2] These names are evidently very corrupt: in Pseudo-Callisthenes (Müller, p. 57) we find Cynaegirus, Antiphon, and Mnesochares or Mnesicharmus.

they were silent, he said to them: "Fellow citizens,—I do not call you Athenians, because I myself am an Athenian and not a stranger,—ye know that our lives are the life of the commonwealth and that our death in the same way (is its death). Therefore it becomes us with great deliberation to give the advice which will give life to the commonwealth. For this reason too it is necessary for us to conquer. If we are able to fight with Alexander, let us fight; but if we are not able, let us submit to him. Now Aeschines, who has made a speech, has spoken to you craftily; he did not say (to the people) to fight with Alexander, neither did he say not to fight. He is a very aged man, and has given many good and fitting counsels in many assemblies. On the other hand, Demades is a young and inexperienced man, and therefore he has said, 'O Athenians, we —(to wit) Antiphon, and Krintmâkhos, and Kandnâkir, and Amnismâkhos, and Kardânâkêlos,—[1] turned back Xerxes the mighty king and the rest of those vast crowds and many kings.' But the people of the Athenians of whom thou hast made mention, who were famed of old for their prowess, O Demades, we have not with us now; those mighty warriors whose names thou hast called to mind as having been of old with us in Athens, that we might fight against Alexander trusting in their strength. But as they are long dead, and we have no other warriors in Athens like unto them, I do not wish that we should fight with Alexander, for every time has its own strength. We orators then, our strength and our weapons are words, but in power to fight we are weak. O Demades, what thou didst say, thou saidst rightly. During the time that he was king, the mighty Xerxes was defeated in many battles; but Alexander has carried on thirteen wars and has not been defeated in one of them, on the contrary he has seized many countries without any fighting and has captured famous cities. Demades has said, 'The Tyrians are of no use in battle; and the Thebans, who were never before defeated in battle, were weary and worn out and exhausted, and therefore they were defeated; the Peloponnesians were defeated on account of the scarcity and famine, and not by the hands of Alexander.' He heard that

---

[1] These are the same names that appeared above, with the addition of Krintmâkhos = Klitomachos.

there was a famine in their land, and he, who was ready to go
against them in war, sent them clothes and food from Macedonia; and when the general Antigonus saw Alexander (doing
thus), he said to him, 'Dost thou send clothing and food to
people with whom thou wishest to make war?' Alexander said,
'It is much better that I should fight with them and subdue
them than that we should fight with them in a starving
condition and utterly destroy them.' Now as regards this ruler
in whose stead Alexander commanded another to be put, why
are ye angry? He is a king, and that ruler wished to withstand
him. If ye judge the case rightly, ye will all be grateful to
Alexander in this matter, and will be angry with the ruler,
because he is a (mere) ruler, and when he removed a priestess and
prophetess of the gods, Alexander restored her to her place."

IV. And when Demosthenes had spoken such words as
these, and had given the people of the country this advice in
this speech, he received much praise from the Amphictyons and
was applauded in a variety of ways. Demades stood silent,
while Aeschines applauded; Lysias agreed with Demosthenes,
and Plato said, "This is my opinion too." Dadnadḳinôs said,
"I too am persuaded by this advice;" and Herliṭâ said, "Let
it not be otherwise[1];" while to the rest of the people of the
country what Demosthenes had said appeared good.

And again Demosthenes said: "As Demades said, king
Xerxes filled the land of the Persians with Greek captives; and
he praised and applauded Xerxes, who turned the Greek
captives into slaves for the Persians. And now he wants to
make war with Alexander, who is a Greek, and wishes to bring
the Persians into subjection to the Greeks. Demades in his
speech praised him that is an enemy, and wishes to make an
enemy of him that is a friend and fellow countryman. Consider this too, ye Athenians: no king has ever carried war into
Egypt, except Alexander the son of Philip alone, and even he,
when he went, did not go with the object of making war, but to
consult the oracle, in what place it was granted to him to build
a city after his name, from which his name should never be

---

[1] The Syriac translator has taken ܩܘܢܘܡܪܕܝ݁ and ܗܘ݂ܠܝܬܐ to be
names of single persons, but the Greek text has οἱ Ἀμφικτύονες for the former
and οἱ Ἡρακλεῖς (?) for the latter.

forgotten. He received the oracle, and built the city, and
completely finished it; and [it is] the [Alexandria] which is in
the country of Egypt that was under the Persians[1]. [The
Egyptians] entreated him that they might be with his army as
auxiliaries against the Persians. Then Alexander, filled with
wisdom, made answer to them, saying, "It is far better for you,
ye Egyptians, to remain dwelling in your own country by the
banks of the Nile, and to till your land by its overflowings,
than to put on the weapons of Arês and to march far away to
war. So the Egyptians came under Alexander's rule, and he
built a city in the land of Egypt and gave it to the Greeks.
It is for this reason that, when the army of the Macedonians is
under service and engaged in fighting, the Egyptians supply it
with clothing and corn. In this manner he made Egypt subject
to the Greeks, and brought men of all nations to it and made
them dwell therein. Just as that land is abundant in crops and
tillage, in the same way that city too is become very populous,
and they pay large taxes and tribute to the Greeks. If then
the Egyptians, who are loved by the Greeks, have taken upon
themselves to give tribute to Alexander the Greek, and have
counted him to be their lord, why do ye, who are Greeks, wish
to be enemies of Alexander and fight with him? Go forth then
to fight with Alexander; but Fortune is his slave[2]."

V. And when Demosthenes had spoken these words, the
Athenians were unanimously convinced, and they sent to Alexander a golden crown of victory weighing fifty pounds, together
with a letter of thanks and gratitude and praise. They wrote
down too therein the speech and opinion of each man upon this
matter, and sent them to him. And they chose the oldest
and best known men from among the Athenians and sent
them on an embassy to him, but the ten orators they did not
send to him. Then the ambassadors went to Alexander at
Plataeae and laid the crown and the letter before him. When
Alexander had read this letter and had heard the counsel of
Aeschines and the teaching of Demosthenes and the bold words
of Demades and the consenting of the people and the praise of
the Amphictyons, Alexander composed another letter to them

[1] The Syriac text is evidently defective in this passage.
[2] Literally, "time has given him the hand (of submission)."

and wrote to them as follows: "From Alexander the son of Philip and Olympias to the Athenians. I will not write to you as king until I make all cities subject to the Greeks; but I write to you to send me the ten orators; not that I am going to do them any harm, but that I may salute them as masters and teachers. It is no plan of mine to come against you with weapons and troops, lest ye should count me an enemy; but I think of coming to you with those ten orators, instead of with nobles and princes, and of setting you free from many anxious thoughts and cares. Ye however think otherwise, because ye know your own minds and thoughts, and are aware that ye are guilty in regard to us. At the time when the Scythians[1] fought with the Macedonians, ye were auxiliaries to the Scythians; but when the Corinthians made war with you, the Macedonians assisted you and delivered you from the hands of the Corinthians. We erected a statue of Athene in Macedonia, while ye have swept away from its place the statue of my mother which stood in the temple of Athene in your city. Do ye think that this recompense is just which ye have made unto us? because ye remember all these things, therefore ye are in trouble, saying, 'Alexander will seek revenge upon us.' And because your own minds and thoughts and the deeds which are done by your hands are perverse and crafty continually, therefore ye expect the same behaviour from others. Moreover ye have not left a single man of the glorious and honoured men that are among you whom ye have not despised and ill treated. Ye confined in prison Euclid; and ye cruelly oppressed Tirmastênis (?)[2], who was the counsellor of right measures, who went to king Cyrus as an ambassador on your behalf. Did ye not disgrace Alcibiades, who was a good general over you. Did ye not also slay Socrates, who was a herald in Hellas? Philip my father too, who assisted you in three wars, ye treated ungratefully. And now ye blame Alexander, who took vengeance for you upon a ruler who had removed your priestess of the goddess Athene, whereas I reinstated her and dismissed the doer of the deed and

---

[1] Read, as in the Greek text (Müller, p. 60, col. 1), *Zacynthians*.

[2] AE *Tirmastenis*, BCD *Tirmtênis*. The single MS. of the Greek text has Ἰσσοθένης, but the Latin translation gives, *Demosthenes*, which Müller follows (p. 60, col. 2).

set up another in his stead. I have read the letter which ye
sent me, and by the speeches made the counsel given in your
assemblies I have learned of your disturbance. Now Aeschines
gave you good advice, and Demades courageously and bravely
invited you to war, and Demosthenes gave you excellent
counsel. Now then let the Athenians be brave, and let them
have no fear of me, and let them fight for freedom; for it would
be a disgraceful thing that, while I am fighting for your freedom, ye should not be fighting for yourselves. At present
however I require nothing from you, until I conquer Darius."

VI.[1] Then Alexander departed from thence and went to
Macedonia [Lacedemonia]. And he came to the border of
Persia and encamped by the river Tigris. And Alexander went
on an embassy to Darius as far as Babylon. And the Persians
came and informed king Darius; and when they had spoken,
and Darius had seen Alexander, he bowed himself down and
did reverence to Alexander, for he imagined him to be the god
Mithras, who had descended (from heaven) and had come to
assist the Persians, for his aspect resembled that of the gods;
for the crown of gold that was fastened on his head resembled
the rays (of the sun), and the robe which he had on was woven
with fine gold, and the pieces of armour which were upon his
arms were wrought with fair silver, and his sandals were of gold,
and his belt was made of pearls and emeralds[2]. And Darius was
standing and examining his apparel, and ten thousand horsemen, who formed his body guard, were standing near him.
Then Darius asked Alexander, "Who art thou?" Alexander
said, "I am the ambassador of Alexander and I have brought a
message from him to thee. Thus he says: 'Thou hast delayed
to make war on me, and the Macedonians say that because the
heart of Darius is timid in battle, therefore he is reluctant
(?) to fight.' Now therefore, do not delay but send word to
me when thou desirest to come to battle." Then Darius said

---

[1] The first sentence of this chapter corresponds with the first sentence
of Chap. VI. in Müller's Greek text (p. 61, col. 1), but the Syriac text passes
on immediately to Chap. XIV. of the Greek (Müller, p. 69, col. 1). Perhaps a
couple of quires had fallen out of the Greek MS. from which the translation was
made.

[2] In the Greek text it is Alexander who well nigh bows down before Darius,
and the subsequent description is that of the Persian king.

to him, "Peradventure thou thyself art Alexander, and not
an ambassador"? for Alexander spoke very boldly, and not
gently like an ambassador. Darius said to him, "I am not
frightened at thy words. Do thou now, according to the custom
of ambassadors, partake of a meal with me, for so did Alexander
treat my ambassador." Then Darius reclined upon his couch,
and his nobles and princes sat at meat before him[1]. The
first was Darius, the second Bar-nôrag his brother, the third
Vashingî, the fourth Dôzyâg, the fifth Bâmar, the sixth Zâdmihr,
the seventh Vârdâr, the eighth Ḳnî'ar[2], the ninth.........the
king of the barbarians, the tenth Prôdis the chief of the host,
the eleventh Prîyôz the general, the twelfth Rĕbîthmâs; and
opposite Darius, in the middle, sat Alexander who was the
ambassador.

VII.[3] And all the people were wondering at him because
he was small in stature, but his words were very keen. And
when they had eaten, they called for wine in a jar. Every
golden cup which they passed to Alexander, he poured the
wine upon the ground and placed the vessel in his bosom;
when they saw what he was doing, they told Darius; and
Darius, when he heard it, rose from his couch, and came to
Alexander and said to him, "O doer of valiant deeds, why
dost thou act in this manner, putting all the drinking cups
in thy bosom?" Alexander said, "When my master Alexander
makes a feast for his nobles, he gives all the golden drinking
cups to them, and I thought that thou wouldst act in the
same way; but now, since thou hast not a similar custom,
behold the drinking-cups are before thee, command and I
will restore thy gold to thee." Then Darius said, "I too
command that they leave thy gold to thee." Meanwhile
all the Persians were looking at Alexander and marvelling,
because his words were mighty and full of knowledge. When
then a certain lord, whose name was Pûsâk [Pasargês], who
had once been sent by Darius to Macedonia, on an embassy
to Philip, Alexander's father, had carefully scrutinised

1 Compare the text of Codex A in Müller, p. 69, note 23.
2 This name Ḳnî'ar is no doubt corrupt; and instead of the name of the
king of the barbarians we have the Syriac words we-m'ḁʻḭḭḭḭḭ, meaning "and
the middle."
3 Chap. XV. of the Greek text (Müller, p. 70).

Alexander, he recognised him, and said to Darius in the
Persian language, "O doer of good things, king Darius, give
orders that they guard this ambassador most carefully, for he
himself is Alexander, and I recognise him by his appearance
and know that it is he." When Darius and his nobles and
princes heard this, they began to speak with one another, and
to watch Alexander closely. Then Alexander perceived this,
and rose up from the banquetting hall, and sprang towards
the king's gate, with all the vessels of gold, which he had
in his bosom; and at the king's gate he found a sentinel,
holding in his hand a flaming torch of cedar-wood, and he
slew him and took it from him. And he mounted a horse
and dug his heels into its flanks, at the same time holding
the blazing torch of cedar-wood before its eyes; and the horse
by the light of the fire galloped furiously down the road and came
to the bank of a river. Then messengers went out after him
in haste, but the greater part of them fell into pits and holes
because of the darkness of the night. Now Alexander by the
might of the gods crossed the river, but when he had reached
the other side and the fore feet of the horse rested on dry
land, the water which had been frozen over suddenly melted,
and the hind legs of the horse went down into the river.
Alexander however leaped from the horse to land, and the horse
was drowned in the river. When the messengers came to the
bank of the river and saw that Alexander had crossed over,
while they were unable to pass over after him, they marvelled
and said one to another, "Great is Alexander's luck, which has
given him a passage over so great a river and he has been
able to cross it." And when they returned, they came to
Darius and informed him of Alexander's escape and of his
crossing the river. Darius was in great trouble, and a sign
suddenly appeared to him; for the picture of king Xerxes,
whom Darius loved, was painted on the wall of the banqueting
room, and suddenly it peeled off from the wall and fell to
the ground under the very eyes of Darius. After Alexander
had crossed the river, he rested from his running and from
his toil, and getting on his feet, he walked on; and in the
darkness of the night he saw Âmôrôs [Eumêlus] the general
standing by himself, in great trouble because of Alexander and

weeping. Then Alexander told Amôrôs all the things which had befallen him.

VIII. And then he took him and went to the army, and commanded the whole army to be gathered to one place, and he himself stood in the midst of them. And when he saw that his army was despised in the sight of Darius, he said to himself, "O heavenly Zeus, give victory to this small band of Macedonians;" and when he had counted them, the army of Macedonians consisted of a hundred and thirty thousand, besides the rest of the peoples that were with him; and they were all skilful and brave. Then Alexander went up to a high place and said to his troops: "My fellow-soldiers and friends, I know that our army is small, but it is not right for us to be afraid on this account, for one man of us through his bravery is better than a hundred of them. The bees that make honey are very numerous, and whithersoever they fly they darken the air by their flight, but when a little smoke comes near them, they all flee away and are dispersed. Now the army of Darius is like nothing but a swarm of bees; therefore fear them not." And when Alexander had spoken thus to his troops, he inspired them with courage and stirred them up and incited them to fight.

IX. And he departed from thence and came to the river Estrakînôs [Strangas]. Then Darius encouraged his troops, saying, "Fear not, though ye be very few in number;" and Darius was troubled on account of the smallness of his army. And when he found that the river was frozen, he crossed the river and commanded the heralds to cry with a loud voice and to invite the Macedonians to battle. Now the troops of the Persian phalanx were without number and were prepared for war with weapons of all sorts and with chariots and with long scythes. Then Alexander clad in armour came at the head of the Macedonians, and he was riding upon the horse called Bucephalus, which no man dared to approach, for the power of the gods was upon him. Then from the camps of both sides the horns and trumpets sounded the fearful blasts of war, and the two armies closed with one another. And from the second to the fifth hour the fight was so fierce that the whole river side and the valley and the

ravines were filled with the corpses and blood of the slain.
Now although such was the case, the troops of the Greeks did
not turn their faces from the fight. And when Darius saw
that a great number of the mighty men of his army were
dead, and that the Macedonians did not turn their faces from
the battle, fear fell upon his heart, and he turned the reins of
the horses of his chariot, and the whole host of warriors turned
back after him. Then Alexander's foot soldiers armed with
long scythes pursued them and mowed them down like corn in
the field. And Darius being vanquished came to a certain river,
and finding it frozen, he himself crossed over it in his chariot;
but when the army of Darius came to the bank of the river,
the troops began to cross over it, and suddenly the ice of the
river melted under them, and the army was drowned in the
river, and those that remained upon the other side of the river
were slaughtered by the Macedonians. Then Darius went into
his palace, and threw himself upon his face on the ground, and
began to weep for the army of the country, for all the warriors
of the country were dead and had perished, and for the land
which had been emptied of its mighty men; and he began
to say: "Woe is me, which of the stars is it that has destroyed
the kingdom of the Persians? I, Darius, who subdued many
lands and cities and nations, and reduced a multitude of
islands and towns to slavery, have now entered my palace
in flight and discomfiture. I who with the sun traversed the
world—but in brief, it is not right for a man to rely upon
his destiny, for if his luck turn and there be an opportunity,
it lifts up and exalts the most despised of men and seats
him above the clouds, while it brings down the lofty from
his height and casts him into the depths." And when he
had said this, he rose up from his palace and collected his
thoughts, and composed a letter to Alexander and wrote to him
thus: "From Darius the king to my lord Alexander. Know
first of all that thou art born a man; and I will give thee
this token that even thou mayest not meditate anything too
great for thee. Because even the mighty Xerxes, who shewed
me the light,—he whom the Greeks so loved, as thou must
have heard[1],—meditated something too high for him, and

---

[1] The Syriac text appears to be corrupt in this passage.

afterwards, having given his mind to greediness, he who lacked nothing, neither gold nor pearls, nor precious stones nor statues of brass, when his good luck left him, returned from Hellas defeated. And now, call thou these things to mind, and be gracious to us and have mercy upon us, for we have now fled to thee for refuge. Behold now my mother and my wife and my daughter, those who have been given to me by the gods as a joy from the god of gods; they were famed and honoured throughout the whole world; do thou take them as thy slaves. And I will shew thee the treasures which my ancestors laid up from the beginning upon the earth. And I will entreat the gods that henceforth thou mayest be master over the Palhâyê [Parthians], and the Persians, and the rest of the nations of the world, all the days of thy life; because Zeus hath exalted thee. Farewell."

And when Alexander had read this letter, he gave orders to assemble the troops that they might consider the matter together. And when they were gathered together, Pllmthiôn [Parmeniôn] the general said: "O king, if we receive the treasures and possessions and land which have been wrested from us, we must deliver up to him his mother and wife and daughter. But Darius ought to have sent this message before the battle. I know this, if he had been victor in this struggle, he would not only have asked for his mother and wife and daughter, but would have taken away our land from us. And know, O king, that Darius offended us first and took our land from us; and now it is right and just and lawful if we avenge ourselves on Darius, who seized a land which did not belong to him, and has held it until now. We know also, O king, that thou camest forth from thy country to seek thine own dominions. Had he restored to us our land, thou, O king, would'st never have come hither." Then Alexander said, "The matter is exactly as thou hast said," and he straightway gave orders to attend to those who had been smitten and wounded in the battle, and to bury the dead. He bade them also to offer sacrifices to the gods of the land, and to burn the palace of Xerxes, the like of which for beauty and magnificence existed not in the whole country; but after a short time Alexander repented and gave orders to extinguish the fire in the palace of Xerxes.

X. And he saw there many graves of the Persians with
vessels of gold and cups of silver in which wine was mingled.
He saw also the grave of king Pâḳôr, which was built with stones
and lime in the form of a tower and had no roof, and there was
a large chamber made in it, and over the chamber was an upper
room ; and in that upper room was a golden coffin, in which was
laid the body of king Cyrus (Kôresh), and a slab of crystal was
cast so as to fit it exactly, and the hair and the body of Cyrus
were seen through the crystal. Now in this tower certain Greek
artisans[1] were imprisoned, some with their hands or ears cut off,
and some with their noses slit, and their feet were bound with
fetters. When the Macedonians had gone to that building,
those who were imprisoned therein cried out in the Greek
tongue to Alexander, "Have mercy upon us, and take pity on
thy servants and thy countrymen." And when Alexander saw
that their limbs were mutilated and their appearance was
horrible, he let the tears fall from his eyes and was very grieved
for them, and bade them to be loosed from their fetters. He
gave orders too that a thousand zûzê[2] should be given to each
one of them with meat and food, and that they should return to
their own country. But after they had received the zûzê from
the king, they begged as a favour that land and water might be
given them, and that they might not return to their own country,
lest, by reason of the defects of their bodies, they should become
a reproach and a disgrace to their brethren. Then Alexander
ordered that the best and most excellent of land and water
should be given to them, and that to each man should be given
six working oxen together with other property.

XI. After these things Darius made ready for war, and he
wrote a letter to Porus, the king of the Indians. "From Darius
the king of kings to Perus the king of the Indians, greeting. I
have written letters to thee before, asking for assistance in the
ruin of my house, because the savageness and fury of this evil
beast, which is come against me, do not, as it seems to me,
resemble man's ; it casts itself into the sea, and loves battle by
water, and does not wish to give back to me my mother and my
wife and my daughter, neither does he desire to make peace

---

[1] The Greek text has "certain Greeks, Athenians" (Müller, p. 75, col. 1).
[2] Zûzâ is the equivalent of the Arabic *dirham*, δραχμή.

with me in any way whatsoever. Therefore I have no resource
but of necessity am bound to fight with him. Now thus will I
do; either I will take his country from him, or I myself will no
longer go about among the living in this world. Have pity
then upon me at this time, and avenge me that am despised.
Remember too the mutual love and friendship, and confidence
which existed between our fathers, and give orders to gather
together troops from every place and bring them with thee to the
Caspian gates, which are called Vîrôphhâgâr; and I will give to
every single man of those who come to my assistance every month
three horses and six darics and corn and straw and hay and
whatever food he requires; and to thee will I give the half of
whatever spoil and booty they make. I will give to thee too
the horse called Bucephalus upon which Alexander rides; and I
will give thee the royal lands together with his royal palace and
one hundred and seventy concubines with their ornaments and
trinkets and clothing." Then the report (of this) reached
Alexander, and he straightway armed his troops and set out
from thence, and went forth to the country of the Parthians.
And when Darius heard that Alexander was come from the place
which was called Beṭmĕthâ[1], he arose and wished to flee before
Alexander; and when Alexander heard this, he pursued after
him quickly.

XII. And when he was come nigh, the nobles of Darius
acted treacherously, and Bâgîz and Ânâbdêh[2], Darius's generals
wished to slay him that they might receive gifts from Alexander,
as from a man whose enemy they had slain. Then with drawn
swords they rushed upon Darius, and Darius knew their
treachery and answered and said to them: "My lords, who
aforetime were my servants, in what have I offended you that
ye wish to slay me? Do not do to me anything worse than
what the Macedonians have done to me, and let not your hands
be against me like those of Alexander. See too that I am
perpetually in tears and in great trouble; my fortune is evil and
treacherous. Peradventure, if ye slay me, and Alexander comes

---

[1] The Greek text has Ἥκουσι δὲ Δαρεῖον εἶναι ἐν Ἐκβατάνοις, with the var
ἐν Βαρδᾶις, Lat., in Bathanis.
[2] The Greek equivalents are ὁ Βῆσσος καὶ ὁ Ἀριοβαρζάνης (Müller, p. 7,
col. 2).

and finds a king slain by the treachery of his troops, he will take
fierce vengeance upon you; for it is not right that a king should
see a fellow king treacherously slain by his troops and should
overlook it and not avenge his cause. When Darius had spoken
these words, Bâgîz and Ânâbdêh stabbed him with their swords,
driving them right through his back, and Darius fell to the
ground. When the army of the Macedonians came up,
Alexander commanded them to halt, and he went up to Darius
alone. And when Bâgîz and Ânâbdêh saw Alexander at a
distance, they left Darius their lord half dead, and fled, that
they might see how pleased Alexander would be by reason of
the death of Darius. But when Alexander came up to Darius,
and saw that he had been mercilessly stabbed and was lying on
the ground, he let fall tears from his eyes upon Darius, and
spread over Darius the purple garment with which he was
clothed, and sat down by him, and laid his hand upon the breast
of Darius, and said to Darius sorrowfully: " Rise up, Darius: be
lord again over thy land, and take the royal crown of the
Persians, and be again renowned for greatness. I swear an oath
by all the gods that I say this in sincerity and do not speak
falsely; I will restore and give to thee alone the crown and
kingship, because I ate salt at thy table when I came to thee as
a spy. And now stand up and play the man; for it does not
become a king to be in trouble because his luck turns away
from him for a little while. We are all men, and are yoked to
fate, and as fate wills so it exalts us. Arise now, and play the
man, and take thy country, and henceforth thou shalt have no
trouble or sorrow through me. Say then now, who these are
that stabbed thee, and I will take vengeance for thee upon
them."

    When Alexander had spoken all these words, Darius heaved
sighs and let fall tears from his eyes, and took Alexander's hand
from his breast and brought it to his mouth and kissed it, and
said to him: " My son Alexander, never let thy mind be lifted up
by vainglorious arrogance; for thou doest and performest and
orderest all deeds and works and orderings like the gods, and
thou mayest imagine in thy mind that thy hands have reached
heaven. Then it will be necessary for thee to fear what may
happen in the hereafter. Because of this it is certain to me

that fate is known neither to the king nor to the meanest
among men, and that the final destiny of men is hidden and
concealed from all.  Look now what I was, and what I am: I
who proudly subdued and captured countries and lords and
many kings of the earth trembled at me; and now I am cast
away like the lowest of all men.  And of all the host of my
generals and officers and ambassadors, not one is near me now to
close my eyes, except these hands of thine, O king, doer of good
things.  Let the Macedonians and Persians sit in mourning for
me, and let the two armies become one, and let the seed of
Philip and Darius be one.  And as for Ariôdocht [Îrândokht][1]
my mother, regard her now as if thou thyself wert born of her,
and consider my wife as thy sister, and take my daughter
Rôshnâk [Roxane] for thy wife, that the seed of Darius and of
Philip may be mingled in her."  Then Alexander brought his
hand to the face of Darius, who said, "Into thy hands I
commend my spirit[2];" and straightway his soul departed.

XIII.  Then Alexander gave orders to wash the body of
Darius, and to array him in royal apparel, and that all the
officers of the Macedonian and Persian armies should march in
full armour before Darius; and he together with the Persian
nobles bore the bier of Darius, and he went on foot to the
grave, and the bier of Darius was carried to the grave upon
their shoulders.

When the Persians saw these things, they applauded
Alexander's care for Darius; and their minds were led away by
love for him.  And when Alexander had buried Darius with
honour and had returned from the grave, the whole army of the
Persians submitted to him.  Then Alexander ordered a proclamation to be written to the rest of the people in the land of
Persia as follows: "From Alexander the king, whose father is the
god Ammon and whose mother is the queen Olympias, to all
the Persians that dwell in the cities and towns of the land of
Persia, greeting.  I desire that all men should live and not die
an evil death; and now God has made me master of the country

[1] See Chap. XIV. near the beginning.
[2] Literally, "in thy hands I leave my spirit."  These words seem to contain
a reminiscence of S. Luke's Gospel, ch. xxiii. 46, and so betray the Christian
translator.  The Greek text (Müller, p. 78, col. 1) is ἔξεστιν τὸ πνεῦμα ἐν ταῖς
χερσὶν Ἀλεξάνδρου.

of Persia, and has exalted me over you. Let the lords, the
nobles of your country, who served of old in the army of Darius,
come now and march with me in my army, even as they
formerly marched with Darius. Let them not accept any other
master in their thoughts save me, Alexander. And I will give
orders that every single man of you shall retain his own
religion and gods and laws, and shall keep his festivals and his
sacrifices, and no one shall be allowed to do anything to you by
violence. Every one shall rejoice in his own possessions, save
the gold and silver which we command to be gathered together
and to be conveyed to our city to be coined into money and
into dínárs bearing my image; and we order that, if zúzê or
darics be found with you, even though our own money be struck,
they shall be left there with you. Let all the lords [satraps]
and generals, together with the rest of the people who are fit
for war, come to help my army. Nation shall not be mingled
with nation, neither shall one man go from his own land to
another, except those who travel for the sake of merchandise,
and even of these not more than ten or twenty shall be allowed
to go. Till the land and dwell in it in prosperity as in the days
of Darius the king; for we desire that prosperity and abundance
should be in your land. Whosoever of you desires to go to
Hellas to trade and to come back from Hellas to the land of
Persia, shall be allowed to go and to come. And I command
the lords [satraps] and all the inhabitants that are on this road
from the bank of the Euphrates to Hellas to divide and measure
the road in equal portions, to pave it with stones and lime, to
set up mile stones, and to write directions at the turnings of
the roads, that every man may know by the writings whither
the road goes, and may not have trouble and be compelled to
ask questions on the road. And we command that what Darius
gave every year, year by year, to the temple of the ministers of
the gods for the salvation of his soul, shall now be given each
year where it is due, from the crops and taxes of the land, for the
salvation of his soul. And let them make a feast and offerings
every year on his birthday as they do upon the birthday of king
Cyrus. And we command that damsels, the daughters of free
men, virgins whom men have not known, shall enter into
the temple of the god whom my mother Olympias worships, for

the space of one year for the service of the gods; and when
they have arrived at the age for marriage, they shall go forth
from the ministry, and shall receive a dowry of five thousand
dinârs from the treasury of the god, and shall marry. And we
command that all youths and men who are in the country of
the Persians shall train themselves continually in warlike
exercises and arms until we come to them and select from
them those that please us. And if there be any one now
who is well trained in horsemanship and arms, weapons shall be
given him out of the armoury of the king, and a war horse, and
a beaker of gold worth twelve dinârs, each weighing eight
*mithkâls*, and five cups of silver, each of them holding what a
man can take at a draught, and one suit of Persian raiment, and
a belt of gold; and he shall be sent to the army. And if there
be any one of them who is trained in war and who has made
himself a famous name, there shall be given to him a Persian
crown of gold, and a suit of white raiment, and two cups of gold,
and one hundred darics, and seventy staters; and his likeness
shall be painted and shall be sent to the temple of the god
of Alexander. We command too that the priests of the gods
shall be held in honour by all men, and they shall set a crown
of gold upon their heads, and shall wear purple clothing,
especially on festival days. We desire also that ye shall bring
before the priests any dispute which ye may have one with
another, and they shall decide it, and terminate the matter for
them with moderation."

After Alexander had composed this writing, he turned and
looked upon the hosts of the Macedonians and Persians with
a sad face, and he made known to them and said, " He whom I
have removed from his kingdom was a great and mighty king,
but he was not my lord, neither did I slay him. Now the
men who slew him are those whom I know not, and it befits
me to give them great gifts, and high posts, and honours,
and lands, and many men, because they have slain mine
enemy." When Alexander had made this speech, every Persian
regarded his fellow, and the colour in their faces was changed
by reason of fear, and one said to another, "Alexander is trying
to search out our minds, wishing to know who it is that slew
Darius." And again he said to them: " I am Alexander.

6—2

Him that slew mine enemy I seek to honour, whether he
be Macedonian or Persian; let him come and fear not; for
I swear by the gods, and by the life of my mother Olympias,
that I will make renowned and great him that slew Darius, and
I will exalt him over my troops." When Alexander had sworn
this oath, the Persian host began to weep. Then the evildoers Bágīz and Ánâbdêh came near to Alexander of their
own free will and answered and said to him, "O king, doer
of good things, it is we who slew Darius." When Alexander
heard this, he commanded that they should be bound, and
should be carried to the grave of Darius, and impaled upon
a lofty stake. Then these evildoers said to him with a
loud voice, "Our lord, the oath which thou hast sworn by
all the gods and by the life of Olympias thy mother is false."
Then Alexander said: "I spoke not this word of persuasion
for your sakes, but for the sake of the armies who stand
listening, because I was unable to bring you into the way
of justice in any other manner than this. Had I not done
so, I should have appeared to be rejoicing in the death of
Darius, the more so as I accounted him an enemy. But my
supplication and entreaty to the gods was this, that I might be
enabled to destroy him that slew Darius; for how can a man
who was not true to his lord, but who slew his lord audaciously
and unmercifully, be true to us? See then, we do not lie
with respect to the oath which we have sworn; for now,
just as I sware to you, I will make you a spectacle and a
marvel to the whole camp, and I will lift you up on stakes."
So he straightway commanded them to be led away and
impaled upon high stakes. Then all the hosts of the Persians
applauded Alexander.

XIV. After a few days Alexander wrote a letter to the
mother and wife of Darius as follows. "From king Alexander
to Írândokht and Estĕhar[1] [Statira] greeting. At the time
when king Darius opposed us with hostility, we sought to
avenge ourselves according to the will of God. Although we

---

[1] So the name is pointed in Syriac, but the letter ܘ should rather be
taken as the equivalent of a Greek vowel. If we write ܐܣܬܗܪ, we have
an adequate representation of the form Στάτειρα, more commonly Στάτειρα (or
Στάτειρα, MSS. Στατίρα), for ܘ is constantly = ε.

sought the victory over Darius, we did not desire his death.
On the contrary, our desire was that he might live and be
under our dominion. We found him however stabbed by the
hand of his troops and lying upon the ground, with very
little life left in him. I was very grieved for him, and because
of my sorrow I threw over him the purple robe with which
I was clothed, and covered him. And I asked him, 'Who
is he that slew thee?' But when he had begun to give me
instructions concerning his mother and his wife and Rôshnâk
[Roxane] his daughter, his life departed from him, and he
was unable to speak to me concerning other matters. We
therefore sought out the evildoers by stratagem, and found
them, and slew them as they deserved. We ordered the
body of Darius to be buried and to be guarded honourably
and fittingly. And we commanded a new grave to be made
beside the grave of his father, and his body to be embalmed
with spices, and to be laid in the grave. And now we bid
you keep yourselves from sorrow and grief, for we will re-
establish you in your royalty; therefore remain where ye
are, until we have arranged the matters which require arrangement. We command also that Rôshnâk the daughter of
Darius be our consort; therefore do reverence to Rôshnâk
as to the wife of Alexander." Then they made answer to
him and wrote to him as follows: "From Îrândokht and
Estěhar to king Alexander greeting. We make supplication
to the heavenly gods, the gods whom Olympias your mother
worships, the gods who have bowed down the crown of Darius
and brought it to the ground, and have taken the supremacy
and dominion from the Persians, that they may make you
lord of the world for ever and aye, and that they may exalt
you and magnify you in words and in knowledge and in
power above all nations. We know that we shall live happily
under your wings; and we wish that we may find your luck
to be good, and the days of your life without number, because
you have not treated us as enemies are wont to treat their
captive enemies when they fall into their hands. We have
therefore no anxiety in our minds, for in seeing you we see
Darius; and from henceforth we will write that all the people
that are in the land shall make supplication and prayer to

the gods that you may rule the land and the world for ever
and aye, and may your dominion be like that of Hormizd
[Ahuramazda]. Rôshnâk [Roxane] greets you with reverence
because it has pleased you that she should be your consort;
and we shall be very joyful on the day that we see your
marriage feast, and Zeus gives you Rôshnâk to wife." And
they wrote another proclamation to all the hosts of the
Persians, as follows: "Do not suppose that Darius is dead,
for Darius is alive, because the kingdom belongs to Alexander,
and Rôshnâk, the daughter of Darius, is the wife of Alexander.
Therefore take ye all the gods that are in Persia, and go
to meet Alexander, and honour him as a god, and pray to the
gods on his behalf that his dominion may be for ever and aye;
for the kingdom of the Persians belongs to Alexander, and he
has exalted it greatly." When Alexander had read this writing,
he said: "These words are strange and useless; I do not
seek that men should honour me as they do the gods, for
I am a mortal man, and I am afraid of anything like this,
for there is a heavy penalty for a man when he goes beyond
his proper limit. I applaud you and praise your knowledge, for
when I made trial of your wisdom it pleased me; and I wrote
a letter to Olympias my mother and begged of her the favour
that she would come to my marriage feast, if it so pleased her."

On this account......[1] Alexander wrote a letter to Rôshnâk
as follows: "From Alexander to Rôshnâk my sister greeting.
I send thee clothes and other ornaments for thine own self,
and to Îrândokht the mother of Darius, and Estĕhar [Statira]
his wife, for themselves. Accept then and keep for thyself
these clothes and ornaments. First of all be pleasing to the
gods; then pay due reverence to Îrândokht and Estĕhar, and
hold them in honour; and fear thou the command of Olympias
my mother, and do not exalt thyself beyond measure. If thou
doest these things, both I and thou shall be praised exceedingly
and all the gods be well pleased with us." Then Alexander
took Rôshnâk to wife[2].

[1] The meaning of the words ‫ܐ‬? ‫ܡ‬ (if correctly written) is not known
to me. We should expect some epithet applicable to Alexander, as φρονῖμη
and the like.

[2] The remainder of Book II. (see Müller, p. 82) is wanting in the Syriac
translation as well as in the Latin.

# BOOK III.

I. AND Alexander heard that Porus the king of the Indians had prepared troops and was wishing to come to the assistance of Darius, but when he heard that Darius was dead, he returned to his own land. And Alexander with all his hosts offered up sacrifices; then taking his army and troops, he went against Porus the king of the Indians. Now when he had gone round about and had marched for many days through a desert and torrents and terrible places and many rivers, all the chiefs of the army were worn out and said among themselves, " We have fought a great deal, we have had enough of war, and there is no need for us to fight any longer. We rightfully fought with Darius, for he imposed tribute upon us, and used to required impost and poll-tax from us every year, and we therefore destroyed Darius as was meet. But now this war is unnecessary, because we are marching against the Indians, who never at any time made war with the Greeks, through this fearfully desert country, being weary and fatigued and worn out with toil. Alexander is brave and a lover of wars, and he wishes to seize all foreign countries; but why should we, who have toiled all this time and are worn out with many battles, go about with him ?" And when Alexander heard these things, he commanded that all his forces should be assembled, and he gave orders for the Persian army to stand by itself, and for the Greek and Macedonian armies to stand by themselves. And Alexander said to them with a loud voice: " To you I speak, ye Macedonians and Greeks, my fellow soldiers and auxiliaries. Ye know that the Persian troops are now in my hands, and are neither enemies of mine nor yours. If ye give me orders and it pleases you that I should go by myself, I will go by myself; but I will speak now to you and call to your mind that I by myself was victor in the

previous wars; and henceforth, with whomsoever I choose to
fight, I by myself will be victor. In the war with Darius ye
were encouraged by my knowledge and my thoughts, because ye
did not understand the customs of the Persians neither did
ye know their skill. I stood at your head, and it was I who
first went to Darius, and I escaped from the hands of Darius,
from the river Gûsh[1] and from my other straits. Turn now
and go to Macedonia, and guide yourselves wisely if ye are
able, for there is no enemy in your way. If I hear that ye
have been able to guide yourselves and to arrive safely in
Macedonia, I shall know and believe and be convinced that
bravery is yours." And when he had spoken these words, all
the hosts of the Greeks and Macedonians fell upon their faces and
entreated Alexander, saying, " Be reconciled to us, and put away
anger from thy heart, and forgive us this folly, and we will be
with thee unto the end."

II. Now after a few days Alexander arrived with his
troops at a flourishing district in the territory of the Indians.
And at that time the letter carriers of Porus the king of the
Indians came to him, and brought a letter from Porus to
Alexander, in which was written as follows: " From Porus the
great king of the Indians to Alexander. I have heard of
thee, that thou doest damage in countries and cities, but what
art thou able to do to the gods and how canst thou fight
against them? Fate came to Darius king of the Persians;
thou didst hurl thyself against him, and so thou thinkest
that just as thou didst become strong and didst lift thyself
up against Darius, so thou art able to exalt thyself against
others. But I am he that has never been conquered; I am
not only king of men but of the gods also; and the proof
(I give) to thee is this, that the god Dionysus returned defeated
by the hands of the Indians. I do not now advise thee, but I
command thee to go quickly to Hellas thy country, for thou
art not able to intimidate me by the war which thou didst
carry on with Darius and with the other nations through whose
feebleness thou hast become exalted; and so thou thinkest that
thou art a mighty man and more exalted than king Porus, the

---

[1] See Book II., chap. 7.

lord of gods and men. Turn now, go back, and depart to thy
country Hellas. If we had wanted Hellas, we would have
taken it before king Xerxes. But because it is a wretched
place and has nothing worthy of a king, we have scorned
and despised it and have not subdued it. Therefore I say
to thee, every man desires to acquire whatever is good and
excellent, and never desires what is hateful. So now for the
third time I say to thee, turn and go back, for thou art not able
to do anything, therefore do not covet."

Then Alexander commanded that this letter should be read
before his troops, and he said to them: "My fellow soldiers, let
not your minds be afraid because of these words of king Porus
which he has written to me in his letter. Be mindful too
of those words which Darius used to write to me. Verily I
say unto you that the barbarians and dwellers in all these
regions are all as stupid and as ignorant as the wild beasts
that live in their country. Leopards and lions and elephants
and panthers are over confident by reason of the strength of
their bodies, and it is well known that they can be easily
captured by the knowledge of man with stratagems and artifices.
In the same way the kings who dwell in these regions, and all
the barbarians, are proud by reason of the number of their
troops, but they will be easily defeated by the knowledge of the
Greeks."

When Alexander had spoken to the troops in this manner,
he encouraged them mightily and he made answer to Porus by
letter as follows: "From Alexander to Porus, the king of the
Indians, greeting. The minds of all the troops that are with
me have been made proud by these words which thou hast
written to me, and their desire has been made the more
ready for war by what thou hast said, that there is nothing
beautiful and noble to be found in Hellas. By thy saying
too that the desire and longing of each man goes after what is
beautiful, by reason of this saying I and my forces now long
to do battle and to make war with thee. Thou hast by thy
words greatly encouraged us against thee, for we Greeks are
poor, and there is nothing costly in our land, while ye Indians
are rich and what is costly abounds in your land. And now
our mind and longing and desire are set upon the fair things

which are to be found in your land, and we will fight with
all our heart until we take that which belongs to you. Thou
didst also write that thou art king of gods and men, and thou
hast exalted thyself above the gods; but I am going to contend
in war with thee as with a warrior, and I am not going to do
battle with thee as with the gods; for all the weapons in
the world are unable to contend against the gods, and how
can mortal man contend with Him, before the cold of whose
winters and the crashes of whose lightnings and thunders
the world is unable to stand? And just as thou art not
afraid (of me) by reason of the war which I carried on with
Darius and with other nations, even so I am not afraid of these
perverse words which thou hast written to me."

III.   After Porus had seen this letter, he commanded the
whole army to be assembled, and a number of elephants to be
brought to the conflict, and mighty wild beasts with them.
And when the Macedonians and Persians drew near and came to
the ranks of Porus, they saw and trembled, for they observed
that the ranks were formed of wild beasts and not of men;
and even Alexander himself was afraid, because he was accustomed to fight with men and not with wild beasts.   Then he
sat down and reflected in his mind, and gave orders to bring
such brazen images as could be found among his troops.   And
when the images were collected, which were in the form of
men and quadrupeds,—now they were about twenty-four thousand in number—he ordered a smith's furnace to be set up;
and they brought much wood and set fire to it, and heated
those images in the fire, and the images became glowing coals
of fire.   Then they took hold of them with iron tongs, and
placed them upon iron chariots, and led the chariots before the
ranks of the warriors; and Alexander commanded horns and
trumpets to be sounded.   When the wild beasts that were
in the ranks of the king of the Indians heard the sound of
the trumpets, they rushed upon the ranks of Alexander's army;
and since the brazen images which were full of fire were in the
van, they laid hold of them with their mouths and lips, and
burnt their mouths and their lips.   Some of them died (on the
spot), and some of them retired beaten and fled away to the
camp of the king of the Indians.   The wise Alexander, having

turned back the wild beasts by this artifice, began to fight with the Indians themselves. Now the battle by day time was very fierce, and the Persian troops prevailed over the Indians in fighting on horseback and with bows and arrows, and many men died on both sides. The horse which was called Bucephalus, upon which Alexander rode, by the sorcery of Porus threw Alexander off his back. Then by reason of this Alexander was in great tribulation, and he went on foot, holding and leading with his hand the horse which was called Bull-head, for he thought, "Peradventure he may fall into the hand of the enemies." And the troops of Alexander did battle with the Indians continually for twenty days, and they were weary and sore enfeebled, and because of their fatigue they wished to surrender to the Indians.

IV. When Alexander perceived that his forces were desirous of doing this, he commanded them to cease [fighting]. He then drew near to the van, and cried with a loud voice to Porus and said to him: "O Porus, king of the Indians, there is neither renown nor glory when a king destroys his troops; but if thou art now willing, let the troops rest, and I and thou alone will fight together." When Porus heard this speech, he rejoiced and agreed with him to do so, saying, "I will fight with thee alone;" for he saw that Alexander was very small in stature, while he himself was very tall. Now Porus was five cubits high, and Alexander three cubits. Then Alexander commanded his troops to stand in order, and Porus also commanded his troops to do likewise. The two came to the contest on foot; and when they had approached one another, there was suddenly a confusion and a great noise in the ranks of the Indians; and Porus was alarmed and turned round and looked upon his forces. When Alexander saw that Porus had turned round and was looking behind him, he ran at him and stabbed him under the shoulders and drove the weapon out beneath his navel and slew him. When the Indians saw that Porus was slain, they came to fight. Then Alexander said to the troops of the Indians, "Ye wretched Indians, your king is dead, and will ye fight?" The troops of the Indians answered and said to him, "We are fighting that we may not become captives." Then Alexander said to them: "Return to your city and do

not fight, because I will leave you free and will impose no tax
upon you ; for I know that the offence was not of you, but of
Porus." Now Alexander said this because he saw that his
own troops were few and he was not able to meet in battle the
legions of the Indians. Then Alexander commanded the body
of Porus to be buried honourably, and he made ready to go to
another place, which was called Ratnirôn, that he might fight
with them, for he heard that they were sages and naked and
that they dwelt in huts and holes of the earth.

V. When these people heard that Alexander was come,
they sent certain sages that were among them to Alexander
with their letter. And when he saw their letter, he found
written therein as follows. "From the Brahmans, the naked
sages [gymnosophists], to the man Alexander greeting. We
write to thee thus: if thou desirest to come in order to make
war with us, thou wilt gain nothing at all from us, for we have
no property at all that can be taken away from us by war; and
if thou desirest to take away that which we have, thou canst
[only] take it away by entreaty, for our property is knowledge,
and knowledge cannot be taken away by war; but even this
thou art not capable of learning, for the heavenly will
distributed and gave to thee war, and to us knowledge."

When Alexander had read this letter, he went to them
peaceably, and he saw that they were all naked, and that they
dwelt under booths and in caves, and that their wives and
children went about the plain like sheep.

VI. Then Alexander asked one of them, "Have ye no
graves here ?" The Brahman said, "The place where we live
is our house, and it is also our grave; here then we lie down,
and bury our bodies continually in it, that our training and our
teaching may be in this world and that the term of our life in
yonder world may be for ever and aye." And he asked another
Brahman, "Which men are the more numerous, those that are
dead or those that are alive ?" The Brahman said, "Those
that are dead are the more numerous, for those who will
hereafter come are not to be counted among those who are now
alive; and you must know of yourself what innumerable
myriads have died through thee and these few legions that
are with thee." He asked another Brahman, "Which is the

mightier, death or life?" The Brahman said, "Life; for when
the sun rises and becomes warm like life, he covers over the
feebleness of night by the beams of his radiance, and becomes
strong. So also they who are dead are fallen beneath the
darkness of death; but when life rises upon them like the sun,
they will again come to life." He asked another Brahman,
"Which is the older, the earth or the sea?" The Brahman
said, "The earth, for the sea too is placed upon the earth." He
asked another Brahman, "Which is the most wicked of all
living things?" The Brahman said, "Man." Alexander said,
"Tell me how so." The Brahman said, "Ask thyself how many
beings go about with thee, that thou mayest wrest the lands
and countries of other living beings, thy fellow creatures, from
their owners, and hold them thyself alone." Alexander was not
enraged at this speech, for he wished to hear. He asked
another Brahman, "What is kingdom?" The Brahman said,
"Greed and brief power, and arrogance, and the insolence of
wicked doings." He asked another Brahman, "Which existed
first, night or day?" The Brahman said, "Night; for a child
is first of all created in darkness in the womb of his mother, and
then when he is brought forth, he sees the light." He asked
another Brahman, "Who is he whom we cannot deceive by
lying?" The Brahman said, "He to whom all secrets are
revealed." He asked another Brahman, "Which limbs are the
better, those on the left side or those on the right." The
Brahman said, "Those on the left; for the sun shines on the left
side; and a woman suckles her child first from the left breast;
and when we sacrifice to God, we make our offering to him with
the left hand; and kings hold the sceptre of their kingdom in
their left hand." And when Alexander had asked this question,
he said to them, "Whatsoever ye desire ask of me all of you at
once, and I will give it you." The Brahmans said, "We ask of
thee immortality." Alexander said, "I am not master over
immortality, because I am mortal." The Brahmans said,
"Since thou art mortal, why dost thou make all these wars and
battles? When thou hast seized the whole world, whither
wouldst thou carry it? for since thou art mortal, it will remain
with others." Alexander said, "All these things happen by the
providence and the will of heaven, and we wait on the heavenly

command; for just as the waves of the sea are not lifted up
unless the wind blows upon them, nor do the trees shake when
there is no wind, so neither are men able to do anything
without a command from above. I very much desire to rest
from wars, but......'. If all men were of one mind and one will,
the whole world would be a wilderness and without cultivation;
no man would sail on the sea in ships, neither would any
cultivate the earth, and there would be no generation of
children. How many unlucky men are there, who have got
mixed up with these wars which I have carried on, and whose
possessions have perished from them! And on the other hand,
how many lucky men have there chanced to be, who have
become enriched by the possessions of others! Every one of us
then who plunders something from another leaves it again to
some one else, and we depart naked and empty." When
Alexander had spoken these words, he turned away from the
Brahmans, and he was much fatigued and worn out by the
journey, for the country through which he was marching was
pathless, and no one had ever marched through it before.

VII.' Then Alexander composed a letter to Aristotle his
master concerning everything that had happened to him, and he
wrote to him thus: "From Alexander to our master Aristotle
greeting. I desire, O my teacher, to write and inform thee of
what has happened to me in this land of the Indians. When
then we had drawn near to the place (called) Prasiakê, which,
as they say, is the great city of the Indians and at a distance
from the shores of the Great Sea', we saw figures of men; and
when we came close up to the spot, we saw men feeding upon
the shores of the sea, and their faces were like those of horses,
and they lived upon fish. And when we had called aloud to
some of them, for we wished to enquire of them concerning that

---

[1] Some words have been accidentally omitted, corresponding to the Greek
ἀλλ' οὐκ ἐᾷ με ὁ τῆς γνώμης μου δεσπότης (Müller, p. 101, col. 2).

[2] This is chapter xvii. of the Greek text (Müller, p. 120, col. 2). Parts of
it have been edited in Syriac by the late Professor Roediger of Halle in his
*Chrestomathia Syriaca*, 2nd ed., pp. 112—120; and considerable portions have
been translated by the late Dr J. Perkins in the *Journal of the American
Oriental Society*, vol. IV., p. 394 sqq.

[3] Just the reverse of the Latin translation, which has *mari imminet subjacenti*
(Müller, p. 190, col. 2).

place, we perceived that their speech was barbarian. And we saw in the midst of the sea something of which they said that it was the grave of the ancients and very old, and that there was much gold in it[1]. And I desired much to go in a boat to the island, but those barbarians suddenly hid their boats, and did not leave more than twelve. Then I gave orders to seize those twelve boats, and I was going to embark in them and go to the island, but my dear friend Philôn, and Hephaestiôn, and Karṭil [Craterus], and other friends, would not allow me to embark in a boat and go to the island. Philôn said to me, ' Bid me go in a boat first and cross over to the island; and if (which God forbid) there be anything evil, I shall die before thee; and if it be otherwise, I will come back and do thou also pass over; for if Philôn perishes, Alexander can find many friends like Philôn, but if (which God forbid) Alexander were to perish, his like could not be found in the whole world.' Then I gave way and bade them embark in the boats and go over to the island; and when they had embarked in the boats and had drawn near the island, the thing turned out to be an animal and not an island at all; and it sank and vanished suddenly in the sea, and my friend Philôn disappeared in the vortex of the waters and perished; and I was in great trouble and deep affliction. Then I ordered those barbarians to be seized, but they fled away and hid themselves. And we remained where we were for eight days. And we saw a wild beast like an elephant, but its body was much larger than an elephant's; and when we saw it, we ran at it with our weapons, but it suddenly fled away from our sight. And when we saw this, we came from thence to Prasiakê disheartened and in sorrow. And since we have traversed a number of the countries of the world, and have seen many wonderful sights, I thought that I would write and inform thee, O my teacher; for I have seen beasts of all kinds and shapes, and wonderful sights, and marvels, and various and divers species of reptiles; but the most wonderful thing of all was this, that I saw the failing of the sun and of the moon, which takes place in its appearance, which is in winter and

---

[1] See Book II. ch. xxxv. in Müller's ed., p. 87, col. 2.

from time to time[1]; and so I thought it necessary for me to write to thee about each one of these things.

Now when I had slain Darius and had taken his country and had traversed it, I found therein a number of treasuries, and there was much gold therein, ingots and cups of gold for mixed wine, which were set with gems of various sorts; some of them held ninety measures of wine, and some fifty measures; and there were goods of various kinds.

And we began our march from the Caspian gates unto the border of the Indians; and we heard that that country was a desert and a wilderness, and that wild beasts and snakes and other kinds of evil reptiles were abundant therein. And I commanded the trumpeters to sound at the tenth hour of the day, and to beat the drums; and from the tenth hour [of the day] to the third hour of the night the phalanx was marching, and so we went on the whole night. When it was day and the sun had spread abroad his rays, I commanded the trumpeters to sound, and the whole phalanx to encamp until the third hour of the day; and I commanded the horsemen and foot soldiers to wear shoes and greaves and breastplates and armpieces of raw hide on account of the evil reptiles of that country, for no man was able to walk about without such clothing, lest perchance he himself should become the cause of his own death. Having marched along so strange a road as this for twelve days, we drew near to a city which was situated between rivers; and we commanded a ditch to be made along the banks of that river. We saw in that river a reed the height of which was thirty[2] cubits, and its thickness as that of a garland which a man puts on his head. The whole city was overshadowed by these reeds; and when we observed the city, it was not built upon the ground, but upon the reeds. We found in that river a boat, and when we had embarked therein, we went and observed, and it was exactly as we had seen at a distance. When we tasted the water of the river, it was more bitter than bitter herbs; and I was very much annoyed when I observed its

[1] The meaning of this sentence is not clear. See Müller, p. 121, col. 1, at the foot.

[2] The Greek text (Müller, p. 121, col. 2) has "four cubits," Δ being an error for Λ.

bitterness, for I did not find sweet water in that place. My ditch was dug along the bank of the river for two miles; and some of my fellow soldiers, thirty and six in number, scornfully cast off the skin garments from their backs, and wished to bathe in the river. When they had gone down to the water, a number of reptiles rose up against them, and seized those men, and dragged them into the river, and killed them in the water. When I saw these things, I crossed over again to the other side of the river. And when I saw the innumerable reptiles, I was in every way afflicted and distressed, and I departed from that place. And I commanded the horns to sound [a halt] from the sixth hour of the day until the eleventh. I saw too that the foot-soldiers and horsemen were drinking their own urine because of thirst.

Now when we had departed thence, another obstacle fell in our way, for we drew near to a lake, and we found therein every species of animal and reptile. When we tasted those waters, we perceived that they were sweeter than honey, and we were very glad. And when the phalanx halted and went on foot towards the lake, they saw upon its shore a pillar with an inscription which ran thus: 'I Siusiníkòs [Sesonchosis], the ruler of the world, have caused this lake to be made for the watering of those who live on and travel by sea.' When the night drew nigh, I ordered a couch to be prepared and a fire to be lighted around it, and I commanded that each horseman and foot-soldier should likewise light a fire by the side of his head. When I lay down upon my couch, the moon rose soon after,—it was about the third hour of the night,—and wild beasts of various kinds came forth from the jungle and came to the lake. Out of the earth too and from the sand white and red scorpions issued, each of which was a cubit long. And in the midst of the phalanx there sprang up snakes with horns on their heads, some red and some white, and they bit and killed a number of the men, and there was a great outcry and weeping heard from within the camp. We saw a lion that came to drink water, and he was larger than the oxen that are in our country; and we saw beasts with horns on their noses, and they were larger than elephants. We saw also wild boars that were larger than the lion, and the tusks of each of which

were a cubit long; we saw too wolves and leopards and panthers
and beasts with scorpions' tails, and elephants, and wild bulls,
and ox-elephants, and men with six hands apiece; and we saw
men with twisted legs and teeth like dogs and faces like women.
And we were afflicted in our soul and were in grief. Then
I commanded my troops to put on every man his skin clothing.
to take his weapons in his hand together with wood and fire,
and all to go in a body to the jungle and set it on fire. When
we had done this, a great number of reptiles hastened of their
own free will to the fire, some of which were burnt therein, and
some were slain by the hands of my troops and perished. Of
the wild beasts we slew some and others fled away. After the
moon had set and it was dark, an animal which was bigger in
its body than an elephant and which they call *Mashkelath*[1] in
the language of the country, came into the ditch and wished to
spring upon us, but I straightway called out to my troops to
take courage and stand ready. Now the longing and desire of
the animal was to enter the ditch and to kill men, and suddenly
it rushed into the ditch and killed twenty-six men, and amid
loud noises and struggles it too perished by the hands of my
troops; and after it was dead, we with three hundred men
dragged it with great toil from the ditch and lifted it out. And
we looked amid the darkness and saw reptiles which they call
night-foxes, the length of which was from six to eight cubits.
We saw also water crocodiles, the length of each of which was
twelve cubits; and we saw bats which were as big as eagles,
and their teeth were like those of men. We saw likewise night-
ravens, the beaks and claws and talons of which were like those of
eagles, and they sat around the lake, and did not harm human
beings, neither did they come near the fire. My troops killed a
great number of them, and when it was day they all hid themselves.

And we departed from thence and came to a wood[2], and

[1] The *mashkelath* is the *odontotyrannus* of the Latin translation (Müller,
p. 123, col. 1). The same creature is mentioned in the Greek text of Book III.
ch. x. (Müller, p. 105) as a huge amphibious animal, big enough to swallow
an elephant whole, which renders the crossing of the river Ganges very
unsafe. This description seems to point to the *alligator*, and it is just possible
that ܡܟܪܐ may be a corruption of *mukara*, in Hindustání *magar*.

[2] See Book II. ch. xxxii., about the middle (Müller, p. 86, col. 1).

in that wood there were trees bearing fruit, and their fruit
was very luscious; and within the wood there were wild men,
whose faces resembled ravens, and they held missiles in their
hands, and their clothing was of skins. When they saw us,
they cast missiles at my troops and slew some of them; and I
commanded my troops to shout and to charge them at full
speed; and when we had done this, we slew six hundred and
thirty-three of them, and they slew of my horsemen one hundred
and sixty-seven. And I ordered the bodies of those that were
dead to be taken up and to be carried to their own country.
We remained in that place three days and fed upon the fruit of
the trees, because we had no other food.

And we departed thence and came to a river in which
there was a copious spring of water; and I gave orders to
encamp there that my troops might have a little rest. At
the ninth hour of the day, behold a creature half beast half
man[1], which in its body was (like) a wild boar reared upright;
and it was not at all afraid of us. I commanded my troops
to catch it, and when they drew near to it, it was not
at all afraid and did not run away from them. Then I
ordered a naked woman to go towards it, that we might
easily seize it; but when the woman went up to it, the beast
took hold of the woman and rent her, and began to devour her.
When we saw this, we went against it at full speed, and smote
it and killed it. Then we departed from the country of the
beast-men, for there was a countless number of men like this in
it, and we slew myriads of them, because we all stood ready
with arms. And I gave orders to cut down all their wood and
to set it on fire, and we burnt them together with their wood.

And we departed thence and arrived at the country of
the people whose feet are twisted; and when they saw us, they
began to throw stones, and they threw accurately and aimed at
us. When I saw that they slew some of my troops, I ran at
them alone with my sword drawn, and by great good luck I
stabbed the chief of those people with twisted feet. The rest
were afraid, and ran away, and hid themselves under the rocks
in various places; and there were some among them with asses'
legs.

[1] Compare Book II. ch. xxxiii. (Müller, p. 86, col. 2).

7—2

We set out again from thence and came to another place where there were men with lion's heads and scaly tails[1].

From thence we set out again and came to a river[2]. And upon the bank of the river there was a tree, which grew and increased from dawn until the sixth hour, and from the sixth hour until evening it diminished in height until there was nothing to be seen of it. Its smell was very pleasant, and I gave orders to gather some of its leaves and fruit, when suddenly an evil wind burst forth upon my troops and distressed them pitilessly; and we heard the sound of violent blows, and swellings and weals appeared upon the back of my troops; and after this we heard a voice from heaven like the sound of thunder which spake thus: 'Let no man cut ought from this tree, neither let him approach it, for if ye approach it, all your troops will die.' And there were birds too which were like partridges. And I commanded that they should not cut ought from that tree, nor kill any of the birds. There were also stones in that river, the colour of which when in the water was deep black, but when we brought them out, they were quite white, and when we threw them in again, their colour (again) became deep black.

And from thence we set out and halted by a spring. And when we had marched through a desolate wilderness[3], we arrived at the ocean which goes round the whole world. And while we were going along the shores of the sea, I commanded the phalanx to encamp; and I heard the voice of men [speaking] in the Greek tongue, but I did not see them, nor did we see anything else in the sea except something like an island, which was not very far from us. Then a certain number of my troops desired to go to that island by swimming; and when they had stripped off their clothing and plunged into the sea, beasts in the form of men, but whose bodies were very large, came up from the deep and seized twenty of my soldiers, and plunged down into the depths.

Then we departed thence through fear, and came to a

---

[1] The word here rendered "scaly" literally means "an oyster" or "oyster shell."

[2] Compare Book II. ch. xxxvi. (Müller, p. 88, col. 2).

[3] See Book II. ch. xxxviii. (Müller, p. 89, col. 1).

certain place. And the people who were in that place had no head at all, but they had eyes and a mouth in their breasts, and they spoke like men, and used to gather mushrooms from the ground and eat them. Now each mushroom weighed twenty pounds. And those men were like children in their minds, and in their way of life they were very simple.

And from thence we set out and came to a certain place which was waste; and in the midst of that place there was a bird sitting upon a tree without leaves and without fruit, and it had upon its head something like the rays of the sun, and they called the bird the 'palm bird' (phoenix).

Then we set out from thence and came to a place amid groves of trees which were large, and in these woods there were wild beasts like the wild asses of our own country. Each of them was fifteen cubits in length, and as they were not dangerous, my troops killed a number of them and ate them.

Then we marched on our road sixty-five days, and arrived at a place which they call Obarkia (?). And on the seventh day we saw two birds', the bodies of which were very large, and their faces were like the face of a man; and suddenly one of them said in the Greek language, 'O Alexander, thou art treading the land of the gods;' and again it said to me in the same language, 'Alexander, the victory over Darius and the subjection of king Porus are enough for thee.' And when we had heard such words as these, we turned and came back from the country of the Obarkĕnâyĕ (?).

Then I gave orders to set out from this place, and we came thence to the foot of a certain mountain. This mountain was very high, and a temple had been built on the top of it, the height of which was a hundred cubits. When I saw this, I marvelled greatly. It was girt round with a chain of gold, and the weight of the chain was three hundred pounds. I gave orders to open the door of the temple that I might go in with my troops'. When we went in, we found in it two thousand five hundred steps of sapphire, and we saw inside a very large chamber the windows around which were of gold, and in them

¹ See Book II. ch. xl. (Muller, p. 90, col. 2).
² Compare the description in Meusel's text, p. 785, at the foot of the page (Book III. ch. xxviii.).

there were thirty figures of gems and of ...... of gold. And
when we drew near to the chamber, we saw that the whole
temple was of gold, and over its windows there were golden
images, figures of Pan and the Satyrs, who were musicians, and
in the windows there stood dancers.  In the temple a golden
altar was placed, and by it stood two candlesticks of sapphire,
the height of each of which was forty cubits.  Lamps of gold
were set upon them, which shone like the light of a lamp.  And
upon the altar instead of fire was placed a lamp made of stone,
which shone like a star.  In the temple a couch of gold was
placed, which was set with gems; its length was forty cubits,
and cushions of great value were laid upon it; the form of a
huge man reclined thereon, and an effulgence shot forth from
him like the lightning flash.  Over him was spread a garment
worked with gold and emeralds and other precious stones in the
form of a vine, the fruit of which was of gold set with gems, and
before the couch an ivory table was placed.  When I saw this,
I was unwilling to draw near hastily and uncover his face and
see who it was.  Then I sacrificed in the temple to the god and
did reverence, and I turned away and came out.  And when I
had come out and was in the doorway of the temple, there was
suddenly a terrible sound like the noise of thunder, and like
the noise of the uproar and billows of the sea.  And when that
roaring noise ceased, I heard a voice from within the temple which
said to me thus: 'King Alexander, rest and cease from thy toils;
enter not the temple of the gods, neither reveal their mysteries;
for he whom thou hast seen upon this couch is I Dionysus, and
I tell thee that it is given to thee to conquer in this war for
which thou art prepared, and to come to our country to rest,
and they shall reckon thee among our number.'  When I heard
a voice like this, my mind was in fear and joy, and I again
sacrificed and did reverence to him; and I went out to go about
that place and to record this sight in it.

Then I gave orders to kill those fifty Indians our guides,
who had led us astray in such roads and places, and to throw
them into the sea; and we turned to the road towards
Prasiaké[1], and arrived at a region abounding in trees, where I

---

[1] See Book III. ch. xvii. (Muller, p. 122, col. 2, ll. 16, 17).

commanded my troops to rest a little. And when I desired to set out from thence, at the sixth hour of the day, a wonderful sign happened to us; now this sign took place on the third day of the month of Âb. First there came suddenly a mighty wind, which tore up all the tents in our camp from their places, and we all fell upon the ground. Then I commanded my troops to pitch their tents again, and to make firm their tent pegs and to keep carefully on the watch. But before their tents were pitched, a dense and black cloud appeared, and its mist was so dark that no one could see his fellow. And we saw in the midst of that dense cloud in the air a fire burning in the darkness; and we also saw in front of that fire about the distance of two miles a black cloud; and when the fire drew nigh, the fire blazed forth from within that black cloud until the whole was fire. This sign appeared continually in this manner for three days; and for five days we did not see the light, but snow fell upon us; and out of the mass of my troops some were caught in the snow outside of the tents and died, and when the sun rose, many of our men perished. We desired to set out from thence but were unable, because the country was a plain, and the snow stood three cubits high from the ground; so because of the difficulty and hardness of the journey we remained where we were thirty days. And after staying thirty days where we were, we set out from thence, and on the fifth day we came to the city of the Prasiakâyê, and took the treasury and the goods which were in it.

Then all the Indians who lived in that city came to me of their own free will and spake to me thus: 'O great king, no living man has ever walked in the cities of the kings, and the mountains of the nations, and the temples of the gods, which thou hast seen and in which thou hast walked; and henceforth there is no king in the world who may be compared with thee. Command us now to do whatever seems right to thee, for we too will be obedient to thee, and will lay all the gold and silver that is in our country before thee.' Then said I to them, 'If there be anything renowned, or any marvel in your country, which a king ought to see, shew it to me, and I will not ask any other thing of you.' Then a certain Indian said to me, ' King Alexander, we have something famous, which it is right

that thou shouldst see. We will shew thee therefore two
talking trees', which talk like human beings.' And as soon as
he had said this speech, I commanded them to beat him, as one
who had said something which he was not able to shew. Then
he said to me, 'O king, doer of good things, I have not lied in
what I have said to thee.' Then I rose up from there and went
a journey of fifteen days with the Indian, and we arrived at a
certain place, and thus he spake : 'This is the end of the south
quarter of the world, and from here onwards there is nothing at
all except a wilderness, and ravening beasts and evil reptiles,
and none of us is able to advance beyond this place.' When
he had said this to me, he brought me into a beautiful garden,
the wall of which was not of stones nor of clay, but trees were
planted round it and were so dense that not even the light of
the sun or the moon was seen through them ; and in the midst
of the garden there was another enclosure which was hedged
round, and they called it the temple of the sun and of the
moon. And two trees were there, the like of which for
length and breadth I had never seen. Their length was
immeasurable, and so I thought that their tops were near unto
heaven. Their appearance was like unto the cypresses which
are in our country, and they grew up within the enclosure ; and
they said that one of them is male and the other female. They
said of the male that he is the sun, and that the female is the
moon, and in their language they call the one *Mitôrd*, and the
other *Mâyôsd*². Skins of all kinds of animals were lying there,
before the male skins of males, and before the female skins of
females; but no vessels of iron or brass or tin or clay were found
there at all. And when I asked them, 'Of what are these the
skins?' they said to me, 'Of lions and leopards, because those who
worship the sun and moon are not allowed to wear any other
clothing but skins.' Then I asked them about these trees, 'When

---

[1] Colonel Yule in his *Book of Ser Marco Polo*, vol. i. p. 131, has a long
discussion about these talking trees of the sun and moon, and about the
"dry tree," and has translated the passage from Müller's *Pseudo-Callisthenes*
relating to them. He has also reproduced a curious old drawing of the two
trees.

[2] In the Greek (Müller, p. 123, col. 2, l. 2) μιτθοῦ ἱμασίαι (var. μυθία
μαθσίη).

do they speak ?'   And they said to me, 'That of the sun in the
morning and at midday and towards evening, at these three
times it speaks; and that of the moon in the evening and at
midnight and towards the dawn.'   Then the priests that were
in the garden came to me and said to me, 'Enter, O king,
purely, and do reverence.'   Then I called my friends Phormiôn
[Parmeniôn], Artarôn [Craterus], Gôrôn (?), Philip, Miktôn
[Machetes], Tarnsargôthâ [Thrasyleôn], Thirtakith [Theodektês],
Philêa [Diiphilus], and Khadkliôn [Neoklês]; twelve[1] men I
took, and we began to enter the temple.   The chief priest said
unto me, 'O king, it is not meet to bring into the temple tools
of iron.'   Then I bade my friends take their swords and put
them outside the enclosure, and I ordered these twelve alone of
all my troops to go in with me without their swords, but I gave
orders that they should first go round about the trees, because I
thought that they might have brought me there treacherously;
but after they had come in and had gone round about, they
said to me, 'There is nothing at all here.'   Then I took hold of
the hand of one of the Indians and went in there, that when
the tree spoke, the Indian might interpret for me; and I swore
to him by Olympias my mother, and by Ammon, and by the
victory of all the gods of the Macedonians, 'If I do not hear a
voice from this tree as soon as the sun sets, I will slay you all
with the sword.'   As soon as the sun had set, a voice came from
that tree in a barbarous tongue; and when I asked the Indian
'What is this voice from this tree ?' he was afraid to explain it
to me and wished to hide it.   Then I straightway understood,
and I took hold of the Indian and led him aside and said to
him, 'If thou dost not explain this voice to me, I will kill thee
with a hard and bitter death.'   And the Indian whispered in
my ears, 'The explanation of the voice is this: thou wilt shortly
perish by thy troops.'   Then I and my friends went again into
the temple by night, and when I had drawn near to the tree of
the moon, and had done reverence to it, and placed my hand
upon it, again at that moment from the tree a voice came in
the Greek tongue, 'Thou shalt die at Babylon.'   And when I
together with my friends were marvelling at this wonder, my

---

[1] Only nine names are given in the text.

mind was troubled and sorrowful, and I desired to put the
glorious and beautiful crown which was upon my head in that
place; but the priest said to me, 'Thou canst not do this, unless
thou choosest to do it by violence, for laws are not laid down
for kings.' Then, as I was in trouble and sorrow because of
these things, my friends Parmâôn [Parmeniôn] and Philip tried
to persuade me to sleep and to rest myself a little. I did not
consent however, but remained awake the whole night. When
the dawn was near, I and my friends together with the priest
and the Indians again entered the temple; and I and the priest
went to the tree, and I laid my hands upon it and questioned it,
saying, 'Tell me if the days of my life are come to an end;
this too I desire to know, if it will be granted me to go to
Macedonia, and to see Olympias my mother, and to ask after her
welfare, and to return again.' And as soon as the sun had risen
and his rays had fallen upon the top of the tree, a loud and
harsh voice came from it, which spake thus, 'The years of thy
life are come to an end, and thou wilt not be able to go to Macedonia, but thou wilt perish in Babylon after a short time by the
hands of thy kinsfolk, and thy mother too will die a hideous
death by the hands of thy kinsfolk, and in the same way thy
sister also; but do not ask further concerning this matter, for
thou wilt hear nothing more from us.' Then I took counsel
with my troops, and we set out again from thence and marched
along the road a journey of fifteen days. And when we had
gone straight forward on our march, we arrived at the country
of Prasiakê[1], I Alexander with these Indians and with my troops.
The Indians who dwelt in that land brought offerings to us,
and they brought offerings to us also from far countries. They
brought to us skins of fishes which were like leopard's skins,
only they were larger, and there were in them teeth, some of
which were one cubit long and some three cubits; the ears
(gills) of these fishes were each six cubits long, and the weight
of each of them was a hundred pounds; and the teeth of
these fishes were some of them two cubits long and others

---

[1] Here ends the epistle of Alexander to Aristotle in Müller's ed., p. 125,
col. 2. What follows appears to be no longer extant in the Greek MSS.
The narrative continues in the first person, as if this were still part of the
epistle.

three. [They also brought things] like oyster shells, each of which held fifty cups of water, and which were very beautiful in appearance; and thirty purple sponges, and fifty white ones, and various other things.

Then we set out from the country of Prasiakê, and set our faces straight for the east. And when we had gone a journey of ten days along the road, we came to a high mountain; and some of the people that lived on the mountain said to us, 'King Alexander, thou art not able to cross over this mountain, for a great god in the form of a dragon lives in it, who protects this country from enemies.' And I said to them, 'In what place is the god?' They said to me, 'He is a journey of three days from here by yon river.' And I said to them, 'Does this god change himself into another form?' And they said to me, 'Enemies never dare to come to this country through fear of him.' And I said to them, 'Is he able to keep off enemies from all your coasts?' And they said, 'No, only on that side where his dwelling is.' And I said to them, 'Has this god a temple? and do ye go to his presence and know him?' And they said, 'Who can go near unto him that can swallow an elephant by drawing in his breath?' And I said, 'Whence know ye this, since ye go not near him?' And they said, 'We know that a number of people are swallowed up by him every year, besides two oxen which they give to him regularly every day for food from our land, and he also kills men.' And I said, 'How do ye give him these two oxen to eat?' They said, 'He that is set apart for the service of the god selects oxen from the land, and takes two of them each day in the morning, when as yet he has not come forth from his temple, and goes down to the bank of the river; and he ties the legs of the oxen, and throws them upon the bank of the river, and he goes up to the top of the mountain; and when the god comes forth from his temple, he crosses over that horrible river, and swallows up those oxen.' And I said to them, 'Has this god one place for crossing, or does he cross wherever he pleases?' And they said, 'He has but one place for crossing.' Then I bethought me that it was not a god but a phantasy of wicked demons. I took some of the people of the land (with me), and set out from thence, and came to the bank

of that river. And I commanded them to place the oxen as
they were accustomed to do, and I and my troops stood upon
the top of the mountain. And we saw when the beast came
forth from his den and came to the bank of the river. When I
saw the beast, I thought that it was a black cloud which was
standing upon the bank of the river, and the smoke which went
forth from its mouth was like unto the thick darkness which
comes in a fog. And we saw it crossing the river, and when as
yet it had not reached the oxen, it sucked them into its mouth
by the drawing in of its breath, as (if cast) by a sling, and
swallowed them. When I had seen this, I gave orders next
day that they should put two very small calves instead of the
two big oxen, that the beast might be the more hungry on the
following day. After it had found the two calves, it was
obliged to cross over again on that day; and when it had
crossed over for the second time, by reason of its hunger, it
went wandering from this side to that but found nothing.
And when the beast desired to come on towards the mountain,
all my troops with one voice raised a shout against it; and
when it heard the shout, it turned and crossed the river. Then I
straightway gave orders to bring two oxen of huge bulk, and to
kill them, and to strip off their hides, and to take away their
flesh, and to fill their skins with gypsum and pitch and lead
and sulphur, and to place them on that spot. When they had
done this, the beast according to its wont crossed the river
again, and when it came to them, it suddenly drew both of
the skins into its mouth by its breath and swallowed them. As
soon as the gypsum entered its belly, we saw that its head fell
upon the ground, and it opened wide its mouth, and uprooted a
number of trees with its tail. And when I saw that it had
fallen down, I ordered a smith's bellows to be brought and balls
of brass to be heated in the fire and to be thrown into the
beast's mouth; and when they had thrown five balls into its
mouth, the beast shut its mouth, and died. And we set out
from thence and came to a region in which was a high mountain, and a river which they call BarsAtls (?) went forth from it;
and they told us that there was a god in this mountain, and
that the whole mountain was of sapphire. Then I and my
troops ascended the mountain, and it was full of fountains and

springs of water; and the people of that country said to me, 'Do
not march confidently in this mountain, for its gods are mighty.'
Then I ordered sacrifices to be offered to that place, and suddenly
from the mountain there came a multitude of kinds and sounds
of singing. When I heard this, I again did reverence; and I
heard a voice from the mountain which spake to me thus in the
Greek tongue, 'King Alexander, go back, and advance no farther;
for from here onwards the country belongs to men who by their
knowledge and power have conquered and subdued a number
of armies.' And I answered and said, 'Since it has pleased you
thus [to speak], inform me whether, if I go by myself, I shall
return alive from thence.' And the gods answered and said to
me, 'Go thyself, for it is given to thee to see something beautiful.' I answered again and said, 'What is the beautiful thing
which I shall see?' And the gods said to me, 'Thou shalt see a
king, a son of the gods, from whose country an honoured priest
goes to a number of countries, and thou shalt learn how from
something small something so noble may arise.' When I had
heard this, I commanded a city to be built by that mountain,
and a brazen statue to be erected upon it, and [I ordered] it to
be named 'Alexandria, the queen of the mountains.'

And I commanded my troops to remain in that place, and I
with twenty of my friends arose and arrived at a place which
they call Ḳâtôn[1]; and we stayed where we were three days, and
we set out from thence and marched a journey of ten days
through mountainous roads and watery lands. And again we
marched a journey of fifteen days through a desert and arrived
at the confines of Ṣîn (China). When we arrived in China, I
gave myself the name of Pithâôs[2] the ambassador of king Alexander. When we approached the gate of the king of China[3],
they went in and informed him of my arrival, and he gave
orders to question me outside. Then Gundâphâr[4], the chief of
his army, questioned me concerning my coming to China, and I

[1] Perhaps *Cathay*, in Arabic الخطا.
[2] Πιθέας or Πόθων?
[3] That is, the royal palace.
[4] On the name of Gundaphar, or Gundaphor, i.e. Gondophares, see in particular the article by Professor A. von Gutschmid in the *Museum für Philologie*,
n. F. XII., pp. 161—170.

said to him, 'I am an ambassador of king Alexander.' And
Gundáphár said to me, ' Why hast thou come hither ?' And I
said, ' I have been sent to the king of China; my message is to
him; and it is not right for me to utter the message which I
bring from my master before thee.' Then Gundáphár went in
to the king of China and informed him, and the king ordered
the palace to be decorated, and silk curtains to be hung up, and
a golden couch to be prepared; and he bade them call me.
When I entered his presence, I did not make obeisance to him,
and he questioned me, and said to me, ' Whence comest thou ?'
I answered and said, ' I am the ambassador of king Alexander.'
And he said to me, ' Who is Alexander ?' I said, ' He is a
Macedonian, the lord of the world, and the bearer [of the
sovereignty] of the Persians and Indians.' And he said to me,
' Where is the land of Macedonia ?' I said, ' In the western
quarter of the world, at the place where the sun sets.' And he
said to me, ' Where didst thou leave this [Alexander] ?' And I
said, ' He is near, and not far off; lo, he is by the river Bîrsâ-
tôs (?).' And he said to me, ' Why has he sent thee ?' And I
said, ' My lord Alexander has been set by the gods as lord over
the kings of the world, and I am come to bring thee to him,
and my message is this: Thus saith Alexander, I have been
established over all the kings of the world by the will and
decree of the heavenly gods, and over all rulers will I be chief
and commander; whosoever accepts willingly this my sovereignty,
his whole territory shall remain his and he shall continue in his
dominion; but whosoever receives me not, his country and his
dominion are no longer his. And if thou dost not believe me
that it is so, ask and learn what greatness and renown Darius
the king of Asia had in the world, for he was a warrior and
a conqueror, and yet afterwards, because of his obstinacy, to
what a place was he abased and degraded ! Porus too, the king
of the Indians, who was so great and mighty, and fertile in
artifices and stratagems, and versatile and rich in every craft,
and so thought that he was not only lord of men but also chief
and lord of the gods, learn what an end befell him through
his obstinacy. Now I have heard concerning thee that thou hast
good and great knowledge and understanding, and I thought
that I would not come against thee with camps and troops as

against an enemy, but I have sent an ambassador to thee as to
a friend, that thou mayest come to me of thine own free will,
and that I may see and taste of the treasure of thy knowledge
by the fruit of thy words from the gates of thy mouth; and if
there is anything worthy of being seen in thy land, bring it
with thee that I may see it.' Then he questioned me and said to
me, 'Is King Alexander mighty in body?' And I said to him,
'No; on the contrary, he is very small.' And he said to me,
'To-day thou must make merry with me after the manner of
ambassadors, and to-morrow thou shalt receive the answer to thy
message.' When the hour of the banquet was come, the king
of China commanded, and they made me sit in the banquetting
hall among the lower seats. When the banquet was finished,
he ordered them to prepare a sleeping apartment in the royal
palace, and bade me sleep there; and in the morning, while it
was yet dark, he ordered me to be brought in before him.
When I entered, I did reverence to him. When he saw that I
made obeisance to him, he was perplexed concerning me, and
ordered me to be questioned again. When I had repeated
my message afresh before him, he said to me, 'Thy message is
that of yesterday, but thy deeds are not those of yesterday;
yesterday thou wast one thing, and to-day thou art another.'
I said to him, 'Thou hast spoken rightly, O king, for
yesterday I myself by the words of my message was clothed in
the person of Alexander; in me, O king, thou didst see
Alexander, and in the speech of my lips thou didst hear that of
Alexander; but to-day [I am] Pithâôs the ambassador.' Then
he commanded and they brought a cloak, and he said to me,
'Shew me how Alexander is formed in stature.' And I said,
'In stature Alexander resembles me.' And he said to me, 'Is
not the king taller than thou?' And I said, 'No.' Then he
gave orders to measure my height and breadth and to cut the
cloak according to my measure. And when they had cut it, he
ordered it to be rolled up and sealed, and he said to me, 'Pithâôs,
go and carry this answer from me to king Alexander, and say to
him: I have heard thy message which thou hast sent to me,
and of thy fortune, thy bravery, and thy exaltation. Thy victory
then over Darius, and thy might, and thy victory over Porus,
and thy subjection too of a number of nations—I do not think

that such exaltation as this is caused by thy good fortune alone, but I imagine that it arises from their bad luck, and particularly because everything that comes to pass is given by fortune. Now to thee fortune and luck have been given by fate, and such elevation as this, which was not granted to Darius and Porus who were before thee. Therefore it is meet for thee to know that thou shouldst have no confidence in fortune, and that thou shouldst not weary thyself more, and that thy hands should not become the executioners of those who have drawn nigh to and reached the end of the days of their life, for the name of executioner is a disgraceful one. And as regards thy message to me concerning my coming to thee, behold, by the words of my mouth I stand before thee, and I speak with thee by the tongue of Pithâôs. Be not angry then because my body comes not to thee, and do not come to our country with warfare, for we have never at any time surrendered. I do not speak these things for thy sake, as if we were stronger than thou art, but I say this on my own account; for shouldst thou come against us, and our luck let go its hold of us, as it did of Darius and of king Porus, thou wilt slay us all, and thy hands will be our executioners, for none of us will accept bondage in his lifetime. And let this also be in thy mind, that, if thy luck turn somehow against thee, this great name of thine and might of thine will perish by fate, for this lying fortune does not remain constantly in one place. We men then who thus work and plan, and by a great deal of expense and toil and executioner's work slay a number of men of our kind and race, and seize a number of countries, afterwards, whether we will or no, everything leaves us and departs, and of the number of countries which we seize, and the numerous regions which we subdue, a piece of land the size of this cloak comes to us.' Then he straightway gave the cloak into my hands, and a crown of gold studded with pearls and jacinths, and ......' a thousand talents; ten thousand pieces of undyed silks, and five thousand brocaded silks; two hundred figures of cane, and one hundred painted (?) skins, and one thousand Indian swords; five wild horses, and one thousand skins of musk, and ten snakes' horns (?), each of which was a

---

¹ I do not know the meaning of the words ܡܟ̈ܠ ܚܣܡܐ.

cubit long: and he said to me, 'Carry this offering from me to Alexander.' Now I was minded not to accept them, but I thought afterwards, 'If I do not take them, peradventure he may have doubts of me and may find out that I am Alexander.'

So I and my friends returned from thence and came to the body of my troops; and I commanded them to set out from thence, and we came through mountains and a difficult country to a plain and a desert region. And from thence we marched a journey of twelve days through the desert. And in that desert we saw numbers of wild animals which were like our gazelles, but their heads and their teeth were different, and they were like foxes. And [we saw] the animals from whose navels they take the musk. On the thirteenth day we arrived at a camping place of savage barbarians, who were very well furnished with horses and arms. When those savages saw us, they came against our encampment with arms and war; and when we saw that they had come for war, I commanded my troops to make ready, and when they had come near, my troops shouted and we joined in battle together. Now when we had closed with one another in fight, by good luck it so happened that I slew the chief of those thieves with the sword; and when they saw that their chief was slain, and that many were killed on both sides, they turned their backs and fled from us. And I commanded my troops that the wives and children of these savages should be slain and their possessions pillaged.

And we set out from thence and came to a country which they call ṢĕbâzÂz (?). All the people of that land, together with the priests of their gods, came to us with offerings and spices, and we remained in that country ten days, and I commanded all the priests of that land to offer sacrifices.

And we set out from thence, and came to a country which they call Sôd [Sogd][1], and the country was very populous. I saw there a large river going forth on the south-west quarter, and that river was difficult to cross; indeed there was no means of crossing it whatever. I was greatly troubled and supplicated all the gods that are in Macedonia and Ammon the

---

[1] That is, the Sughd of Samarḳand, الصُغَد or الصُغْد.

god of Lybia, and I vowed that if they would aid me to cross
this river with my troops, I would build a city on the other side
and set up a temple of the gods in it.   When the people that
were in that country heard [of our coming], they sent to me
saying, 'Do not pass over into our territory, for we will not
allow thee to come into our territory.'   And when I heard
this message, I ordered those ambassadors to be bound and
guarded; and I asked them, 'Where is he that is ruler and chief
in this land? and in what town does he dwell? and how many
of the nobles of the land has he with him?'   The ambassadors
said, 'Swear to us by the gods that thou wilt do us no harm,
and we will carry thee and shew thee the spot, for all the
nobles of this country are in that place.'   Then I sware to them
by all the gods, saying, 'If ye shew me rightly, I will not kill
you; but if ye say ought otherwise, I will kill you together
with the others that are in the towns.'   And as the gods willed,
I gave orders to take each of those eight ambassadors by
himself and to question him, and when we got the statements
of all of them, [we found that] they agreed.   I ordered my troops
to get ready and Kôkaros (?), the chief of the host, to question
one of the ambassadors who was bound; and with fifty horsemen
I set out early in the night to go and spy out the road and to
observe the town, because it was night and we did not know
the custom of the country, and owing to this I was afraid.
Then a kundâkôr[1] went and explored the way; he returned
and came to me and said to me, 'The road is easy and the town
is not large.'   Then I and my troops went to the town, and I
commanded the horns to be sounded and the troops to encircle
the town; and I ordered much wood to be brought and fire to
be kindled around the whole of the town, and the troops to stand
outside the fire; and I commanded them also to kill every one
who should flee from the town.   When the people that were in
the town heard the sound of the horns, they came forth from
the houses and saw the fire round about the town, and some
of them wished to flee; and as they fled from the town, they
died by the hands of my troops.   Then their chief and the
nobles that were in the town came forth from the town and

[1] This word is glossed in one of the MSS. (B) by the Persian word *sardâr*
" chief, commander."

said with a loud voice, 'King Alexander, let thy wrath turn to favour, and do not order thy servants to be slain.' Then I commanded them to come to me; and when they came, I gave orders to guard them vigilantly.

And we came to the country of the Sundîkâyê[1]; and when I saw that the whole country yielded to me, I commanded a city to be built there and to be called Samarkand. I ordered a temple to be built therein to the goddess Rhea, whom they call Nânî[2], and when they had built it, I ordered it to be painted with gold and with the choicest paints, and a Greek inscription to be written thereon; and I commanded that all the Sundîkâyê should come to that place and should make a feast to Rhea and offer sacrifices to her. When the Sundîkâyê had done this in their country, they were firmly reconciled to Alexander in friendship and love.

And again we set out from thence and went to the river Barṭêsîṭôs (?), the interpretation of which is 'crystal.' When the king[3] saw that the river was large and difficult to cross, he ordered all the carpenters and artificers that were in Sôd to be brought, and bade much wood to be given to them; and he commanded Espisṭâhândos (?) to build a thousand Alexandrian boats. And he ordered the bows of the boats to be very sharp (?), and he bade two cables to be made of the bark of trees, each of them fifty cubits in thickness, and ordered men to cross over to the other side of the river in boats and to construct a kind of tower there. When they had made it, I gave orders to measure the breadth of the river, and to bring all those boats to the bank thereof, and to fasten them all to the one rope, and to one another with planks of wood; and to the other rope they fastened thousands of bags of ox-hide filled with air; and [I commanded] them to take the rope across and to fasten the end of it to the tower. When they had fastened

[1] That is, the inhabitants of the *Sughd*.

[2] See Hoffmann's *Auszüge aus syrischen Akten persischer Märtyrer*, p. 130 sqq. and p. 295; Lagarde, *Gesammelte Abhandlungen*, pp. 16, 143; *Armenische Studien*, p. 110. In Cureton's *Spicil. Syr.*, p. ܩܠܒ, l. 8, read ܚܠܒܐ for ܚܠܒ, and also in ZDMG. xxix., p. 111, l. 7, for ܚܠܒ.

[3] The translator departs from the direct narrative more than once in the course of this description.

the rope, he ordered a strong rope to be tied to the boats from
the one side to the other, and a number of men to pull with
ropes from that side.   And when the head of the boats reached
the middle of the river, the boats went on and were stretched
out by the force of the current (?), and the bridge became
straight.   And he commanded a number of men to pull on this
side and on that, and in the middle, with the rope which was
fastened on the bank of the river, lest the boats, with the rope
by which they were tied, should knock upon the stones and be
broken.   And when the bridge reached the rope, the ships at
first struck the skins with violence, but the shock was broken
and lightened by the skins.   Thus he constructed the bridge by
his skill and craft, and he ordered the troops to pass over.

When we had crossed the river and had gone a journey of
two days, I saw a river that was copious and abundant in its
flow, and towns with numerous hamlets and country houses
were round about it, and the people of that country were simple
in mind, and the country was rich in crops, and there was plenty
of corn and fruit therein.   I commanded the phalanx to halt in
that place, and we remained where we were for five months.
I ordered a large city to be built there; and on account of the
beauty and desirability of the country, I commanded that it
should be named afresh, and to the city I gave the name 'a part
of Cûsh,' which is called in Persian *Behli*[1].   And I ordered two
temples to be built in the city, the one to Zeus, and the other
to Rhea; and I commanded them to be constructed with lime
and stone and at much outlay; and I commanded a statue
to be made in brass of myself and another of my friend
Îdmâlos (?), and to be set up in those temples.   And by reason
of the fairness and beauty of the country, some of the Greek
troops that were with me desired to stay there; and I gave
orders that five hundred men should remain and dwell there,
more particularly for the honour of those temples; and I
commanded sacrifices (to be offered) and a great feast to be
made.

And from thence we set out and came to a river, on the bank
of which I commanded the phalanx to encamp, and we rested

[1] There seems to be something radically wrong in this sentence, but the
MSS. agree.

where we were for five days. And when I gave orders to set out from thence by night, Paryôg the.........and his band came against us. My soldiers had let loose their horses and cattle to graze quietly along the bank of the river, and Paryôg and his band seized all the horses and cattle, and went into a wood, and led them away from the bank of the river. When I heard these things, I took a band of foot-soldiers and some Macedonian troops, and we pursued after Paryôg that day along the river by means of the prints of the horses' hoofs which had been imprinted on the bank; and we went after him a journey of one day, but we did not overtake him. Then I made a vow to the god Ammon and made supplication to him, saying, 'If we overtake Paryôg and his band, in the place where I overtake him I will build a city to thy name, O Ammon, and will set up in it a temple to thee.' When I had gone five miles along the road, the earth was covered with water, and the hoof marks of the horses were no longer seen. I ordered the foot-prints of the horses to be sought for around the water and the wood; and when they had looked for the foot-prints but did not find them, I knew that the god Ammon would come to our assistance. And I ordered them to set fire to the skirts of the wood all round, so that Paryôg and his troop were not able to bear the flame of the fire. Then they all came out from the wood, and my conquering troops fought with Paryôg and slew him, and he died. And of Paryôg's band some died by the fire, two hundred and seventy men, and a thousand and three hundred others perished by the hands of my troops; and we got our horses and our cattle. We made the whole camp rest there, and I commanded earth to be brought for all the waters which were detained there, and the place where all the waters were to be filled up, and a city to be built upon it, and a temple to be made therein to the god Ammon. And we were in that spot four months, and when the city and the temple were finished, I commanded men to be brought from various places to dwell therein, and I called its name Margiôs (Μαργιανή), that is Mârô (Merv), and I offered sacrifices to the god Ammon there.

VIII. When then we were ready to go from the country of Margiana to the land of the Persians, I desired also to go quickly[1]

[1] Here begins ch. xviii. of the Greek text (Müller, p. 125, col. 2).

and without delay to the country of the Samrâyè[1] and to see their kingdom, for the kingdom of the Samrâyè was renowned among the Athenians and in the land of Hellas, and they were wont to say of it that all the walls of the city were of whole stones, the length of each being three stadia, which make a mile. It has one hundred and twenty gates, and the gates are all bound with iron and brass outside, for iron is abundant in their country; and all the houses that are built in that city are of hewn stone from their foundations to their roofs. Over their country a woman reigned, who in her appearance was very beautiful; she was of middle age, and was a widow; and she had three sons, and her name was Kundâkâ [Candace], the lady of the Samrâyè. To this lady Alexander composed a letter and wrote to her thus: "From king Alexander to queen Candace greeting; and to the generals of the country of the Samrâyè greeting. When I went to Egypt, I saw there your graves and dwelling-places; and when I asked the priests of that country, they told me that ye dwelt in Egypt a long time, and that the god Ammon was with you as a helper. And after some time, by the oracle of Ammon, the god of his own accord sent to our border, [saying,] that I should go to your border and should sacrifice to him. If it pleases you, do ye also come to the border with the images, that we may hold a festival together."

Then Candace, when she had read this letter, made answer to him thus: "From Candace, the queen of the Samrâyè, and from all the generals of the Samrâyè, to king Alexander greeting. When of old we went to the land of Egypt, we went by the command of the oracle of Ammon, and he himself was with our army. Now too he has commanded us, saying, 'Beware lest ye move me from my place; neither shall ye go to another spot; but if any man shall come to your country, fight with him as with an enemy.' Thou wilt not catch us with this impudent speech of thine, for we are inspirited with the same spirit as thyself, even more than the illustrious and renowned who are in thy army[2]. I have troops to the number of eight

---

[1] In the Greek (Müller, *loc. cit.*) ἐπῆγε τὰ στρατεύματα ἐπὶ τῆς Σεμιράμεως βασιλεία, Lat. *ad Semiramidos regiam*.

[2] The Greek text is very different (Müller, p. 126, col. 1): Μὴ καταγνῷ ἡ

hundred thousand, who are ready and prepared to fight with
the evil one. Thou therefore hast done well, since thou hast
proposed this in honour of the god Ammon; but if thou
desirest to offer sacrifices to the god Ammon, do thou come by
thyself, and let not an army come with thea. Farewell." And
my ambassadors brought from her one hundred solid missiles'
of gold; five hundred ass-goats', which they call in Persian
*khar-bôz*; of different kinds of the bird which is called *pâipâ*
(parrot) two hundred; two hundred apes; a crown of gold set
with emeralds and pearls for the god Ammon who is within
the border of Egypt; twenty unpierced pearls; thirty unpierced
emeralds; and eighty small boxes of ivory. And she sent to
us of different kinds of beasts three hundred and fifty elephants;
three hundred leopards; eighty animals which are called rhinoceros, and in Persian *markêdad* or *bargêdad;* four thousand
hunting bears and leopards; three thousand dogs that eat men;
three thousand buffaloes for killing; three hundred leopard-
skins and one thousand three hundred teak rods: and she said
thus, "Do thou take these things, and inform me in writing if
thou art lord over the whole world."

IX. Then Alexander accepted these things and sent to her
Ḳdimiôn [Kleomenês] the Egyptian as an ambassador with a
letter to the queen. And when Candace heard from Alexander
how he had taken different countries and captured cities and
overcome and subdued mighty kings, she bade a certain painter
of hers, a Greek, arise and go to the place where Alexander was,
and paint for her his face and figure accurately, without the
king's being aware of it, and bring it to her. And when the
painter had gone and painted the portrait of Alexander and
brought it to her, Candace took the likeness and hid it in a
certain place. Then it fell out that a son of Candace, whose
name was Ḳandâros [Candaules], with his wife and a few horsemen, came to the country of the Amazons to perform the
mysteries of the gods; and it came to pass that the chief of the
Marnikâyê' slew his horsemen and took his wife, and Candaules

τοῦ χρώματος ἡμῶν· ἰσμὲν γὰρ λευκότεροι καὶ λαμπρότεροι ταῖς ψυχαῖς τῶν παρ'
ὑμῶν λευκοτάτων.

¹ The Greek has πλίνθους, Lat. *laterculos.*
² The Greek says Αἰθίοπας ἀσήβους φ', Lat. *Æthiopas impubes quingentos.*
³ In the Greek ὁ τύραννος τῶν Βιβρύκων (Müller, p. 127, col. 1). Of the

escaped with a few horsemen, and came to the camp of Alexander. Then the guards of Alexander's camp took him and brought him before Ptolemy, the second in the kingdom, Alexander being asleep. Then Ptolemy questioned him, "Who art thou?" Candaules said, "I am the son of queen Candace." He said to him, "What art thou doing here?" Candaules said, "I and my wife, with a few horsemen, came to the country of the Amazons, as is our wont every year, to perform the mysteries of the gods; this time, however, the chief of the Marnîkâyê saw my wife, and came against me with a large troop, and wrested my wife from me, and slew a number of the horsemen that were with me; and now I am come back that I might fetch a number of troops and do battle with him." And when Ptolemy heard this, he arose and went in to the king and awoke him, and related these things which he had heard before him. When Alexander heard this, he rose up early in the morning, and gave his crown to Ptolemy, and arrayed him in his purple robe, and said to him, "Go before me, as if thou wert king, and call me Antôgnâyâ [Antigonus], the chief of the host." And when they had gone out, Alexander spake before Ptolemy these words which he had heard. So Ptolemy went forth and looked upon the troops; and the troops thought that it was Alexander, and grief and trouble fell upon their hearts, and they said one to another, "What else pray is this Alexander who is rich in plans meditating?" When Candaules saw this, fear took hold of him, for he thought, "Peradventure they will slay me." And Ptolemy gave orders and questioned Alexander after the manner of kings, saying, "Antigonus, who is this man?" Antigonus said, "This is Candaules, the son of queen Candace, from whom, while he was journeying along the way, the chief of the Marnîkâyê carried off his wife by force; what, O king, dost thou counsel and command me to do?" The king said, "I counsel and command thee that thou shouldst take my troops, and go and fight with the Mârônikâyê, and deliver his wife from thence. On account of the dignity and wisdom of Candace his mother, thou shalt rescue his wife, and give her back to him."

---

different readings ܠܡܪܘܢܟܝܐ, ܠܡܐܪܘܢܟܝܐ, ܠܡܪܘܢܩܝܐ, ܠܡܪܘܢܩܝܐ, the second is perhaps the best, and may mean the people of Mârô or Merv.

When Candaules heard this, he was glad. Antigonus said, "Since it is pleasing to thee, O king, I will go and carry out this matter; only do thou give orders that they supply me with troops."

X. Then Ptolemy in the guise of Alexander commanded troops to go with Antigonus. Antigonus came to that place while it was yet day, and said to Candaules: "Come, let us hide ourselves on one side until it is the night, for if the Mûrkâyê see us, they will speedily tell their chief, and he in his anger will slay the woman before the fight, and what joy will there be in our victory when thy wife is dead? Let us tarry now, and enter the city at night; and we will set fire to it, and in the midst of the crush in the city, they shall bring thy wife to thee, for our fight is not with the country, neither is it for the government of the city, but for the sake of bringing back one woman." When Antigonus had spoken these words, Candaules fell upon his face and made obeisance to him, saying, "How admirable is this wisdom and knowledge of thine, Antigonus! It were right that thou thyself shouldst be Alexander, and not merely the chief of the host." When it was night, they went to the city; and when the people of the city were awakened out of their sleep and asked concerning the cause of the conflagration, Alexander commanded his troops to shout with a loud voice, "It is Candaules the king with his vast army, and he commands you, saying, 'Either restore my wife to me, or I will burn your whole city with fire.'" Then the people by reason of their fear went in a great crowd to the palace of their chief, and carried off the woman from his bed, and brought her and gave her to Candaules. Then he made obeisance to Antigonus, and praised his counsel, and thanked him, and they returned together to the camp of Alexander. And Candaules embraced Antigonus, and said to him, "O my lord, trust thyself to me and come with me to my mother that I may give thee gifts." Then Antigonus rejoicing at this speech said to him, "Ask permission for me from the king, for I myself am desirous to come and see the city." Then he sent to the king saying, "Send Antigonus as an ambassador to my mother." Ptolemy called Candaules and said to him, "Do thou, O Candaules, salute thy mother in writing, and receive Antigonus my general

as ambassador, and send him back to me too in health, for he
restored thee along with thy wife, and will carry thee to thy
mother." And Candaules said, "O king, I accept this man
from thee on these conditions, as if he were Alexander, and I
will send him back to thy kingdom to thee in health with gifts."

XI. Then Alexander took with him one division of the
army, with cattle and chariots, and went. And as they were
marching along the road, they saw a mountain of beryls, which
in its height reached the clouds, and it was thickly crowded
with lofty trees and fruits, but its trees were not like the trees
which are in the country of the Greeks. The apples for
example which we saw were as large as the citrons which are in
the country of the Greeks; the clusters of grapes were like the
clusters of dates in our country; and the nuts were as big as
melons. Snakes were coiled round the greater number of the
trees, and each of them was as big as a ferret with us; the apes
upon the trees were larger than bears with us; and there were
a number of animals of different kinds; and the mountains
were the caves and paths of ibexes. Then Candaules said to
me, "Antigonus, this place is the temple and dwellingplace of
the gods, and many times they appear in these spots. Now
then, if thou pleasest, when thou art on the way back, offer up
a sacrifice to them that they may reveal themselves to thee."
When Candaules had said this, we journeyed on and arrived
at the royal palace. And when we drew near, his mother and
brethren came to meet us; and when they wished to embrace
Candaules, he said to them, "First of all salute the saviour and
deliverer of myself and wife, Antigonus, the ambassador of
Alexander king of peace." And when he went on to tell them
severally of the carrying away of his wife and of the assistance
which came from Alexander's army and of the knowledge and
wisdom of Antigonus, his mother and brethren embraced and
kissed Antigonus, and prepared a great and splendid feast for
him, and they ate.

XII. On the following day Candace put on the royal
apparel, and set the crown upon her head, and was so
ornamented that, when Alexander saw her, he thought that he
was looking upon Olympias his mother. The whole roof of the
house in which she sat was painted with gold, and its walls

were all set with precious stones and gems, and the cushions which were in the house were all woven with silk and fine gold; the legs of the couches were of magnificent beryls, and the tables in the house were of ivory, and the pillars of the house, their bases and their capitals, were made of precious beryl stones; statues of Corinthian brass stood upon the tops of the pillars, and the pillars were of purple stone, and representations of chariots and of men were engraved upon them; and these carvings were so marvellous that every one who saw them thought that the horses were going to run. Some of the stones were wrought in the form of elephants, which were standing in battle and holding enemies in their trunks. Statues of all the gods of the nations stood round the whole house, and others were standing on pillars; and the roof of their house appeared from the inside as if all the plane-trees and cedars of the earth were growing there; and there was the representation of a lake round about it, so that the whole house was reflected by the waters that were painted in it. When Antigonus (that is to say Alexander) saw this, he marvelled and wonder laid hold on him. And Candaules entreated his mother that gifts and offerings should be given to this ambassador as befitted the greatness of his knowledge. Then on the following day Candace took Alexander by the hand, and led him into a chamber. The whole chamber was inlaid with white marble like the heavens, and by reason of the splendour of the marble every one who saw it thought that the sun was shining in it; and the beams of the roof were of a wood which they call ôbmiôn[1], which wood no woodworm attacks, neither does it burn in fire. The foundations of the house were not laid upon the ground, but upon square beams which were very thick; and beneath it, at its four corners, were chariot wheels, and elephants were drawing them; and whithersoever the queen went to war, she dwelt in it and lived in it. Then Alexander said to Candace, "O queen, all these things would be worthy of admiration, if they were in the country of the Greeks, but here they are not very marvellous, for there are many mountains like these here, in which are to be found beryl stones

[1] Perhaps a corruption of the Greek word ἀμίαντος, as the text (Müller, p. 132, col. 1) has the words ἐξ ἀμιάντου φύλων.

of divers colours and variegated in many ways." Candace
answered with indignation and said to him, "Thou hast spoken
rightly, Alexander." When Alexander heard that Candace
called him by his own name, he was troubled and he turned
his face backward. Candace said to him, "Wherefore dost thou
turn thy face backwards because I called thee by thy name
Alexander?" Alexander said, "My lady, Antigonus is my name,
and Alexander is the king who sent me hither." Candace said,
"I know that Alexander is the king, and thou thyself art Alexander, and now I recognise thee from the look of thy picture;"
and straightway she took him by the hand and led him into
another chamber, and shewed him the likeness, and said to
him, "See if thou canst recognise the face in this painting."
When Alexander saw the painting of himself, his mind was
perturbed, and he began to gnash his teeth. Candace said to
him, "Why art thou troubled, and why dost thou gnash thy
teeth at me, O bearer (of the sovereignty) of the Persians and
Indians, who hast gained the victory over the Persians, and
triumphed over the Parthians? Without war and without an
army hast thou now fallen into the hands of queen Candace.
Know then, Alexander, that it is not right for a man to glorify
himself in his mind as though all wisdom and knowledge
belonged to him alone, for though his wisdom be very great, one
may be found who is wiser than he." When Alexander heard
this, he stood up in a rage and gnashed his teeth, and Candace
spake thus to him: "Why art thou angry? and for what reason
dost thou gnash thy teeth, O thou who art so great a king?"
Alexander replied: "I am a wretched man, inasmuch as I have
no sword." Candace said to him: "Suppose thou hadst a
sword, what wouldst thou be able to do?" Alexander said: "If
I had a sword, I would either slay thee, that thou mightest no
longer be in the world, or I would stab myself, because I of my
own freewill have exposed myself to ridicule." Candace said to
him: "Thou hast spoken these words also valiantly and
royally; but now weary not thyself, neither let thy mind nor
thy will be perturbed, for as thou hast rescued my son and my
daughter-in-law, and hast brought them in safety to me, so also
will I protect thee from the barbarians, and will send thee away
from here under the name of Antigonus. For if the barbarians

should hear that thou art Alexander, they will slay thee, because thou didst slay Porus the king of the Indians, for my daughter-in-law is a daughter of Porus. Henceforward let thy name be called Antigonus, and I will keep this secret."

XIII. And when she had spoken these words to him, they both went out; and she called her son and daughter-in-law and said to them, "Son Candaules, and thou too, my daughter Mâlâpsâ', had ye not obtained the help of Alexander's troops, we should never have seen one another, neither you me, nor I you. Now therefore it is right that thou shouldst send this ambassador of Alexander's away from here with honour and glory." Then her other son Kĕrâtôr² said: "My mother, Alexander has delivered my brother and his wife; but my wife is angry and says, 'Alexander slew my father Porus, and I now desire that thou wilt slay this ambassador of Alexander to avenge my father'." Candace said: "My son, what profit wilt thou gain by this, that this ambassador be slain here? for though thou shouldst slay this ambassador here, Alexander will not be grieved." Candaules said: "I will not allow him to die, because he delivered myself and my wife, and it is right that I should send him away (safe) from hence to Alexander." Then Kĕrâtôr said, "If thou send this man away from here, there will be war between thee and me." Candaules said, "I do not desire this; but if thou seekest war, I too am ready." Now Candace was in great trouble and affliction because of this matter, for she thought that peradventure her sons would fight with one another on this account, so she called Alexander privily and said to him: "O Alexander, thou hast been on every occasion astute and abundant in knowledge and fertile in expedients and skilled in contrivances; and now art thou able to do nothing to prevent these my sons fighting with one another for thy sake?" Then Alexander answered and said: "Hear ye, Kĕrâtôr and Candaules; if ye slay me here, do not imagine that Alexander will be distressed on my account, or that he will sorrow for me, (though it is not right to

¹ The Gr. Codex A has μαρίρσα, the others ἀρσινσα, ἀρσινα, or ἀρσινσα, the Latin translation *Margis* (see Müller, p. 133, col. 2).

² Called in the Latin translation *Charagos* (Müller, *loc. cit.*). In the Greek MSS. no name is given.

kill an ambassador even in war,) because, if ye slay me here, Alexander has many ambassadors like me. But if ye desire that I should deliver Alexander into your hands without trouble, I am able to do it; but do you now promise me what ye will give me, and how many towns and cities ye will give, that henceforward I may live with you in this country, and I will go and persuade Alexander to come hither, as if ye had asked him that ye might honour him with great and excellent offerings; and I know that I am able to bring him hither without any body of troops, and when he comes here, ye can easily take him and revenge yourselves on him." When Kĕrâtôr heard these words of his, he was persuaded and promised Alexander a number of his own towns. Then Candace, marvelling at the knowledge and understanding of Alexander, called him secretly and said to him, "O Alexander, would that thou also wert my son, for by the knowledge and wisdom which thou hast thou art able to subdue all nations." And next day Candace dismissed Alexander and gave him gifts, a royal crown of gold set with ......[1] and a breastplate of gold set with beryls and chalcedonies and other precious stones, and a purple cloak like stars woven with gold; and she sent some of her own horsemen with him.

XIV. Then he went forth from thence and arrived at the hill of which Candaules had told him that it belonged to the gods. He offered sacrifices in that place, and he went into a cave, and saw in that cave a blackness out of the midst of which stars were shining, and suddenly he heard behind him a noise of dead bodies[2] and the sound of an uproar. Then Alexander trembled and stood up silently to see what it was; and suddenly the darkness disappeared, and he saw the form of a man reclining upon a couch, and his eyes were like sparkling stars. And he said to Alexander, "Peace be with thee, Alexander; dost thou know who I am?" Alexander said, "Nay, my lord, nay." Then he said to him, "I am Sĕsânḳôs (Sesonchosis), the ruler of the world, and from the time that I

---

[1] I do not know what ܣܘܼܟܿܘܿܠܠ means. The Greek text is στέφανον διαδήτων χρόνων (Müller, p. 134, col. 2).

[2] So in the Syriac.

died I am with the gods; I, who am immortal, am not so renowned as thou art." Alexander said to him, "How so, my lord?" He said to him: "I took the whole world and subdued a number of nations, yet now there is no remembrance of me on earth; but thou art renowned on account of the city of Alexandria the Great which thou hast built; thy name will be famed for ever. But now come within and see the Maker of all natures." And when Alexander had gone within, he saw a fiery cloud and the great god Serapis seated upon a throne. And Alexander said, "My lord, I saw thee in the vision at Thebes as thou didst sit, and behold I see thee here too." Then Sesonchosis said, "My lord Serapis dwells in one place, but reveals himself everywhere." Then Alexander said, "My lord, how many years longer shall I live?" Sesonchosis said: "It is well for mortal man when the day of his death is hidden from him; for when he learns when his death shall take place, from the day that he knows concerning his death he considers himself as already dead. But as for thee, when thou establishest and completest a great and famous city, thou shalt enter it, whether with death or without death, and the people of the city will receive thee, and will do reverence to thee as to a god, and thy grave shall be in that spot."

XV. When Alexander had heard these words from the messenger (or angel), he set out on his road, and the generals of his forces came to him on the way, and straightway put his crown upon him, and arrayed him in royal apparel. Now Alexander had made ready to go to the country of the Amziôs (Amazons), which was the land of women. These Amazons are women, who have one breast like a man's and one like a woman's. When Alexander drew near and had arrived in the country of the Amazons, he composed a letter and wrote to them as follows: "From Alexander to the Amazons greeting. Ye have heard concerning the war which we had with Darius, and of that with Porus the king of the Indians, and how I slew them. And after I had slain them, I went to the country of the Indians, and saw there the Brahmans and their sages, and received tribute from them, and allowed them to remain in their own land, and they sacrificed to the gods on my behalf. And I turned away from them, and now I have made ready to

come to you.  Come ye then to meet me and receive me, for I
am not coming to make war nor to do anything evil; but I
come to see your country, and I will benefit you."

When they had read the letter, they wrote him an answer
as follows: " From the Amazons and the chiefs of the hosts of
our camp to Alexander greeting.  We write to thee that thou
mayest know, before thou comest hither and before thou
enterest our country, that perhaps when thou comest hither,
thou wilt be obliged against thy will to retreat and turn back.
In this letter too we will inform thee of all our affairs, and
what is the condition of our country, and in what state it is.
By our nature we are women, but owing to our bravery we are
superior to men.  We live upon an island in the sea Meznikos',
and there is a sea round about it, the beginning and end of
which are unknown, and there is only one place of crossing
over to us.  We who dwell in the island are in name virgins,
and are in number two hundred and eighty thousand.  We
have no man with us, and no male is found among us; for
our husbands live on the other side of the sea.  At the time of
the year when we slay horses and offer sacrifices to Zeus and to
Hephaestos, during that festival we cross over to the other side
of the sea, and we make a feast together with the men for
thirty days, and those who wish to stay with their husbands
stay.  She that conceives remains where she is until she gives
birth to a child; and if she bears a female, she leaves it with
fosterers on the other side of the sea for seven years, and
then they bring her over to this side to us.  Should any
unfriendly people come against us in battle, and it be necessary
for us to make war with them, we go forth to battle one
hundred and thirty thousand strong upon equipped horses, and
the remainder keep watch in the camps and on the islands.
Our husbands come after us; and if it happen that some
women of us die while we are doing battle with the enemy, our
husbands take their bodies and carry them to the islands.  If
the troops of the enemy be mighty and powerful and numerous,
and do battle with us for many days, should any of our women

¹ No doubt corrupted from 'Αμαζονιs.  In the Arabic version بكر (are)
might stand for river, as in بكر النيل.

lay any of the enemies' host, we give them a crown from the
altar of Zeus. If it fall out that we rout an enemy who is
stronger than we, and that they are conquered by us, it is a
great disgrace to those mighty and powerful enemies that they
are conquered by the hands of women and turn their backs in
flight; but on the other hand, should it happen that the enemy
has the advantage over us in war, and we turn and come to
our islands in discomfiture, it is not accounted a brave deed to
those men, neither is their victory deemed creditable to them,
because it is merely women whom they have conquered. Do
thou therefore consider this, for peradventure it may happen
thus even to thee. My lord the king, if it please thee, retire,
and we will each year give thee as a gift what is right. Do
thou then make a reply to our letter on this subject as thou art
bound to do, and we are in our camp on this summit[1] prepared
and ready."

XVI. When Alexander had read this letter, he smiled, and
ordered an answer to be made to this letter of theirs as
follows: "King Alexander to the Amazons greeting. We
have taken and subdued three ends of the world, and have
been victorious over them; and now it would be a great
disgrace to us if we did not come to your country. Now,
if ye desire your own destruction and that of the rest of the
people in your land, remain where ye are upon the top of
the mountain[2]: but if ye desire to live and to dwell in your
country, and are not desirous to experience a trial of our
strength, cross over to this side, and [come to] see us with your
husbands in the plain, and receive us, and I swear by the soul
of my mother and by the fortune of Hêra the mother of the
gods, and by Athênê the lady of battles, and by Artemis the
great goddess, that I will do no evil unto you. But whatever
tribute ye are willing to give for the benefit of my troops, I
will accept it from you. Let as many horsewomen as ye please
come to my army, and I will give each of you five dinârs as
the pay of each month, besides the food of the horsewomen
and of the horses; and I will keep them in my army one

---

[1] Müller's text has καὶ εὑρήσεις ἡμᾶς τὴν παρεμβολὴν ἐπὶ τῶν ὀρέων (p. 137,
col. 1) but the translator evidently read ὀρέων for ὁρίων.

[2] Reading again ἐπὶ τῶν ὀρέων for ὁρίων.

year, and then I will send them away to their own places,
and do ye send others in their stead."

When this letter had been read and they had taken counsel
among themselves, they made answer to him as follows: "From
the chiefs of the Amazons and all the generals to Alexander
greeting.  We grant thee power to come and see our country.
And afterwards we will give to thee each year a thousand
pounds of gold for a crown; and those who bring them to thee
shall remain in thy camp a year.  If it should happen that any
of them fall in love with men, let them marry them and dwell
in the land.  Do thou send to us the number of the women who
die and of those who remain, that we may send to thee other
women in their stead.  And henceforward we will obey thee
far or near, for we have heard of thy excellence and thy goodness
and thy might and thy power.  And what are we more than
the rest of the world that we should not receive thee as lord ?
Farewell."

XVII.  Then Alexander made ready, and when he drew
near to the country of the Amazons, Zeus rained so great a
rain upon them that the hoofs of all the cattle and horses
rotted away by reason of the quantity of rain, and the saddles
of the horses and the packsaddles of the cattle were destroyed.
After the rain had ceased, a fierce and powerful heat came upon
us, which no one of us was able to endure; and then came
lightnings and thunderings and mighty sounds from heaven to
such a degree that many of the horsemen fell upon their faces
through fear.  When we had crossed over the river[1] Zûtâ (?)
and saw the country, the whole country was decorated with
temples and altars, like the land of the Indians.  When we saw
the abundant rain, we remembered the snow which fell upon us
in the country of Prasiakê; and when the people that were dwelling in that land saw all the rain and the ill, they said that
it happened because of Alexander.  They came to Alexander
and said to him, "O good king, depart from our land, and
we will give thee sixty mighty elephants trained to war and
one hundred thousand chariots."  Then Alexander gave orders
to accept them from them, and he departed thence.  Then

---

[1] In the Syriac ܢܗܪ, read = ܢܗܪ.

those five hundred horsewomen came to meet him, bringing
the gold, and they stood in Alexander's presence and laid the
gold before him.    When Alexander had seen the country of the
Amazons, he ordered sacrifices to be offered to all the gods that
were in the land.

And he set out from thence, and on the way a letter met
him.  "From Aristotle to Alexander greeting.  I have heard
that thou hast laboured in many battles and wars, and that
thou hast also taken and subdued a number of countries and
many cities.  Thou hast been able to do all these things by the
aid of the gods, for at present thou art but thirty years of age,
and by the assistance of the gods thou hast performed such
deeds as no other lord has been able to do in a number of years.
Therefore thou art under many obligations to the gods, and now
the time has come for thee to pay them back with sacrifice and
incense, for great is thy debt to the gods who have honoured
thee, and thou wilt not be able to pay it in a short time."

When Alexander had read this letter, he and his host
returned to Babylon.    And when he had drawn near to
Babylon, he wrote a letter to his mother Olympias in which he
wrote as follows.  "From Alexander to Olympias my mother,
greeting.  In a former letter I informed thee accurately concerning the things which I did previously, from the beginning
as far as the country of Asia ; and now it appears to me that I
ought to inform thee by writing of all that took place afterwards,
after I arrived at Babylon.  I Alexander took my forces [con-
sisting of] brave and mighty warriors one hundred thousand,
and I made ready to depart from Babylon.    In ninety-five days
I arrived at the cave of Hêraklês, and I saw two statues, one
of gold and the other of silver ; the length of each was twelve
cubits and the breadth two cubits ; and I did not believe them to
be solid but [thought that they were] cast.   Then I commanded
the troops of my army to halt, and I sacrificed to Hêraklês,
and I ordered the golden statue to be bored with a borer; and
when I perceived that it was all of gold and that it was solid,
I commanded that the shavings from the boring should be
weighed, and they weighed one thousand three hundred mithḳâls
of gold.    And we set out from thence and marched to a mountainous place, and came to a broken country, and in that place

the darkness was so dense that the troops were unable to see one another. We remained in that place seven days, and from thence we came to a warm region. In that place there was a great river in a level plain, and on the banks of that river women dwelt in the guise of Amazons, but they surpassed the Amazons in their bodies and their beauty; they were clothed in black garments, and they all went armed on horseback; and all their arms were of silver, for in the place where they dwelt there was neither iron nor brass. They dwelt on the bank of the river on the other side, and when we came to the bank of the river, we found no crossing whereby we might pass over to the other side, for the river was very deep and very wide, and upon its bank on this side there were a number of savage animals. These women crossed over to this side of the river by night and carried off some men of my troops, and we were unable to cross over [after them] to the other side.

XVIII   And from thence we departed and began to come to the shore of a great sea; and we arrived at a place on the right of which was a high mountain, and on the left the sea; and in that place we sacrificed a number of white horses to Poseidon, the divinity[1] of the sea, and we made a hunt there. And from thence we departed to a place, the ground of which was not visible to us by reason of the darkness and blackness; and thenceforward there was no land. We found five ships, and having embarked in them we put to sea. On the third day we arrived at a city, of which they say that it is the city of the sun, and the circumference of that city is twenty miles. In the middle of it was an altar, and upon it there was a chariot, which was made of fine gold and emeralds, and a priest of the sun stood upon it; and in that place we sacrificed to the sun. From thence we came a journey of one day, and found a great darkness, and there was no road, so I gave orders to light branching[2] lamps of silver, and to carry them before my troops. And we retired from thence and arrived at the river Sakhan[3], which divides Asia and Europe; and thence we made ready and came to the palace of Khusrau and king Pâkôr[4]; and in that

[1] Literally, *the luck* or *good fortune*.
[2] Literally, *outspread*.
[3] In Cod. A and the Latin version, *Tanais* (Müller, p. 141, note 13).
[4] In Cod. A and the Latin version, *Xerxes and Cyrus* (Müller, *loc. cit.*).

palace we saw a number of ingenious things which are needed
for great purposes. And there was a room made within it,
and a statue of one of the gods of the Greeks stood there, and
they say that at the time that king Xerxes was alive, when
any of his enemies were preparing to come to his land with
war and battle, a voice issued from this statue. And a cage
of gold was suspended from the ceiling of the room, within
which cage a golden dove was confined; and they say that
when the voice came from the statue in the speech of men,
this dove interpreted it. When I desired to take this dove
from thence and to send it to the country of the Greeks, they
said to me, ' Do not take it, because this dove counsels this
god.' And I also saw something worthy of admiration in the
palace of Shôshan the fortress; for I saw there large globes
of silver, each of which, they say, would hold three hundred
and sixty measures of wine, and on the outside round about
there were carved horses and their riders fighting, and in the
middle the gods sitting in assembly; and they say that they
brought these globes from Egypt, the country of Zeus, at the
time when the Persians were masters over Egypt. When I
desired to know how great were these globes, I offered
sacrifices to the gods, and commanded one of the globes to be
filled with wine, and I gave orders to my troops to sit down,
and at that meal there was not used more than one globe
full of wine. Now when they had consumed the wine, it
happened according to what I had heard. And I entered a
large house, and I found there a very large cup, and upon
it was carved [a representation of] the battle which king
Xerxes fought in ships with the Greeks. And in the house
a seat of gold was placed, which was set with gems, and there
was a sort of canopy over it, and a golden harp with strings
was placed upon it; and they said that this harp used to play
of itself, without anyone striking it. Around [the throne]
were thirty cups of gold, and it had eight steps, and over
it there stood a golden eagle whose wings spread over the
whole of it. A root was there like a vine, out of which
sprouted seven shoots, and the bunches of grapes were wholly
of fine gold set with gems. But why need I write to thee
of the abundance of the gold and silver? Gold and silver

are so abundant that I am unable to describe the quantity
thereof."

XIX.[1]  When he had sent this letter to Olympias his
mother from Babylon, the day of his death was come, and a
sign to this effect happened as follows. A certain woman,
one of the inhabitants of that country, gave birth to a child,
who from his buttocks upwards had the form of a man, and
from his buttocks downwards a number of forms of animals,
all of them separate, that is to say, a lion, a leopard, a wolf,
and a wild dog, all the heads apart and separate; they were
so well defined that every one who saw them knew at once to
what beast each head belonged; and the human body died as
soon as it was born. Then the woman, as soon as she had
given birth to it, covered it over and carried it to the palace
of Alexander; and she said to one of Alexander's servants,
" Speak to him about bringing me into his presence, that I
may shew the king a wonderful sign, the like of which he has
never seen." Now Alexander was asleep within, and it was
noon; and when he had been roused up from his sleep, and had
heard concerning the woman, he commanded that she should
be brought in before him. Then the woman said, " Give orders,
O king, that every one go forth from before thee." And
when every one had gone forth from the king's presence,
she uncovered it and exhibited it before the king, saying to
him, " Look upon this prodigy, O king, to which I have
given birth." When Alexander had seen it, wonder and
amazement laid hold on him, and he straightway commanded the Chaldeans who were skilled in portents to be
called. When they came, he said to them, " Tell me exactly
what this sign indicates, for if ye do not speak the truth, your
heads shall be taken off." Then one of those skilled in
portents sighed, and having waited a little said to the king,
" O king, thou wilt not live any longer, and they do not allow
thee to remain among the number of the living, as this sign
portends." When Alexander heard this, he praised him and
said, " Explain how thou understandest this sign." He

[1] Corresponding to ch. xxx. of the Greek text (ch. xxix. is wanting in the
Syriac). See Müller, p. 148, col. 2.

said to him, "O ruler of all men, the sign is thus: this human body and this child are thyself, and these bodies of beasts are all the nations  As soon as it was born, this human body died, while those of all the beasts are alive.  Now thou, O king, who art lord of all nations, art about to die, whilst they all, being alive, will escape from under thy hands.  Therefore, O king, when I saw that this sign referred to thee, I was deeply grieved."  When he had spoken these words, he went forth from Alexander's presence; and the woman took the child, and carried it out, and burned it with fire.  When Alexander had heard all these things, he was in grief and trouble, and sighing, he said, "O Zeus, it would have been right that I should have finished all my plans and then died; but since it has appeared good to thee thus, command that they receive me as the third dead."  This speech he said for this reason: Dionysus was a man, and because of the name and fame and power that he made for himself, he was reckoned when dead among the number of the gods; and in like manner Hêraklês; therefore Alexander spake of himself as 'the third dead,' because these had not gained such name and fame and might as Alexander.

XX.  At this time Olympias the mother of Alexander sent him a letter containing an accusation against Antipater, and Alexander was very grieved because of his mother's anger against Antipater.  When Antipater knew that Alexander was angry with him, and became aware that he wished to slay him, he sent Alexander a quantity of gold.  Alexander commanded that it should be accepted; but although he took the gold, he did not set right his mind with Antipater. When Antipater knew the secret plans that Alexander had formed against him, he dissolved a deadly drug in a vessel, and gave some of it to his son Keshandrôs (Cassander), and furnished him with many offerings and sent him to Alexander, bidding him to seek some means and in one way or other to give the poison to Alexander.  When Cassander arrived at Babylon, he found Alexander offering sacrifices, and a feast was prepared for the generals of the provinces.  Then Cassander drew near to Ôliyâs (Iollas), the chief of the king's cup-bearers, and entered into a secret plot with him.  Now

this Iollas had been scourged a few days before for some cause
by Alexander, so that his mind was excited against him, and
therefore Cassander found an opportunity against Alexander.
They took Mitrôn (Médius) with them into the secret—now
this Mitrôn was Alexander's chief friend—, and he took upon
himself to administer the poison to him. When Alexander
and his friends were sitting at table and were drinking and
talking cheerfully — now on that day Alexander was very
merry, for many of his friends had come to him from various
countries, and had brought him crowns of victory—after they
had finished the meal, Mitrôn drew near to Alexander and
said to him, " O king, since to-day thou hast had great joy
with the rest (?) of thy friends, bid thy dearest friends, who
love thee most, to drink wine with thee in a chamber." When
Alexander heard the speech of Mitrôn, he ordered Priskôs,
Markânos, Lôsios (Lysias), Pritôn, Rêkithâros, Ksîdâros (Cassiodôrus), Nicolaus, Krimîos, Harklitandîs, Tarkânâ, Philip,
and Mônîdâros (Menander) to be invited[1]. Now of all these
persons only Priskôs, Krimîos, Harklitandîs, Cassiodôrus, and
Lysias, were unacquainted with the secret, but all (the rest)
were eager participators in it, and were with Iollas the chief of
the cup-bearers and Cassander in the matter, and had sworn
oaths among themselves. When Alexander had sat down, and
they had all taken their seats in his presence, Iollas the chief
of the cup-bearers mixed the poison and gave the cup to
Alexander. When Alexander had drunk, he straightway felt
great pain; he immediately commanded some of that wine to
be brought and to be poured out to all his friends. Although
he was grievously tortured by the intensity of the pain, he
bore up and was neither excited nor alarmed ; and his friends
also continued drinking. After his friends had gone out from
his presence, he thought that perchance he was seized with
pain by reason of the quantity that he had drunk, and he took
birds' feathers and put them into his throat, for so he was accustomed to do from time to time. After he perceived that
nothing did him good, for the poison had flown through all

---

[1] Most of these names are horribly corrupt. See the Greek text, Müller,
p. 144.

his body, he was unable to restrain his groans, for the pain was too strong for his body. On the following day at dawn he desired to take counsel with his friends, but he was unable to make a testament, because his tongue was paralysed. Then Cassander wrote to Macedonia to his father Antipater, "the deed for which I came hither has taken place, and has received a glorious consummation."

When Alexander had been seized at Babylon with a grievous sickness, he commanded at night every one to go forth from the chamber in which he was lying, and he also commanded Rôshnâḳ (Roxana) his wife to go to another chamber[1]. Now one of the doors of the house opened on to the river Euphrates, and he ordered that door to be opened, and said, "There is no need for the guards to keep their watch." When every one had gone forth and it was mid-night, he rose up from his bed, and extinguished the lamp which was burning before him and went forth by that door, and crawled on his hands and feet to the bank of the river, and was going to cast himself in. Then his wife Rôshnâḳ hastened at once and took hold of him, and with weeping and loud and mournful sighs said to him, "Hast thou left me, Alexander, and art thou become thine own executioner? Bitter is the lot which has fallen to my share, and evil and cruel is that which has happened to me by fate. I was left an orphan by my father Darius in my childhood, and now in my youth I shall be left by thee a widow." Then Alexander said, "Be not distressed, O Rôshnâḳ, for everything happens in its season; but be silent, and tell this secret to no one." Then Rôshnâḳ took Alexander by the hand and led him back to his bed. And when it was day, Alexander commanded Ḳrisḳôs[2], and Lysias, and Ptolemy to come into his presence alone, and every one else to be put out[3]. And they came into his presence. Then he ordered a testament to be written. And Ḳrisḳôs was doubtful in his mind, for he thought, "Peradventure he will give all his possessions to Ptolemy alone, for he loved him very much during his life, and Olympias

---

[1] For what follows see Müller, p. 146, note 1 on ch. xxxii.
[2] A little above the name was written Prisḳôs.
[3] See Meusel, p. 780, at the foot.

his mother loved him." Then Ķrī·ķôs swore an oath with
Ptolemy, "If Alexander gives all his property to me, thou
shalt have one half of it; and if he gives it to thee, do thou
give me a half." And having written the document, they
were commanded to write the testament.

XXI. Then a report of an uproar and tumult among
the Macedonian soldiers was heard; and they all came clothed
in armour to the gate of Alexander, for they thought that
Alexander had not been seized with sickness, but that the
generals of the army had slain him by treachery; and they
were going to fall upon them and kill them. When Alexander
heard the outcry and uproar, he asked, "What is this disturbance?" Then Ķriskôs informed him concerning the uproar
and tumult. When Alexander heard of the real love and
affection of the Macedonian soldiers towards himself, he ordered them to carry him and to convey him to the hippodrome.
And he commanded that the troops of the Macedonian
camps should be armed, and that they should pass before
him in their suits of armour. Then Ķriskôs went out from
before the king, and told the Macedonians, and convinced
them that Alexander was not dead, but had been seized by
sickness. "But (said he) put ye on your armour, and go to
the royal hippodrome, for there ye are to pass before him in
review." When the Macedonians heard this, they girded on
their armour and went to the hippodrome. And they carried
Alexander thither on his bed. So the Macedonians passed
in their armour before Alexander; and when they lifted
up their eyes and saw Alexander, suddenly the colour of
their faces was changed, and their hearts were so oppressed
by weeping and mourning that, in the face of that sadness
and suffering and grief mingled with sighs, even the light of the
sun became obscure and dark. Then Pināķlêôs (Phainoclês?),
an old Macedonian warrior and hero, wept aloud when he saw
Alexander, and said to Alexander in the Greek tongue, "O
king, doer of good things, Philip thy father ruled over us
kindly and firmly, and thou too, O king, hast been likewise
good and merciful and kind to us. But since we love thee,
and thy rule is pleasing to us, and we desire and enjoy it,
why dost thou wish to forsake us, and to part from us and

to leave us? for through thy departure from us all Macedonia will be destroyed, and by thy death we ourselves will all perish. It is better that we should die with thee, for thou hast made us renowned and famous; through thee we have subdued countries and kingdoms, and through thee we have brought enemies into subjection. Henceforth what is the good to us of weapons of iron and brass, when we have lost thee, O most skilled in weapons? With thee we have marched through deserts and dark mountains, through rough and difficult and hard and impassable places; and now we will go to the next world with thee." When he had spoken these words, tears streamed down from Alexander's eyes, and each one of the Macedonians drew his sword and was going to slay himself. Then Alexander sprang up from the couch on which he lay, and sat upon the cushions, and said to the Macedonians, "O my servants and friends and fellow-soldiers, why do ye add pain to pain so that I should taste death by dying before my own death?" Then he commanded the troops of the Macedonians to go to their camps, and he bade them bear him upon his bed and carry him to his palace.

XXII. Then they bore him and carried him to his palace, and he commanded Priskôs to bring the testament and to read it before him. Then Archelaus the scribe brought the testament, and in it there was written as follows: From Alexander to Ammon and to my mother Olympias, greeting. Inasmuch as the gods have willed that I should be taken from the assembly and dwelling of men to the assemblies and dwellings of the gods, I too have thought that it would be expedient and helpful for me, and I have thought that it would be right for me to inform you thereof. Do thou then, my mother, not be grieved nor distressed at my departure, for such is the will of God, but console thyself in thy wisdom and be glad. I have appointed and sent all my generals for thy honour that they may make thee exceedingly glad. I Alexander in this testament command: the Macedonians and the Greeks shall keep themselves in training and guard the country from enemies and be always vigilant; they shall keep the temples of the gods and the royal palace, and preserve them in prosperity and in joy. Let there be given every year to the princes that are in Egypt darics [to the amount of] one hundred pounds from the crops and taxes of the country, for I have commanded my body to be carried thither; and let the expenses which are requisite and necessary for the grave in which my body is laid be given to the priests according to their desire from the revenues of the kingdom. I also command that the offence wherewith the Thebans offended me be forgiven them, and that three hundred talents of gold be given them for the restoration of their city. I also command that there be given from Egypt every year twenty thousand bushels of wheat, and from Asia twenty thousand bushels. I also command that Krêtênôr (Craterus) shall be ruler and governor of the Macedonians; and over Egypt shall be Ptolemy; and over Asia Kriskôs (Perdiccas). I also command that seventy talents of gold be given to the army of the Macedonians. I also command that Archelaus take this testament and carry it to the temple of the god Ammon. And let there be in the land of Alexandria food and abundance of corn, and let skilful workmen of all kinds be ready, and when Ptolemy comes thither bringing my body, let them prepare quickly a grave for the burial of my body, and let there be no hindrance nor delay to him. I also command that if Rôshnâk (Roxana) my wife give birth to a son, he shall be king, and they shall call his name after one of the kings of the Macedonians, according as they please; but if she give birth to a girl, let the Macedonians choose and set up as king whomsoever they please; and if they find (?) Bêlîrôs the son of Milêkôs (?), he shall be lord over them. Olympias my mother shall dwell in Rhodes, and Lysimachus shall rule over the country of Thrace; and his wife shall rule over the Thessalonians, because she is my sister, the daughter of Philip the king of the Macedonians. Over Hellas Piṭasdrôn (?)[1] shall rule; and over Pamphylia and Lycia Antigonus shall rule; and over Great Phrygia Andreas shall rule; and over Cilicia Piôr (?); and over Syria and as far as the Rivers Pythôn shall rule; and Seleucus clothed in armour shall rule over

---

[1] Most of these names are horribly corrupt. See the Greek text, Müller, p. 145.

this Babylon, and his wife over Nicaea; and Âdîmîs (Eumenês) shall rule over Paphlagonia and Cappadocia; and Mempath (Meleager) shall rule over Phoenicia and Coelosyria; and over Egypt Ptolemy, and Cleopatra the sister of Alexander's wife shall be given to him; and my wife Rôshnâk shall rule from this Babylon of mine to the country of Adôrbaijân and Persia and Media, and I command that she shall be given to Priskôs (Perdiccas) to wife. And I command that they shall make for the interment of my body a coffin of fine gold, two hundred and fifty talents [in weight], and let them lay the body of me Alexander the king of the Macedonians in it; and let them fill it with white honey which has not been melted, and let them deliver it to the Macedonians. Let them send one suit of my royal apparel and my golden throne to the city of Athens, to the temple of the virgins; and let them send all my arms to Persia, with one hundred and fifty talents of gold; and let them send to the temple of the gods which is in Macedonia the dragons' heads of gold [weighing] one hundred talents, and one hundred signet rings of gold, and a thousand ivory cups. [Let them send] one hundred and fifty talents [of gold] to the Philippians (Milesians) for the restoration of their city; and the remainder of the gold and silver, and the whole of the possessions which I have brought from the country of the Indians, let them be given to my mother Olympias. Let them deliver over Sôd—that is to say Samarkand—to Philip; and let them give Abarnshahr and Gurgân to Pîtâpôlis (?), and Garmânîâ (Kermân) to Thlipaitmôs (Tlepolemus); and as for Persia let the lords of the various provinces hold them, and let Pisôn (?) be ruler over them. I also command that they shall bring some of the Dôsîn, who dwell in tents, and call them "sojourners in Alexandria." Now as I have said above, they shall lay my body in a golden coffin, and they shall lift it on to a chariot, and sixteen docile mules shall draw it, and the army of the Macedonians, with Ptolemy and the other generals, shall guard it, and carry it [to Egypt]; and they shall give for the expenses of the journey one thousand talents of gold from the revenue of the kingdom, and for the mules which shall draw the chariot one thousand six hundred talents.

XXIII. When Alexander had given these commands, he

straightway died; and they did even as Alexander had commanded. And when they had taken the body of Alexander and
placed it upon a chariot, all the Macedonians in Babylon began to
make a mourning and outcry with bitter weeping and sore lamentation. And when he had arrived at Mephyâ [Memphis], when
the people of the land heard it, they came to meet him with all
kinds of music, and they praised the body of Alexander with
doleful voices, saying, "Thou art welcome, O god Sîsnâkîs
(Sesonchosis), ruler of the world." They kept the body of
Alexander in that place twelve days, and each day they made
elegies and lamentations and weeping over him afresh; and
they wished to retain his body there. Then the priests of
Serapis said to them, "This body of Alexander must not be laid
here, but they must carry it to the city which he built; for in
the place where the body of Alexander is laid, there will be
wars and contests continually, for in his lifetime he had
continually the desire for war and battle." So Ptolemy made a
grave for the body of Alexander in Alexandria, as he had been
ordered, and there did he lay the body of Alexander; and they
call that place "The tomb of Alexander" unto this day.

XXIV. Alexander waged numerous battles and great wars,
and he defeated and routed and put to flight mighty and
powerful kings. He lived in this world thirty-two years and
seven months, and of these he had rest for only eight years in
this world. He subdued of the barbarians twenty-two kings,
and of the Greeks thirteen. He built thirteen cities, some of
which are flourishing to this day, but some are laid waste. The
first is Alexandria which was built after the name of the horse
called Bucephalus, the interpretation of which is Bull-head; the
second is Alexandria the fortified Rôphôs (?); the third is
Alexandria the Great; the fourth is Alexandria in the dominion
of king Porus; the fifth is Alexandria in the land of
Gôlênîkôs[1]; the sixth is Alexandria in the country of the
Scythians; the seventh is Alexandria on the shore of the sea
(or river); the eighth is Alexandria which is near Babylon; the
ninth is Alexandria which is in the country of Sôd, that is to
say, Samarkand; the tenth is Alexandria which is (called) Kûsh,

---

[1] Apparently "apud Granicum" (Müller, p. 151, col. 3).

that is Balkh; the eleventh is Alexandria which is called Margenîkôs, that is to say Môrô (Merv); the twelfth is Alexandria which is upon the farther bank of the rivers in the country of the Indians; and the thirteenth is Alexandria which is in Egypt[1]. And after Alexander died in Babylon by poison, the name of the day [upon which he died] was called "The slayer of young men," for Alexander was a young man[2]. Alexander reigned as king twelve years and seven months, and there was none among all the kings on earth that fought and made war and conquered like Alexander until the day he died[3].

---

[1] The Greek codices give the names in different order. See Müller, p. 151, col. 1. See also Droysen, *Geschichte des Hellen.* Vol. 2 pp. 591—651 Die Gründungen Alexanders; Pauly *Real Encyclopaedie* Vol. 1, *Art.* Alexandria (twenty-two Alexandrias are here enumerated); Bunbury, *History of Ancient Geography,* Vol. 1, pp. 415, 576, 621, 623, and the map in Vol. 1, facing p. 464. See also the Arabic list in Yâkût's البلدان معجم. ed. Wüstenfeld, 1. p. 100, or in the *Mushtarik,* ed. Wüstenfeld, p. ۲۲, and the list in the "Life of Alexander" published by Prof. Paul de Lagarde, *Analecta Syriaca,* pp. 205—208.

[2] See Müller, p. 152, col. 2, ll. 5, 6.

[3] The scribe adds: "May the Lord God make his soul to rest with the believing kings [DC add "who have trodden in his steps"] the lovers of Christ, and may the hearers and listeners and readers and writers obtain mercy and remission of transgressions and sins. Yea and Amen."

# A CHRISTIAN LEGEND CONCERNING ALEXANDER[1].

An exploit of Alexander the son of Philip the Macedonian, [shewing] how he went forth to the ends of the world, and made a gate of iron[2], and shut it in the face of the north wind, that the Hûnâyê [Huns][3] might not come forth to spoil the countries: from the manuscripts in the house of the archives of the kings of Alexandria.

In the second year, or the seventh, of the reign of Alexander, he set his crown upon his head and arranged himself in his royal apparel, and sent and called those who wore his royal

---

[1] A metrical version of this legend by Jacob of Sěrûgh has been printed by Knös in his *Chrestomathia Syriaca*, pp. 66—107.

[2] This gate was probably made at the Pass of Derbend. See Yule, *The Book of Ser Marco Polo*, Vol. I. p. 51 sqq., and also his notes on Alexander's wall near the Caspian.

[3] ܗܘܢܝܐ, ܗܘܢܝܐ, Οὖννοι, Χοῦνοι. The name Huns is a collective one applied to several nomad Scythian tribes who appear to have belonged to the Mongolian family. The original seat of the Hiong-nu, or Huns, appears to have been in the provinces of Shensi and Shansi in the north-west of China and their power remained unbroken until the year 93 A.C. It was to protect China from the inroads of this barbaric race that the famous wall of China was built about two centuries and a half before our era. See D'Ohsson, *Histoire des Mongols*, t. 1, p. 2. Their early history has been written by de Guignes, *Histoire des Huns*, ii. pp. 1—124. For native Syriac explanations of the name Huns see Payne Smith, *Thes. Syr.* col. 994. See also Gibbon, *Decline and Fall*, chap. xxvi; Wright, *Chronicle of Joshua the Stylite*, p. 9 (Syr. text); Nöldeke, *Geschichte der Perser und Araber zur Zeit der Sasaniden*, p. 72; Karl F. Neumann, *Die Völker des Südlichen Russlands*, pp. 23—30.

:rowns[1], the generals, and Priskos and......[2], and all his forces;
ind he questioned them and said, "Hear, all ye officers of my
palace." They said to him, "Speak, O wise king, king of the
Greeks, and whatsoever thou commandest us shall come to
pass." He said to them : "This thought has arisen in my mind,
ind I am wondering what is the extent of the earth, and how
high the heavens are, and how many are the countries of my
fellow kings, and upon what the heavens are fixed; whether
perchance thick clouds and winds support them, or whether
pillars of fire rise up from the interior of the earth and bear the
heavens so that they move not for anything, or whether they
depend on the beck of God and fall not. Now this I desire to
go and see, upon what the heavens rest, and what surrounds all
creation." The nobles answered and said to the king, "Bid us
speak;" and he commanded them, and they spake and said to
him; "As to the thing, my lord, which thy majesty (or thy
greatness) desires to go and see, namely, upon what the
heavens rest, and what surrounds the earth, the terrible seas
which surround the world will not give thee a passage[3]; because
there are eleven bright seas, on which the ships of men sail, and
beyond these there is about ten miles of dry land, and beyond
these ten miles there is the fœtid sea, Ôkěyânôs (the Ocean),
which surrounds all creation. Men are not able to come near to
this fœtid sea, neither can ships sail thereon, and no bird is
able to fly over it, for if a bird should attempt to fly over it, it
is caught and falls and is suffocated therein[4]. Its waters are
like pus; and if men swim therein, they die at once; and the
leaves of the trees which are by its side are shrivelled up by the
smell of these waters as though fire licked them." So the
nobles spake to king Alexander; but he said to them, "Have ye

[1] Literally knotted, tied, bound.

[2] These words seem to be corrupt. ܩܣܦܝܘ looks like ܩܣܩܝܘ,
an alteration of *Perdiccas* (which we met with above), but we should hardly
expect a single proper name in this place. As for ܣܩ, the word means
nothing in Syriac but *whips*.

[3] See Knös, *Chrestomathia Syr.*, p. 69.

[4] Compare the description of the Asphaltites Lacus by Tacitus (*Hist.* v. 6)
Lacus immenso ambitu, specie maris, sapore corruptior, gravitate odoris accolis
pestifer, neque vento impellitur neque pisces aut suetas aquis volucres patitur.

gone on your own feet and seen that the sea is thus!" They
made answer to him: "Yea, O wise king. This very thing of
which thy majesty has thought occurred to us also, and we
went to see upon what the heavens rest, but the fœtid sea
would not give us a passage." Alexander said to them: "I do
not account you as liars; but although ye went and the sea did
not give you a passage to cross, yet I too will go and see all the
ends of the heavens. If there be a king whose lands are more
than mine I will take his lands and slay him, even if it be one of
the quarters from whence the spoilers come forth." Then all
the officers of his palace accepted what Alexander said to them,
and straightway the trumpets sounded in Alexandria, and the
troops were numbered that went forth with him, three hundred
and twenty thousand men. And king Alexander bowed himself
and did reverence, saying, "O God, Lord of kings and judges,
thou who settest up kings and destroyest their power, I know in
my mind that thou hast exalted me above all kings, and thou
hast made me horns upon my head[1], wherewith I might thrust
down the kingdoms of the world; give me power from thy holy
heavens that I may receive strength greater than [that of] the
kingdoms of the world and that I may humble them, and I will
magnify thy name, O Lord, for ever, and thy memorial shall be
from everlasting to everlasting, and I will write the name of
God in the charter of my kingdom, that there may be for Thee
a memorial always. And if the Messiah, who is the Son of God,
comes in my days, I and my troops will worship Him. And if
He does not come in my days, when I have gone and conquered
kings and seized their lands, I will carry this throne, which is a
seat of silver upon which I sit, and will place it in Jerusalem,
that, when the Messiah comes from heaven, He may sit upon my
kingly throne, for His kingdom lasts for ever. And seven
hundred pounds of gold shall be before the Messiah as a

---

[1] "Possessor of two horns" is a well-known name of Alexander. In the
Ethiopic version Alexander is always referred to as ሕበሰላ: ሰፈርነቲሁ:
"the two horned." See Spiegel, *Die Alexander Sage*, p. 57; Kor'ân, Surah 18.
Some say that the "two horned" mentioned in the Koran is Alexander, while
others say that a contemporary of Abraham is meant, who was king of Persia,
and others that he was a king of Yemen. For a discussion on this point see
*Z.D.M.G.*, vi. s. 506; vIII. ss. 412—450; ix. ss. 214—223.

present when He comes; and whether I die in one of the [other]
regions of the world, or here in Alexandria, my royal crown
shall be taken and hung upon that seat which I have given to
the Messiah; and the crown of every king who dies in
Alexandria shall be taken and hung upon that silver seat which
I give to the Messiah."

And they went forth and came to mount Sinai[1], and encamped
there and rested.  And they put ships to sea[2] and crossed over
to Mesrên, that is to say, Egypt.  And scouts went up and
looked [to see] if the seas and their waves were visible or not.
And the chiefs of the hosts answered and said, "King Alexander,
the host is unable to march without smiths.  Give orders
that they may go with us from Egypt, for there are no smiths
upon all the face of the earth like unto those of Egypt."  So
Alexander called Sarnâ ̱kôs[3] (?) the king of Egypt and said to
him, "Give me seven thousand[4] smiths, workers in brass and
iron, to go with me; and when I come from the countries
whither I am going, if they wish [to return] hither, I will send
them, and if they wish [to stay in] one of the countries under
my sovereign rule, I will grant it them, and they shall not give
tribute to the king, but they shall give.........to us."  And
Sarnâ ̱kôs the king of Egypt chose seven thousand men, workers
in brass and iron, and gave them to Alexander, and they ate
bread with one another.

And they put ships to sea and sailed on the sea four months[5]
and twelve days, and they arrived at the dry land beyond the
eleven bright seas.  And Alexander and his troops encamped,
and he sent and called to him the governor who was in the
camp, and said to him, "Are there any men here guilty of
death?"  They said to him, "We have thirty and seven men
in bonds who are guilty of death."  And the king said to the
governor, "Bring hither those evil doers."  And they brought

---

[1] Knös, p. 104, l. 1.

[2] Knös, Chrestomathia Syr., p. 70.

[3] This name is spelt ܩܐܡܣ in Knös, Chrestomathia, p. 71.

[4] Twelve thousand, ibid. p. 71, l. 5.

[5] According to Jacob of Sěrûgh Alexander made his way towards India where
he landed after four months.  See Knös, p. 71, ll. 16, 17.

them, and the king commanded them and said, "Go ye to the shore of the fœtid sea, and hammer in stakes that ships may be tied thereto, and prepare everything needful for a force about to cross the sea." And the men went, and came to the shore of the sea. Now Alexander thought within himself, "If it be true as they say, that everyone who comes near the fœtid sea dies, it is better that these who are guilty of death should die," and when they had gone, and had arrived at the shore of the sea, they died instantly. And Alexander and his troops were looking at them when they died, for he and his nobles had ridden to see what would happen to them, and they saw that they died the moment that they reached the sea. And king Alexander was afraid and retired, and he knew that it was impossible for them to cross over to the place where were the ends of the heavens. So the whole camp mounted, and Alexander and his troops went up between the fœtid sea and the bright sea to the place where the sun enters the window of heaven; for the sun is the servant of the Lord, and neither by night nor by day does he cease from his travelling. The place of his rising is over the sea, and the people who dwell there, when he is about to rise, flee away and hide themselves in the sea, that they be not burnt by his rays; and he passes through the midst of the heavens to the place where he enters the window of heaven; and wherever he passes there are terrible mountains, and those who dwell there have caves hollowed out in the rocks, and as soon as they see the sun passing [over them], men and birds flee away from before him and hide in the caves, for rocks are rent by his blazing heat and fall down, and whether they be men or beasts, as soon as the stones touch them they are consumed. And when the sun enters the window of heaven, he straightway bows down and makes obeisance before God his Creator; and he travels and descends the whole night through the heavens, until at length he finds himself where he rises.

And Alexander looked towards the west, and he found a mountain that descends, and its name was "the great Mûsâs¹"; and [the troops] descended it and came out upon Mount Ḳlaudiâ.

¹ ܩܡܣܡܢ ܦܠܐ ܩܡܣ (Kuäs, p. 72) "Mâsâ, a high mountain."

and ate bread there. Then they went down to the source of the Euphrates, and they found that it came forth from a cave; and they came to Halûrâs[1], where the Tigris goes forth like the stream which turns a mill, and they ate bread in Halûrâs. And they departed from thence and went to the river Kallath[2]; and they ascended the mountain which is called Râmath, where there is a watch-tower. And Alexander and his troops stood upon the top of the mountain and saw the four quarters of the heavens. And Alexander said, "Let us go forth by the way to the north"; and they came to the confines of the north, and entered Armenia and Âdarbaijân and Inner Armenia. And they crossed over the country of Tûrnâgiôs, and Bêth-Parḍiâ, and Bêth-Teḳil, and Bêth-Drûbîl, and Bêth-Ḳâṭarmên, and Bêth-Gebûl, and Bêth-Zamraṭ. Alexander passed through all these places; and he went and passed mount Mûsâs and entered a plain which is Bâhî-Lebtâ, and he went and encamped by the gate of the great mountain. Now there was a road across it by which great merchants entered the inner countries, and by it did Alexander encamp. And he sent heralds of peace on horseback, and they rode about and proclaimed through the whole country: "The king of the Greeks is come to this country, neither slaying, nor burning, nor destroying; let every man dwell in peace. Let three hundred men advanced in years be chosen, and let them enter my presence, says king Alexander, that I may learn what I require, and let every man dwell in peace." When the people of the country heard what the heralds of peace were proclaiming, they were not afraid, and they chose three hundred aged[3] men, who went into Alexander's presence as soon as he had encamped in the country; and he himself commanded the people not to flee before him. And when the aged men, natives of that land, had come into his presence, he asked them, "Who are ye? and to whom do ye give tribute? and what king rules in this land?" The old men answered and said to the king, "This land belongs to Tûbûrlâḳ the king of the Persians[4], who is of the race of the

---

[1] ܡܚܘܪܣ Knös, p. 79, l. 6.

[2] See Wright, *Chronicle of Joshua the Stylite*, p. 57.

[3] Knös, *Chrestomathia*, p. 78.

[4] Tûbarlîḳâ is called by Jacob of Sěrûgh "Great King of the territory of the Persians and of the Âmôrâyê" (ܐܡܘܪܝܐ), Knös, p. 79, l.

house of Ahshôrah[1], and to him do we give tribute." Alexander
said to them, "How far does this mountain descend in this
direction?" They answered him, "This mountain extends
without a break, passing by the sea of Bêth-Ḳaṭrâyê, and goes
on and comes to an end in outer Persia near India; and from
this road and upwards the mountain goes to a great river on
this side of the sea. And there are narrow paths there
which a man is unable to pass through unless he be on
horseback. And people who pass through the mountain are
unable to do so without bells that ring, for animals come up
from the sea and from the rivers and descend from the mountains and crouch in the path, and if men go to pass through it
without bells that ring, they perish immediately." Alexander
said, "This mountain is higher and more terrible than all the
mountains which I have seen." The old men, the natives of the
country, said to the king: "Yea, by your majesty, my lord the
king, neither we nor our fathers have been able to march
one step in it, and men do not ascend it either on that side
or on this, for it is the boundary which God has set between us
and the nations within it." Alexander said, "Who are the
nations within this mountain upon which we are looking?......"
The natives of the land said, "They are the Huns." He said to
them, "Who are their kings?" The old men said: "Gôg[2] and
Mâgôg and Nâwâl the kings of the sons of Japhet; and Gig
and Tĕâmrôn, and Tiyâmrôn, and Bêth-Gamlî and Yâphô'bar,
and Shûmârdâḳ, and Glûsiḳâ, and 'Ekshâphâr, and Salgaddô,
and Nislik, and Âmarphil, and Ḳâ'ôzâ, these are the kings of
the Huns[3]." Alexander said, "What is their appearance, and
their clothing, and their languages?" The old men answered
and said to the king: "Some of them have blue eyes, and their

---

[1] ܐܫܚܘܪܐ probably means Xerxes, like Ahasuerus (for אֲחַשְׁוְרשׁ is a
corruption of אֲחַשִׁירֶשׁ, i.e. חַשִׁירֶשׁ, as the name is written in the stele of
Bakhârâh, Khshîyarsh).

[2] In Enôs (p. 80) this word is spelt ܓܘܓ.

[3] The names of the twenty-two kingdoms which were imprisoned within the
northern gate by Alexander are, according to the Book of the Bee (ed. Budge, p.
128), as follows:—Gôg, Mâgôg, Nâwâl, Eshkênâz, Dênâphâr, Paḳḷâyê, Wêlôtâyê,
Humnâyê, Parzâyê, Daḳlâyê, Thaubêlâyê, Darmêtâyê, Kawhêbâyê, Dog-men
(Cynocephali), Emdêrâthâ, Garmîdô, Caunibals, Therḳâyê, Âlânâyê, Piselôn,
Denḳâyê, and Saḷrâyê.

women have but one breast apiece; and the women fight more
than the men, for they wound a man with knives. They hang
knives upon their thighs and arms and necks, so that, if one of
them should get into a fight, wherever she stretches out her
hand she can lay hold of a knife. They wear dressed skins;
and they eat the raw flesh of everything which dies of theirs;
and they drink the blood of men and of animals[1]. They do not
besiege or fight against cities and fortresses, but they run to the
paths and gates of fortresses and cities, and they surround the
men who come out to meet them outside. They are swifter than
the wind that blows, and ere the rumour of their going forth to
battle is heard, they outstrip the whole world; for they are
sorcerers, and they run between heaven and earth, and their
chariots and swords and spears flash like fearful lightnings.
They carry maces in their hands, and each has two or three
horses;......between fifty and sixty men, and they go before
and after him, and the noise of each one's outcry is more
terrible than the voice of a lion; for it is the will of God that
delivers the nations into each other's hands, and the terror of
the Huns is fearful upon all creatures that see them, for they
are no lovers of mankind. When they go forth to war, they
fetch a pregnant woman, and pile up a fire, and bind her in
front of the fire, and cook her child within her, and her belly
bursts open and the child comes forth roasted. Then they lay
it in a trough and throw water upon its body, and its body
melts away in this water; and they take their swords and
bows and arrows and spears, and dip them in this water.
And to every one whom this water touches, it appears as if
there were a hundred thousand horsemen with him; and by the
side of every hundred men there seem to stand one hundred
thousand bands of demons, for their sorceries are greater than
those of all kingdoms. And of this too, my lord, we inform thy
majesty," said the old men to Alexander, "The Huns go not
forth to spoil except where the anger of God goes up that He
may slay the fathers and the children and that the Lord may
smite the earth in His anger, for they are fiercer than all the

[1] Comedent carnes hominum et bibent sanguinem bestiarum sicut aquam.
See Methodius (ed. Brant). Adventus Gog et Magog.

kings in their wars[1]." Alexander said to the natives of that
country, "Have they come forth to spoil in your days?" The
old men answered and said to the king: "May God establish
thy kingdom and thy crown, my lord the king! These fortresses
which have been overturned in our lands and in the lands of the
Romans, have been overthrown by them; by them have these
towers been uprooted; when they go forth to spoil, they ravage
the land of the Romans and of the Persians, and then they
enter their own territory." Alexander said to them, "Who are
the nations that live beyond these?" The old men replied,
"Those of Bêth-Âmardâth and the Dog-men; and beyond the
Dog-men is the nation of the Mĕnīnê; and beyond the nation
of the Mĕnīnê there are no human beings but only terrible
mountains and hills and valleys and plains and horrible caves,
in which are serpents and adders and vipers, so that men
cannot go thither without being immediately devoured by the
serpents, for the lands are waste, and there is nothing there
save desolation. Within all these mountains the Paradise of
God appears afar off. Now Paradise is neither near heaven nor
earth; like a fair and strong city, so it appears between heaven
and earth; and the clouds and darkness which surround it are
visible afar off, and the horn[2] of the north wind rests upon it."
And Alexander said to them: "How do the four rivers go forth?"
The old men replied: "My lord, we will inform thy majesty.
God made four rivers to go forth from the Paradise of Eden.
Because God knew that men would dare to seize the rivers, and
would go by means of them to enter Paradise, He drew the
rivers within the earth, and brought them through valleys and
mountains and plains, and brought them through a number of
mountains, and made them issue forth from the mountains, and
there is one which He made to flow from a cave. And He
surrounded Paradise with seas and rivers and the Ocean, the
fœtid sea; and men are unable to draw near to Paradise, neither
can they see where the rivers go forth, but they see that they
go forth either from the mountains or from the valleys."

[1] "Each one
of them stands six or seven cubits high." Knös, p. 60, l. 15.
[2] It is the point or quarter from which the north wind blows.

When Alexander had heard what the old men said, he marvelled greatly at the great sea which surrounded all creation; and Alexander said to his troops, " Do ye desire that we should do something wonderful in this land ?" They said to him, " As thy majesty commands we will do." The king said, " Let us make a gate of brass and close up this breach." His troops said, " As thy majesty commands we will do." And Alexander commanded and fetched three thousand smiths, workers in iron, and three thousand men, workers in brass. And they put down brass and iron, and kneaded it as a man kneads when he works clay. Then they brought it and made a gate, the length of which was twelve cubits and its breadth eight cubits[1]. And he made a lower threshold from mountain to mountain, the length of which was twelve cubits; and he hammered it into the rocks of the mountains, and it was fixed in with brass and iron. The height of the lower threshold was three cubits. And he made an upper threshold from mountain to mountain, twelve cubits in length; and he hammered it into the rocks of the mountain, and fixed in it two bolts of iron, each bolt being twelve cubits [long]; and the bolts went into the rock two cubits; and he made two bolts of iron from rock to rock behind the gate, and fixed the heads of the bolts into the rocks. He fixed the gate and the bolts, and he placed nails of iron and beat them down one by the other, so that if the Huns came and dug out the rock which was under the threshold of iron, even if footmen were able to pass through, a horse with its rider would be unable to pass, so long as the gate that was hammered down with bolts stood. And he brought and hammered down a lower threshold and hinge for the gate, and he cast therein bolts of iron, and made it swing round on one side like the gates of Shûshan the fortress. And the men brought and kneaded iron and brass and covered therewith the gate and its posts one by one, like a man when he moulds clay. And he made a bolt of iron in the rocks, and hammered out an iron key twelve cubits long, and made locks of brass turn therewith. And behold the gate was hung and stood[1].

[1] See Müller, p. 143, col. 1, l. 20; Bar-Hebraei Chron. Syr. ed. Bruns, l. p. 39; and Knös, Chrestomathia Syriacae, p. 87.
[2] According to Marco Polo the defile in the mountains where Alexander

And king Alexander fetched [an engraver] and inscribed upon the gate: "The Huns shall go forth and conquer the countries of the Romans and of the Persians, and shall cast arrows with......, and shall return and enter their own land. Also I have written that, at the conclusion of eight hundred and twenty-six years, the Huns shall go forth by the narrow way which goes forth opposite Halôrâs, whence the Tigris goes forth like the stream which turns a mill, and they shall take captive the nations, and shall cut off the roads, and shall make the earth tremble by their going forth. And again I have written and made known and prophesied that it shall come to pass, at the conclusion of nine hundred and forty years,...... another king, when the world shall come to an end by the command of God the ruler of creation. Created things shall anger God, and sin shall increase, and wrath shall reign[1], and the sins of mankind shall mount up and shall cover the heavens, and the Lord will stir up in His anger the kingdoms that lie within this gate; for when the Lord seeks to slay men, he sends men against men, and they destroy one another. And the Lord will gather together the kings and their hosts which are within this mountain, and they shall all be assembled at His beck, and shall come with their spears and swords, and shall stand behind the gate, and shall look up to the heavens, and shall call upon the name of the Lord, saying, 'O Lord, open to us this gate.' And the Lord shall send His sign from heaven and a voice shall call on this gate, and it shall be destroyed and fall at the beck of the Lord, and it shall not be opened by the key which I have made for it. And a troop shall go through this gate which I have made, and a full span shall be worn away from the lower threshold[2] by the hoofs of the horses which with

built the Iron Gate extended four leagues. The pass referred to is probably the Pass of Derbend. "apparently the Sarmatic Gates of Ptolemy, and *Claustra Caspiorum* of Tacitus, known to the Arab geographers as the Gate of Gates (باب الأبواب), but which is still called in Turkish Demir-Kâpi or the Iron Gate, and to the ancient Wall that runs from the castle of Derbend along the ridges of Caucasus, called in the East *Sadd-i-Iskandar*, the Rampart of Alexander." Col. Yule, *The Book of Ser Marco Polo the Venetian*, I. p. 55, note 3.

[1] Kuša, p. 92.
[2] *Ibid.* p. 96.

their riders shall go forth to destroy the land by the command of the Lord; and a span shall be worn away from the upper threshold by the points of the spears of those that shall run over it and go forth. And when the Huns have gone forth, as God has commanded, the kingdoms of the Huns and the Persians and the Arabs, the twenty-four kingdoms that are written in this book, shall come from the ends of the heavens and shall fall upon one another, and the earth shall melt through the blood and dung of men. Then the kingdom of the Greeks shall move itself, and shall come and take a hammer of iron in its right hand, and a hammer of brass in its left, and the kingdom of Greece shall smite the hammers one upon the other, and as iron which is melted by fire, and as brass which boils in the flame, so shall the power of the kingdoms melt away before the might of the kingdom of the Greeks which is that of the Romans. And the kingdoms of the Huns and of the Persians shall be desolated the one by the other; only a few of them shall escape who shall flee to their country; and what remains of them the kingdom of the Romans shall destroy. And my kingdom, which is called that of the house of Alexander the son of Philip the Macedonian, shall go forth and destroy the earth and the ends of the heavens; and there shall not be found any among the nations and tongues who dwell in the world that shall stand before the kingdom of the Romans. Lo, I Alexander have written and made known [these things] in my own handwriting, and verily I have not lied in what I have written; but perhaps the nations and the world will not believe that what I have written will come to pass; but if ye will not receive my word, receive [that of] Jeremiah the prophet who long ago pointed out that kingdom in his prophecy, and spake thus in his book[1], 'Evil shall be opened from the north upon all the inhabitants of the land.' And behold I have a sign, which is wrought by God: on the rock which is within the gate on the one side,......[2] and as it rises from the rock it is narrow; and on the other side there hangs a sponge full of blood, and the blood descends upon the

---

[1] Jerem. i. 14. The land of the north shall be opened on the day of the end of the world. Knös, p. 92, l. 2.

[2] Some words seem to have been omitted here.

rock, and the Huns come and smear their heads with it, and return.  And this testimony is set there by God that men may see and fear; for as that blood descends from that sponge, so shall the blood of man be shed upon the mountains and the hills."  So Alexander and his troops marvelled at the gate which they had made.  Then the people of that country went down and said to Tûbârlâḳ[1] the king of the Persians, "Alexander the son of Philip the Macedonian, the king of the Greeks, is come hither and has made a gate of iron in the face of the Huns; but arise, take thy army, and come and slay him, and take whatever he has."  And Tûbârlâḳ arose and sent to Měshazběrî, the king of Inner India, and to Bar-Sidaḳ, the king of Ḳâdêsh, and to Hûrazdân, the king of Javan; and he sent to Armenia, and to all the countries that were obedient to him, and hired and brought eighty-two[2] kings and their armies, one million one hundred and thirty thousand men.  And they took counsel together before Tûbârlâḳ and before all the kings and their hosts, and decided to come.  Now it was the time of summer, and Alexander's whole camp was lying down and at rest.  And the king himself had scarcely lain down, when lo, the Lord came to Alexander and found him asleep, and He called him and said to him, "Rise up from there."  And the king arose and knelt down and did reverence to the Lord; and the Lord said to him, "Behold, I have magnified thee above all kingdoms, and I have made horns of iron to grow on thy head that thou mayest thrust down the kingdoms of the earth with them; and upon me thou didst rely when thou wentest forth to war and to see the countries.  But lo, a multitude of kings and their armies are coming against thee to slay thee; call upon me that I may come to aid thee, for I am the Lord, and I help all those that call upon me."  And the Lord departed from Alexander.

And the king aroused his troops and said to them, "Behold, the spoilers are coming against us.  Let now the watchmen go up to the top of the mountain, and spy and see, for the Lord has appeared to me in this hour."  And the watchmen went up and saw the troops and their kings, a host without end.  And

---

[1] ܛܘܼܒܲܪܠܵܩ Knös, p. 82, l. 9.
[2] Sixty-two, Knös, p. 88, l. 3.

they ran and said to the king, "O king, we perish; but God,
who knows their number, will slay them." And king Alexander
straightway commanded the army to be numbered, [to see] how
many were dead and how many were alive. And the camp was
numbered, and there were found therein three hundred and
sixteen thousand, and four thousand had died; for when they
went forth from Alexandria, there were three hundred and
twenty thousand men. And Alexander commanded every man
of his troops over whom he had power, saying, "Let every man
who is here offer an incense offering upon sherds or upon stones
to the Lord, for the Lord will surely come to our assistance, and
He will come and find the odour of the camp pleasant with the
incense of spices." Then Alexander took his crown and his
purple robes and laid them before the Lord, and said, "Thou, O
Lord, hast power over my life and my kingdom, and to thee
belongs dominion. Do thou deliver thy servant and his camp
from his enemies." And while Alexander was praying, the
kings and their armies surrounded them. And Alexander.
answered and said, "Victory is the Lord's"; and the camp cried
out and said, "O God, come to our aid." And Alexander said,
"O Lord, who didst appear to me in this land, help us." Then
the Lord appeared, coming upon the chariot of the Seraphim,
and the watchers and the angels came before Him with praises.
And He led His host upon the camp of Alexander, and the Lord
appeared standing on the west. And the whole of Alexander's
camp looked towards the Lord, and the Lord became a helper
to the camp, and the people were strengthened, for the Lord
had come for their deliverance. Then a terrible fight arose, the
people crying out, "This battle is the Lord's, who has come
down and stood in it." And the Lord again appeared to
Alexander and said to him, "Fear neither the kings nor their
troops, for behold I am with thee." And the voice of the Lord
went along thundering among them, until the kings and their
armies trembled before the camp of God. And Alexander and
his troops slew sixty kings and their hosts, and those that fled,
fled, and those that were scattered, were scattered; and he
took Tûbârlâk the king of Persia, but slew him not.

Then Alexander and his troops stood up, and Tûbârlâk the
king of Persia, being bound[1], and the nobles of all Persia; and

¹ Knös, p. 86, l. 4.

Tûbârlâḳ brought forth gold and silver and beryls and pearls and precious stones of sapphire, and gave them to king Alexander. And Alexander subdued all Persia upon the sea of Darkness. And he was going to slay Tûbârlâḳ; and Tûbârlâḳ said to him, "What wilt thou gain, if thou slayest me? Take the gold that I have, and I will pledge Persia to thee that she shall give thee tribute fifteen years; and then, after the fifteen years, Babylon and Assyria shall be......" And Tûbârlâḳ and Alexander sat down, and took counsel together and said that six thousand men of the Romans, and six thousand men of the Persians, should go and guard that gate of iron and brass which is in the north, and that every man should eat and drink at the expense of the king who sent him. And Tûbârlâḳ the king of Persia brought sorcerers and enchanters, and the signs of the zodiac, and fire and water, and all his gods, and made divination by them; and they told him that at the final consummation of the world the kingdom of the Romans would go forth and subdue all the kings of the earth; and that whatever king was found in Persia would be slain, and that Babylon and Assyria would be laid waste by the command of God. Thus did king Tûbârlâḳ make divination, and he gave [it] in his own handwriting to king Alexander. And he put down in writing with Alexander what should befall Persia, that the king and his nobles prophesied that Persia should be laid waste by the hand of the Romans, and all the kingdoms be laid waste, but that that power should stand and rule to the end of time, and should deliver the kingdom of the earth to the Messiah who is to come.

And Alexander and his troops arose and went forth from Persia, and they went up by the wilderness, and he came and encamped in the mount of the Romans. And Alexander brought the smiths whom he had fetched from Egypt, and gave them Bêth Dêma and Bêth-Dôshar to cultivate and live in, and they were not to give tribute to the king. And Alexander went up and worshipped in Jerusalem, and put ships to sea and went to Alexandria, and when he died, he gave his royal throne of silver to be in Jerusalem.

Here ends the history of the Achievements and Wars of Alexander the son of Philip, the king of the Greeks.

# A BRIEF LIFE OF ALEXANDER.

The Life, or history, in brief terms, of Alexander, king of the Macedonians[1]. King Alexander was the son by adultery of Nectanebus, the last king of Egypt, and of Olympias, the wife of Philip, king of the Macedonians. According to the deception by which his father deceived his mother when he committed adultery with her, the son was attributed to Ammon, the god of Thebes, who was the forefather of all the Egyptian kings. This [youth] was victorious in many contests before he became king, and also in divers wars against hostile nations, who were constantly rebelling against Philip and against the Macedonians. He became king over the Macedonians after Philip, when he was twenty years old. First of all he persuaded all the nations of the Greeks and their kings and chiefs to receive him as king, and that he should reign over them. As he subdued many of them merely by words, he was only compelled to reduce some few by arms and war. Afterwards, however, when he went to Italy and entered Rome, being received with great honours and with crowns by the inhabitants of Rome, he subdued for them the Africans, who were in rebellion against them. When he had come from thence to Egypt, and had recognised the statue and image of his father, and learned the augury about Nectanebus, and made known to the Egyptians concerning himself and concerning his descent from their king, he persuaded them to be subject to him. And when he had come from thence to the regions of Palestine and Judaea and Phoenicia and Syria and Arabia, and had subdued and conquered them, he made war with Darius, the king of the Persians, in Cilicia, who at that time was master of these countries. And when he had overcome him, he subdued

[1] Translated from the Syriac text in Prof. P. de Lagarde's *Analecta Syriaca*, pp. 205—208.

the countries which were under him, I mean Cilicia and Cappadocia and Galatia and Asia and all the earth as far as Pontus.
And he immediately spread with a sudden onslaught over all
the territory of the Persians, and fought a second battle with
King Darius and overcame him.  And when Darius had been
slain by treachery by enemies who were under his rule, he
punished those who had slain him; and either by kindness or
by force he brought all the nations that were subject to the
kingdom of the Persians to be subject to him.  And he took
Roxana, the daughter of King Darius, to wife.  When he had set
out from thence to the northern regions, and had gone to Media,
and from thence to the gates of Kaspia, and had passed through
all the countries of the Scythian nations that were in the north,
he made a sudden onslaught with the Macedonians and Persians
upon Porus the king of the Indians.  When Porus had gathered
together a large army against him, in the first battle he was
overcome and subdued by him.  In the second battle however,
after Porus had rebelled against him, when he fought in single
combat with Alexander, he was conquered by him and slain.
Afterwards, when Alexander had set out from thence he went to
the country of the Brahmans, the naked sages.  And when he
had discussed many things with them, he departed from thence,
going round about all the territories of the Indians.  And
he saw divers places, and terrible and destructive beasts and
deadly reptiles; and he passed through numerous and divers
nations of barbarians, and underwent many toils.  After these
things he went also to the king of the Sináyé (Chinese); and
from thence he went against all the northern nations.  He also
passed by the Serici who [live] in......[1]  And when they had
received him and become subject to him, he built a city there
and named it Samirkir (Samarkand).  From thence he came to
the country of the Soghdians, and there too he built a city and
named it Kûsh.  From thence likewise he came to Merg (Merv),
and there too he built a city and called its name Margiánós.
After all these things, when he had returned to the land of the
Persians, he went from thence to see the kingdom of the country
of Shebá, over which a woman reigned whose name was Candace.
And when he had gone and had been received nobly, he

[1] ــمـیـﻊ

approached also from thence to the realm of the Amazon women. And when he had accepted many gifts from them, he returned to the city of Babylon in the land of the Chaldeans. While he was there, Cassander, the son of Antipater, one of his generals, arrived from Macedonia, and administered a deadly poison to him while drinking, and killed him. All the days of his life were thirty-two years and seven months, and of these he reigned twelve years and seven months.

He built thirteen cities and named them after his own name. The first, Alexandria Bucephalus; the second Alexandria the fortified; the third Alexandria which is in the land of the Persians; the fourth that which is in the country of king Porus; the fifth that which is in the land of Gâlikôs; the sixth, that which is in the land of the Scythians; the seventh, that which is upon the shore of the great sea; the eighth, that which is near Babylon; the ninth, Alexandria which is in the land of Seriei, which is called Samîrkîr (Samarkand); the tenth, Alexandria which is in the land of the Soghdians, which is called Kûsh and Babel; the eleventh, Alexandria which is called Margiânôs (Merv); the twelfth, that which is upon the bank of the rivers on the road to the Indians; the thirteenth, the great Alexandria which is in Egypt.

Now when he was about to die in Babylon, he made a testament and commanded and distributed his dominions among twelve of his servants. He gave to Kartados (Craterus) Macedonia; to Ptolemy all Egypt; and to Priscus (Perdiccas) Asia. He appointed Lysimachus over Thrace; Dôrân over the Hellespont; Antigonus over Pamphylia and Lycia; Andreas over Great Phrygia; Pîrôs over Cilicia; Python and his wife over Syria and as far as Mesopotamia; Adomnos (Eumenês) over Paphlagonia and Cappadocia; and Seleucus over Babylon. He commanded that Manpath (Meleager) should rule over Phœnicia and Coelesyria; and he made his wife Roxane mistress over all the country of the Assyrians and Media and Parthia, and he commanded that she should be given in marriage to Priscus (Perdiccas). And after he was dead, his captains brought his body to the great Alexandria which is in Egypt, as they had been commanded by him, and they buried him there.

A DISCOURSE COMPOSED BY MÂR JACOB[1] UPON
ALEXANDER, THE BELIEVING KING, AND UPON
THE GATE WHICH HE MADE AGAINST ÂGÔG
AND MÂGÔG[2].

5 Through Thee, O splendour of the Father, I begin to speak,
By Whose victory the righteous have been victorious in their
  wars[3].
In love, O Lord, give me speech from Thy doctrine[4],
That the speech of wonder may run among the listeners[5].

---

[1] I.e., Jacob of Sêrûgh. He was born at Kurtam, a village on the river
Euphrates, in the year 451, and he died at Batnân, the chief town of Sêrûgh, on
the 29th of November 521, aged seventy years. For a summary of his life and
writings see the Article Syriac Literature by Prof. Wright in the Encyclopaedia
Britannica, 9th ed. vol. xxii. pp. 824—856.

[2] Translated from the Syriac text of this discourse published by Knös,
Chrest. Syr. 1807, pp. 66—107. There is a German translation of it by A. Weber
entitled Des Mor Yaqûb Gedicht über den gläubigen König Alexandrus, Berlin,
1852. The edition of the text by Knös contains numerous misprints and the
manuscript from which it was edited seems to be very faulty. Dr. Zotenberg of
the Bibliothèque Nationale, Paris, has most kindly collated a large number of
the faulty passages in the printed text with the original manuscript, and I have
given the results of this collation, together with the corrections of some misprints,
at the foot of the pages of the English translation which follows. The Syriac
extracts which occur in the footnotes are taken from Brit. Mus. Add. MS.
14624, ff. 20b—34a, col. 1, (see Wright, Catalogue of the Syriac MSS. in the
British Museum, vol. ii. p. 782); a number of variant readings which will help
to make clearer the text published by Knös have also been added.

[3] These two first lines are wanting in Add. 14624.    [4] Read ܡܚܒܠܝ

[5] Add. 14624 has ܗܘܬܐ ܕܪܘܢ ܠܘܪ̈ܝ ܥܠ̈ܝܟܐ ܠܬܗܘ ܕܪ̈ܐ ܚܝ ܩܡܬܐ ܠܫܡܥܐ.

Through the knowledge which is sanctified[1] from corporeal
thoughts

10 Will I sing[2] to Thee [with] sounds of glory in the congrega-
tions.

p. 67 From Thee shall my pain-bearing tongue put on armour[3],

With understanding and the word full of life and of all good
things[4].

Overshadow[5] my feebleness with the compassion of Thy
sweetness,

And we shall possess[6] riches from Thy gift full of beauties.

15 And Thee, O Lord, shall my feeble mouth preach with a loud
voice[7].

O Jesus, the Light, Who redeemed creation by His crucifixion,

Thee are the fiery hosts eager[8] to praise,

With glory and power will I sing unto Thee bowing low in
adoration.

The fiery Cherubim bear Thee, O Lord, upon their wings[9],

20 And the fiery ranks ascribe to Thy name all adoration.

The watchers of the height bow down[10] in trembling to praise
[Thee].

But how can I, the feeble one, speak of Thee?

The fiery hosts bless Thee, O Lord, with holiness,

And with them the assemblies of the house of Gabriel ascribe
honour [to Thee].

25 The terrible Seraphim adore Thee, O Lord, with their hymns[11],

But I, the wretched one, how can I bring forth glory to Thy
name?

---

¹ Add. 14624 ܚܡܝܪܐ ܘܡܩܕܫ    ² Add. 14624 ܐܡܪ    ³ Add. 14624

⁴ Add. 14624 ܡܟܠܝܠ ܘܣܘܡܟܠܐ    ܠܟܚܣ ܠܚܣܝܣ ܣܝܛܐ

⁵ Add. 14624 ܐܨܠ    ⁶ Add. 14624 ܢܐܠܝ ܣܝܠܐ    ܣܝܐ ܘܚܠܐ ܠܩܕܐ

⁷ After this line Add. 14624 has ܡܙܪܡܣܝܢ ܠܚܠܟܐ ܘܗܐܢ ܡܪܚ

ܣܝܐ ܡܩܝܩܕܐ ܀ ܠܟܪ ܡܬܡܪܣ ܕܠܐ ܫܝ ܠܚܣܘܕܐ ܕܐܐ

⁸ Reading with Add. 14624 ܬܝܟܚܣܝ    ⁹ Add. 14624 ܘܣܘܪܝܘܢ

¹⁰ Add. 14624 ܣܝܢ    ¹¹ Add. 14624 ܡܙܪܐ ܘܣܝܛܠܐ ܘܡܠܚܕܣܐ

The captains of the hosts and the hosts of heavenly beings,
p. 68 Glorify [Thee] with trembling, though their songs are beautiful.
O Good One, Who bindest on the crowns of kings and
governors,
30 Grant that I may speak about the kingdom of the son of
Philip'!

This king, full of wisdom, gathered together to his dominion[s]*
The captains of the hosts* and the hosts with their ranks.
And when the captains of thousands and all the wise men were
gathered together*,
35 Lords and governors and warriors,
Then began Alexander, the son of Philip,
To speak with them, while they marvelled at his discourse*.
The king, the son of Philip the Macedonian, said,
"I desire* greatly to go forth and see countries,
And also what is the condition of lands far away,
40 I will also go forth and see seas and boundaries and all the
quarters of the world';
And more than all [I desire] to go in and see the Land of
Darkness,
If* it is in truth as I have heard it is*."
All these things were spoken by the king"
To the captains of the hosts" and to the captains of thousands
and to the lords".

ܚܠܬܐ܂ܩܕܡ ܚܡܘܙ ܡܣܐ܂ ܡܕܡܕܢܣܘܢ ܕܡ ܫܡܪܡܣ ܟܢ ܢܩܪܡ.
ܠ ܡܘܚܒܣܐ ܡܠܟܣܡܚ [ܠܟܪ] ܡܙܪ ܣܟܐ ܚܢܩܩܣ ܝܣܢ. 1 After this line
Add. 14624 has ܟܢ ܠ ܡܙܐ ܡܠܟܠܐ ܘܐܝܘܙܬ ܐܢܩܐ ܚܐܡܣܪܬܝܣܘܢ ܗܕ
ܣܡܘܣܚܘܣ. ܘܐܡܕ ܚܠܐ ܡܠܚܣܡܠܐ ܘܚܪ ܗܣܠܣܚܣܣܗ 3 Add. 14624 ܚܐܘܣܪ,ܢܣ
2 Add. 14624 ܐܚܣܒܟܡ * ܠܝܚܒ ܣܢܠܐ 3 Read ܠܝܒܐ
6 Read ܘܪܐܚܣܟܠ 5 Add. 14624 ܢܣܠܐܝ,ܝ 7 Reading with Add.
14624 ܐܣܢ ܗܣܠܐ ܗܚܠ ܐܩܣܚܘ ܐܚܩܩܐ ܠܒܘ/ܐ ܡܩܣܚܐ ܘܐܗܣܘܡ 8 Add.
14624 ܐ—ܝ 9 Read ܢܣܘܠܐܝ 10 Add. 14624 adds ܠܚܣܚܪ,ܚܣܢ
ܣܚܣܪ,ܥ 11 Add. 14624 ܣܢܠܐ ܚܣܚܣ 12 Add. 14624
adds ܚܣܚ/ܠܚܣܗ ܐܝ,ܥ ܠܘܩܐ ܘܐܩܩܐ ܘܣܪܚܠܚ ܠܣܣܚܝܣܘ

43 And after he had subdued Macedonia which had rebelled[1]
    against him,
He went down and dwelt[2] in the chief town of all[3] Egypt,
And he bound on the crown, and he became greater and
    stronger[4] than all kings.
When the question went forth from him to the chiefs[5],
They said to him, "Master, the terrible seas which surround[6]
    the world

50 Will not allow[7] thee to go over and see the land."
The king marvelled at what he had heard from his subjects
    (lit. dominion),
And he began to speak to his hosts like[8] a wise man.
The king said, "Have ye been and seen the seas[9]
Which, according to what ye say, surround the whole earth?"

55 They say to him, "Master, within these terrible seas
Is the fœtid sea, which, of a truth, is full of quaking.
And unless men decree death to their lives with great wrath
They never come to the fœtid sea."
The king said, "Let us go and see if, of a truth[10],

60 The terrible seas and the fœtid sea [are] as we have heard."
p. 70 They say to him, "Master, thy wisdom hath well commanded;
Let us gather together[11] the hosts and go and see the countries."
The command went forth[12] from the king speedily,
And he assembled[13] straightway the hosts in great multitude.

65 He gathered together[14] riders, and captains of thousands, and
    lofty seats,
And ready soldiers, and mighty men[15] dressed in armour,

---

[1] Read ܐܬܬܙܝܥܬ݀    [2] Add. 14624 ܘܣܠܩ ܗܘܐ    [3] Read ܕܟܠܗ̇

[4] Add. 14624 ܘܣܠܩ̈ܣ    [5] Add. 14624 adds ܬܚܘܡܐ ܒܬܪ

[6] Add. 14624 ܕܚܕܪܝܢ ܠܗ and omits ܠܟܠܟܡ ܘܬܠܡܝ̈ܕܐ    [7] Add. 14624 ܠܐ ܡܫܒܩ

[8] Read ܐܡܪ] here and in lines 53 and 56.

[9] Reading with Add. 14624 ܐܠܟܡ̈ ܐܢܘܬܢ ܐܡܪ ܘܐܟܪܘܢ ܗܠܝܢ̈ ܝܡܡ̈ܐ

[10] Add. 14624 ܗܢ ܐܝܟ    [11] Add. 14624 ܟܢܫ    [12] Add. 14624 ܕܚܡܬ ܐܚܕ

[13] Read ܢܗܘ    [14] Add. 14624 ܘܟܢܫ

[15] Add. 14624 ܘܡܚܝ̈ܠܝ ܥܩ̈ܠܬܐ

And horses and men; and the king marvelled at his forces.
Then the wise king in his wisdom commanded,
"Let ships be prepared for the host'.
70 Let also men be taken who have gone and seen the land
And the countries and the terrible seas and the fœtid sea."
He made ready a great multitude of ships for his hosts',
And he filled them with all kinds of food' for horse and man:
The believing' king Alexander, the son of Philip,
75 In his wisdom did' this, and his heart rejoiced
Because the people were gathered together to him quickly'.
He took the number of his troops of the Âmôrâyê',
p. 71 One thousand three hundred and many more with polished
armour'.
And he sent and told Sôrîk' the king of all Egypt
80 To send to him from his dominions all the artificers,
Workers in brass and iron, men full of skill,
For the Lord had beckoned to him to make a gate against Mâgôg.
Twelve'" thousand cunning workmen
Did Sôrîk" the king of Egypt send to the son of Philip.
85 King Alexander made ready iron and brass a great quantity,
And, in his wisdom", he filled" the ships therewith.
He" alone knew this mystery,
Which" Jeremiah, in his prophecy, had prophesied concerning
him.

¹ Add. 14624 has ܗܘܐ ܩܛܠܐ܂
² Reading with Add. 14624 ...
³ Add. 14624 ...
⁴ Add. 14624 ...
⁵ Reading with Add. 14624 ...
⁶ Add. 14624 omits this line.
⁷ Add. 14624 ...
⁸ Add. 14624 ...
⁹ Add. 14624 ...
¹⁰ Add. 14624 ...
¹¹ Add. 14624 ...
¹² Read ...
¹³ Reading with Add. 14624 ...
¹⁴ Add. 14624 ...
¹⁵ Reading with Add. 14624 ...

The great king went forth[1] with his subjects[2],

90 The horns sounded[3] and the thousands and the ranks were
gathered together and went forth.

The camp rose up and went forth, and the king marvelled[4],

And his hosts began to go down into the great sea.

The earth[5] was astonished at the rumour of king Alexander.

The king[6] set his course on the sea towards India[7];

72 95 After four months the king and his host went up from the sea,

And spread[8] abroad in the land, and creation was filled with
their hosts.

Quaking fell upon the lands and their inhabitants

By reason of the multitude[9] of the hosts which terrified them.

And they went and came and drew near to the border of the
foetid sea,

100 And they departed[10] by reason of its stench, they fled away
from its noise, and the king's soul was astonished[11].

And he made straight his way towards the lofty mountain
Māsīs[12],

---

[1] Read ܘܩܒܠܘ

[2] Add. 14624 : ܥܡ ܣܓܝܐܐ ܕܐܬܐ ܗܝ ܡܢ ܣܒܝܣܘܬܗܘܢ
ܘܩܡ ܐܬܐ ܡܘܥܕܐ ܘܬܪܥܐ ܕܥܠܡܐ ܠܡܣܪܚܘܗܝ:

[3] Add. 14624 ܡܘܣܓܐ ܩܠܐ ܘܡܢ ܟܢܝܫܐ ܥܡ̈ܪ̈ܐ ܡܢ ܣܓܝܐܘܬܐ

[4] Add. 14624 ܘܬܗܪ ܡܠܟܐ ܐ ܒܟܣܝܐ ܥܡ̈ܘ̈ܗܝ ܢܒܥܐ ܠܘܬܗ • ܘܠܕ ܡܠܟܐ

[5] Add. 14624 ܬܗܪ ܐܪܥܐ ܐܢܕܐ ܘܣܥܐ ܘܣܥܡܐ ܘܡܠܟܐ ܡܠܟܐ ܘܟܠ ܕܥܡܡܗܘܗܝ

[6] ܣܚܐ ܡܘܩܪ ܐܚܕ    [7] Add. 14624 adds ܒܚܛܘܦܝܐ    [8] Add. 14624 adds ܒܟܣܝܬܗ

[9] Read ܗܘܐܠ    • ܘܣܚܝܗܘܡ ܕܐܢܕܐ ܘܚܝܕܗ ܐܢܕܐ • Add. 14624 ܐܬܪܘܬܐ

[10] Read either ܘܪܚܩܘ or ܘܥܪܩܘ

[11] Add. 14624 ✧ ܡܦܢܝ̈ܬܗ ܘܡܟܠ ܠܥ̈ܢܐ ܡܣܬ̈ܟܠܝܢ ܗܘ
ܘܡܗܡܕ ܟܠܐ ܡܢܝܗܝ ܘܦܥܡ ܗܪܢܐ ܐܣܪ ܕܐܢܟܠܟ ܗܘܐ:
ܚܪܩ ܡܢ ܕܢܝܒܘܬܗ ܕܣܢܠܐ ܡܢ ܡܟܗ ܘܬܪܥܐ ܕܥܡܡܗ:

[12] Add. 14624 ܡܣܝܣ

He ascended the mountain and stood upon its summit and
   looked at the lands,

And with him were all the thousands and ranks and hosts.

The king, the son of Philip the Macedonian, said

105 To the hosts, "Let us straightway go forth by the way of the
   north."

The king went in and took possession of (lit. stood upon) the
   lands, and [the people] feared him,

And fled[1] away from him, for his great fame made them flee
   away[2].

When the king saw that the inhabitants of the land trembled
   at him,

He sent before him some of his ambassadors to proclaim[3]
   peace, [saying]

110 "Let the people remain[4], and let no man flee before them
   (i. e., the hosts)."

He gave the word and swore by his life through the heralds,

p. 73 "I will not slay, nor carry away captive, nor destroy."

The heralds cried, "Alexander the great king

Has come to this land in peace, neither slaying,

115 Nor leading away into captivity, nor carrying away spoil[5],

Let every man dwell in his habitation in peace and without
   fear!

Let the nobles and the aged men of the country go[6] to him,

For he has given the word of his mouth which never lies."

He in his wisdom gathered together and brought the nobles
   and the aged,

120 That he might learn from them of the matter of the secrets of
   the land[7].

Three hundred old, greybeaded men were gathered together
   to him, ·

---

Intelligent men who knew the secrets of the land[1].

They went in and stood before the glorious king, and did
  reverence unto him[2],

And they saw his glory and his speech and his strength, and
  they feared him,

125 And they entreated him and besought him to have mercy
  upon them[3].

They say to him, "Master, may thy crown be magnified over
  all the world,

May thy fame and name overthrow kings and their dominions[4]!"

The king[5] rejoiced to be blessed by the old men[6],

p. 74 And he commanded them to sit on his right hand and on his
  left[7].

130 When they had sat down according to the command of the
  great king,

He began to question [them] wisely, saying,

"One thing my soul asketh you to show[8] me,

Where is the Land of Darkness[9]? I wish to see it."

They say to him, "Master, why seekest[10] thou the Land of
  Darkness?

135 Every one who hears the mention[11] of it flees that he may not
  enter therein.

---

[1] Add. 14024 adds ܐܚܪ : ܘܚܟܝܡܘܗܝ ܚܟܡܬܐ ܗܘܘ ܡܠܟܐ|

[2] After this line Add. 14024 adds ܥܠ ܒܝܬܗ؟ ܡܨܝܕܢ ܘܒܪ ܒܪ ܬܡ
ܘܡܘܪܫܘܗܝ ܘܕܝܢܐ؟ ܐܢܘܢ. ܥܠ ܡܠܟܬܗ ܘܐܝܢ ܩܥܝܕܘܗܝ
ܡܘܕܥܝܢ ܗܘܘ ܚܟܡܝ ܥܠܝܡܘܗܝ ܘܡܘܪܫܘܗܝ ܒܐܝܕ؟ ܡܥܒܕ ܕܠܐ ܐܩܪܘܢ..

[3] Add. 14024 ܕܐ ܡܪܘܡܐ ܡܝܬ ܡܚܣܐ ܠܘܬܗ

[4] Add. 14024 ܠܩܘܗܕܟ ܪܡ ܘܢܟܬܐ ܢܟܣܘܣܡ

[5] Read ܚ      [6] Add. 14024 adds ܘܢܣܒ ܣܒ؟ ܡܪܝܐ؟ ܡܝܬ    ܢܟܬܐ
ܒܝܪܝܗ؟ ܡܠܟܐ ܘܢܟ؟      [7] Add. 14024 ܩܘܪܣܝܗ ܥܠ ܣܡܠܗ

[8] Add. 14024 ܒܣܥܬܐ؟      [9] Add. 14024 ܕܚܫܘܟܐ؟ ܟܪ ܐܝܟܐ ܠܡܢ. ܟܡܐ؟ Add. 14024 ܘܥܒܕ؟ ܠܣܥܬܐ؟

[11] Add. 14024 ܬܘܟܪܢ؟

Some men, in their audacity, dared to enter therein,
And they went and perished and unto this day have not re-
 turned and come forth."
The king said, "Our coming to this land was on account of this,
And there is no other way' for me but to see it."
140 The old men say, "There is a great mountain
The length of the road to which from here is twelve days'."
The king said, "Give me men who know the country,
And as for the way, however far it may be, it will not be
 tedious to me."
There was one old, greyheaded man there
145 Who knew the way and was experienced' in the mysteries of
 the country.
p. 75 This old man answered and said to Alexander,
"I will go with thy majesty and show' thee."
Then the heart of the king rejoiced and his face became glad;
And he took the old men and the nobles and they went' with
 · him.

150 And when he had come to the country in which was the Land
 of Darkness'
While as yet they were ten parasangs distant from the place,
One wise old man who knew mysteries' answered and
Said to the king, "Reveal to me the mystery and hide not it
 from me,
What is thy quest in the Land of Darkness? what [will it]
 profit [thee]?
155 And why hast thou come to the land in which there is no
 light'?"

¹ Add. 14624 ܠܘܢ ܠܠ ܠܡܠܘܣ ܠܚܣܡܩ

² Add. 14624 ܡܚܚܝܚ ܚܡܙ܂ ܡܠܙܘܣ ܚܡܩܠܝ   ³ Read

with Add. 14624 ܡܚܢܩܣ  ⁴ Read with Add. 14624 ܠܠ ܠܚܚܩܩ

⁵ Add. 14624 ܩܢܠܠܝܩ?  ⁶ Add. 14624 ܙܚܣܚܙ? ܠܣܩܢ ·

⁷ Reading with Add. 14624 ܠܝܠܝ ܤܚܙ?

⁸ Add. 14624 ܡܩܩܚܣܚܚ ܚܙ ܚܚܚܩܡܩܣܙܠܚܚܣܙܠ ܠܚ ܠܩܢ ܠܡܩܚ ܩܚܩܩܩ
ܠܩܢ ܙܠܠ܂ ܚܣܠܝܝ ܡܚܠܝܝ ܠܚܣܩ? ܚܚܚܣ ܟܚ ܠܢܩܚ . ܚܩܩ ܡܩܩܛܠ ܠܩܢܙܠܚ

The king said, "I have heard that therein is the fountain of
    life,
And I desire greatly to go forth and see if, of a truth, it is
    [there]."
The old man said, "There are many fountains in the country,
And no man knoweth which is the fountain of the water of
    life."
160  The king said, "Do not dispute with me' concerning this matter,
For there is no other way for me but to go in and see the
    country."
Then the old man answered and said to him in his wisdom,
p. 76  "Since the matter is thus, seek out beasts from among the
    she-asses,
All of whom have' young and give suck.
165  According to the number of the men whom thou wishest to
    go into [the land] with thee
Let them bring beasts, and let them also bring their young
    with them."
The command went forth from the king full of wisdom,
And the people of the country went forth from him and
    gathered' together and brought five hundred beasts from
    among the she-asses.
After these things the old man said to the son of Philip,
170  "Command thy cook' to take with him a salt fish, and
    wherever he sees a fountain of water let him wash the
    fish';

ܐ܊ܠܝ؟ ܚܣܟ ܚܣܚ     ‎    ‎‏     ‎   ‎      ‎     ‎  * Read ܚܣ ܟܚܣ ‎    ‎  1 Add. 14624 ܐ܊ܣ ‎22 ‎[ܐ܊ܠ]‏

ܣܚܣܣܢ ܩܣܒܣܚ ܐ܊ܩܐ ܚܟܣܐ [ܐ܊ܠܟ]؟ ܚܣܢ ܣܚ܊ܠܝ ‎‏[ܐ] ‎ *Reading with Add. 14624

ܟܚܣܚ ;ܣܟܚ‏ *Reading with Add. 14624 *Reading with

ܣܐܣܐ؟ ܪܢܐ؟ ܢܨܚܐ ؛ܕܟܟܣ؟ ܣܒܢܟ ܣܣܢܚ ܟܢܚܣܐ.. Add. 14624

And if it be that it comes to life in his hands when he
    washes it,
That is the fountain of the water of life which thou askest
    for, O king."
And when he arrived at the door which goeth into the Land
    of Darkness[1],
The king said to his cook[2], "Take thou a dry[3] fish,

175 And where thou seest a fountain of water, wash it.
And if it be that the fish comes to life in thy hand when thou
    washest it,
Reveal it to me and show me which is the fountain when thou
    hast found it."
The old man said, "Let the foals remain outside the door,

p. 77 For if they come in with us we shall perish[4]."

180 The king mounted and the chosen people that were with him,
And they began to go in, and they left the young asses out-
    side the door;
And they then began to go down into the darkness,
Without knowing whither they were travelling in the land[5].
And when the cook[6] came to water he alighted and began to
    wash

185 The salt fish; and it did not come to life in his hand as had
    been said[7].

---

¹ Add. 14624 adds ܠܘ ܪܢܟܠܟ ܗܘܘ ܘܟܠܟܘܢ ܐܚܣܢ ܠܐܗܣܬܐ ܕܚܣܡܕܐ

² Reading with Add. 14624 ܠܟܡ ܣܚܘ

³ Add. 14624 ܠܘܡ ܕܚܠܟܣܢ ܘܣܘܪܬ ܗܠܝ ܩܪܣ ܣܩܟܠܚܣ

⁴ "The Tartars however sometimes visit the country, (i.e., the land of
Darkness) and they do it in this way. They enter the region riding mares that
have foals, and these foals they leave behind. After taking all the plunder that
they can get they find their way back by help of the mares, which are all eager
to get back to their foals, and find the way much better than their riders could
do." *Marco Polo*, ed. Yule, ii. p. 485.

⁵ Add. 14624 ܗܘ ܠܐ ܩ ܫܣܣܥ ܣܝ ܕܘܒܐ ܣܡܩܒܘܐ ܩ ܢܙܒ ܟܣ ܣܡܟܝܘ
⋮ ܠܪܠܐ        ⁶ Reading with Add. 14624 ܣܟܘܪܣܐ        ⁷ Add. 14624 adds
ܡܚܠܐ ܩ ܘܐܙܐ ܣܚ ܕܐܠ ܣܟܬܐ ܗܘܐ ܠܐ ܕ ܟܠܪܐ ܣܚܕܝ ܣܟܬܐ ܗܘܐ ܘܠܐ ܣܝܢܐ ܠܘܒ ܕܣܚ
ܣܚܬܐ ܗܠܣܝ ܠܐ ܣܢܬܐ ܕܘ ܗܘܘܢ.

Finally he came to a fountain in which was the water of life,

And he drew near to wash the fish in the water, and it came to life and escaped.

The faulty one feared lest the king would require at his hand

That he should return to him the fish which came to life without impediment',

190 And he leaped down into the water to catch² it, but he was not able.

And he went up from the fountain to tell³ the king that he had found the [fountain of life].

He cried out⁴ and they heard him not, he went to the mountain and then they heard him⁵.

Then the king rejoiced that he had heard of the fountain,

And he went back to bathe in it as he had asked.

195 He went to the mountain in the darkness but he did not stand upon it,

p. 78 And it was not granted to him by the Lord that he should live [for ever],

And he was grieved about this even unto death⁶.

And when the old man saw that he was afflicted with grief,
 [he said],
"The Lord hath not turned His face away from thee, O king."
200 The old man said, "Let us turn our beasts and let us go forth
 from here;
For the Lord does not wish thee to bathe in the fountain[1]
 and live for ever."
They turned[2] the beasts and they whipped them and they went
 out to their young ones.
The king turned being grieved that he had not accomplished
 the matter.
And the nobles came and comforted him by reason of [his] grief
 [saying][3],
205 "Master, be not afflicted on account of this, and let it not
 be grievous unto thee.
Look, master, and observe the early and middle generations,
That to each one of them has come its end and it has passed
 away and gone."

And Alexander in his wisdom began to ask questions, [saying,]
"What are these nations who are beyond you?
210 Has any king obtained[4] sovereignty in this land[5]?"

<hr>

[1] Read ܟܚܚܠܐ        ܟܘ. ܘܠܐ ܐܘܘ ܗܘܐ ܡܪ.

[3] Add. 14624 ܐܗܢܗ   [2] Add. 14624 ܟܪܒܣ   ܡܐܬ ܡܟܟܐ ܡܟ ܘܢܒܣ

[4] Add. 14624 ܟܐܢܐ ܡܟܟܐ ܡܠܐ

[5] Add. 14624 adds ܗ.ܟܢܚܗܡ ܕܟܝܝܗ ܘܟܝܘ ܡܟܟܐ ܠܟ ܗܘܐ ܐܟܪܝ

The wise men[1] looked upon this king full of wisdom [and saw]
How joyful he was at the advice of the old men and nobles
    of the country.

p. 79 The old men say, "This is the dominion of Tûberlîkâ[2]
The great king of the house of the Persians and of the
    Âmôrâyê[3].

215 Within it are the peoples of the house of Japhet and of the
    house of Mâgôg,
A cunning nation, a flayed nation, an uprooted nation[4]."
The king said, "Have we a mountain from here onwards[5]?"
The old men say, "As far as the river Kallath[6] and [as far as]
    Halôris[7] [are]
Fearful, savage and lofty mountains with great terror,

220 And beyond them terrible mountains, a great boundary[8]
Which God hath set between us and them from all eternity."
The old men say, "It is altogether a difficult land
In which there are dragons and wild beasts and serpents[9],
And unless men pass the sentence of death upon their lives

225 They are not able to dwell with dragons and snakes[10]."

---

[1] Reading with Add. 14624 ܐܟܣܡܐ ܒܣܠܡ ܚܟܝܡܐ ܚܕܒܘ ܣܚܝܣܟܐ ܟܪܘ

[2] Add. 14624 ܟܠܣܪܘܐ؛

[3] Add. 14264 ܠܣܦܖܘܐ ܖܘܣܖܘܐܘܪ        [4] Reading with Add. 14624 ܟܣܐ
ܚܣܐ ܚܣܟ ܟܟܣܣܟ        [5] Add. 14624 ܟܟ ܐܣ ܐ ܟܘܐ܂ ܐ ܟܠܣܐܠ
ܟܣܟܐ ܟܣܐ ܠܪܒܘܪ        [6] See Wright, Chronicle of Joshua the Stylite, p. 56.

[7] Add. 14624 ܚܣܟܟܣܐܖܘܣܐ    Halôrôs or Halôris is a place near the source
of the Tigris, a journey of two days and a half from Âmid (Diarbekir)

هلورس موضع عند مخرج دجلة على يومين ونصف من آمد

See مراصد الاطلاع ed. Juynboll, t. III. p. ٣٣٣

[8] Add. 14624 reads ܣܟܣܣ ܣܣܟܣܘ ܣܟܐ ܐܣܐ܂ ܐܣܐܘܪ

[9] Reading with Add. 14624 ܣܟ ܐܬܣܐ ܣܟܝ ܣܣܣܐܠ ܣܣܣܐ܂

[10] Reading with Add. 14624 ܠܐ ܣܟܘܣ ܕܣܟܝܣ ܚܣܐ ܠܬܣܐ ܣܣܣܐ܂ .

Then the great king Alexander answered
In his wisdom, "How can we pass through¹ the mountains?"
He commanded and they brought armour², and he made every
    beast to carry [some of it].
The horses rattled the bells and the armour, and they passed

p. 80    through the land³.

230   The old men say, "Look⁴, my lord the king, and see a wonder,
This mountain which God has set as a great boundary."
King Alexander the son of Philip said,
"How far is the extent of this mountain⁵?"
The old men say, "Beyond India it extends in its appearance."

235   The king said, "How far does this side come?"
The old men say, "Unto all the ends of the earth."
And wonder seized the great king at the counsel⁶ of the old
    men,
And he began to ask questions to learn more about everything.
The king said, "Who are these kings

240   And the terrible peoples which are beyond this mountain?"
The old men say, "Listen⁷, O Master, and king; and we will
    tell thee.
Behold, the family of Âgôg and the family of Mâgôg are be-
    yond us,
Terrible of aspect, hateful of form, of all heights,
The stature of each one of them is from six to seven cubits;

245   Their noses are flat⁸ and their foreheads hateful.

¹ Add. 14624 ܣܘܢ܊ܣܝܢ؛ ܢܟܚ؛ ܐܝܢܬ؟ ܗܘܐ ܐܠ̈ܗܦ،ܣ ܣܪܐܩܣܣܝܢܒ

ܠܗܝܣ ܐܘܣ ܚ ܥܘ̈ܢ    ² Read ܐܦ̈ܐܐ

³ Add. 14624 reads ܣܪܢܠܟ ܚܚܠܟܣܚܢ؟ܝܒܚܕܣ ܟܠܣܟ̈ܣ ܐܘܐ ܣܥ
ܐܚܐ. ܣܠܟܣ ܐ̈ܝ ܚܚܠܟ ܚܕܚܚܐ ܐ̈ܡܚܝ ܚܚ؛ ܣܟ؛ܥܚ̈ܣ ܣܪܐ؛ܥܚ̈ܣ
؟ܣܢܠܟ̈ܚ ܟܣܣܪ ܩܟܕܐ ܣܪܘܐܚ. ܚܚܠܐ ܐܝ ܠܚܝ ܣܘܪܐܩܣ ܐܢܐ
❖ ܐܠܢܒ܊ܝ ܣܚܚܝ̈ܣ    ⁴ Add. 14624 ܙܣܝ    ⁵ Add. 14624 ܐܚܐܠ
ܐܘܢ ܐܝܣܩ؟ ܣܪܣܣܐܘܙ ܠܝ̈ܢ    ⁶ Add. 14624 ܣܪܐܠܠܣܣܚ

⁷ Read ܐܢܣ܊ܣ    ⁸ Add. 14624 ܣܟ̣܊ܚ̈ܣ

They bathe in blood, and in blood wash they also their heads;

p. 81 They drink blood and eat the flesh of men;

They wear skins, sharpen weapons and forge wrath,

And are more ferocious and have more wars than all other nations[1].

250 Where[2] the wrath of the Lord rises he sends them;

And they overturn the land, and uproot mountains, and devour men."

Then the son of Philip was grieved because he heard these things,

And he marvelled at this greatly within himself a long time.

Little by little he learned and understood everything which he asked[3],

255 And he had it in his mind to make there a great gate.

His mind was full[4] of spiritual thoughts,

While taking advice from the old men, the dwellers[5] in the land.

He looked at the mountain which encircled the whole world,

The great boundary which God had established from everlasting.

260 The king said, "Where have the hosts come forth

To plunder the land and all the world[6] from of old?"

They show him a place in the middle of the mountains,

A narrow pass which had been constructed by God.

p. 82 The king looked upon the narrow pass with wonderment,

265 And [saw] that the mountain extended[7] and was terrible in its strength on all sides.

Above it he saw a river of blood flowing down[8],

[1] Add. 14624 ܡܢ ܟܠ ܡܠܟܐ ܚܡܝܨܝܢ

[2] Read ܘܐܬܪ    [3] Add. 14625 ܡܢ ܡܠܟ ܗܘܐ ܡܗܠܐ ܕܡܩܐ ܟܚܒ ܕܝܠܝܐ. ܗܝܪܒܝܠ ܗܝܠ ܘܐܙܠܘ ܚܡܝܐ ܚܢܘܗܝ ܘܡܒܠܐ. ܕܡܠܝܐ ܡܠܝܐ ܐܢܠܟ ܡܠܟܐ ܡܢ ܒܚܩܩܐ :·

[4] Read ܡܠܐ    [5] Read ܟܡܝܪ    [6] Add. 14624 ܐܡܪ ܡܠܟܐ

ܐܢܠܘ ܐܙܠܐ ܘܒܗܨܒ ܡܢܘ ܣܟܩܐ ܘܡܨܒ ܠܡܟܐ ܐܙܠܐ ܡܠܟܐ ܟܠܗ

[7] Read ܚܡܠܟܘ    [8] Read ܡܒܠ ܐܪܗܝ ܗܝ ܡܕܡ ܕܕܡ ܡܒܠ ܒܠܐ

And like a torrent of water flowing on against the people.
He examined it that he might make there a great door
Full of wonder in all the world to him that sees it.
270 The Spirit of the Lord stirred up the king, the son of Philip,
With all' thoughts to restrain wickedness from the land.

Letters went to Tûbarlikî' the king of Persia, [saying,]
"Alexander the great king is in thy country,
He is not carrying away captive, nor slaying, nor spoiling,
275 Though he has with him countless hosts' of men.
He dwells peacefully in thy land' as if it
And the royalty and the dominion were his own."
When the king of Persia received this report
From the ambassadors who went into his presence with the
p. 83    · letters,
280 Wonder took hold of the king of Persia on account of this,
And he trembled and was disturbed by the noise of the rumour
    of the great king'.
And he sent and gathered together the forces that were in his
    dominion,
And he assembled and brought sixty-two other kings
To come to his aid and to help him with their hosts;
285 And they all gathered together and covered the earth like
    locusts.
And in great wrath all the kings took counsel
To go up against him and destroy him and blot out his name.

When all the kings with their hosts arrived,
And drew near to go in and throw war into the camp,
290 King Alexander, the son of Philip, lay down to sleep,
And he saw in his dream an angel saying' to him,

---

¹ Read ܚܕܐ   ² Add. 14624 always ܙܘܒܪܠܝܩ

³ Read ܡܒܘܙܐ]   ⁴ Reading with Add. 14624 ܐܢܚܢܘ؟

⁵ Add. 14624 adds ܗܘ ܐܝܟ ܢܦܫܗ ܕܡܢ ܗܘܐ ܘܗܝ؟ ܗܘܐ ܘܐܚܣܢܬ

⁶ Read ܐܡܪ ܕ

12—2

"Behold Tûbarlik! the king of Persia has gathered together
a host,
And has also hired him sixty-two other kings:
Arise, prevail over their hosts, and destroy them',

295   For, behold, God has come and stood within thy camp,
He will make thee victorious, and will help thee, and will make
thee to triumph.

p. 84   Thou shalt conquer them all through the right hand of the
Lord that is with thee'."


Then Alexander awoke and rose up from his sleep,
And he called to the nobles and the captains of hundreds and
the captains of thousands,

300   And he began to speak' and command his troops, [saying,]
" Behold, the Lord hath come to our aid and to our help,
Come, let us stand praying to the Lord with strength'."
And the king commanded all the people to take incense,
And they burned there a sweet odour to the Lord among their
ranks.

305   The king and the nobles and the hosts that were with him
Carried' upon stones and sherds fire and sweet incense.
And after they had burned incense' in the camp,
The king began to speak and to exhort his troops, [saying,]
" Behold the time of great strife and battle [has come],

310   Put on your breastplates and gird upon you all your armour,
Put your helmets upon your heads and stand up for war' like
men.

---

¹ Reading with Add. 14624 ܐܢܐ ܩܘܡܘ

² Reading with Add. 14624 ܪܟܬܒܪ       ³ Add. 14624 ܪܐܟܠܐ

⁴ Add. 14624 ܠܘ ܢܩܘܡܐ ܚܠܝ ܕܡ ܡܘܝܟܕܠܝ ܟܐܝܠܐ ܚܣܡܝܐ   In Rous
the order of this and the following line is inverted.     ⁵ Read ܟܠܒܐ

⁶ Add. 14624 ܡܣܟ ܚܠܝܐ ܪܬܡܣܟ ܪܐܟܕܝ ܪ

⁷ Add. 14624 reads ܟܚܣ.  ܘܢ ܚܢܠܝ ܪܡܢܝ ܐܕܐ ܠܐܐ ܪܝܘܩܕܢܠܝܐ.
ܝܐܪܟܚܐ ܡܣܘܦܐ ܟܠܚܚܐ ܚܠܚܐ ܐܢܠܐ. ܡܣܘܩܐܝܠ ܐܘܝܡܐ ܡܣܩܕܝܡܐܪ ܝܐܟܚܐ;

For behold Tûbarliḳ! the king of Persia has gathered to himself a host,
And has also hired sixty-two other kings.
p. 85 And behold they are all gathered together like one man with
 their hosts,
315 That they may come against us and wipe out our name and
 our kingdom.
Stand up then to war like men and warriors,
And receive triumph and a fair renown for evermore."
He made ready and furnished the hosts, the children of Rûm'
With armour and breastplates that they might not be terror-
 stricken in the fight.
320 The wise king encouraged his hosts
That they should neither be terror-stricken nor moved by the
 enemies' hosts, [saying.]
"I have hope in God, Whom I serve,
That He will make us victorious and triumphant in [our] wars
 with them'."
When Alexander had finished speaking
323 And encouraging his hosts for the battle,
His hosts stood up and put on [their] armour and breastplates,
And were ready to fight like' men.
Then the king' of Persia looked from' the top of the mountain,
And these sixty-two kings with their hosts
330 Descended and came against the camp of Alexander.
p. 86 And he made there a great slaughter among their ranks,
And the believing king Alexander prevailed,
And slew sixty-two kings and a multitude of the host,
Tûbarliḳ! the king of Persia he captured alive,
335 And he fettered him with heavy iron fetters and bound him
 prisoner near to him.

---

ܩܘܡ܂ ܟܠܒܝܬܐ ܗܕܐ ܩܡܬܐ ܡܘܡ ܟܘܡ The passage in Knös is utterly
corrupt. The Paris MS. has ܟܠܒܝܬܐ     ¹ I.e., the Byzantine
Greeks. See Wright, Chronicle of Joshua the Stylite, p. L.

² Add. 14624 adds ܟܢ ܩܡܬܐܘ؟ ܡܗܝܪܐ ܩܡܬܐ ܟܠ ܟܠܒܝܬܐ

³ Reading ܐܘܠ with Add. 14624.   ⁴ Read ܟܠܒܬܐ   ⁵ Add. 14624 ܟܠ

Then the hosts which remained fled away from him,
And forsook their king and escaped to another land.

And when Alexander had thus gained the victory[1],
He buried the slain and took their arms.
340 Then he courageously took pains and made a door
Against Âgôg and the family of Mâgôg, and bound them
  [inside].
He took iron and brass, a great quantity, and made it ready
For the making of the door that he might shut [it] in the face
  of the people.
He gave [his] commands to twelve thousand skilled, ready
  workmen
345 Whom Sôrîk[2] the king of Egypt had given to him from his
  dominion[3],
He, the wise man, called the workmen and taught them
p. 87 How they should make[4] the length and breadth [of it], with
  great strength.
He measured the ground of the narrow pass between the mountains,
That he might shut[5] in the peoples of the house of Mâgôg until
  the end.
350 The king in his wisdom measured from mountain to mountain,
Twelve[6] cubits in the strength of his power.
The king said, "Make ye a threshold for the whole pass,
And let it be sunk in the mountain on this side and on
  that."

---

[1] After this line Add. 14624 reads ܐܘܪ ܣܡܠܐ ܡܟܬܐ ܕܟܡܝ ܡܡܐ ܕܗܠܐ܀
ܕܣܪܠܐ. ܘܣܪܝ ܗܡܪ ܗܘܐ ܡܟܬܐ ܡܗܘܪܐ ܟܣܝܕܩܠܐ ܢܥܟܝܣܘ
ܗܪܙܢܨܘ    [2] Add. 14624 ܐܢܝ ܠܐܢܩܐ ܨܗܢܬܠܐ ܘܢܗܗܘ ܐܝܠܐ ܀

[3] Add. 14624 ܗܘܟܨܪܗ    [4] Add. 14624 ܠܘܩܣܒ

[5] Read ܘܢܣܟܘܗܒ    [6] Add. 14624 ܐܟܐܝ ܣܪܠܘ̈ܨ ܚܗܪܝ
  ܚܕܘܡܠܐ ܘܢܗܪܨܡ܀

They made it of great height (i. e. thickness) and breadth, four cubits',

355   Its length and extent [was] twelve cubits of a strong man.

On each side of the mountain he sunk the head of the threshold,

On both sides two cubits of a strong man'.

He made a lintel (lit. threshold) over the door over all the pass,

And sunk it in the mountains on both sides for the whole [width of the] door'.

360   He made [it] six cubits wide and six cubits high with skill,

Of iron and brass, a marvellous work, the like of which there is not.

The hosts erected and fixed the door there

In all the threshold, above and below', as in clay (sic).

p. 58   He put bolts into' the threshold and into' the door,

365   And sunk them in so that no man knew where they fitted together.

For all the lintel' over the door against the wind

The king made strong posts' of brass and iron.

On this side of these he made bolts of great strength,

Twelve cubits was its length and two cubits its breadth,

---

¹ Reading with Add. 14621 ܚܒܪܘ ܟܠ ܒܪ ܒܘܩ̈ܘ ܐ̈ܚܕ̈ܐ ܐ̈ܚܕ̈ܐ ܐ̈ܚܕ̈ܐ ܐ̈ܚܬ̇

² Add. 14621 adds ܟܒܢ̈ܝ ܗܘܐ ܐ̈ܚܒܐ ܕܒܓ ܡܠܟܐ ܡ̈ܚܘܬ
∴ ܐ̈ܝܢ̈ܕܬ ܟܠܟܕܗ ܒܟܝ̈.   ³ Add. 14624 omits this line.

⁴ Add. 14624 ܘܡܟ̈ܐ̈ܚܘ   ⁵ Add. 24624 ܚܠܠܐ   ⁶ Add. 14624 ܚܡܠܐ

⁷ Add. 14624 ܒܟܝ̈ ܥܟ ܟܚ ܪܘܢܐ ܕܒܩܐܚ sic. ܐܡܘ̈ܡܗ

⁸ Reading with Add. 14624 ܒܓ ܕܒܓ ܡܗܪ̈ܘ ܒܣܢ̈ ܒܣ̈ܝܪ̈ܬ ܗܘܐ ܒ̈ܝܢܬܗ

370  A cubit and a half was the thickness' of the bolt with cunning
        work,

And it held fast the wood (posts)' and the bolts and the door
        and the two sides of the mountain that they might not be
        unloosed'.

The king fixed (lit. threw) doors and beams and bolts in the
        two sides of the mountain,

And another bolt of brass and iron, in his wisdom.

He fixed (lit. threw) the door, and wonder and quietness and
        rest and silence

375  [Came] over the peoples of the house of Mâgôg who had not
        perceived the building.

King Alexander made haste and made the door

Against the north, and against the spoilers and the children
        of Mâgôg.

In the sixth month he finished the building of the whole door.

And the king and all his army marvelled and their hearts re-
p. 89      joiced,

380  That the whole work of the royal building had been built,

A work of which wisdom and intelligence had laid [the foun-
        dations].

Ambassadors went forth into the countries and lands and pro-
        claimed

The great work of the terrible door which the king had made'.


After these things the king, the son of Philip said,

385  "It is meet that we make a great feast to the Lord' in this
        land,

For He came to help us and destroyed our enemies,

And He has helped' us and straightway completed this building.

---

¹ Read ܟܣܗܘ     ⁴ Add. 14624 ܣܩܦܐ     ⁵ Add. 14624 reads

ܐܬܓܙܐ ܡܢܓܘܠܐ ܡܘܐܬܓܙܐ ܡܘ ܘܐܓܘܐ ܡܨܡܐܬܓܙܐ ܡܨܡܨܬܓܙܐ ܡܨܡܟ ܣܢܡܐ ܠܓܚܘ

ܘܐܓܐ ܡܟܚܐ ܘܚܨ ܘܐܬܠܐ and omits the two lines which come after

ܠܐ ܡܐܓܙܐ in Knös which I have translated here, but which seem to be

corrupt.     ⁴ Lines 373—382 are omitted by Add. 14634.

² Reading with Add. 14624 ܠܐܓܟܚܟ     ⁶ Read ܓܪ,

It is He that hath restrained and silenced the children of Mâgôg

That they shall not go forth through this pass during the whole length of the time."

390 The king said, "Let us take incense, and let all the people

Burn it here for a sweet smell to the Lord among their assemblies."

The king and the nobles and the hosts that were with him

Carried fire and sweet incense upon stones and sherds,

They burnt pure incense among the ranks and the thousands and the assemblies,

395 On the new festival upon which was built the great work.

The king said, "If the Lord come into our camp,

And find it of sweet odour, peradventure He will dwell therein."

p. 90 And after [they had burnt] incense king Alexander commanded

That all the people of the palace should rejoice and be glad.

400 The king set in order rich foods for all his hosts

And gave .........¹ to the captains of thousands that they might .........¹

The king commanded that there should be set forth meat for the assembly of his hosts,

And that they should make glad at the table according to their ranks.

He made a feast for the old men and the nobles and the captains of thousands,

405 And they made glad at the table in a loving manner.

The king rejoiced in that building full of cunning works,

Because he had become triumphant through the victory which God had given him.


And having thus rejoiced at the table,

At midday, at the time of noon, the king rested,

410 On a couch (?) of gold, in perfect love and belief.

Then the Lord answered him in a vision, with great wonder,

And He sent a watcher of fire to him* beyond all expectation.

The king saw that fiery being in a dream, and feared,

¹ The words ‏ܗܩܡ‎ and ‏ܩܨܬܢܘܢ‎? do not make good sense here.

² Read ‏ܗܪܡܘܢ‎

p. 91    And he spake with him all hidden and terrible things.

415    The watcher said, "The Lord sent me that I might come to thee,

And inform thee what it is meet for thee to do with Tûbarlîḳî.

Rise up and make peace with Tûbarlîḳî, the king of Persia,

And take away from him the land of Egypt[1] and the land of Jâbûs.

Take from him the land of Palestine[2] and the Hebrews' country

420    And the whole land of Syria and Mesopotamia.

Take from him Phoenicia and Cilicia,

Cappadocia, Galatia and Phrygia,

Also Asia and the territory of the Greeks and Seleucia,

Take his dominion until thou comest to Ḳalkîdîâ,

425    Take his dominion and set the river Kallath as a boundary for yourselves[3].

And let not one of you pass over the boundary which ye set for him."

The Lord spake by the hand of the angel, [saying] "I will magnify thee

More than all the kings and governors in all the world.

p. 92    This great gate which thou hast made[4] in this land

430    Shall be closed until the end of times cometh.

Jeremiah[5] also prophesied concerning it and the earth hath heard,

'The gate of the north shall be opened on the day of the end of the world,

And on that day shall evil go forth on the wicked.

---

¹ Read ܐܘܣܝ ܐܪܥ?    ² Read ܦܠܫܬ

³ Add. 14624 has as the equivalent of lines 388—424 ܘܐܡܪ ܠܗ ܗܘܐ ܗܠܝܢ ܟܠܗܝܢ

ܟܣܝܬܐ ܥܡ ܕܚܝܠܬܐ. ܘܐܡܪ܂ ܕܠܗܘ ܐܘܣܝܐ ܟܕ ܐܢܬ ܥܬܝܕ

ܡܠܟܘܬܗܘ :. ܐܡܪ ܗܘܐ ܠܗ ܗܘ ܗܠܝܢ ܟܠܗ ܐܠܘ :܂ ܘܗܘܐ

ܡܠܟܘܬܗ ܕܝܢ ܕܗܢܐ܂ ܡܩܡܟܬܐ ܠܡܩܡܗ : ܡܣܡ ܠܐ ܕܗܘܐ

ܠܟܠܗܘ ܣܝܡ ܠܟ ܡܠܟܘܬܗ : ܘܗ.

⁴ Add. 14624 ܕܐܒܝܕ?    ⁵ Add. 14624 ܐܚܟܡ

There shall be woe to those who are with child and to those
who give suck[1].'

'435 The Lord says, "In that the seven thousandth year
Shall there be rumours and dire quakings in all countries.
Sin and wickedness and all evil things shall increase in the
world,
Envy, craftiness, adultery, murder and all hateful things,
Lying and slander of the children of wickedness.

440 Fraud and pride[2] shall increase in the earth,
And haughtiness and lasciviousness and infidelity[3],
And schisms and contentions shall fall among the children of
men.
The heavens shall be like darkness and the earth shall quake,
And the love of many shall wax cold in these days[4].

445 And wars and captivities and death shall increase among the
children of men.
And there shall be famines and cruel wars in various countries,

p. 93 And there shall be also tumults in the islands that are in
the sea.
And the sun and the moon and the stars shall be dark in their
risings,
And the earth shall be devoured by fire[5] and locusts and mighty
hail,

450 The ends of the earth shall tremble with the noise of the thun-
dering in all lands,
And winter and winds and storms and lightnings and mighty
earthquakes.
The heavens shall become like smoke through darkness,
The sea shall be troubled[6], and wickedness shall increase in
all the world.
Towns and cities and villages shall dwell in mourning,

455 Through the terrible quakings of all the horrible signs[7].

---

[1] Jeremiah i. 14 ; S. Matt. xxiv. 19.    [2] Read ܠܩܘܒܠܐ    [3] Add.

14624 ܟܪܣܘܬܐ    [4] S. Matt. xxiv. 12.    [5] Reading ܒܢܘܪܐ with

Add. 14624.    [6] Reading with Add. 14624 ܘܬܬܕܠܚ

[7] Add. 14624 ܘܩܪܝܐ ܘܩܘܪܝܐ ܟܠܗ ܥܡ ܣܘܟܪܬܐ

And when these things have come to an end and passed away[1]
>    before the end

The earth shall quake and this door which thou hast made
>    be opened[2].

At the end of times creatures and men shall make evil to
>    increase,

And wickedness shall wax strong in all quarters of the earth,
>    and the Lord shall be grieved[3],

460    And anger with fierce wrath shall rise up on mankind.

And the earth and vineyards and oliveyards and all plants shall
>    be laid waste,

And woods and gardens; and the earth and mankind shall
>    dwell in mourning[4],

And destructive winds shall go forth against creation;

p. 94    And the Lord shall visit evil upon the world, upon the fertile
>    lands[5].

465    And the nation that is within this gate[6] shall be roused up,

And also the hosts of Âgôg and of the peoples of Mâgôg shall
>    be gathered together.

These peoples, the fiercest of all creatures,

Of the mighty house of Japhet [are they] of whom the Lord
>    spake, [saying], 'They shall go forth on the earth

And cover all creation like[7] a locust.'"

470    The king marvelled at these things which he had heard from
>    the angel

Whom the Lord had sent to him in a vision to teach him these
>    things.

The watcher said, "When all the things that are written have
>    been completed,

---

[1] Read ܐ̈ܢܐ ܟܠܗܘܢ ܡܢ ܕܝܢ ܚ̈ܠܡܬܐ ܥܡܕܘ     [6] After this line Add.

14624 adds ܐܗܕ ܚܡܪ܏ ܠܚܕܐ ܣܡܡܬ ܡܠܟܐ ܘܕܐ     [2] Read

ܘܐ̈ܟܠܬܗ Add. 14624 has ܐܚܕܘ

[4] Add. 14624 ܡܠܬ ܚܕܝܪܐ ܘܐܢܡܐ ܕܐܝܢܐ ܕܐܝܢܐ     [3] Read ܐܩܠܗ

[6] Read ܐܕܝܪ     [7] Read ܐܝܟܡܐ Add. 14624 ܐܣܕܝ ܗܕ ܡܢ ܩܡܕܝ

The Lord will command, and by His beck will be opened[1] this
door.

When the anger of the Lord waxes hot to slay men,

475 In His ill will He will rouse up the people of the house of
Mâgôg against the lands.

In the seven thousandth year, in which the heavens and the
earth shall be dissolved,

The hosts and troops shall go forth from their lands.

The thousands and the ranks and the assemblies without
number shall come

And shall stand behind this door, and shall give voice with

480 An exceeding great cry stronger than the wind and the loud
thunder [saying],

p. 96 'O Lord, our Lord, open to us the gate that we may go forth
on the earth.'

The mountains and the earth and mankind shall tremble at
that time

By reason of that wrathful and angry and terrifying voice.

At that time the cry shall go forth among their ranks,

485 And the voice of the Lord shall overthrow the height of this
door.

Over the threshold which carries this strong door,

The hosts of horses and men shall tread and go forth.

Another host which shall go forth after the hosts

.....................................................................[2]

The door and the bolts shall the Lord destroy and carry away.

490 The hosts which shall go forth from thence shall cover the earth.

In anger shall the hosts and the assemblies and the thousands
go forth,

With drawn swords and bent bows and sharp arrows,

With wrath and murder and eager horses and pointed spears.

---

[1] Add. 14624 ܡܣܬܬܚ ܕܛܪܥܐ ܗܢܐ    [2] A line appears to

have fallen out here, for Add. 14624 reads ܡܢܐ ܐܣܪܐ ܕܬܦܣܩ ܗܘ
ܡܣܟܩܐ. ܘܢܦܩ ܣܢܕܐ ܕܡܢܐ ܒܬܪ ܗܘ ܡܢ ܣܢܕܐ. ܠܬܪ
ܡܣܟܬܐ ܕܣܒܣܘܣ ܢܘܣܡܣ ܡܕܘܣ ܣܢ

With great wrath shall each one of them pursue a thousand,
495 And through fear ten thousand shall flee away before two.
They will fly and settle down upon the quarters of the whole
    world,
And kings and hosts shall flee away before them.
p. 96 The tips of the spears shall rub away the strength of that
    lintel (lit. threshold),
And the beam which thou hast made with great strength
    above the door.
500 This door which thou hast made shall not be opened by a
    key.
At the end of times shortly [before the end] shall they go forth
    [over] the earth[1],
They shall not desire gold or silver or cattle,
Neither possessions, nor the riches of this world.
These people shall go forth for slaughter and blood and strife,
505 And shall fly and fill the face of the world with wars and
    slaughters.
The assemblies of warriors shall not be delivered from them,
The whole creation shall totter[2] and fall under the ruin[3].

---

[1] Add. 14624 reads ܠܗ ܗܘܟܠܐܝ ܘܕܚܠ ܡܟܠܐ ܟܠܟܣ ܡܗܦܟܗܣ ܠܟܠܐ ܗܘܐ
ܘܐܣܡܣܟ ܚܐܩܒ ܐܝܗܝ ܘܪܚܣ ܥܠܝܗܝ. ܚܣܝ ܠܚܕܐ ܐܩܕܝ
ܡܗܣܝܣܐܠ ܡܪܡ ܡܘܟܡܐ. ܚܪܡܟܐ ܘܡܟܢܠ ܠܗܦܟܣܘ ܠܟܠܐ
ܚܪܝܗܠܐ ܐܕܐ ܚܕܐ ܡܘܗܣܘ ܚܩܡܟܐ ܡܣܟܠܩܐܠ ܩܠ ܡܟܣܣܐ. ܢܣܗܣ
ܠܐܕܐ ܘܠܐܘܪܠܠܐ ܗܟܣܝ ܠܘܘܪܠܐܠ ܡܣ ܚܢܩܐ. ܘܐܟܗܐ ܡܣ ܠܩܡܘ ܢܦܣܣ ܡܟܠܐ
ܟܠܐܚܠ ܗܘܐ ܠܣܗ ·:·          [2] Add. 14624 ܚܪܗܠ

[3] After this line Add. 14624 (fol. 80 a. 2) adds ܚܪܡܟܐ ܗܡܟܝ ܦܟܣܚܣ
ܠܐܕܐ ܚܪܝܗܠܐ ܐܕܐ. ܗܟܣܝ ܩܠܠ ܡܗܟܣ ܗܘܐ ܡܟܟܐܠ ܡܣ ܡܟܠܐܠܐ :
ܘܡܟܠܠ ܟܡܟܣ ܚܕܣܘܪܐ ܘܐܕܐ ܟܠܐ ܚܡܩܣܐܠ ·:· ܐܩܕ ܚܣܪܐ ܘܪܗܐܕܐ ܟܚܟܟܚܠ
ܠܐܕܚܡܣܪܗܣܡܗܣ. ܚܣܝ ܐܚܩܐ ܚܪܝܗܠܐ ܠܘܘܪܠܐ ܠܐܕܐ ܗܘܐ. ܢܩܣܗ
ܡܟܣܣ ܡܟܢܩܐ ܘܣܢܠܐ ܘܠܐ ܡܟܣܣܠܐ. ܚܣܩܐܣܐ ܠܐܟܣܣܐ ܡܟܠܐܠ ܣܚܠܠ

Concerning that day Isaiah[1] cried and the earth heard,
'They shall not be eager for[2] gold and silver and pearls,
310 Nor riches[2] nor fine raiment nor possessions.
They shall dash weaned children on the stones without sparing,
And they shall rip up women with child and cast them down
  with their offspring.'
The rivers of the whole world shall be accounted nothing by
  them,
And rough mountains and valleys and gorges shall not restrain
p. 97   them.
515 They shall rise up and go forth and fill the earth with their
  assemblies, and with
War and captivity and strife and blood and great slaughter.
When the anger of the Lord waxes hot against the wicked,
He will send over the earth the people of Âgôg and the people
  of Mâgôg.
Before the end of the world shall they go forth to destroy,
520 The earth will be drunk with the tumult of men and the mountains shall tremble.
He[4] will come to Persia and will strip it and destroy it,

ܐ. ܘܗܐ ܐܝܟܐ ܘܘܝܚܢܐ݂ ܪܚܟܢܗ ܠܡܐ ܡܥ ܠܚܡ݂ ܗܡܬ݀ ܐ ܘܘܘܘ ܘܝܪܐ؟    [1] Isaiah xiii. 17, 18.

[2] Add. 14624 ܡܚܝ݂ܝܚܡ           [3] Read ܕܚܚܡܘ݂ܗ

[4] I. e. the nation of Âgôg and Mâgôg.

He will come to India and will cut it in pieces and destroy it,
He will overthrow Syria and pass over and terrify it,
He will destroy and lay waste and overthrow Cilicia,
525 He will make an end of Cappadocia and will slay [the people
    thereof] with terror.
And tremblings shall fall upon countries and upon their inhabi-
    tants,
And the earth shall be a desolation and a captivity and a
    whistling.
They shall cover[1] the earth with arms and spears and polished
    swords[2],
And kings and governors shall not be able to stand before
530 Those who from God have received power over creation.
The voice of each one of them is stronger than that of a lion,
p. 98 And one shall pursue a thousand, and two of them ten thousand.
Hateful and terrible, cruel and bitter and warlike [are]
The hosts of the children of Âgôg and of the people of Mâgôg[3],
535 Tumultuous, evil, sinful, excitable, proud, unclean,
Filthy, haughty and full of woe and great judgment.
They rend and devour the flesh of men and of beasts,
They all wash in blood which has flowed from mankind[4]."

And when all these things had been spoken by the angel
540 To the wise king Alexander, the son of Philip,
The angel[5], in the spirit of the revelation of prophecy, told him
To write down these things and teach the world that these
    things would happen.
And when all these things had been said by the angel,
The Spirit of the Lord rested upon[6] the king as upon Jeremiah,

<hr />

¹ Read ܘܡܪܩ̈ܬܐ

ܘ ܣ̈ܟܝܢܐ ܕܡ̈ܦܬܟܬܐ

² Add. 14624 adds ܘܗ̈ܝ ܐܫܕ ܕܡ̈ܐ ܐܚ̈ܝ

³ Add. 14624 omits this line.

⁴ After this line Add. 14624 reads ܘܕ̈ܚܠ ܐܟܡ ܡ̇ܪ̈ܝ ܡ̈ܐܟܠܐ ܕܗܝ̇

ܕܡܚܣܪ̈ܝܢ. ܘܚ̈ܒܝ ܘܒ̈ܝ̈ܫ̈ܐ ܘܡ̈ܚ̈ܒܠܝܢ ܕܡ̈ܬܠܐ. ܐܡ̇ܪ ܟܕ

ܕ̈ܡܐ ܨ̈ܪܒ ܕܡ̈ܫܟܢܬܐ ܘܕ̈ܒܨܡܨ. ܘܒܚ̈ܫ̈ܒ ܐܢ̈ܝ ܗ̈ܦܟ ܕܚ̈ܠܡ

ܕܗܘ̈ܢ ܫ̈ܝܘܠ ܀    ⁵ Read ܡ̈ܠܐ̈ܟܐ    ⁶ Read ܥܠ

545 And he wrote down hidden things like Daniel[1] and like Isaiah.
He wrought mighty deeds and destroyed kings in their wars,
He destroyed idols like Hezekiah[2] and like Josiah[3],
The just king who served truth and righteousness.

p. 99 The earth shone through his wisdom full of beauties,

550 And he wrote[4] and showed everything that was to come like Daniel.
Alexander the king, the son of Philip, said,
"Let the kings and their ranks and their dominions tremble,
On the day on which these people go forth over the earth at the end of times.
And men and all the quarters of the earth will anger the Lord of Hosts,

555 And His anger will rise and blot out the earth with an evil desolation.
Mighty Rûm from her greatness He shall throw down to the depth[5].
The seas shall roar, the earth shall cry out, and the mountains shall shriek,
The valleys shall fear, and towns and villages shall be desolated.
The vineyards shall be destroyed and stupor shall fall upon the planters thereof,

560 Joy shall come to an end, and the power of all mighty men shall fall.
Beautiful things[6] shall perish, riches shall fail and power shall vanish,
Fountains shall fail, streets shall be destroyed, and the valleys shall be useless.
The hosts and filthy[7] assemblies of the children of Mâgôg shall stand up,
And all creation shall become and remain a ruin.

---

[1] Daniel, chap. vii—xii.      [2] 2 Kings xviii. 4.

[3] 2 Kings xxiii. 4—14.      [4] Read with Add. 14624 ܣܠܒܩ

[5] Add. 14624 reads ܠܘܣܘܪܝ ܘܥܠܟ ܠܐܘܪܙܠܠܗ ܣܪܚܒܣ ܗܣܘܣܗ
ܠܢܪܙ ܐܝܣܠ      [6] Reading with Add. 14624 ܠܪܣܗ

[7] Reading with Add. 14624 ܠܪܚܗ

B. A.                                    13

563  And from the signs and bitter rumours
He that is wise will understand concerning the end.
Lebanon and Sânîr and their fellows shall be accounted nothing
    to him, [i. e. to the nation of Gog and Magog]
The mountains of Carmel shall not restrain the host that is
    with him.
His voice thunders, the rumour of him is terrible, and his
    strength is fearful,

570  His appearance is evil, his form huge and altogether harsh.
Deformed is his visage, violent is his strength, and dark is his
    colour,
His form is long, his weapon is sharp, and the whole of him
    is death[1].
Evil sounds and tremblings and rumours shall run before him,
And horrible things and captivities and famines and deaths
    and all evil things.

575  He shall quench the beauty of the sun and of the moon and of
    all luminaries,
The hills and the valleys shall put on darkness[2] and sadness.
Laws shall come to an end and the whole earth shall dwell in
    mourning,
And the world shall become like a desolate and a sterile
    thing.
Depict in me, O our Lord, the beauty of Thy word in a loving
    way,

580  That I may preach the sign of the day of Thy coming as far as
    I am able.
That great nation[3] which is perverse in its works,
And bears woe and is full of wrath and slaughter and death,

p. 101  For evil captivity and destruction do they prepare with great
    wrath,
For spoil and slaughter are they all [i. e. the nation] ready
    without ceasing.

585  They all threaten with power and there is wrath in their
    cursings,
Mountains and valleys and plains tremble at them.

---

[1] Add. 14624 omits this and the preceding line.

[2] Reading with Add. 14624 ܚܫܟܐ    [3] Read with Add. 14624 ܥܡܐ

And great woe [shall be] upon those who are with child and
those who give suck,

And mourning and pain upon young men and maidens,

Weeping for the children being slain through the cutting off of
hope,

And for the youths also being cut off by the baleful ones.

The heavens and the earth will put on pain[1] and sadness,

And the assemblies of celestial beings will be astonished in
those days[2].

Quaking will fall upon the living and the dead at that time,

Through the slaughter and blood of the children of Mâgôg
before the end.

A renowned people will stir up strife in the lands,

And cast tumult among cities and towns,

An ugly people, a people flayed and uprooted[3] and full of
blemishes,

Of the children of Âgôg and of the house of Mâgôg with their
fellows.

In abundance will they come to Palestine madly,

They will uproot and destroy its cities and slay [its] people.

The race of men, nation after nation, will roar and cry out[4],

Joy and gladness shall cease and woe will reign,

Weeping and spoiling and wickedness and all sadness shall
increase.

They will uproot walls and towers and streets and towns,

And they shall become mounds, and stupor shall fall upon all
creation.

Come, O Jeremiah, the prophet of the Spirit and of revelation,

And take up bitter cries of lamentation concerning that day.

The prophet says, 'Woe to thee, O land, for a mighty nation

Is sent against thee; with arms and captivity shall he destroy
thy children[5].'

---

[1] Add. 14624 ܠܒܣܐ

[2] Read ܣܘܠܡܐ ܗܘܐ

[3] Read ܡܠܟܝ ܘܚܣܕ ܒܨܝܪ|

[4] Add. 14624 adds ܣܘܠܒܣܠܟܝ

ܠܒܨ ܒ ܡܟܣܡܣܝܣܝܒ ܡܢ ܗܘܪܝ|

[5] Jeremiah v. 15—17.   Add. 14624 reads ܐܟܕ| ܒܚ ܒ ܢܨܠ ܐܟܕ|

13—2

610  The prophet says, 'Thus shall all creation be
    For a great astonishment and for a treading down, for slaugh-
       ter and disgrace.
    All creation shall kneel and fall down before that nation
    And the earth shall be destroyed of its inhabitants with great
       slaughter.
    The priests and their flocks shall seize a place of respite
615  And take up tears and lamentation bitterly[1].
    Flocks and herds and cows and oxen shall dwell in mourning.'
p. 103  The prophet says 'Woe to thee, O earth, what is this nation
    Harsh of speech which slays and destroys without sparing?
    The keepers of vineyards shall weep over the vineyards[2]
       through sorrow,
620  And all the dwellings of the shepherds shall dwell in mourning.'
    The earth shall say, 'Woe is me, for I have seen all revolutions
    With evil quakings and disturbed horrible things full of misery.'
    For to them will the Lord cry in anger at the end of times[3],
    And as with a broom will the Lord sweep and purge it,
625  And He will overturn it and rend it and destroy it.
    Gloomy and sorry and full of darkness shall be the days and
       months,
    Before the coming of the sinful people of the children of Mâgôg.
    In these days the living will ascribe happiness to the dead,
    By reason of the disturbance and quaking and slaughter and
      blood.
630  They shall not, however, enter into Jerusalem, the city of the
      Lord.

ܪܚܡܐ ܕܐ ܚܠܚܢܒ ܡܠܡܐܙ. ܨܪܝܐ ܡܪܝܐ ܠܒܨܠܐ ܡܠܪܝܢܪ
ܐܡܪ ܢܒܝܐ. ܡܚܐ ܠܘܢ ܠܚܐ ܚܚܠܢܗ ܐܙܐ ܚܠܡܠܢܐ ܐܙܐ.

       [1] Add. 14624 reads ܠܒܨܨܐ ܒܡܐ ܚܡܐ ܡ̄ܘܪܙܝܗ̄ ܚܪܢܐ ܒܚܚܡ

ܡܥܡܢܟ ܙܡܢܐ ܐܗ ܚܨܐܪ ܙܚܝܪܐ. ܒܚܚܡ ܠܘܐܙܐܪ ܚܠܐ ܡܥܚܚܟ

ܡܪ. ܡܕܚܚܡ ܚܠܐܡ ܚܚܗ. ܪܚܠܚܐ ܚܚܗ;       [2] Reading with Add. 14624

ܚܝܠܐ ܐܚܝܐ. ܒܚܚܡ ܙܪܚܚܡ       [3] Add. 14624 ܒܚܚܡ ܚܡܚܐ ܚܠܐ ܚܪܚ ܚܪܒܐ

ܗܡ̄ ܠܐܙܐ ܥܡܠܠ ܡܪܝܐ ܡܨܠܐ ܐܚܐ. ܐܝܪ ܡܚܚܚܐܠܐ ܗܘ̄

For the sign (i.e., the Cross) of the Lord shall drive them
away from it, and they shall not enter it.
All the saints shall fly away from them to mount Sânir[1],
All faithful true ones and the good and all the wise.

p. 104 They shall not be able to approach mount Sinai, for it is
the dwelling place of the Lord,

635 Nor to the high mountains of Sinai[1] with their shame[2].
By Jerusalem shall fall by the sword the hosts
Of the children of Âgôg and of the house of Mâgôg with great
slaughter.
After these things shall the days full of trouble decrease[3],
And evil shall come and stand in the world with great trembling.

640 And the earth shall be drunk with the blood and slaughter
of their ranks,
For the sword of a man shall fall upon his fellow with great
amazement.
And if it were possible for the mountains and the earth and the
stones
And the sea and the dry land to weep, they would weep for
the whole world.
O how much more bitter than the slaughter of the sword and
the blood of the spear,

645 Is the affliction of the cursed children of the great family of
Japhet!
For[4] they shall lead away captive and subdue the earth and
all people.

---

[1] Add. 14624 ܟܘܪ̈ܝܣ̈ܡܠܟܠ   [2] Reading with Add. 14624 ܐܛܠ ܟܘܪܐ̈

ܡܟܪܐ ܐܡܬܩܣ̈ܡܚܐ Compare ܣܘܢ̈ܩܣ̈ܡܚܐ • ܬܡܟ? ܬܡܟ܀

ܬܫܦܚ̈ ܠܘܡ "The Lord shall uncover their shame," Isaiah iii. 17.

[3] Reading with Add. 14624 ܟܣܚ ܟܝܢ̈ܠܟܡ ܐܟܡ ܟܝܬܐ̈ ܣܠܟܘܬ ܐܬܟ?ܡܚܘ

[4] Add. 14624 reads ܟܣ ?ܟܚܘܡܘ ܘܚܘܬܨ̈ܡܚ ܠܟܐܠ ܐܟܝܠ ܘܠܐܡܚ

ܟܚܣܘܡ. ܘܣܪܡ ܢܩܠܟ ܣܢܐܠ ?ܠ̈ܘܥܝ ܘܬܨܕܐ ܡܚ?ܥܝܘܦ܀ ܠܘܬ

ܢܩܠܟ ?ܡܚ?ܐ ܚܣܨܘܚ ܬܟܡܐ ܚܟܡܐ. ܚܡܬܛܐ ܦܠܐ?ܡܘ ܐܣܣܘܐܠ

ܬܣܘܟܣܚܐ. ܘܐܟܐ ?ܐܟܐ ܟܠܠܡܘܣܡ ܣܪܐ ?ܠ?ܘܦ ܠܥܚ܀

Then the hosts of Ágôg and of the house of Mágôg shall go forth,

And man shall fall upon his fellow, and nation upon nation,

And the quaking of the earth and the sword of anger shall be there.

650 On the skirts of Zion shall the bodies of the dead[1] [lie] in heaps.

p. 105 And after these things the earth shall be desolated of mankind,

Villages shall be destroyed and all towns and cities;

The scattered ones only remain in the earth as a remnant.

Then shall Antichrist rise upon the whole earth,

655 Through that gate shall go forth and come that rebel;

That lying one shall Christ overthrow as is promised[2].

There shall stand up before him demons and spirits and wicked devils,

And they shall gather together all creation to their cursed master.

The earth shall cry out, 'I entreat Thee, O Lord, in Thy mercy to spare me,

660 For, behold, I am sick and persecuted with all wounds.'

These things which I have spoken shall come to pass before the end of the world,

And let him that hath an ear of love listen to them."

These beautiful things did king Alexander interpret,

That they should all take place before that day at the end.

665 "And after these things the heavens and the earth will put on pain[3],

And times and days and months in their courses will cease,

p. 106 And will not again return to the earth from whence they came.

When the assemblies of the thousands of the children of Ágôg and of the house of Mágôg,

---

[1] Read ܘܩܛܝ̈ܠܐ

[2] Add. 14624 ܘܣܡ: ܐܢܕ ܕܐܢܐ ܡܠܟܐ ܐܣܟܢܕܪܘܣ ܣܡ ܗܢܐ ܠܘܩܒܠ ܘܗܘ ܡܪܘܕܐ ܗܘ ܕܐܠܝܗ. ܗܘ ܡܪܝܡ ܡܚܡܣܢ ܘܣܡ ܠܗܠܝܢ.

[3] Add. 14624 ܘܟܕ ܫܠܡ ܟܠܗ ܕܚܝܠ ܡܠܟܐ ܐܠܟܣܢܕܪ

Have destroyed all constituted things with a great slaughter,
670 Creation, weeping and lamenting, will cry out [saying], 'What
    wilt thou do [more]?'
The earth will say, 'Let the assemblies of the height entreat
    for me
Thy great name', the power which bears the height and the
    depth.'"

O Jesus, look upon me in mercy and love, I entreat Thee,
May I see Thee in peace when Thou risest with Thy angels!
675 "The whole creation shall totter and fall with great quaking,
By reason of the signs; the end cometh, it is not far off.
By Jerusalem shall perish and come to an end the hosts
Of the children of Àgôg and of the house of Màgôg together
    with their fellows,
And there shall that lying one be put to shame in his infi-
    delity',
680 And the whole baneful company of idolatry shall be overcome.
Little by little shall be filled the web of all this world,
That it may incline and come speedily to' the end.
The Lord will look upon the earth with wrath and great anger,
And it shall pass away and become nothing; but He shall not
p. 107     pass away.
685 Out of the north then shall come evil to all the earth,
And Isaiah cried to creation on account of this'."


O Jesus, O King in Whose hands are the height and the
    depth,
In Thee shall the Church and her children take refuge from
    trouble'.
Blessed be the Good One Who stretched out the height and
    Who laid out' the earth.

¹ Add. 14624 ܐܕܳܬ ܟܝܘܠ ܝ ² Add. 14624 ܘܪܐ̈ܣܡ ³ Read ܝܪܡ

⁴ Reading with Add. 14634 ܐܡܕ ܚܠ ܣܪܒ ]ܐܕܚܐ[ ܗܒܐ ]ܗܢ ܘܗܠܠܣܡ Isaiah
xiii. 4—19.

⁵ Add. 14624 reads ܘܗ ܬܣܕܠܣܡ ·]ܠܕ ܐܡܚ ܐ̈ܝܠܣ ܐܕܠܟܦ ܢܐܘ
.]ܣܩܢ]ܐ ]ܚܐ ܠܣܟܐܙ ܪܚ .ܟܟܡܟܡ     ⁶ Read ܘܢܠܣ

G90  They shall pass away but Thou shalt stand, O Lord, our Lord.

.....................................................................

And power to all His servants and the victory (?) of might[2].
From the celestial and from the terrestrial beings to Thee be
    praise,
For [Thy] grace and compassion and mercy upon sinners.
Blessed be the Lord who gave victory to Alexander,

695  And he conquered and destroyed the inhabitants of the lands.
Grant unto me, O Lord, a mouth that I may preach Thy great
    glory,
That it may cry out before Thee on the day of Thy revelation,
    "Glory to Thee,"
And to the readers and the writer [of this book] may there
    be remission of sins,
And to the hearer and the doer may there be propitiation.

700      Here endeth the discourse upon Alexander
    And upon the gate which he made towards the north.
    Yea and Amen[1].

[1] The discourse in Add. 14624 comes to an end with the words ܥܠܝ ܠܟܡ

ܐܠܟܣܢܕܪܘܣ

[2] This appears to be the meaning of the line, but I suspect that either one
or more lines before it have been omitted.

[3] Dr. C. Bezold has kindly called my attention to a German translation of
this discourse by P. Pius Zingerle. It was made in 1871 and was privately
printed by the care of J. Zingerle in 1882 under the title of *Ein altes Syrisches
Alexanderlied.* Druck von Rudolf M. Rohrer in Brünn. Pius Zingerle was
unable to find a publisher for his translation and, when an editor of a scientific
journal wished to publish it with an introduction and description of the manuscripts, he wrote, "Von der Bekanntmachung meiner Uebersetzung der Alexandersage stehe ich gerne ab. Da werden allerlei gelehrte Forderungen gestellt, zu
denen ich nicht aufgelegt bin. Ich bin leider nicht gewöhnt, bei meinen Arbeiten
so gründlich zu Werke zu gehen." I have not been able to find any Syriac
equivalent for the passage entitled *Fortsetzung über Alexander's Geschick,*
printed on pp. 15—17 of Zingerle's pamphlet.

# GLOSSARY.

# GLOSSARY.

# GLOSSARY.

ܐܒܒ ܐܰܒܽܘܒܳܐ Ar. أنبوب, *reed pipe, flute*, p. 103. 7.

ܐܒܪ ܐܰܒܳܪܳܐ Ar. آبار, *lead*, p. 193. 3.

ܐܶܓܳܪܳܐ *pass, close*, plur. ܐܶܓܳܪ̈ܶܐ p. 15. 7, where ܒܓܕ̈ܘܗܝ is explained by ܐܓܪ̈ܘܗܝ

ܐܰܓܽܘܓܳܐ *pipe, watercourse*, plur. ܐܰܓܽܘܓ̈ܶܐ p. 106. 11.

ܐܓܘܪܣܐ *hamlet*, plur. ܐܓܘܪ̈ܣܐ p. 206. 5.

ܐܕܡܘܣ ἀδάμας, *adamant*, p. 9. 2.

ܐܶܕܪܝܰܢܛܳܐ, ܐܰܢܕܪܝܰܢܛܳܐ *image, statue*, p. 60. 9, 10, 19; 67. 6; 68. 8, 10; 70. 12, 17; 76. 8; 77. 1; 126. 10; 194. 14; 206. 15; 233. 9; 236. 3; plur. ܐܶܕܪ̈ܝܰܢܛܶܐ p. 136. 14; 161. 5, 6; 181. 12; 218. 16; 233. 5.

ܐܘܪܡܣܝܢ A kind of wood which "no woodworm attacks," p. 219. 17. The word is perhaps a corruption of the Greek word ἀμίαντος.

ܐܘܚܕܢܘܬܐ *power, rule*, p. 103. 20. The text actually has ܐܘܚܕܢܘܬ

ܐܘܚܕܢ see ܐܚܘܕܢ

ܐܘܩܝܢܘܣ ὠκεανός, *sea, ocean*, p. 20. 5; 256. 12; 266. 17.

ܐܚܪ. ܐܚܪ̈ܢܝܬܐ for ܐܚܪܢܝܐ *another*, p. 10, note 4.

ܐܛܡܘܢܐ *thongs*, p. 48. 8; 135. 4. In B this word is glossed by ܬܣܡܬܐ, Pers. تسمه

ܐܛܪܘܓܐ Chald. אֶתְרוֹגָא, Arab. أُتْرُجّ, *citron*, plur. ܐܛܪ̈ܘܓܐ p. 217. 5.

ܐܝܬܘܬܐ *being, existence*, p. 104. 6.

ܐܟܕܢܐ *viper*, plur. ܐܟܕ̈ܢܐ p. 266. 2.

ܐܟܠ ܩܪ̈ܨܐ, ܡܐܟܠ ܩܪ̈ܨܐ *calumny*, p. 55. 5.

ܐܟ̈ܠܝ ܒܢ̈ܝܢܫܐ *cannibals*, p. 97. 18.

ܐܟܦ. ܐܘܟܦܐ Ar. إِكَاف, *packsaddle*, plur. ܐܘܟ̈ܦܐ p. 231. 6. The form ܐܘܟܦ̈ܢܐ is given by Duval, *Lexicon Syriacum auctore Hassano bar Bahlule*, col. 61.

ܐܠܟܣܢܕܪܝܐ, ܐܠܟܣܢܕܪܝܬܐ plur. ܐܠܟܣܢܕܪ̈ܝܬܐ *Alexandrian* ships, p. 205. 1.

ܐܠܦ. ܡ̈ܠܐ ܝܠܝܦܬܐ *words learnt by heart*, p. 107. 11.

ܐܠ̈ܦܐ ܕܬܠܬܐ *triremes*, p. 63. 8.

ܐܡܘܢ *Egypt.* 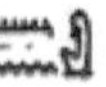 Ȧmen, Ἀμμοῦν, Heb. אָמוֹן, *Ammon*, p. 22. 4. For pictures of the various forms of this god as found on Egyptian monuments see Lanzone, *Dizionario di Mitologia Egizia*, plates XVII—XXI.

ܐܡܣܬܐ *spade*, plur. ܐܡ̈ܣܐ p. 101. 4. D and E have ܐܡܣܬܐ

ܐܡܢ. ܐܡܝܢܐܝܬ *continually, perpetually*, p. 12. 9.

ܐܢܢܩܐ ἀνάγκη, *necessity*, p. 140. 7; plur. ܐܢܢ̈ܩܐ p. 61. 19; 62. 12; ܐܢܢ̈ܩܣ p. 156. 20.

ܐܢܬ. ܓܢܬ, ܓܢܬܐ, plur. ܓܢ̈ܬܐ *effeminate men*, p. 100. 18.

ܐܣܐ *wall*, plur. ܐܣ̈ܐ p. 218. 11.

ܐܣܛܒܪܩܐ Arab. إِسْتَبْرَق, Pers. إِسْتَبْرَك, *brocaded silks*, p. 200. 9. The word is glossed in B by ܕܡܫܐ ܕܡܠܘܟܐ (Ar. دَسْت, Pers. دَشْت).

ܐܣܛܘܢ, ܐܣܛܘܢܐ Ar. اسطوانة, Pers. استون, *pillar*, *pedestal*, p. 60. 8; 173. 15; plur. ܐܣܛܘܢ̈ܐ, ܐܣܛܘܢ̈ܐ, p. 219. 5; 256. 1.

ܐܣܛܝܪ, ܐܣܛܝܪܐ, *στατήρ*, *stater*, plur. ܐܣܛܝܪܝܢ, p. 147. 17. The Egyptian form of the word is  *setetert*, Coptic сатєєрє and саѳнрı. See Brugsch, *Zeit. Aeg. Sprache*, 1889, p. 9.

ܐܣܛܪܛܠܛ̈ܐ *officers*, p. 144. 2.

ܐܣܟܡܐ *σχῆμα*, *apparel*, *dress*, p. 4. 17; ܐܣܟܝܡܐ *caste*, p. 31. 2.

ܐܣܩܘܦܬܐ *threshold*, p. 267. 10, 12, 13; 268. 4, 6; 269. 16.

ܐܘܨܪܐ *barn*, *storehouse*, p. 75. 6.

ܐܣܦܘܓܐ f. *σπόγγος*, *sponge*, plur. ܐܣܦܘ̈ܓܐ, p. 190. 8.

ܐܣܦܝܪܐ *ball*, p. 80. 17; 81. 11; 87. 10; 237. 8, 9, 10; plur. ܐܣܦܝܪܝܢ p. 193. 11; ܐܣܦܝܪ̈ܐ p. 193. 9; 237. 1, 5, 7.

ܐܣܦܠܐ *beaker*, p. 147. 11.

ܐܦܕܢܐ Ar. فَدَن, Heb. אַפֶּדֶן *palace*, p. 11. 12; 13. 8; 17. 1; 29. 14; 58. 12, 14; 59. 2; 197. 12. We have ܐܦܕܢ̈ܐ given once for the sing. (p. 2. 8). The Babylonian form of the word is *Ap-pa-da-an* and occurs in the inscription of Artaxerxes Mnemon, line 8. See Bezold, *Die Achämenideninschriften*, p. 44.

ܐܩܘܒܝܛܘܢ, ܐܩܘܒܝܛܢ *ἀκούβιτον*, *couch*, 51. 6, 12.

ܐܩܡܐ *ἀκμή*, *age*, p. 10. 16; 14. 14. D has ܐܩܡܝ p. 14, note 7.

ܐܪܕܟܠܐ p. 181. 10. I do not know the meaning of this word in this passage; it is probably corrupt. ܐܪܕܟܠܐ usually means "architect," and has been thought by some to be derived from the two Assyrian words *arad êgal* "man, or servant, of the palace."

ܐܪܕܟܠܘܬܐ *architects*, p. 74. 4. This word is explained in this passage by ܕܟܘ ܢܓܪܐ "chiefs of carpenters."

ܐܪܕܟܠܝܕܐ p. 268. 14. I do not know the meaning of this word in this passage.

ܐܪܡܠܬܐ. Ethpa"al part. ܡܬܐܪܡܠܐ *to be made, or become a widow*, p. 244. 9.

ܐܪܡܛܝܒܕܐ for ܐܪܡܝܕ (?) ܐܣܩܕܟܠܡܕܐ p. 42. 15.

ܐܫܟܪܥܐ Chald. אַשְׁכְּרֹעַ *acacia wood*, p. 8. 4.

ܐܫܘܬ ܐܫܘܬܐ *adder* (?) p. 266. 3; plur. ܐܫܘܬܐ p. 275. 2

ܐܫܬܘܦ *would that!* p. 26. 10; 96. 14; 224. 9.

ܐܒܝܕ Pe'îl part. pass. plur. ܐܒܝܕܝܢ p. 46. 4.

ܐܬܠܝܛܘܬܐ L *ἄθλησις, athletic exercises*, p. 110. 10; 111. 5.

ܒܓܠ. Pa"el ܒܓܠ *to complain*, p. 36. 20; 37. 13, 14. Part. plur. masc. ܡܬܒܓܠܝܢ p. 38. 3; ܡܬܒܓܠܝܢ *to complain bitterly*, p. 37. 13.

ܒܓܠܬܐ *blame*, p. 36. 4.

ܒܕܩ. Pa"el ܒܕܩ *to spy out, to search out*, p. 3. 16. Part. masc. ܡܒܕܩ p. 10. 10.

ܡܒܕܩܢܐ *scout*, p. 3. 14.

ܒܗܪ. Eshtafal ܐܫܬܒܗܪ *to boast*, p. 40. 7; 62. 13.

ܒܪܪܒܘܬܐ *boasting*, p. 83. 6.

ܒܘܙ Pers. بز, *goat*, p. 211. 8.

ܒܘܙܝܩܐ, ܒܘܙܝܩܐ Arab. باز *hawk*, p. 14. 11; 15. 7.

ܒܘܠܣܐ *castanets*, p. 89. 21.

ܒܘܩܝܢܐ *trumpet*, plur. ܒܘܩܝܢܣ p. 134. 21; 161. 20; ܒܘܩܝܢܣ p. 134. 16; 261. 14.

ܒܝܬ. ܒܝܬ ܕܘܩܐ *watchtower*, p. 261. 3.

ܒܝܬ ܗܠܟܬܐ *place for walking*, p. 39. 15.

ܒܝܬ ܙܝܢܐ *armoury*, p. 147. 10.

ܒܝܬ ܓܙܐ *treasure house*, p. 77. 8.

ܒܝܬ ܡܠܦܢܐ *school*, p. 38. 5.

ܒܝܬ ܝܠܕܐ *birthday*, p. 146. 19; *horoscope*, p. 9. 9, 10; 10. 10; 27. 2. ܚܙܝ ܒܝܬ ܝܠܕܐ *casters of nativities*, p. 7. 6.

ܒܝܬ ܣܘܦܝ ܫܡܝܐ *place of the ends of heaven*, p. 260. 1.

ܒܝܬ ܪܗܛܐ *hippodrome*, p. 42. 9; 43. 5; 46. 14; 49. 12; 245. 12, 17; 246. 1.

ܒܝܬ ܪܟܫܐ *stable*, 38. 16.

ܒܠܐ. ܒܠܝܐ *decrepit*, p. 30. 4.

ܒܝܐ. ܒܘܝܐܐ *consolation*, p. 30. 15.

ܒܠ Assyrian Bêl, Heb. בֵּל, Βῆλ, *the god Bel*, p. 20. 6; 22. 6; 27. 14. The native lexicons say that Bel is ܙܘܣ but B glosses this name twice (p. 22. 2; 27. 22) by ܝܘܦܛܪ *Jupiter*.

ܒܠܕܪܐ Pers. بريد, *letter carrier*, plur. ܒܠܕܪ̈ܐ p. 157. 10.

ܒܝܪܬܐ *palace*, p. 236. 12; 268. 8. The Assyrian form of the word is *birtu*. See Strassmaier, *Alphabetisches Verzeichniss*, p. 192 ff.

ܝܠܝܕܬܐ *wood worm*, p. 219. 18.

ܢܘܓܗ *Venus*, p. 27. 13; ܢܘܓܗ p. 31. 1, 3; 26. 7.

ܒܢܐ. Pa''ēl part. pass. ܒܢܝܐ ܕܬܘܪܐ *built with oxen* (?) p. 105. 1.

ܒܣܪ. Part. pass. ܒܣܝܪܐ *despised*, p. 31. 8.

    Af'ēl ܐܒܣܪ *to neglect*, p. 95. 6; part ܡܒܣܪ p. 61. 19.

    ܒܣܢܝܐܝܬ *scornfully*, p. 173. 2.

ܒܣܝܣ, ܒܣܝܣ *bases*, p. 67. 8; 218. 15.

ܒܥܩܬܐ *see* ܒܥܩܬܐ

ܒܥܪ. Af'ēl ܐܒܥܪ *to go away, flee away, depart*, p. 5. 7; 170. 15.

ܒܥܪ. ܒܥܝܪܐ, ܒܥܝܪܐ *savage, wild*, plur. ܒܥܝܪܐ p. 176. 10; 180. 10; 201. 6; plur. fem. ܒܥܝܪܬܐ p. 159. 5.

ܒܨܪ. ܒܘܨܪܐ ܕܫܡܫܐ ܘܣܗܪܐ *failing of the sun and moon*, i.e. "eclipse" ? p. 171. 2.

ܒܨܠܬܐ *see* ܒܨܠܬܐ p. 89. 10.

ܒܪ, ܒܪܐ, ܒܪܐ ܐܢܐ ܕܒܪܟ *I who am your son*, p. 54. 18.

    ܒܢܝ ܐܪܙܐ *partners in a secret*, p. 57. 12.

    ܒܪ ܦܝܪܐ p. 153. 9. I do not know the meaning of this word. Here the text is probably corrupt.

    ܒܢܝ ܕܪܥܐ *armpieces*, p. 172. 5.

    ܒܪ ܘܫܩܐ *a greave, legging*, plur. ܒܢܝ ܘܫܩܐ p. 129. 1; 172. 4.

ܒܪ ܟܢܫܗ *kinsman*, p. 81. 4.

ܒܢܝ ܘܠܦܢܐ *fellow learners*, p. 117. 9.

ܒܢܝ ܠܘܝܬܐ *companions, fellow travellers*, p. 82. 10.

ܒܪ ܟܢܬܗ *consort, companion*, p. 34. 16; 81. 5; 86. 1;

ܒܪ̈ܬ ܩܘܡܬܐ p. 151. 12; ܒ̈ܢܝ ܩܘܡܝܬܐ p. 152. 11.

ܒܢ̈ܝ ܡܠܬܐ *partisans*, p. 57. 16.

ܒܪ ܢܘܗܪܢܘܬܐ *son of light*, p. 86. 2.

ܒܢ̈ܝ ܫܘܢܝܘܬܐ *children of the same age*, p. 81. 11; 93. 6.

ܒܪ ܢܗܝܪ̈ܐ *son of the luminaries*, p. 81. 5.

ܒܪ ܦܨܘܨܐ *counterpart*, p. 86. 4.

ܒܢ̈ܝ ܦܠܚܘܬܐ *fellow soldiers*, p. 83. 4; 103. 12; 156. 9; 158. 17; 173. 2.

ܒܢ̈ܝ ܦܠܛܝܢ *officers of the palace*, p. 255. 9.

ܒܪܬ ܫܡܫ *daughter of the Sun*, p. 21. 6.

ܒܪܓܕܢ = Pers. کرگدن *rhinoceros* ? p. 211. 15.

ܓܐܘܡܛܪܝܐ γεωμετρία, *geometry*, p. 23. 15.

ܓܓܪ. ܓܓܪܬܐ *throat*, p. 243. 7.

ܓܕ. ܓܕܐ, Ar. جاد *luck, fortune*. ܒܝܫܘܬ ܓܕܐ *ill-luck*, p. 81. 7; ܒܝ̈ܫܝ ܓܕܐ *unlucky men*, p. 168. 5; ܛܒ̈ܝ ܓܕܐ *lucky men*, 168. 6; ܓܕܗ ܕܙܘܣ *the luck of Zeus*, p. 100. 11; ܓܕܗ ܕܝܡܐ *the luck or divinity of the sea*, p. 234. 13. Part. ܓܕܝܕܐ *to cut off*, p. 114. 10.

ܓܕܘܕܘܬܐ *boyhood*, p. 24. 2.

ܓܕܐ. ܓܕܝܐ *luck, chance*. ܓܕܝܗ ܕܝܢ ܐܠܗ̈ܐ *the luck of the gods*, p. 178. 4; 201. 11.

ܓܗܢ. Ethpĕ'ĕl ܐܬܓܗܢ *to bow oneself*, p. 257. 11; part. ܡܬܓܗܢ p. 260. 13.

ܓܘܐ *commonwealth*, p. 120. 2, 6.

ܓܘܣ. ܡܓܘܣܘܬܐ *scarcity*, p. 121. 14.

ܓܚܟ. ܡܓܚܟܢܐ *jester*, p. 51. 5.

ܓܠܘܣܩܡܐ γλωσσόκομον, *coffin*, p. 250. 8.

ܓܡܣ. Af'ēl ܐܓܡܣ *to dare*, p. 91. 16.

ܓܘܡܣܢܐ, ܓܘܡܣܢ *audacious one*, p. 116. 2.

ܓܘܡܣܢܘܬܐ *insolence, impudence*, p. 117. 18.

ܓܡܨ. ܓܘܡܨܐ *pit*, p. 27. 16; 28. 2; 29. 12; 30. 11; plur. ܓܘܡ̈ܨܐ p. 132. 4.

ܓܡܫܐ, Pers. گاومیش, گامیش, *buffalo*, plur. ܓܡ̈ܫܐ (ܓܘܡܫܐ) p. 212. 2.

ܓܢܐ. Pĕ'al part. pass. ܓܢܐ p. 50. 14; plur. ܓܢܝܢ p. 50. 12.

ܓܢܝ. ܓܘܢܝܐ, ܓܘܢܝ *disgrace*, p. 229. 17.

ܓܦܣܘܣ, ܓܘܦܣܘܣ γύψος, *gypsum*, p. 193. 3, 7.

ܓܨܐ Ar. جصّ *lime*, p. 138. 14; 146. 12; 206. 14.

ܓܪܡ. ܓܪܡܢܐܝܬ *actually, really, of a certainty*, p. 10. 6; 16. 7; ܓܪܡܢܐܝܬ ܗܘܐ ܕܝܢ ܥܪܡܢܐܝܬ p. 11. 17.

ܓܪܡ ܦܝܠܐ *elephant's tusk, ivory*, p. 8. 3; 182. 8; 211. 13; 218. 14; ܟ̈ܣܐ ܕܓܪܡ ܦܝܠܐ *ivory cups*, p. 250. 16.

ܓܫ. ܓܫܘܫܐ *spy*, (= ܓܘܫܐ) p. 3. 3, 13; 4. 3.

ܓܫܪ. ܓܫܪܐ ܓܫܪ *to construct a bridge*, p. 206. 2.

ܕܒܪܐ *desert*, p. 21. 11.

ܕܠ, ܕܘܠ *to rise up*, p. 269. 4. ܚܘܫ̈ܒܐ ܕܠܝܢ ܗܘܘ ܒܗ̇ *thoughts were stirring in her*, p. 25. 13. Cf. also ܕܠ ܚܘܫܒܐ ܒܡܕܥܗ ܗܿܦܟܬܐ ܕܢܐܙܠ ܠܐܬܪܗ *the thought that he would go to*

*Bagdad arose in Mâr Yabalâhâ*. See Bedyan, *Histoire de Mar Jab-Alaha*, Paris, 1888, p. 29, l. 7.

ܕܘܩ, ܕܩܐ. ܕܳܘܩܳܐ *watcher, spy*, plur. ܕܳܘܩܶܐ p. 258. 11; 272. 22; ܕܳܩܽܘܩܶܐ p. 272. 18, 19. ܕܫܳܥܶܐ ܕܳܘܩܳܐ *watcher of the hours*, (= τὸν εἱροσκόπον, Meusel, p. 708, l. 35) p. 8. 12; 9. 6.

ܕܘܪܳܬܳܐ *spear*. ܕܪܘܪܬܝ ܡܫܩܠܢܐ ܐܢܐ ܒܠܫܢܗ (p. 42. 6) = δόρατί σε λήψομαι (Müller, p. 18, col. 2, l. 18; Meusel, p. 718, l. 31) and we have ܒܠܫܢܗ ܕܕܘܪܬܐ p. 100. 14. ܒܠܫܢܗ ܕܕܘܪܬܝ is glossed in B by ܪܫܐ ܕܪܘܡܚܝ "*tip of my spear*."

ܕܚܠ. ܕܚܘܠܬܢ *timid*, p. 119. 15; plur. fem. ܕܚܘܠܬܢܝܬܐ p. 117. 12.

ܕܚܘܠܬܢܘܬܐ *fear, timidity*, p. 4. 13; 117. 14.

ܕܚܘܠܬܢܐܝܬ *timidly, fearfully*, p. 3. 16.

ܕܪܐ. ܡܕܪܝܐ *razor*, p. 23. 10.

ܕܠ. ܕܠܝܠܐ plur. ܕܠܝܠܐ, ܕܠܝܠܐ ܙܘܥܐ *few earthquakes*, p. 72. 20.

ܕܠ. ܕܘܠܐ *Aquarius*, p. 22. 4.

ܕܠܒ. ܕܘܠܒܐ, Pers. and Ar. دُلب *plane tree*, plur. p. 219. 7.

ܕܡܐ. Ethpa‘‘al ܐܬܕܡܝ *to become like*, p. 17. 5.

ܕܡܘܬ ܩܪܢܬܐ *horned*, p. 20. 8.

ܕܡܟ. ܕܡܟ *sleeping*, p. 12. 8; ܕܡܟܐ p. 11. 18.

ܕܡܥ. Pa‘‘êl part. ܡܕܡܥ *weeping*, p. 54. 2.

ܕܩܠܐ = ܕܓܠܐ *brook, stream*, p. 261. 1; 268. 17.

ܕܩܩ. ܕܩܕܩܐ *little, small*, plur. ܕܩܕܩܐ p. 2. 11; plur. fem. ܕܩܕܩܬܐ p. 2. 11.

ܕܶܩܰܢܰܘܣܶܐ *decani (the thirty-six)*, p. 8. 17.

ܕܪܡ. ܡܕܰܪܡܳܐ *crafty, cunning*, plur. fem. ܡܕܰܪܡܳܢܝܳܬܳܐ p. 236. 1.

ܕܪܫ. Pa"ēl part. pass. ܡܕܰܪܰܫ *trained, skilled*, p. 25. 10; plur. ܡܕܰܪܫܶܐ p. 39. 6; ܕܪܰܫܘ *they talked*, p. 11. 11; 27. 8.
ܕܽܘܪܳܫܳܐ *training, practice*, p. 25. 6; 35. 18; 36. 7.
ܡܕܰܪܫܽܘܬܳܐ *skill*, p. 3. 1; 25. 8.

ܗܶܕܪܳܐ *bloom, flower*, p. 93. 11.

ܗܰܠܒܝܬܳܐ *halfbred*, p. 18. 7.

ܗܕܐ. ܗܳܕܽܘܝܳܐ *guide*, plur. ܗܳܕܽܘܝܶܐ p. 183. 5; ܗܳܕܽܘܝܳܬܳܐ p. 183. 20.

ܗܰܘܢܳܐ. ܐܬܳܐ ܠܘܳܬ ܗܰܘܢܳܐ *to come to one's senses, regain self-possession*, p. 16. 17.

ܗܰܝܟܠ, ܗܰܝܟܠܳܐ, Accadian E-GAL, Heb. הֵיכָל *palace, hall*, p. 2. 9; 4. 9; 17. 6, 13; 58. 13; 70. 8; 71. 2; 98. 14; 99. 5; 105. 2; 126. 12; 202. 11; 216. 3; 247. 15. Plur. ܗܰܝܟܠܶܐ p. 108. 1; 113. 3; 147. 2; 206. 13; 231. 11. ܗܰܝܟܠ ܒܶܝܬ ܡܰܠܟܽܘܬܳܐ "*royal palace,*" p. 6. 6.

ܗܡܐ. Af'ēl ܐܰܗܡܝ *to overlook*, p. 142. 3.

ܗܢܝܘܟܐ ἡνίοχος *charioteer*, plur. ܗܢܝܘܟܶܐ p. 46. 7. This word is glossed in B by ܡܕܰܒܪܳܢܶܐ ܕܡܰܪܟܒܳܬܳܐ *drivers of chariots*.

ܗܦܟ. Part. pe'īl pass. ܗܦܝܟ *perverse*; plur. ܗܦܝܟܝܢ p. 126. 17; ܕܓܰܪܡܶܗ ܗܦܝܟ ܠܡܶܚܦܰܪ *whose bones ought to be dug up*, p. 115. 16.

ܦܽܘܪܝܳܐ *coffin*, p. 138. 16.

ܘܠܐ. ܘܳܠܺܝܬܳܐ *what is right, fitting*, p. 36. 11, 18; 37. 18; 93. 4; 240. 4.

ܘܠܝܐܝܬ *rightly, fittingly*, p. 53. 6; 103. 17; 138. 1; 155. 10.

ܬܚܘܡܐ *limit*, p. 165. 12; *confines*, p. 195. 1; ܠܣܛܪ ܕܡܪܟܒܬܗ "*close to his chariot*," p. 48. 5.

ܙܒܢ. ܙܒܢܐ plur. ܙܒܢ̈ܐ *articles of sale*, p. 75. 14.

ܙܓ. ܙܓܐ *bell*, plur. ܙܓ̈ܐ p. 262. 14, 16.

ܙܓܘܓܝܬܐ *glass*, p. 138. 17, 19.

ܙܕܩ. Adv. ܙܕܩܐܝܬ *rightly*, p. 137. 15; 151. 5.

ܙܗܪ. Ethpa"al ܒ ܐܙܕܗܪ *to guard, care for*, p. 32. 9.

ܙܘܗܪܐ *care*, p. 183. 14.

ܙܗܝܪܐܝܬ *carefully*, p. 131. 10.

ܙܗܪܐ *light*, p. 132. 1.

ܙܘܝܬܐ *corner*, plur. ܙܘܝ̈ܬܐ p. 219. 20.

ܙܘܓܐ ζυγόν, *a suit*, ܚܕ ܙܘܓܐ ܕܠܒܘܫܐ ܦܪܣܝܐ *one suit of Persian clothes*, p. 147. 13; ܙܘܓܐ ܕܠܒܘܫܐ ܚܘܪܐ *a suit of white clothes*, p. 147. 16.

ܙܘܪ *to grasp, to hold tightly*, p. 101. 12.

ܙܘܪܐ *fist*. ܡܠܐ ܙܘܪܐ *handful*, p. 88. 15; 94. 14, 16.

ܙܚܪ. ܙܚܘܪܝܬܐ *scarlet*, plur. ܙܚܘܪ̈ܝܬܐ p. 43. 13.

ܙܝܛܘܣ p. 101. 5. The meaning of this word is unknown to me.

ܙܟܐ. ܙܟܝܐ, *conqueror*, plur. ܙܟܝ̈ܐ p. 229. 16.

ܡܙܕܟܝܢܘܬܐ *defeat*, p. 135. 19; 136. 15; 158. 2; 161. 18; 170. 15; 229. 5.

ܠܐ ܡܙܕܟܝܢܘܬܐ *invincibility*, p. 1. 14.

ܙܠܓ. ܙܠܝܓܐܝܬ *lustfully*, p. 7. 12.

ܙܠܓܦܬܐ *oyster shell.* ܕܘܢܒܝ ܙܠܓܦܬܐ *tails of oyster shells*, p. 178. 8;
ܡܐܢܝ̈ܐ ܕܙܘܠܓܦܬܐ *oystershell vessels*, p. 190. 6.

ܙܡܢܐ p. 207. 6. This word is glossed in B by ܟܢܫܐ, Ar. جَمَاعَة *troop, band.*

ܙܡܪܓܕܐ *emerald*, plur. ܙܡܪܓܕ̈ܐ p. 9. 4.

ܙܦܬܐ Ar. زِفْت, Heb. זֶפֶת *pitch*, p. 193. 3.

ܙܩ. ܙܩܐ, Ar. زق *bag*, plur. ܙܩ̈ܐ p. 205. 8; 206. 1.

ܙܩܪ. Infin. ܠܡܙܩܪ *to weave*, p. 114. 8; part. fem. ܙܩܪܐ p. 113. 5; 114. 7; part. pass. ܙܩܝܪ *woven*, p. 129. 1; fem. ܙܩܝܪܬܐ p. 224. 15; plur. ܙܩܝܪ̈ܢ p. 218. 12.

ܚܒܫ. ܚܒܫܐ *crowd, swarm*, p. 81. 16; 216. 2; plur. ܚܒ̈ܫܐ p. 92. 3.

ܚܓܠܐ, Ar. حَجَل, Heb. חָגְלָה, *partridge*, plur. ܚܓܠ̈ܐ p. 179. 1.

ܚܕܝ ܚܕܝܐܝܬ *gladly, joyfully*, p. 63. 1.

ܚܕܪ ܚܕܘܪܘܬܐ *mendicity, begging*, p. 20. 7.
ܚܕܪ̈ܐ *circles*, p. 8. 5.

ܚܘܪ, ܚܪ *to be ashamed*, p. 94. 7.

ܚܘܐ ܡܚܘܝܢܘܬܐ *demonstration*, p. 30. 11.
ܡܚܘܝ̈ܢܝ ܡܠܘܫܐ *those who show the Signs of the Zodiac*, p. 5. 4.

ܚܘܣ ܚܘܣܢܘܬܐ *mercy*, p. 105. 14.

ܚܘܦ ܚܘܦܐܝܬ *quickly*, p. 90. 4; 158. 3.

ܚܙܐ ܚܙܝ, ܚܙܝܐ *spectator*, plur. ܚܙ̈ܝܐ p. 46. 1.

ܚܛܡܐ *the bow of a boat* (?), p. 205. 1.

ܚܙܘܪܐ *apple*, plur. ܚܙܘܪ̈ܐ p. 217. 5.

ܚܙܝܪ ܒܪܐ *wild pig, boar*, p. 177. 5; plur. ܚܙܝܪ̈ܐ ܒܪܐ p. 174. 11.

ܚܛܪ ܚܘܛܪܐ *rod, stick*, p. 4. 12. In D the word is masculine.

ܚܝܐ. ܚܝܘܬ ܒܪܢܫ *a creature half beast half man*, p. 177. 5.

ܚܟܡ. ܚܟܡ̈ܬܐ *the Sciences*. ܐܪܝܬܡܛܝܩܝ ܡܘܣܝܩܝ ܓܐܘܡܛܪܝܐ ܐܣܛܪܘܢܘܡܝܐ p. 95. 11.

ܚ̈ܠܟܝܬܐ p. 9. 6. The meaning of this word is unknown to me.

ܚܠܛ ܚܘܠܛܢܐ *union, mixing, mixture*, p. 66. 14; 72. 15.

ܚܡܪ ܚܘܡܪܐ, plur. ܚܘܡܪ̈ܐ *gems*, p. 8. 13, 15; 26. 1.

ܚܘܡܪܬܐ *wheel*, p. 101. 11.

ܚܡܬ ܚܡܝܬܐܝܬ *angrily, wrathfully*, p. 21. 4; 221. 7.

ܚܢܐ ܚܢܐ *bosom*, p. 130. 9, 14.

ܚܢܛ Infin. ܠܡܚܢܛܘ *to embalm*, p. 151. 7.

ܚܣܐ Pa''el part. ܡܚܣܝ *innocent*, p. 6. 8.

ܚܣܟ ܚܣܘܟܘܬܐ *parsimony*, p. 38. 1.

ܚܣܠ Ethpĕ'ĕl ܐܬܚܣܠ *to be weaned*, p. 23. 4.

ܚܣܢ ܚܣܝܢܐܝܬ *heavily, mightily, violently*, p. 51. 17; 94. 9; 159. 11. Pam'ĕl ܚܡܣܢ *to be strong, bear bravely*, p. 20. 2; 21. 9.

ܡܚܡܣܢܢܐܝܬ *bravely*, p. 22. 1.

ܚܣܪ ܚܣܝܪܐ, ܚܣܝܪ̈ܐ *needy, poor*, p. 12. 9; 136. 13.

ܚܣܝܪܘܬܐ *need, lack*, p. 12. 10; 28. 12.

ܚܦܛ ܚܦܝܛܐܝܬ *diligently, earnestly*, p. 11. 13; 78. 4.

ܡܚܦܛܢܐ *one who incites or urges on to anything*, p. 61. 4.

ܚܦܢ ܚܘܦܢܐ, Ar. حَفْنَة, Heb. חֹפֶן, *fist*. ܡܠܐ ܚܘܦܢܐ *handful*, p. 88. 12.

ܚܨܦ Afel part. ܡܚܨܦ to act audaciously or daringly, p. 191. 1.

ܚܨܝܦ, ܚܨܝܦܐ impudent, p. 89. 2; 116. 1; 119. 11; plur. fem. ܚܨܝ̈ܦܬܐ impudent things, p. 211. 1.

ܚܨܝܦܐܝܬ audaciously, p. 150. 1.

ܚܪܕܠܐ Ar. حرذون, crocodile, plur. ܚܪ̈ܕܠܐ p. 176. 1.

ܚܪܕܫ to wag the tail, p. 33. 7.

ܚܪܨ ܚܪܨܢܐܝܬ cruelly, p. 30. 4.

ܚܪܒ ܚܪܒܐ astute, p. 76. 11.

ܚܪܦ ܚܪܝܦ, ܚܪܝܦܐ pungent, sharp, p. 93. 15; 95. 2; plur. ܚܪ̈ܝܦܝܢ p. 88. 16; 94. 18.

ܚܪܝܦܘܬܐ sagacity, p. 79. 17.

ܚܪܝܦܘܬ ܡܠܐ sharpness of speech, p. 57. 2; intentness, p. 7. 10.

ܚܪܝܦܐܝܬ sharply. ܐܬܚܡܬ ܚܪܝܦܐܝܬ he was furiously angry, p. 59. 1.

ܚܪܫ. ܚܪ̈ܫܐ sorcerers, p. 7. 6. A name given by the Greeks to the Signs of the Zodiac.

ܚܫܠ ܚܫܠܬܐ, plur. ܚܫ̈ܠܬܐ trinkets, p. 141. 2.

ܡܚܫܠ polished, p. 2. 7.

ܚܬܪ ܚܬܝܪ ܒܩܢܝܢܐ purse-proud, p. 57. 8.

ܚܬܬ ܚܬܝܬܐܝܬ exactly, p. 27. 1; accurately, p. 56. 19; 212, 12; 232. 20; 238. 13; intently, p. 131. 8; in good order, p. 93. 10; promptly, p. 5. 11.

ܚܬܝܬܘܬܐ earnestness, p. 7. 9.

ܣܟܕ . Ethpě'el ‎‎ *to be reported*, p. 29. 1. Glossed in B by
ܗܘܐ ‎‎ *always to be spoken of.*

ܣܟܝܠܬܐ for ܣܟܠܬܐ (?) *dish*, p. 51. 13.

ܣܟܝܠܬܐ *table*, p. 25. 16. Glossed in B by ܕܗܘܡܟܐ ܚ ܗܣܟ ܠܐ
ܗܣܟܐ ܦܕܐ ܕܘܡ ܓܐ *a drum, or a board like the surface of a wide drum.*

ܓܢܣ . ܓܢܣܐ *race, kin*, p. 18. 2; 13. 9; 42. 2; 66. 8; 81. 4;
105. 4; 107. 6; plur. ܓܢܣ̈ܐ p. 1. 5; 66. 12; ܟܠ ܓܢܣ
*every species*, p. 173. 12; ܒܪ ܓܢܣܐ *kinsman*, p. 81. 4;
ܒܪ ܓܢܣܐ ܕܐܠܗܐ *son of the divine race*, p. 104. 5;
ܓܢܣ̈ܐ ܕܐܠܗܐ p. 13. 9; 66. 12; ܓܢܣܐ ܕܟܠܬܐ
p. 83. 8.

ܓܢܬܐ *enclosure*, p. 185. 19; 186. 4.

ܓܒܪܘܢܐ p. 259. 1. The meaning of this word is unknown to me.

ܛܠܠ . Af'ēl part. ܡܛܠܠ *overshadowing*, p. 15. 8; ܡܛܠܠܐ p. 172.
12; ܡܛܠܠܐ p. 172. 23.
ܬܛܠܠܬܐ *huts*, p. 164. 10.
ܛܠܠܐ *roof*, p. 138. 15; 218. 10; 219. 6; plur. ܛܠܠܐ
p. 209. 11.

ܟܟܪܐ *talent*, p. 74. 10; plur. ܟܟܪ̈ܝܢ p. 63. 23; 74. 10; 115.
20; 116. 16; 200. 19; ܟܟܪ̈ܬܐ 74. 18; ܟܟܪ̈ܐ 200. 8;
ܟܟܪ̈ܝܐ 63. 13; ܟܟܪ̈ܐ 115. 10; 116. 2.

ܛܡܪ . Ethpa"al ܐܬܛܡܪ *to be obstructed, choked, filled up*, p. 69.
16; Pa"ēl Infin. ܠܡܛܡܪܘ p. 208. 14.
ܛܡܝܪܐ *solid*, p. 233. 10; plur. masc. ܛܡܝܪ̈ܐ 233. 7;
fem. ܛܡܝܪ̈ܬܐ 211. 8.

ܚܕܪ.　Pə'al part. pass. ܚܕܪ excited, p. 241. 12.

ܚܕܘܕܐ　τραγῳδός, singer, plur. ܚܕܘܕܐ p. 78. 11.

ܚܕܪܐ　Ar. ظر rock, plur. ܚܕܪܐ p. 178. 5.

ܚܕܝܣܡܝܠܐ　τριπκελής, tripod, p. 8. 9; ܚܕܝܣܡܠܝ p. 98. 23; 106. 8; ܚܕܘܣܡܠܝ p. 98. 19; 99. 3.

ܝܗܒ,　ܝܗܒ ܠܐܢܫ to yield to anyone, p. 204. 5; ܝܗܒ ܠܗ ܙܒܢܐ time has given him the hand, i.e., fortune is his slave, p. 124. 18; ܐܙܠ ܠܟ ܝܗܒ ܚܕܢܐ ܠܚܕܐܚܕ he went on to tell severally, p. 218. 3.

ܝܕܥ　ܝܕܥܝ ܐܬܘܬܐ knowers of signs, p. 7. 5.

ܝܕܥܝ ܚܠܡܐ knowers of dreams, p. 16. 6.

ܝܕܘܥܬܐ portent, p. 87. 17.

ܝܠܕ　ܝܠܝܕ ܥܡ ܥܟܙܐ birthmark, p. 33. 9.

ܝܠܦ　ܡܠܐ ܝܠܝܦܬܐ words learned by heart, p. 107. 11.

ܝܡܐ sea.　ܝܡܐ ܣܪܝܐ fœtid sea, p. 256. 12; 257. 2; 259. 11; 260. 2.

ܝܡܐ ܢܗܝܪܐ bright sea, p. 260. 2; plur. ܝܡܡܐ ܢܗܝܪܐ 256. 9; 259. 5.

ܝܡܐ.　ܡܘܡܬܐ ܗܕܐ this oath, p. 42. 2.

ܝܥܐ.　Af'el ܐܘܥܝ to make to spring up, p. 4. 12.

ܝܨܦ.　ܝܨܝܦܘܬܐ care, p. 23. 1.

ܝܨܦܐ care, p. 26. 6.

ܝܩܪ.　ܡܝܩܪܐܝܬ honourably, p. 60. 5.

ܝܬܪ.　Eshtaf'al ܠܐܬܝܬܪܐ to increase, p. 23. 4.

.

ܝܒܣ. ܡܘܬܒܐ *seat used by women in childbirth*, p. 19. 13.

ܝܬܡ. Ethpa'al ܐܬܝܬܡ *to become an orphan*, p. 244. 8.

ܝܬܪ. ܝܬܝܪܘܬܐ *superiority*, p. 20. 5.

ܡܘܬܪܢ *useful*, p. 3. 13.

ܟܐܘܢ, Assyrian *ka-ai-ma-nu*, Ar. كِيوَان, Heb. כִּיּוּן *Saturn*, p. 19. 15; 20. 4; 27. 12; ܒܝܫܘܬ ܟܐܘܢ *fate of Saturn, i. e., ill luck*, p. 40. 11.

ܟܒܪ. *to disgrace*, p. 91. 10.

ܟܘܒܪܐ *disgrace, reproach, shame*, p. 93. 5; 105. 7; 139. 13; 229. 3.

ܟܒܪܝܬܐ *sulphur*, p. 193. 3.

ܟܕܒ. ܟܕܒܘܬܐ *lying, falsehood*, p. 6. 16.

ܟܕܢ. *to yoke*, p. 46. 14; Pə'il part. pass. plur. ܟܕܝܢܝܢ p. 49. 16; 143. 4.

ܟܘܕܢܐ *eagle*, plur. ܟܘܕܢܐ p. 176. 3.

ܟܘܬܐ, Ar. كَ *window*, p. 260. 3; ܟܘܬܐ p. 260. 7.

ܟܘܬܠܐ *ingots*, p. 171. 7.

ܟܘܪܐ *furnace*. ܟܘܪܐ ܕܩܝܢܝܐ *smith's furnace*, p. 161. 8.

ܟܣܕ. ܟܘܣܕܐ *shame*, p. 89. 2.

ܟܬܒܐ. ܟܬܒܐ ܕܝܕܐ *handwriting*, p. 270. 15; 275. 7. ܝܕ ܟܬܒ Brit. Mus. MS. Rich 7203, fol. 61 b, col. 1.

ܟܟܐ *tooth*, ܟܟܐ *teeth*, p. 190. 3, 5.

ܟܪܒܣܐ Chald. כַּרְבּוּשְׁתָא *ferret*, p. 217. 9. M. Duval (*Journal Asiatique*, 8ième Série, t. XIII, p. 351, note 1) translates this word by *ichneumon*. These animals were eaten by the ancients in times of famine. Compare ܠܡܐܟܠ ܘܟܠܒ̈ܐ ܘܫܘܢܪ̈ܐ ܡܢ ܥܘܠ ܟܦܢܐ Bedjan, *Histoire de Mar-Alaha*, p. 177. 7.

ܟܠܒܬܐ, plur. ܟܠܒ̈ܬܐ Ar. كَلَّاب *tongs*, p. 161. 11.

ܟܠܕܝܐ *augur, soothsayer*, p. 78. 2; plur. ܟܠܕ̈ܝܐ p. 75. 9, 11, 18; ܐܦܠܘ ܟܠܕܝܐ *Apollo the augur*, p. 78. 2; ܟܠܕ̈ܝܐ ܡܨܪ̈ܝܐ *Egyptian soothsayers*, p. 75. 9.

ܟܠܕܝܘܬܐ *augury, divination*, p. 19. 8; 76. 17; 98. 19; 99. 3; 110. 3; 114. 1; 210. 7, 14.

ܠܐ ܫܘܝܐ ܠܟܠܕܝܘܬܐ *a woman unworthy of the office of divination*, p. 113. 13.

Af'ēl infin. ܠܡܟܠܕܝܘ *to divine*, p. 109. 7.

ܟܠܡܝܣ *chlamys, cloak*, p. 224. 14.

ܟܡܪ. Ethpĕ'ĕl ܐܬܟܡܪ *to be sad*, p. 94. 6.

ܟܡܝܪܘܬܐ *gloominess*, p. 246. 6; ܐܦ̈ܐ ܟܡܝܪ̈ܬܐ *gloomy face*, p. 61. 13.

ܟܘܡܪܐ *priest*, plur. ܟܘܡܪ̈ܐ p. 147. 18.

ܟܘܡܪܬܐ *priestess*, p. 113. 5, 10, 12; 114. 2, 12, 13; 122. 10.

ܟܘܡܪܘܬܐ *office of priestess*, p. 114. 1, 12.

ܟܢܫ intrans. *to be assembled*, p. 43. 5; 60. 10; 62. 19.

ܟܦܦܬܐ, ܟܦ̈ܦܬܐ *small boxes*, p. 211. 12. Glossed in B by ܬܒܝܒ̈ܬܐ

ܟܘܦܪܐ *asphalt, bitumen*, p. 2. 10; 4. 11.

ܟܪ. Pers. خَر *ass*, p. 211. 8.

ܟܪܐ. part. pass. *mean, little*, ܟܪܝܐ ܒܩܘܡܬܗ *in stature small*, p. 163. 6.

Afĕl ܐܟܪܒ *to be grieved*, p. 94. 7.

ܟܪ̈ܒܐ *ploughed lands*, p. 68. 1.

ܟܪܟ Pĕʿîl part. plur. ܟܪܝܟܝܢ *surrounding, encircling*, p. 69. 6; 70. 5.

Ethpĕʿel ܐܬܟܪܟ *to roll* of an egg, *to go round, to encircle*, p. 18. 11, 12; 66. 18; 171. 5; 187. 10; part. ܡܬܟܪܟ 19. 1, 7; 76. 13; 179. 7; ܡܬܟܪܟܢܐ p. 101. 11; infin. ܠܡܬܟܪܟܘ 183. 4.

Afĕl *to surround with, to bind*, p. 268. 8, 11.

ܟܘܪܟܐ *a bend or turning*, p. 146. 13; ܟܘܪܟܐ ܕܪܗܛܐ *the farthest point* of a chariot course, p. 46. 16, 17.

ܟܪܐ. ܟܪܝܘܬ ܪܘܚܐ *impatience*, p. 117. 18.

ܟܪ̈ܥܐ *legs of a couch or table*, p. 218. 13.

ܟܪܬܐ *green*, plur. ܟܪ̈ܬܐ p. 43. 14.

ܟܫܐ *to pile up*, p. 264. 15.

ܟܫܪ. ܟܫܝܪܐܝܬ *excellently, properly*, p. 3. 15.

ܟܬܢܐ *linen*, p. 5. 3; plur. ܟ̈ܬܢܐ p. 15. 4, 17; 56. 20.

ܟܬܫ. Ethpaʿal part. ܡܬܟܬܫ *striving, contending*, p. 13. 2. ܒܩܠܐ ܡܬܟܬܫ *importunate with voice*, = *συρισμὸν τέμ-νων*.

ܟܬܘܫܘܬܐ *worry, strife*, p. 81. 16.

ܠܒܒ. ܠܒܝܒܐܝܬ *courageously*, p. 3. 16.

ܠܒܕ. Part. pĕʿîl ܠܒܝܕܐ *frozen*, p. 134. 8.

ܠܒܟ. Part. pĕʿîl ܠܒܝܟ (transitive), *to hold*, (like ܐܚܝܕ p. 21. 10); 19. 14; 33. 6.

ܠܚܡ. Paʿʿēl part. ܡܠܚܡ *fitting, fitted*, p. 101. 11; 138. 18.

ܠܚܫ *to mutter charms*, p. 14. 12.

ܠܛܫ. ܠܛܝܫܐ *sharp, pointed*, p. 205. 2.

ܠܛܝܫܬܐ *tip, point (of a spear)*, p. 42. 5; 100. 14.

ܠܟܘܪܡܐ p. 224. 13. The meaning of this word is unknown to me.

ܠܡܝܢܐ λιμήν, *harbour*, p. 39. 9.

ܠܩܢܐ λεκάνη, *bowl, basin*, p. 2. 9, 11, 14, 15; 4. 10; 29. 1; plur. ܠܩ̈ܢܐ p. 190. 6.

ܡܘܓܠܐ *pus*, p. 256. 16.

ܡܓܝܪܘܣܐ μάγειρος *cook*, p. 51. 15.

ܡܕܪܐ Ar. مَدَر, Ethiopic ምድር: *earth*, p. 208. 13.

ܡܪܘܓܠܐ (ܡܘܪܓܠܐ p. 59. 20) *whip*, p. 15. 7; 16. 2, 3; 59. 3. The Egyptian ⋀ χu is here referred to.

ܡܘܢܝܛܐ monēta, *money*, p. 145. 17; 146. 1.

ܡܘܫܟ Ar. مسك, ܡܫܟ̈ܐ ܕܡܘܫܟ *musk skins*, p. 200. 11.

ܡܙܓ. Ethpaʿal part. ܡܬܡܙܓ *to be mixed*, p. 138. 13.

ܡܚܠ. Ethpĕʿēl ܐܬܡܚܝܠ *to be weary*, p. 162. 13.

ܡܚܝܪ *reluctant*? p. 129. 10. This word is probably corrupt.

ܡܘܫܐ *the name of a tree*, p. 186. 7.

ܡܝܛܘܪܐ *the name of a tree*, p. 186. 6.

ܡܝܛܟܣܐ μέταξα, *silk*, p. 218. 12.

ܡܢ ܟܘܠܐ p. 200. 8. The meaning of this word is unknown to me.

ܡܠܐ. ܡܫܡܠܝܐܝܬ *exactly, fully*, p. 90. 1.

ܡܠܟ. ܡܠܟܢܐܝܬ *royally*, p. 221. 16.

ܡܠܟ. ܡܠܟܐ, plur. ܡܠܟܐ *signs of the Zodiac*, p. 5. 4; 8. 5; 20. 2; 26. 7; 27. 15; 29. 4; 30. 11; 275. 3.

ܡܢܐ. ܡܢܐ ܟܘܟܒܐ *counter of stars, astrologer*, p. 7. 8; plur. ܡܢܝ ܟܘܟܒܐ p. 7. 6. A name given to the Signs of the Zodiac by the Greeks.

ܡܢܐ, *string of a harp*, plur. ܡܢܐ p. 237. 16.

ܡܢܟܝܕܘܣ p. 101. 5. The meaning of this word is unknown to me.

ܡܠܩܐܕܐ = ܡܠܩܐܕܐ = μηλοπέπονες (?), *melons*, p. 217. 7.

ܡܨܥ. Pa'él ܡܨܥ *to put in the middle*, p. 48. 3. ܡܨܥܢܐ *mediator*, p. 58. 4. ܐܢܐ ܗܘܝܬ ܡܨܥܝܐ *I am in the midst, i. e., I am mediator*, p. 54. 6.

ܡܪܪ. ܡܪܪܬܐ *gall*, p. 48. 11. ܡܪܪܬܗ ܗܘܐ ܐܬܕܠܚܬ ܒܗ *his gall was stirred up in him*, p. 41. 11.

ܡܪܙ, ܡܪܙܐ, plur. ܡܪܙܘܬܐ *satraps, lords*, p. 55. 16; 56. 3. This word is glossed in B by نجيبان *nobility*, p. 55. 21.

ܡܪܕ - ܡܢܝܕ *to glance off, turn aside*, p. 68. 8.

ܡܪܕܢܐ, ܡܪܕܢܐ *jar*, p. 130. 8.

ܡܪܕ *to knead*, p. 268. 10.

ܡܪܕܩܪܙ *rhinoceros*, p. 211. 15.

ܡܫܐ. ܡܫܘܚܬܐ *age, class (of men)*, p. 103. 5.

ܡܫܢܟܠܐ *name of some large amphibious animal*, p. 175. 9.

ܡܫܪ. Ethpe'él ܐܬܡܫܪ *to straighten oneself out*, p. 17. 10.

ܢܒܘ *Nebo*, p. 21. 9; 27. 14. Glossed in B by ܟܘܟܒܐ *Mercury*, p. 21. 20; 27. 21.

ܢܦܪ. *to start forth*, p. 43. 18. ܢܦܪܘ may be a corruption of ܢܦܩܘ or ܫܘܪܘ

ܢܦܪܙ. Ethpalp. ܐܬܢܦܪܦܙ *to be on fire, to burn*, p. 6. 10; part. ܡܬܢܦܪܦܙܐ *blazing*, p. 131. 19.

ܢܓܠ. ܡܓܠܐ, *scythe*, plur. ܡܓ̈ܠܐ p. 134. 11; 135. 6.

ܢܗܪ. ܢܗܝܪܐ *star, luminary*, p. 182. 1; plur. 81. 5.

ܢܗܝܪܘܬܐ *brightness*, p. 119. 4.

ܢܘܚ. ܢܝܚܘܬܐ *gentleness, quiet*, p. 22. 3.

ܢܝܚܐܝܬ *quietly*, p. 32. 15.

ܢܘ̈ܢܐ Pisces, p. 22. 4.

ܢܘܦ. Af'ēl ܐܢܝܦ *to wave, brandish*, p. 58. 7.

ܢܚܫܝܪܐ Pers. نخجير *a hunt*, p. 107. 4.

ܢܚܫܝܪܬܢܐ, plur. ܢܚܫܝܪܬܢ̈ܐ *hunters*, p. 212. 1.

ܢܛܪܬܐ *cage*, p. 100. 16, 18.

ܢܣܐ. Pa"ēl part. ܡܢܣ̈ܝܐ ܒܩܪܒܐ *men tried or expert in war*, p. 92. 2; ܡܢܣܝܢ̈ܐ for ܡܢܣ̈ܝܐ p. 100. 12.

ܡܣܐܬܐ Libra, *balance, scales*, p. 19. 15; 20. 8.

ܢܣܒ. ܢܣܒ ܐܢܬܬܐ *to take a wife*, p. 58. 17; 106. 2; 154. 4; ܒܢܬܐ ܒܥܐ ܗܘܐ ܕܢܣܒ *he wished to take to wife*, p. 50. 11; ܒܢܬܐ ܠܐܚܪܢ ܡܠܟܐ ܐܬܠܝܗ̇ *I will give her to another king to wife*, p. 50. 17; ܡܢ ܒܢܬܐ ܡܫܒܩܬܐ *divorced*, p. 50. 9; ܐܢܬܬܐ ܐܚܪܬܐ ܒܢܬܐ ܠܡܗܘܢܗ̇ *to take another woman to wife*, p. 53. 9.

ܡܣܒܐ ܘܡܬܠ *taking and giving*, p. 36. 10. Talm. and

Rabb. מְסַב וּמִיתֵּן ; Ar. وطا اخذ Brit. Mus. MS. Rich
7203, fol. 81 a, col. 1.

ܚܣܡ. Pōʻil part. ܡܚܣܡ cast (of images), p. 138. 18.

ܚܚܕܐ raven, plur. ܚܚܕ̈ܐ p. 176. 10.

ܚܣܢ. Paʻʻēl part. ܡܚܣܢ exercised, trained, p. 25. 8.
ܪܟܫܐ ܡܚܣ̈ܢ trained horses, p. 39. 6; ܦܝܠܐ
ܩܪܒܬܢ elephants trained in war, p. 231. 17.
ܡܚܣܢܘ exercise, training, p. 39. 3.

ܚܣܢ. ܒܝܬ ܩܒܘܪܐ tomb, sepulchral monument, p. 68. 14, 15. ܚܣܐܟ
ܕܐܠܟܣܢ = Ταρσούρις of Straba.

ܨܚܝ. Afʻēl part. plur. ܡܨܚܝ clear, p. 26. 17, 18.
ܡܨܚܝܬܐ gloriously, p. 49. 11.
ܡܨܚܝܢܘܬܐ victory, p. 35. 10.

ܨܚܘܪ ܐܝܢܐ ܢܨ̈ܝܚܐ bodyguard, p. 129. 4.

ܨܚܠ. ܡܨܚܠܬܐ cup, vessel, plur. ܡܨ̈ܚܠܬ p. 190. 7.

ܚܣܕ. ܚܣܕܐ the den of an animal, p. 192. 4; plur. ܚܣ̈ܕܐ holes,
p. 132. 4.

ܚܣܟ. Afʻēl ܐܚܣܟ. ܐܚܣܟ ܡܢ ܚܘܕܬ ܠܡܐܡܪ he went on to tell
from the beginning, p. 28. 18; ܐܚܣܟ ܠܣܓܝ ܕܢܡܪ ܠܡܐܡܪ
he went on to tell severally, p. 218. 3.

ܚܨܝܢܐ axe, pick, plur. ܚܨ̈ܝܢܐ p. 101. 4.

ܚܣ. ܚܣܝܢܐܝܬ feebly, p. 83. 14.

ܚܫܫ to hiss, p. 17. 6.

ܚܦܛ to attract, draw, p. 192. 9.
ܚܘܦܛܐ attraction, p. 192. 9.

ܣܬܦ. ܫܘܬܦܐ *sharing*, p. 233. 11.

ܣܦܛܐ. Ar. سفط *a small basket, casket or chest*, p. 8. 9.

ܣܒܗ. Afêl part. pass. ܡܣܒܗ *to be like unto, resemble*, p. 23. 8; 25. 11; 128. 13; ܡܣܒܗܘܬܐ p. 87. 16.

ܣܒܪ. Pĕ'il part. ܣܒܝܪ ܗܘܐ *he thought*, p. 58. 15.

ܡܣܒܪܢܘܬܐ *expectation*, p. 14. 10; 26. 5; 127. 1; ܝܗܒ ܡܣܒܪܢܘܬܐ *he gave the expectation*, p. 58. 6.

ܣܓܐ. ܣܘܓܐܐܝܬ *abundantly*, p. 111. 5.

ܡܣܓܝܐ ܥܠܠܬܐ *abundant of crops*, p. 124. 12.

ܡܣܓܝܐ ܦܘܠܚܢܐ *abundant of tillage*, p. 124. 12.

ܣܕܪ. ܣܕܝܪܘܬܐ *ordering, arranging*, p. 1, 7; 29. 4; ܣܕܝܪܘܬ ܡܠܠܐ *arrangement of speech*, p. 23. 14.

ܣܘܩ. ܣܘܩܐ *a breathing*, p. 191. 6; ܒܣܘܩܗ ܢܓܕ *it drew in with its breath*, p. 193. 6.

ܣܗܪܬܐ, plur. ܣܗܪ̈ܬܐ *palace, country house, summerhouse*, p. 18. 3; 206. 5.

ܣܘܓܪ. ܣܘܓܪܬܐ, plur. ܣܘܓܪ̈ܐ *fetters*, p. 139. 2.

ܣܛܘܪܘܣ σάτυρος, *Satyr*, p. 181. 13.

ܣܟ. ܣܟܪܐ *a bolt*, p. 268. 10.

ܣܟܠ. ܡܣܟܠܢܐ *offender, evildoer*, p. 82. 11; plur. ܡܣܟܠܢ̈ܐ p. 25. 1.

ܣܠܝܢܐ σελήνη *the Moon*, p. 20. 20.

ܣܡ, ܣܡܐ, plur. ܣܡ̈ܡܢܐ *paints*, p. 204. 9.

ܣܡܟ. Part. pĕ'il plur. ܣܡܝܟ̈ܐ *those that sit at meat*, p. 50. 13; 51. 15; 52. 4.

Ethpĕ'ĕl ܐܣܬܡܟ݂ *to sit at meat*, p. 129. 19.

Af'ēl infin. ܠܡܣܡܟܘ *to make to sit down to meat*, p. 85. 2.

ܣܡܟܐ *table.* ܪܫ ܣܡܟܐ *at the head of the board*, p. 50. 14; ܣܡܟܐ ܬܚܬܝܐ *the lower seats*, p. 197. 11.

ܣܦܩ. Pĕ'īl part. pass. ܣܦܝܩܐ p. 15. 14; ܣܦܝܩܬܐ p. 45. 4; plur. ܣܦܝܩܝܢ *empty*, p. 168. 9.

Pa''ēl ܣܲܦܸܩ *to empty*, p. 8. 11.

Ethpa'al ܐܣܬܦܲܩ *to be emptied, deprived of*, p. 20. 5; 21. 11; 135. 16.

ܣܦܠ. Pĕ'īl part. pass. ܣܦܝܠ *decorated, splendid*, p. 13. 4; 104, 6.

ܣܩܪܐ σάκρα *letter*, p. 83. 6; 90. 10; 91. 13; 93. 1, 7; 94. 11; 115. 8; 116. 5; 145. 3; 150. 9; 152. 13; 210. 1; 226. 17; 227. 9; كتاب. رسالة. Brit. Mus. MS. Rich 7203, fol. 123 *a*, col. 2.

ܣܪܐ. Pĕ'īl part. ܣܪܝܐ *foul*, p. 32. 6; ܣܪܝܬܐ p. 32. 7; 256. 12; 257. 2; 259. 11; 260. 2.

ܣܪܓ. ܣܪܓܐ, سَرْج. ܣܪ̈ܓܐ *saddles*, p. 231. 6.

ܣܪܕ. ܡܣܪܕܢܝܬܐ, plur. ܡܣܪ̈ܕܢܝܬܐ *alarming* (*of words*), p. 117. 13.

ܣܪܛܢܐ *Cancer*, p. 20. 4.

ܣܪ̈ܢܐ. Ar. سرن *axle*, p. 49. 8.

ܣܪ. Pa''ēl part. ܡܣܪܣܪܐ *founded*, p. 106. 4.

Ethpa'al ܐܣܬܪܣܪ *to become firm*, p. 93. 12.

ܣܪܩ. ܣܪܘܩܐ *vine*, p. 182. 7, 19.

ܥܒܐ. ܥܘ̈ܒܝܐ *swellings*, p. 178. 15.

ܥܒܝܘܬܐ *thickness*, p. 205. 20.

ܥܒܕ. Shaf'ēl ܫܰܥܒܶܕ *to subdue*, p. 60. 18; part. ܡܫܰܥܒܶܕ p. 5. 15; 64. 7.

Eshtaf'al part. ܡܶܫܬܰܥܒܰܕ *to be subdued*, p. 13. 18; infin. ܠܡܶܫܬܰܥܒܳܕܽܘ p. 52. 1.

ܫܽܘܥܒܳܕܳܐ *submission*, 124. 7.

ܥܒܛ. ܥܒܺܝܛ *dense, thick*, p. 217. 3; ܕܽܘܟܬܳܐ ܥܒܺܝܛܰܬ ܛܰܪ̈ܦܶܐ *a place dense with foliage*, 106. 12.

ܥܒܪ. ܥܒܰܪ ܠܩܽܘܕܡܳܐ *to pass over to the front*, p. 44. 2; 45. 6; ܥܒܰܪ ܠܥܶܒܪܳܐ p. 44. 1, 8.

Af'ēl ܐܰܥܒܰܪ *to make to pass over*, p. 21. 3; 58. 8; 118. 8; 127. 11; 157. 7; infin. ܠܡܰܥܒܳܪܽܘ p. 72. 8; part. ܡܰܥܒܰܪ p. 33. 13; part. plur. ܡܰܥܒܪܺܝܢ p. 228. 9.

Ethpě'ēl ܠܳܐ ܡܶܬܥܰܒܪܳܢܳܐ *impassable*; plur. ܠܳܐ ܡܶܬܥܰܒܪ̈ܳܢܶܐ p. 247. 5.

ܡܰܥܒܰܪܬܳܐ *passage*, p. 47. 8; 191. 19; 227. 18.

ܥܒܽܘܪܳܐ *corn*, p. 124. 10; 135. 6; 140. 14; 206. 7; 249. 6.

ܥܓܠ. Pe'il part. pass. plur. ܥܓܺܝܠܺܝܢ *fallen*, p. 166. 4.

ܥܕܐ. Af'ēl part. ܡܰܥܕܶܐ *removing, taking away*, p. 137. 14.

ܥܕܠ. Ethpa'al ܐܶܬܥܰܕܰܠ *to blame*, p. 37. 13.

ܥܕܪ. Pa''ēl part. ܡܥܰܕܪܳܐ *recovering*, p. 97. 3.

ܥܙܪ. ܥܙܺܝܪ *furious*, p. 32. 5.

ܥܘܩ. ܥܘܳܩܳܐ *hindrance*, p. 249. 8. تاخر Brit. Mus. MS. Rich 7203, fol. 126 *b*, col. 1.

ܥܘܠ. ܥܺܝܠܳܐ *foal, colt*, p. 24. 9; ܥܺܝ̈ܠܶܐ ܕܡܕܰܪ̈ܫܶܐ p. 38. 16.

ܥܺܝ̈ܠܶܐ ܡܕܰܪ̈ܫܶܐ *trained colts*, p. 39. 6.

ܥܩܒ. Ethpe'el part. pass. ܡܬܥܩܒܝܢ *afflicted*, p. 223. 13.

ܥܩܝܒܐ *sad, sorrowful*, p. 25. 11.

ܥܝܪ. ܥܝܪܘܬܐ *watchfulness*, p. 105. 6.

ܥܙܙ. ܥܙܐ *a goat*, ܥܙܐ ܕܒܢܝ *ass-goats*, p. 211. 8.

ܥܙܩܬܐ *ring*, p. 15. 5, 19.

ܥܛܡܬܐ *thigh*, plur. ܥܛܡܬܐ p. 263. 14.

ܥܛܦ. Ethpa'al *to be arranged or wrapped in*, p. 255. 7.

Af'el ܐܥܛܦ *to make to return, to come back*, p. 216, 14.

ܥܡܛ. ܥܡܛܢܐ *mist*, p. 183. 16; 184. 1; 225. 18.

ܥܢܕ. ܥܢܕܐ *vengeance*, p. 10. 11; 12. 2; 15. 1; 52. 6, 10; 60. 2; 80. 11; 138. 1; 142. 1; 224. 5.

ܥܠܠ. Ethpa'al ܐܬܥܠܠ *to enter*, p. 29. 13.

Af'el ܐܥܠ *to bring in*, p. 32. 15.

ܥܠܐ. Pa''el part. pass. ܡܥܠܝ *exalted*, p. 136. 10; plur. ܡܥܠܝܢ p. 99. 14.

Ethpa'al ܐܬܥܠܝ *to go up from a ship*, p. 39. 13.

ܡܥܠܝܘܬܐ *greatness, excellence*, p. 86. 3; 142. 17.

ܥܠܬܐ *elevation*, p. 83. 6.

ܥܠܡ. ܥܠܝܡܐ ܬܕܝܬܐ *inexperienced*, p. 120. 14.

ܥܠܬ. ܥܠܬܬܐ *locks*, p. 268. 12.

ܥܡܕ. *to set (of the sun)*, p. 187. 16; 196. 19.

ܥܡܛ. *to shroud*, p. 94. 6; 246. 6.

Af'el ܐܥܡܛ *to make dark*, p. 119. 4.

ܥܡܘܛܐ *dense, dark*, p. 183. 15; plur. ܥܡܘܛܝܢ p. 185. 17.

ܥܲܡܛܳܢܳܐ *fog, blackness*, p. 183. 17; 192. 7; 225. 4; 233. 14; 234. 15; 235. 7.

ܥܡܨ. Pa''ēl ܥܲܡܶܨ *to close* the eyes, p. 144. 2.

ܥܡܪ. Pa''ēl part. ܡܥܲܡܪܳܐ *making to dwell*, p. 22. 2; ܡܥܲܡܪܳܢܳܐ p. 191. 3.

ܥܡܝܪܳܐ *hay*, p. 140. 15.

ܥܣܩ. ܥܣܝܩ p. 66. 15; ܥܲܣܩܳܐ *difficult*, p. 200. 17; plur. ܥܲܣܝܼܩܳܐ p. 247. 4.

ܥܲܣܩܽܘܬܳܐ *difficulty*, p. 184. 8.

ܥܦܐ. Pa''ēl infin. ܡܥܲܦܳܝܘ *to bury*, p. 138. 7.

Ethpa'al ܐܶܬܥܲܦܳܐ *to be buried*, p. 164. 8.

ܥܦܩ. Pa''ēl part. ܡܥܲܦܶܩ *embracing*, p. 11. 18; ܡܥܲܦܩܳܐ p. 17. 11.

ܥܨܐ *to restrain*, p. 20. 3.

ܥܨܪ *to press, bruise*, p. 11. 14.

ܥܩܒ. Ethpa'al ܐܶܬܥܲܩܲܒ *to be insolent* (?) p. 40. 8.

ܥܩܡ. Pa''ēl part. plur. ܡܥܲܩܡܺܝܢ *crafty*, p. 126. 17.

ܡܥܩܡܢܘܬܐ, plur. ܡܥܲܩܡܳܢܘܳܬܳܐ *perverse, crafty*, p. 160. 14.

ܥܩܪܒܐ, Ar. عَقْرَب, Heb. עַקְרָב *scorpion*, plur. ܥܩܪ̈ܒܐ p. 174. 4, 14.

ܥܪܐ. ܥܲܪܳܐ *cold*, p. 160. 11. البرد الشديد Brit. Mus. MS. Rich 7203, fol. 132 *b*, col. 2.

ܥܪܒ. ܥܲܪܒܳܐ *trough*, 265. 1.

ܥܘܪܒܐ. Ar. غُرَاب, Heb. עֹרֵב *raven*, ܥܘܪ̈ܒܝ ܠܠܝܐ *night ravens*, p. 176. 19.

ܥܪܕ. ܥܪܕܐ *mushroom*, plur. ܥܪ̈ܕܐ p. 180. 1. كَماة Brit. Mus. MS. Rich 7203, p. 132 *b*, col. 2.

ܥܪܕܐ *ass*, plur. ܥܪ̈ܕܐ p. 180. 10.

ܥܪܛܠ. adv. ܥܪܛܠܐܝܬ *naked*, p. 21. 6; 39. 5.

ܥܪܛ. ܥܪܛܐ, *a rough place*, plur. ܥܪ̈ܛܐ p. 247. 4.

ܥܪܣܐ *bed*, ܥܪܣܐ ܕܝܠܕܬܐ *childbed*, p. 19. 11; 21. 12. D has ܡܫܟܒܐ ܕܝܠܕܬܐ

ܥܪܦܠܐ Heb. עֲרָפֶל *darkness, blackness*, p. 192. 7; plur. 256. 1.

ܥܪܝ. Ethpa'al ܐܬܥܪܝ *to be afflicted*, p. 173. 7.

ܥܪܩ. Af'ēl ܐܥܪܩ *to make to flee away*, p. 118. 3.

ܥܪ̈ܩܝ ܪܓܠܐ men with *twisted legs* = ἱμαντόποδες, p. 174. 22; 177. 16.

ܥܫܢ *to be strong*, p. 93. 6.

Pa''ēl ܥܫܢ, part. plur. fem. ܡܥܫ̈ܢܢ p. 23. 11.

ܥܫܝܢ *strong, mighty*, p. 84. 9; ܥܫܝܢܐ p. 59. 19; 231. 7; ܥܫܝܢܬܐ p. 90. 5; plur. ܥܫ̈ܝܢܝܢ p. 176. 3; plur. ܥܫ̈ܝܢܐ p. 252. 17.

ܥܫܝܢܘܬܐ *strength*, p. 32. 12; 159. 6.

ܥܘܫܢܐ *power, strength*, p. 76. 14.

ܥܬܕ. Pa''ēl ܥܬܕ *to make ready, to prepare*, p. 83. 12; infin. ܠܡܥܬܕܘ p. 201. 9; part. pass. ܡܥܬܕ p. 3. 18; plur. ܡܥܬܕܝܢ 90. 2; 201. 7; fem. ܡܥܬܕܐ 211. 3.

Ethpa'al ܐܬܥܬܕ *to be ready*, 81. 6; 95. 7; 164. 8; 209. 1; 226. 14; 233. 4; ܐܬܥܬܕ ܙܟܘܬܐ *he obtained the victory*, p. 50. 1; part. plur. ܡܬܥܬܕܝܢ p. 2. 4; 3. 5.

ܡܣܪܗܒܐܝܬ *readily*, p. 42. 9; 175. 11; 177. 14; 182. 18.

ܥܬܪ *to be rich*, Pe'al infin. ܠܡܥܬܪ *to be rich*, p. 34. 9.

Af'él *to make rich*, part. ܡܥܬܪ p. 34. 11.

ܥܬܝܪܐ *rich*, p. 40. 1; 84. 10; 196. 16; ܥܬܝܪܐ 67. 3; plur.

ܥܬܝܪܐ 160. 2; ܥܬܝܪܐ ܡܝܐ *well watered*, 177. 3.

ܥܘܬܪܐ *riches*, p. 10. 14; 34. 10; 67. 4.

ܦܐܪ. ܦܐܝܐ *beautiful*, p. 6. 7.

ܦܐܝܘܬܐ *beauty*, p. 24. 11; 138. 9; 206. 10.

ܦܓܘܕܐ. ܦܓܘܕܐ *bridle*, p. 32. 15; 33. 5, 8; 48. 13; plur. ܦܓܘܕܐ
p. 38. 17; 43. 17; 48. 8.

ܦܕܓܘܓܐ p. 36. 13; ܦܕܓܘܓܐ παιδαγωγός *teacher, tutor, guardian*,
p. 23, 13; 35. 9; plur. ܦܕܓܘܓܐ p. 89. 7.

ܦܕܓܘܓܐ ܕܡܘܕܒ ܗܘ. ܡܠܟܐ ܗܘ ܘܡܘܪܕܐ ܠܡܠܟܐ ܕܪܘܡܐ
ܕܝܠܟܘܢ ܐܢܬܘܢ ܚܕ ܗܕܐ ܘܡܕܡ ܠܗ ܗܘܐ ܗܟܕܐ مدير الصبيان
Brit. Mus. MS. Or. 2441, fol. 282 b, col. 2. ܦܕܓܘܓܐ =
معلمون ،مودبون ،ومدبرون Brit. Mus. MS. Rich 7203,
fol. 134 b, col. 2.

ܦܕܓܘܓܘܬܐ *education*, p. 35. 23.

ܦܚܡ *to be like unto*, p. 121. 3; 184. 17.

ܦܚܡܐ *like*, p. 86. 9; 103. 18; 138. 9; ܕܒܦܚܡܐ *in comparison with*, p. 88. 5; ܦܚܡܐ ܕܝܠܗ *counterpart*, p. 170. 4.

ܦܛܪ *to finish a meal*, p. 242. 1.

Af'él *to separate*, ܦܛܪ ܣܦܘܬܗ *he parted his lips in
scorn*, p. 41. 18; part. ܡܦܛܪ p. 80. 6.

ܦܓܝܕܐ *untanned*, p. 172. 5.

ܦܓ̈ܝܐ *footsoldiers*, p. 63. 1; 95. 3; 98. 1; 101. 4; 108. 3; 135. 5; 172. 4; 173. 9; 207. 10.

ܦܝܠܐ Assyrian pî-ru. See Strassmaier, *Alphabetisches Verzeichniss*, p. 517, l. 6. Ar. فيل (plur. أَفْيَال , فُيُول) *elephant*, 170. 13; 175. 9; 191. 6; plur. ܦܝ̈ܠܐ 159. 5; 160. 17; 174. 11; 211. 13; 219. 3; 220. 1; ܬܘܪ̈ܝ ܦܝܠܐ *ox-elephants*, p. 174. 14.

ܦܝܠܘܢܐ *cloak*, p. 198. 3, 7; 200. 5, 6.

ܦܝܣܐ the Greek infin. πεῖσαι, *persuade*, Syriacised ܦܝܣܐ *persuasion*.

Hence Afʿêl ܐܦܝܣ *he persuaded*, p. 5. 9; 54. 16; 55. 11; 188. 17; part. act. ܡܦܝܣ 66. 11; part. pass. plur. ܡܦܣܝܢ 242. 10.

Ettafʿal ܐܬܬܦܝܣ *be persuaded*, p. 6. 11; 58. 2; 224. 6; ܬܬܦܝܣܘܢ 116. 10; part. ܡܬܬܦܝܣ 123. 1.

ܡܦܝܣܢܘܬܐ *permission*, p. 91. 18.

ܠܐ ܡܬܬܦܝܣܢܘܬܐ *obstinacy, disobedience*, 82. 13; 196. 13.

ܦܝܠܣܘܦܘܣ, φιλόσοφος *philosopher*, plur. ܦܝܠܣܘ̈ܦܐ p. 18. 6.

ܦܝܠܣܘܦܘܬܐ φιλοσοφία *philosophy*, p. 23. 17.

ܦܝܠܙܘܪ p. 159. 5; 174. 13. See ܦܠܙܘܪ

ܦܟ̈ܐ *tusks*, p. 174. 12.

ܦܠܓ *to divide*, p. 235. 10; 244. 1.

Paʿʿêl part. act. ܡܦܠܓ *dividing, distributing*, p. 35. 9, 14; 37. 3.

Ethpaʿal *to be divided in mind, perplexed, in doubt*, p. 197, 15; 200. 14; 244. 16.

ܦܠܓܗ ܕܝܘܡܐ *midday*, p. 186. 15.

ܦܠܓܗ ܕܠܠܝܐ *midnight*, p. 186. 16.

ܦܠܓ ܙܒܢܐ = μεσῆλιξ *middle age*, p. 10. 17; 14. 15; 16. 5;

ܦܠܓܝ ܙܒܢܗ *a woman of middle age*, p. 209. 13.

ܦܘܠܓ *doubt*, p. 126. 4.

ܦܠܓܘܬܐ *half*, p. 52. 4; 142. 8; ܒܪ ܦܠܓܘܬܐ *a half partner*, p. 245. 1.

ܦܠܓܘܬܐ *doubt*, p. 26. 6.

ܦܠܝܓܘܬܐ *doubt*, p. 67. 4.

ܦܠܓܐ *phalanx* (= ܡܥܪܟܬܐ Brit. Mus. MS. Rich 7203, fol. 108 *b*, col. 2) p. 134. 10; 172. 1, 3; 173. 14; 174. 7; 179, 8; 206. 8; 207. 4.

ܦܠܓܐ *drums*, p. 171. 14. طبول ودفوف ܦܠܓܐ ܘܕܢܒܓܐ Brit. Mus. MS. Rich 7203, fol. 138 *b*, col. 2.

ܦܠܓܕ. ܡܬܦܠܓܕܝܢ *to be dispersed*, p. 134. 1.

ܦܠܚ. Pĕ'îl part. plur. ܦܠܝܚܝܢ *tanned, dressed*, p. 263. 16.

Afēl ܐܦܠܚ *to serve*, p. 63. 1.

ܦܠܚܘܬܐ *army*, p. 156. 9; 158. 17; 173. 2.

ܦܠܛܝܢ παλάτιον, palatium, *palace*, p. 255. 9.

ܦܠܛ. Ethpa'al ܐܬܦܠܛ *to be delivered, to escape*, p. 212. 18; infin. ܠܡܬܦܠܛܘ p. 52. 2; 119. 16; part. plur. ܡܬܦܠܛܝܢ p. 239. 19.

Pa''ēl infin. ܠܡܦܠܛܘ *to escape*, p. 157. 2.

ܦܘܠܛܢܐ *escape*, p. 132. 14.

ܦܠܬܟܦܬ *squares*, p. 74. 8. شَوَارِع، بُرُوب p. 69. 14; ܦܠܬܟܦܬ
Brit. Mus. Rich 7203, fol. 139 *a*, col. 1.

ܦܩܟܣ = πλάκας *tablets*, p. 70. 11.

ܩܒܠ. ܡܕܩܒܠܢܘܬ *restoration, giving back*, p. 215. 10.

ܩܘܒܠ *answer*. ܩܘܢ ܚܟܒܬܟܬ *written answer*, p. 56. 15.

ܩܒܝܠܬ *boundary, quarter of the world*, p. 90. 3; plur. ܩܒܠܬ
p. 3. 10; 90. 12; 115. 2; 159. 4.

ܩܝܡܕܘܪ πάνθηρ, *panther*, p. 159. 20; 174. 18.

ܩܡܪ *lot*, p. 43. 8. القُرعَة Brit. Mus. MS. Rich 7203, fol. 139 *b*, col. 1.

ܩܡܕ. Pě'al intin. ܠܡܩܡܕ *to march*, p. 100. 1.

ܩܡܕܬ *step*, p. 52. 1; 262. 20.

ܩܘܒܩܣܬ *dice*, p. 89. 21. زَرد اللعب Brit. Mus. MS. Rich 7203, fol.
139 *b*, col. 2. ܩܘܩܣܬ ܒܛܪܢܓ ܚܒ. الزرد الذي ܡܬܩܠܒ
ܩܘܩܣܬ ܣܛܪܢܓ ܘܩܘܩܣܬ ܚܠܩܩܣܬ ܦܕܢ ܠܚܡ
ܕܕܓܕ ܗܠܡ ܕܟܘܚܒܝ ܕܗ ܥܠ ܚܬܟܠܬ ܩܕܟܘܡܬ
للعب بالزرد و السطرنج * ܩܘܩܣܬ ܚܕ ܗܕܐ زرد
ܕܗܘܣ ܣܘܩܣܬ زرد ܩܘܩܣܬ ܢܒ ܚܕ ܗܕܐ النَّسِيفَا'
Brit. Mus. MS. Or. 2441, fol. 302 *b*, col. 2.

ܩܡܨ. Pa''ēl *to cut*, p. 116. 7; *to decide a dispute*, p. 148. 4.
Ethpa'al ܐܬܩܨ *to be cut*, p. 205. 22.

ܩܘܡܨܬ *fate*, p. 28. 11.

ܩܡܬܨܬ *brevity*, ܒܩܬܨܝܬ *briefly, shortly*, p. 23. 16; 115. 9;
136. 1.

ܩܡܣܝ *piscina, reservoir*, p. 18. 4. القِناء Brit. Mus. MS. Rich
7203, fol. 140 *a*, col. 1, and Brit. Mus. MS. Or. 2441, fol.
303 *a*, col. 1.

ܦܦܓܐ Ar. بَبغا *parrots*, p. 211. 9.

ܦܨܐ. Pa''ēl ܦܨܝ *to deliver*, p. 62. 10; 221. 18; 222. 13.

Ethpa'al ܠܡܬܦܨܝܘ *to be delivered, to escape*, p. 59. 6.

ܡܦܨܝܢܐ *deliverer*, p. 218. 1.

ܦܩܥܐ *blossom*, p. 93. 11.

ܦܩܥ *to split, to burst*, p. 18. 11.

ܦܩܥܐ *crash*, plur. ܦܩܥܐ p. 160. 11.

ܦܩܥܬܐ *field, plain*, p. 11. 13; 78. 3; 200. 17; plur. ܦܩܥܬܐ 100. 17.

ܦܩܪ. Pĕ'īl part. ܦܩܝܪ *excited*, p. 32. 5.

ܦܪܓܠܐ φραγέλλιον, *whip*, p. 48. 10; 80. 16; 81. 10; 87. 10; 89, 7; plur. 43. 17; 255. 8. ܦܪܓܠܐ درة ,مِقرَعة Brit. Mus. MS. Rich 7203, fol. 141 *a*, col. 1.

ܦܪܕܐ *grains*, p. 82. 6.

ܦܪܕܦܐ *clubs*, p. 264. 8.

ܦܪܚ. ܦܪܚܬܐ ܕܕܩܠܐ = φοῖνιξ *the bird of palm trees*, p. 180. 8.

ܦܪܚܕܘܕܐ *bats*, p. 176. 3. خشافه ,فار الليل Brit. Mus. MS. Or. 2441, fol. 308 *b*, col. 1; خشاف يعني الاصنام التي كانت تعبد ليلاً سراً Brit. Mus. MS. Rich 7203, fol. 141 *b*, col. 2.

ܦܪܙܘܠܐ. Pers. بِرِنج *copper, brass*, p. 9. 7.

ܦܪܢܝܬܐ φερνή, *dowry*, p. 147. 4. ܡܗܪ ܕܝܗܒ ܚܬܢܐ ܠܟܠܬܐ ܐܘ ܫܘܟܠܬܐ ܗܘ ܡܗܪܐ Rich 7203, fol. 310 *a*, col. 2.

ܦܪܢܣ. ܦܘܪܢܣܐ *food*, p. 56. 6.

ܦܪܣ *to spread out*, p. 142. 14; Pĕ'īl part. ܦܪܝܣ p. 182. 6; plur. ܦܪܝܣܝܢ p. 238. 1.

ܩܘܕܣܐ ، ܩܘܪܣܐ, plur. ܩܘܕܣܝܢ, ܩܘܪܣܐ from the Greek πόρος, *way, means, device, scheme, stratagem*, p. 2. 7, 14; 14. 7; 36. 6; 48. 2; 57. 13; 65. 8; 140. 6; 159. 7; 173. 7; 192. 13; 202. 7; 223. 9; 241. 5; ܦܘܪܣܐ ܣܓܝ *fertile in expedients*, p. 223. 8. Hence the verb in Ethpa'al part. ܡܬܦܪܣ *contriver* of inventions, p. 223. 9.

ܦܪܣ Ethpa'al part. ܡܬܦܪܣܐ *famed*, p. 2. 1.

ܦܪܣܬܐ *hoof*, plur. ܦܪܣܬܐ p. 48. 12.

ܦܪܩܕܘ ܠܡܬ p. 35. 18; see ܠܩܘܠܐ

ܦܪܨܘܦ πρόσωπον, *face*, p. 175. 1; ܦܪܨܘܦܐ p. 51. 10; 83. 2; 212. 11; 220. 18; plur. ܦܪܨܘܦܐ p. 169. 5; 176. 10; ܦܪܨܘܦܐ = شخص وجه Rich 7203, fol. 142 *b*, col. 2.

ܦܪܫ. ܦܪܫܐ, Heb. פָּרָשׁ, Ar. فارس *horseman*, plur. ܦܪܫܐ p. 64. 2; ܦܪܫܐ 25. 7; 33. 13; 62. 19; 95. 3; 98. 1; 102. 8; 108. 3; 119. 3; 129. 4; 173. 10; 176. 15; 203. 7; 224. 15; 230. 9; 232. 1.

ܦܪܫܘܬܐ *horsemanship*, p. 25. 7.

ܦܘܪܫܢܐ *separation*, p. 246. 14.

ܦܪܬܐ *dung*, p. 270. 3.

ܦܫܩ. ܦܫܝܩܐ *easy*, p. 203. 11.

ܦܘܫܩܐ *explanation*, p. 253. 3.

Pa''el infin. ܠܡܦܫܩܘ *to describe, explain*, p. 8. 4.

Ethpa'al part. pass. ܡܬܦܫܩ *interpreted*, p. 31. 12.

ܦܫܪ *to explain* dreams, p. 7. 4; 15. 10; *to macerate*, 265. 1.

Pa''el part. pass. ܡܦܫܪ *melted*, p. 250. 11.

Ethpaʻal part. plur. ܡܬܦܟܕܝܢ *cracked, split,* (of houses on
fire) p. 102. 11; 105. 7.

ܦܟܕܐ *explanation,* p. 16. 6.

ܟܦܐ Paʻěl part. pass. ܡܟܦܦܐ *variegated,* p. 220. 7.

ܦܐܬܘܪܐ *table,* p. 8. 1, 9; 51. 12; 143. 1; 182. 8; plur. ܦܬܘܪܐ
218. 14.

ܟܠܐ Paʻěl part. pass. ܡܟܠܠܐ *decorated, ornamented,* p. 13. 4;
231. 11.

ܟܠܝܠܐ *ornament,* plur. ܟܠܝܠܬܐ p. 153. 13.

ܨܘܪ, ܨܪ *to paint,* p. 56. 20; 57. 1; 80. 1.

ܨܝܪܐ *painter,* p. 56. 18; 212. 9.

ܨܘܪܬܐ *picture,* p. 220. 18.

ܨܡܘܥ *to hear, listen to,* p. 41. 6; 99. 11.

ܬܐܡܐ ܬܐܡܐ *Gemini,* p. 20. 4.

ܨܡܚ. Afʻěl part. *sparkling, shining,* p. 182. 5; 219. 9; plur.
ܡܨܡܚܝܢ p. 225. 4.

ܡܨܡܚܢܐ *shining, sparkling,* plur. ܡܨܡܚܢܬܐ p. 225. 8.

ܨܡܪ. ܨܡܘܪܬܐ *vortex,* p. 170. 9. ܨܡܘܪܬܐ كان وخا غمر
ܨܡܘܪܬܐ الما تردور الدايره Rich 7203, fol. 146 b, col. 2;
..... ܬܚܘܝܢ ܕܦܨ. ܢܚܢ ܕܣܘܩܝ ܡܢ ܕܪܡܚܘ
Brit. Mus. ܘܣܘ ܬܕ ܡܕܐ ܚܕܘܚܠܐ ܕܡܢ ܡܠܟܘܬ
MS. Or. 2441, fol. 318 b, col. 2.

ܨܢܥ. ܨܢܥܬܐ *craft, device, artifice, stratagem,* p. 45. 3; 72. 16,
17; 162. 2; plur. ܨܢܥܬܐ p. 2. 7; 8. 14; 58. 1; 93. 3;
159. 7; ܨܢܝܥ ܡܟܝܕ *fertile in artifices,* p. 196. 15.

ܨܢܝܥܘܬܐ *craft, slyness,* p. 79. 17; 206. 2.

ܨܢܝܥܐܝܬ *artfully,* p. 85. 5; 110. 13.

ܨܥܪ. Pa''ēl *to revile, abuse,* p. 114. 18; 118. 7; 127. 6.

ܡܨܥܪܢܐܝܬ *despicably,* p. 21. 7.

ܩܒܘܛܐ κιβωτός, *box,* p. 80. 17; 81. 12; 87. 11.

ܩܒܠ. Af'ēl ܐܩܒܠ *receive, accept,* p. 198. 9.

Estaf'al ܐܫܬܩܒܠ *to be involved in,* p. 168. 5.

ܩܘܒܠܐ *accusation,* p. 240. 13.

ܩܘܒܠ ܛܝܒܘܬܐ *gratitude,* p. 122. 8; 125. 3; 154. 3.

ܩܒܪ. ܩܒܪܐ ܕܐܘܣܝܪܝܣ *grave of Osiris,* p. 74. 12, = Ταφόσιρις.

ܩܕܚ. ܩܕܘܚܐ *borer,* p. 233. 10, 11.

ܩܕܡ. Pa''ēl ܩܕܡ. ܩܕܡ ܢܩܕܡ *to rise up betimes,* p. 15. 10; Part. plur. ܡܩܕܡܝܢ ܡܩܕܡܝܢ *to point out beforetime,* p. 114. 5.

ܡܩܕܡܘܬ ܝܕܥܬܐ *fore-knowledge,* p. 29. 2; 66. 13.

ܩܘܢܐ *purple, dark blue,* p. 113. 4; ܩܘܢܝܐ p. 43. 15. In Rich 7203, fol. 151 *b,* col. 1, ܩܘܢܝܐ is explained by اخضر *green.*

ܩܘܕܪܣܪ p. 203. 10. Glossed in B by Pers. سردار *chief.*

ܩܝܢܝܐ *a smith, metalworker,* plur. ܩܝܢ̈ܝܐ p. 161. 8; 253. 13; 267. 7; 275. 14.

ܡܦܘܚܐ ܕܩܝܢ̈ܝܐ *smith's bellows,* p. 193. 9.

ܩܘܦܐ *poles, carrying bars, fetters for the legs,* p. 59. 11. ܩܘܦܐ is the word used in the Syriac version of the Old Test. to translate the Heb. בַּדִּים, בַּדֵּי, the poles by which the ark was carried, in Ex. xxv. 13 (LXX. ἀναφορεῖς, ed. Lagarde, p. 76), Ex. xxvii. 6 (LXX. φορεῖς), Numb. iv. 6; and the Heb. מוֹט in Numb. iv. 10. ܩܘܦ̈ܐ is explained by نحوق (sing. نحق) in Rich 7203, fol. 152 *a*, col. 2. See also Brit. Mus. MS. Or. 2441, fol. 330 *b*, col. 1, where ܩܘܦ̈ܐ is explained by ܡܘܛ̈ܐ ܕܒܗܘܢ ܡܫܬܩܠܝܢ ܩܒܘܬܐ ܐܘ ܦܬܘܪܐ "*the staves by which a box or table is carried.*" The verb نحق is used in speaking of a dead animal as, for example, of a stag or donkey, *qui est porté par deux hommes au moyen d'une perche qu'on a passée entre ses pieds,* après les avoir liés les uns aux autres. Dozy, *Supplément aux Dictionnaires Arabes*, t. i, p. 466.

ܩܘܦ̈ܐ *apes*, p. 211. 19; 217. 9. ܩܘܦܐ ܗ̄. ܚܝܘܬܐ ܕܕܡܝܐ ܠܒܪܢܫܐ Or. 2441, fol. 330 *b*, col. 1.

ܩܘܨ̈ܬܐ *ringlets*, p. 13. 4. ܩܘܨܬܐ جمم مغاير Rich 7203, fol. 152 *b*, col. 1; Or. 2441, fol. 231 *a*, col. 2.

ܩܛܪ *to bind*, p. 80. 14.

ܩܛܝܪܐ *violence*, p. 53. 5.

ܩܛܝܪܐܝܬ *violently*, p. 145. 15.

ܩܝܛܘܢܐ κοιτών, *bedchamber*, p. 12. 16; 13. 19; 52. 12; 80. 8; 197. 12; 219. 14; 220. 16; plur. ܩܝܛܘ̈ܢܐ p. 13. 7; 101. 1.

ܩܝܬܪܐ κιθάρα, cithara, Chald. קִיתָרֹס, *harp*, p. 237. 16, 17.

ܩܠ. ܩܠܝܠ *little, few*, p. 47. 8; 57. 7; 65. 17; 93. 14; 97. 3; 133. 19; 138. 10; 143. 3; 165. 17; 189. 9; 212. 18; ܩܠܝܠܐ 14. 12; plur. ܩܠܝܠܝܢ 94. 17.

ܩܠܝܠܐܝܬ *swiftly, speedily*, p. 11. 12; 20. 2; 113. 11; 132. 3.

ܩܠܘܒܐ *cage*, p. 236. 6, 8. In Rich 7203, fol. 156 *a*, col. 1, this word is explained by قفص ، مشبك

ܩܠܣ. Pa''ēl part. ܡܩܠܣ *praising*, p. 18. 1.

ܩܠܥ. ܩܠܥܐ *sling*, p. 192. 9; plur. ܩܠܥܐ p. 101. 14, 17; 102. 2.

ܩܠܥܝܐ *slingers*, p. 101. 20.

ܩܠܦ. ܩܠܦܬܐ *bark*, p. 205. 2.

ܩܡܪ. ܩܡܪܐ *belt*, p. 8. 6; 129. 2; 147. 13; plur. ܩܡܪܐ p. 8. 6.

ܩܡܪܐ مِنْطَقَة Rich, fol. 157 *b*, col. 2.

ܩܢܕܝܠ, Chald. קַנְדִּילָא, Ar. قِنْدِيل candēla, *lamp*, *torch*, plur. ܩܢܕܝܠܐ ܩܢܕܝܠ 101. 6; 235. 8.

ܩܢܛ. ܩܢܛܐ *fear*, p. 127. 17.

ܩܢܛܐ *purple*, p. 114. 10.

ܩܢܐ ܥܠܡܐ = ܩܘܠܛܢܐ Libra, *balance*, p. 20. 8.

ܩܘܢܛܐ *band*, *company*, p. 81. 17.

ܩܢܩܠ κάγκελος, cancelli, *fetter*, p. 24. 23; 32. 3, 12, 15; 33. 4.

ܩܣܛܘܢܪܐ quaestionarius, *executioner*, p. 244. 6; plur. ܩܣܛܘܢܪܐ p. 82. 14, 16; 199. 5, 14. This word is explained by حارس ، حانقى in Rich 7203, fol. 159 *a*, col. 1.

ܩܣܛܘܢܪܘܬܐ *execution*, p. 199. 6; 200. 2.

ܩܠܦ. Ethpě'ēl ܐܬܩܠܦ *to be peeled*, p. 132. 18.

ܩܣܝ. Ethpa'al part. ܡܬܩܣܝܢܐ *creditable*, p. 229. 7.

ܩܣܡ. *to divine*, p. 275. 3, 7; infin. ܠܡܩܣܡ *to consult an oracle*, p. 7. 16.

ܩܨܘܡܐ *diviner*, p. 31. 5, 6; 33. 16; plur. ܩܨܘܡܐ p. 7. 5.

ܩܘܣܡܐ *divination*, p. 5. 17, 18; 31. 15; 33. 15; 50. 7; 99. 15; 109. 4; 110. 2; 123. 13; plur. ܩܣܡ̈ܐ p. 5. 11, 15.

ܩܣܘܡܘܬܐ *augury, divination*, p. 29. 1; 106. 8.

ܩܪܒ. ܩܪܒܬܢܐ *warlike, brave*, plur. ܩܪܒܬܢ̈ܐ p. 25. 7.

ܩܪܒܬܢܘܬܐ *art of war*, p. 24. 1.

ܩܪܒܬܢܐܝܬ *warlike*, p. 21. 5.

ܩܪܝܒܐܝܬ *nearly, shortly*, p. 10. 6.

ܩܪ̈ܒܐ *galleys*, p. 119. 3.

ܩܘܪ̈ܒܐ perhaps for ܩܪ̈ܒܝܐ *transport ships*, p. 63. 8; 65. 15. Conf. κάραβος, καράβιον, Ar. غراب . قارب

ܩܪܘܣܛܠܠܘܣ κρύσταλλος, crystallum, *crystal*, p. 9. 1.

ܩܪܛܝܣܐ χάρτης, charta, *charter*, p. 257. 18.

ܩܪܟܕܢܐ χαλκηδών, *chalcedony*, plur. ܩܪ̈ܟܕܢܐ p. 224. 14.

ܩܪܡ. ܩܪܝܡ *inlaid*, p. 219. 14.

ܩܪܢ. ܩܪܢܢܐ *horned*, fem. ܩܪܢܢܝܬܐ p. 21. 10; ܩܪܢܢܬܐ p. 21. 20.

ܩܪ̈ܢܝ ܚܡܪ̈ܐ *rhinoceroses*, p. 211. 14.

ܩܪ̈ܩܦܢܬܐ *skulls*, p. 32. 6. Rich 7203, fol. 163 *b*, col. 2, ܩܪܩܦܢܬܐ الهاما الجماجمه

ܩܫܐ. ܩܫܝܘܬܐ *hardness*, p. 184. 8.

ܩܫܝܐܝܬ *fiercely*, p. 49. 3; 78. 8; 142. 1.

ܩܬܕܪܐ καθέδρα, cathedra, *seat*, p. 258, 1, 7, 9.

ܩܕܩ. ܢܦܠ ܥܠ ܩܕܩܕ *to fall headlong*, p. 44. 7; 49. 10.

ܩܪ̈ܩܦܬ ܕܟܪ̈ܐ *rams' heads*, i.e., battering rams, p. 101. 7, 8.

ܪܒܝ. ܩܪܒܬܢܐ *fosterer, guardian,* plur. ܡܪܒܝܢܐ p. 228. 8.

ܪܬܟ. ܡܪܬܟܐ *squire,* p. 219. 19.

ܪܬܝ. ܪܬܝܐ *strain, force of a current,* p. 205. 13.

ܪܓ. Infin. Pe'al ܡܪܓ *to desire,* p. 158. 15.

Ethpalpal ܐܬܪܓܪܓ *to desire,* p. 6. 4; 107. 3; 206. 18.

ܪܓܝܓܘܬܐ *desirability,* p. 206. 10.

ܪܗܛ. ܪܗܛܐ *runner,* plur. ܪܗܛܐ p. 268. 5.

ܪܗܠܐ *ravine,* plur. ܪܗܠܐ p. 134. 19.

ܪܗܠܐ *river, torrent,* plur. ܪܗܠܐ p. 155. 7.

ܪܓܫ. Af'el *to make perceive,* p. 162. 16; 243. 1; part. act. ܡܪܓܫ p. 86. 6.

ܪܓܫܬܐ *feeling, perception,* p. 68. 11, 13.

ܪܕܐ. ܪܕܝܐ, ܪܕܝܘܬܐ *learning,* p. 56. 17; ܠܐ ܪܕܝܘܬܐ *ignorance* p. 89. 3.

ܪܗܒ. Saf'el part. plur. ܡܣܪܗܒܝܢ p. 3. 11.

Estafa'al ܐܣܬܪܗܒ *to hasten,* p. 11. 13; 102. 12; 243. 4.

ܡܣܪܗܒܐܝܬ *hastily,* p. 132. 2.

ܪܗܝܒܐܝܬ *hastily, quickly,* p. 182. 9; 209. 2.

ܪܗܛܪܐ ῥήτωρ *orator,* p. 117. 1, 11; plur. ܪܗܛܪܐ p. 115. 13; 116. 7; 121. 5; 125. 7; 126. 3.

ܪܗܒ. ܪܗܒܐ *tumults,* p. 57. 17.

ܪܚܡ. Ethpa'al ܐܬܪܚܡ *to be gratified,* p. 33. 4.

ܪܚܝܐ *mill,* p. 261. 1; 268. 18.

ܪܘܟ. ܪܘܟܐ *sprinkling, spattering,* p. 41. 14; 51. 2. تنضيح ﻧﻀﺢ , ﺭﺵ . Rich 7203, fol. 169 b, col. 1.

16—2

ܐܪܙܘܦܛܐ, Chald. אֲרַזפְתָּא, Ar. الرزبة hammer, p. 270. 4, 5;
plur. ܐܪܙܘܦܟܐ p. 270. 6. See Duval, *Lexicon Syriacum
auctore Hassano bar Bahlule*, p. 286, col. 2.

ܪܚܡ. ܐܠܗܐ ܪܚܡ homeloving, p. 20. 11.

ܪܚܡܬܢܐܝܬ lovingly, p. 30. 3.

ܡܪܚܡܢܐܝܬ kindly, p. 246. 10.

ܪܛܢ. to grumble, p. 36. 3.

Af'el part. act. ܡܪܛܢ complaining, p. 36. 4.

ܪܟܒ. Pa''el part. act. ܡܪܟܒ to compose a song, p. 107. 10; ܡܬܟܐ
ܡܪܟܒܬܐ words strung together, p. 107. 11.

ܪܟܒܐ riders, p. 44. 7.

ܪܘܟܒܐ composition, p. 96. 5.

ܪܟܢ. Af'el part. act. ܡܪܟܢ to make to bow, p. 151. 16.

ܡܬܪܟܢܢܝܬܐ placable, p. 103. 13.

ܪܟܫܐ horses, p. 24. 9.

ܪܡܐ. Af'el to throw, p. 52. 4; 118. 1; ܐܪܡܝܬ ܒܝܥܬܐ is laid an
egg, p. 18. 9; Infin. ܠܡܪܡܝܘ p. 111. 2.

ܪܡܙ. to make a sign, p. 48. 1.

ܪܡܙܐ hint, p. 88. 1; 196. 6.

ܪܡܟܐ herd of horses, plur. ܪܡܟܐ p. 24. 8.

ܪܢܐ. ܡܪܢܝܬܐ anxious thought, p. 118. 4; 162. 9; plur. ܡܪܢܝܬܐ
p. 126. 4.

ܪܥܐ. ܐܪܥܘܬܐ reconciliation, p. 204. 2

ܪܓܙ. ܪܘܓܙܐ anger, indignation, p. 220. 7; plur. ܪܘܓܙܐ p.
122. 9.

ܪܦܐ. Af'ēl *to leave, forsake*, p. 4. 16; 90. 16; 101. 12; 108. 17; 168. 8; 169. 12; 195. 19; 202. 12; 207. 8; 244. 5; ܡܪܦܐ ܐܢܬܬܐ ܡܢ *to divorce*, p. 10. 4; ܡܪܦܐ ܠܐܚܕܐ *to let go hold*, p. 199. 13.

ܪܦܝܐܝܬ *sluggishly*, p. 83. 13.

ܪܩܕ. ܪܩܘܕܐ *dancers*, p. 181. 14.

ܡܪܩܕܢܘܬܐ *mourning*, p. 21. 3; 251. 17.

ܪܩܥ. ܐܘܪܩܥܬܐ *rug*, p. 41. 16; رقعة من ثوب See *Duval, Lexicon Syriacum*, p. 94, col. 2.

ܪܫܦ *to glide, crawl, creep*, p. 13. 1; 17. 7.

ܪܬܐ. ܡܪܬܝܢܘܬܐ *admonition*, p. 55. 12.

ܪܬܚ. ܡܪܬܚܢܘܬܐ *abounding*, p. 75. 13.

ܫܐܪܝܐ *silken* curtains, p. 195. 11; 200. 8. ܫܐܪܝܐ حرير ,القز Rich 7203, fol. 174 *a*, col. 1.

ܫܒܐ. ܫܒܝܐ *captors*, p. 164. 1.

ܫܒܩ *to leave*, 194. 16; *to let go* a battering ram, p. 101. 8; *to set fire*, p. 175. 4; *to divorce*, p. 53. 10; ܫܒܝܩܬܐ *divorced*, p. 50. 9.

Ethpĕ'ēl ܐܫܬܒܩ *to be forgiven*, p. 248. 14.

ܫܒܘܒܬܐ *branch*, p. 93. 12; plur. ܫܒܘܒܝܢ, ܫܒܘܒܬܐ p. 238. 2.

ܫܒܫܬܐ *vine branches*, p. 78. 12. In Rich 7203, fol. 175 *b*, col. 1, ܫܒܫܬܐ is explained by شغشه الدقيقه التي في الكرم

ܫܓܐ. Ar. ساج *plane, teakwood*, p. 2. 12; 4. 12; 212. 3.

ܫܓܫ. ܡܫܓܫܢܐ *various*, p. 171. 1. ܡܫܓܫܢܐ = مختلف in Rich 7203, fol. 88 *a*, col. 2.

ܫܕܪ. Ethpa'al ܐܫܬܕܪ *to be sent*, p. 79. 16.

ܫܗܐ. Ethpe'al ܐܫܬܗܝ *to be diminished*, p. 206. 2.

ܫܗܝܘܬܐ *wilderness*, p. 108. 2.

ܫܘܐ. Pa''ēl infin. ܠܡܫܘܝܘ *to lay, to prepare*, p. 195. 12; part. pass. ܡܫܘܝܐ *laid*, p. 182. 4.

ܫܘܒ. ܫܘܒܐ *drought*, p. 72. 18.

ܫܘܛ. ܫܝܛ *despised*, p. 86. 6.

ܫܝܛܘܬܐ *contempt*, p. 149. 9.

ܡܫܬܐܝܛܘܬܐ *ridicule*, p. 221. 15.

ܫܘܝܘܬܐ *equality*, p. 146. 12.

ܫܘܝܐܝܬ *together, equally*, p. 27. 16; 46. 15, 17; 137. 7; 175. 4; 203. 5.

ܫܘ̈ܛܐ *blows*, p. 178. 15.

ܫܛܐ. ܫܛܝܐܝܬ *stupidly*, p. 106. 3.

ܫܚܢ. Af'ēl part. act. ܡܫܚܢ *making warm*, p. 86. 5.

ܫܚܩ. Ethpĕ'ēl *to be vexed*, p. 28. 8.

ܫܚܩܐ *vexation*, plur. ܫܚ̈ܩܐ p. 146. 15.

ܫܬܬ. ܫܬܝܬܐ ܡܢ ܣܥܪܐ *barley meal*, p. 75. 5.

ܫܦܝ. ܫܦܝܘܬܐ *level*, p. 100. 17; 233. 17.

ܫܝܢ. Pa''ēl ܫܝܢ *to make peace*, p. 57. 4; part. act. ܡܫܝܢ *pacify*, p. 54. 19; plur. ܡܫܝ̈ܢܐ *docile, gentle*, p. 251. 9.

ܡܫܝܢܘܬܐ *peace*, p. 140. 6.

ܫܝܦ. Pa''ēl infin. ܠܡܫܝܦܘ *to rub*, p. 33. 3; part. act. ܡܫܝܦ p. 33. 6.

ܫܟܚ. ܫܟܚܬܐ, plur. ܫܟ̈ܚܬܐ *inventions, discoveries*, p. 2. 1.

ܫܟܝܚܘܬܐ *invention*, p. 67. 1.

ܫܟܪ. ܫܟܝܪܐ *bad, foul*, p. 199. 6; ܫܟܝܪܬܐ p. 128. 2.

ܫܟܝܪܘܬܐ *foulness*, p. 107. 14.

ܫܠܐ. Pa"ēl infin. ܠܡܫܠܝܘ *to quiet*, p. 46. 1.

ܫܠܝܐܝܬ *peacefully, silently*, p. 33. 8; 122. 15; 225. 6.

ܫܠܛ *to rule*, p. 65. 3; ܫܘܠܛܢܘܬܐ *dominion*, p. 151. 17.

ܫܠܝܛܘܬܐ *rule*, p. 113. 11.

ܫܠܡ. ܫܠܡܘܬܐ, plur. ܫܠܡ̈ܘܬܐ *perfect*, p. 209. 6.

ܡܫܠܡܢܘܬܐ *betrayal*, p. 29. 2.

ܫܠܩ. ܫܠܝܩ *roasted*, p. 264. 16. In Brit. Mus. Or. 2441, fol. 375 *b*, col. 1,

ܫܠܩܐ is explained by مَطْبوخ، مَسْلوق.

ܫܡܗ. Pa"ēl ܫܡܗ *to call, to name*, p. 16. 13; 109. 1; Part. ܡܫܡܗ *name*, p. 53. 2; ܡܫܡܗܐ *renowned, famous*, p. 39. 4; 142. 17; 225. 15; plur. ܡܫܡ̈ܗܐ p. 211. 2; 247. 1; ܡܫܡܗܬܐ p. 67. 16; 75. 13; 226. 7.

ܡܫܡܗܘܬܐ *fame*, 196. 12.

Ethpa'al ܐܫܬܡܗ *to be famed*, p. 72. 16.

ܫܡܥ. *to be obedient*, p. 2. 3; 230. 19; ܡܫܬܡܥܢܐ *obedient*, p. 174. 8.

ܫܢ. ܫܢܢܐ *rock*, p. 271. 6; plur. ܫܢ̈ܢܬܐ *mountains*, p. 260. 8; 267. 11, 14, 15, 16; 268. 2, 10; 269. 17.

ܫܢܐ. ܫܢܝܘܬܐ *madness*, p. 89. 3.

ܫܥܐ. Ethpa'al ܐܫܬܥܝ *to play*, p. 81. 11; 89. 11; ܐܫܬܥܝ *to be told, narrated*, p. 18. 17.

ܫܥܝܬܐ *game, sport*, plur. ܫܥ̈ܝܬܐ p. 57. 15, 17; 73. 4; ܫܥܝܐ ܕܛܠܝܐ child's *play*, p. 41. 13.

ܫܥܘܬܐ *yellow*, p. 43. 15.

ܫܘܥܠܐ *fist, hand*, p. 83. 17.

ܫܦܠ. *to be timid, weak*, p. 129. 9.

Ethpa'al ܐܫܬܦܠ *to be abased, brought low*, p. 196. 14.

ܫܦܠܐ *mean*, p. 144. 1.

ܫܦܝܠܘܬܐ *disgrace*, p. 91. 4, 6.

ܫܦܥ. ܫܦܝܥ *liberal*, p. 35. 7.

ܫܘܦ̈ܥܐ *overflowings* of the Nile, p. 124. 5.

ܫܩܠ. Af'ēl ܐܫܩܠ *to move on, decamp*, p. 97. 1, 4; 113. 2; 192. 1; 193. 12; 194. 18; 201. 16; 202. 3; 207. 3; 232. 5; infin. ܠܡܫܩܠܘ p. 183. 9; part. act. ܡܫܩܠܐ *marching*, p. 172. 1.

Ethpa'al ܐܫܬܩܠ *to prevail*, p. 118. 17.

ܡܫܩܠܘܬܐ *arrogance, greatness*, p. 86. 3; 143. 12; 151. 17; 198. 14; 199. 1.

ܡܫܩܠܐܝܬ *proudly*, p. 143. 19.

ܫܩܠܐ *tax*, p. 164. 4; ܫܩ̈ܠܐ p. 124. 13; ܫܩ̈ܠܬܐ p. 146. 18.

ܫܩܝܠ ܚܫܚܐ *carefully*, p. 23. 2; 49. 1.

ܫܪ. ܡܫܪܪܐܝܬ *surely*, p. 23. 2.

ܫܪܝܪܐܝܬ *truly, certainly*, p. 6. 15; 11. 17; 15. 14; 53. 16; 61. 11.

ܫܘܪܐ *navel*, p. 163. 15; plur. ܫܘܪ̈ܐ p. 201. 5.

ܫܪܐ. Af'ēl infin. ܠܡܫܪܝܘ *to break up a company*, p. 207. 4.

Ethpĕ'ēl ܐܫܬܪܝ *to be dismissed*, p. 114. 15.

Ethpa'al ܐܫܬܪܝ *to be finished* (of a feast), p. 197. 10.

ܫܪܘܬܐ *feast*, p. 85. 2; 129. 16; 197. 10.

ܫܪܝܢܐ *breastplate*, p. 224. 13.

ܫܪܘܝܢܐ *cypresses*, p. 186. 3.

ܫܪܩ. Pa''ēl part. act. ܡܫܪܩܝܢ *hissing*, p. 17. 7.

ܫܡܫܡ. ܫܘܡܫܡܐ *grains of sesame* (Ar. سمسم) p. 82. 6; 83. 16; 88. 1, 13; 92. 8, 13, 14; 93. 13, 16; 94. 13.

Shafʿēl part. pass. ܡܫܘܬܦ *joined with*, p. 62. 8.

ܫܘܡܫܡܢܐ *ant*, plur. ܫܘܡܫܡܢ̈ܐ p. 92. 3.

ܫܬܐ, ܫܬܬ, ܫܬܣ. ܫܬܐܣܬܐ = ܫܬ *foundation*, + ܐܣܬܐ *wall*, p. 209. 10; plur. ܫܬܐܣ̈ܐ p. 74. 8; 101. 5.

ܫܬܦ. Eshtafʿal ܐܫܬܘܬܦ *to be united with*, p. 11. 7; 20. 9.

ܫܘܬܦܘܬܐ *union*, p. 29. 7.

ܫܘܬܦܐ *associate*, p. 34. 16.

ܬܐܛܪܘܢ θέατρον, *theatre*, p. 58. 3, 4; 110. 13.

ܬܒܥ *to seek vengeance*, p. 10. 12; 12. 1; 15. 1; 52. 6, 10; 60. 2; 127. 10; 138. 2; 142. 1; 143. 7; 224. 5.

ܬܒܥܬܐ *vengeance*, p. 64. 4.

ܬܘܗ. ܬܘܗܝܐ *delay*, p. 117. 2; 249. 9.

ܬܘܒ. Ethpĕʿēl ܐܬܬܘܝܒ *to repent*, p. 82. 11.

ܡܬܬܘܝܢܘܬܐ *repentance*, p. 62. 3.

ܬܟܟ. *to be humbled*, p. 17. 18.

ܬܟܝܟܐ *despicable, wretched*, p. 100. 14.

ܬܚܬ. Ethpaʿal ܐܬܬܚܬܝ *to descend, be brought down*, p. 128. 11; 196. 14.

ܬܩܦ. ܬܩܝܦܬܐ *sore, grievous*, plur. ܬܩܝ̈ܦܬܐ p. 251. 17.

ܬܟܠ. ܬܘܟܠܢܐ *confidence, trust*, p. 61. 18; 199. 3.

ܡܬܬܟܠܢܘܬܐ *trust*, p. 21. 7.

ܬܟܝܠܐܝܬ *confidently*, p. 193. 18.

ܬܠܚ. Ethpa'al part. plur. fem. ܡܬܬܠܚ̈ܢ *torn, rent*, p. 260. 11.

ܬܡܗ. *to wonder*, p. 32. 12; ܬܡܝܗ *wonderful*, p. 2. 3; 66. 15; ܬܡܝܗܬܐ p. 172. 8; 183. 10; ܬܡܝܗܝܢ p. 130. 6; 131. 4; 219. 1; ܬܡܝܗܐ p. 105. 13; ܬܡܝܗ ܐܢܐ *I wonder*, p. 12. 11.

ܬܘܡܗܐ *wonder*, p. 12. 3.

ܬܘܪ̈ܩܐ *breastplates*, p. 172. 4.

ܬܠܠ ܬܠܠܒ̈ܐ = νυκταλώπηκες, *nightfoxes*, p. 175. 17.

ܬܪܥܐ, *stream*, plur. ܬܪ̈ܥܐ p. 70. 4. See ܬܪܥܐ p. 261. 1; 268. 7.

ܬܩܠ. Ethpe'el ܐܬܬܩܠ *to be upset*, p. 44. 9, 12; 45. 9; 49. 9; 68. 9.

ܬܘܩܠܬܐ *a stumbling*, p. 52. 2.

ܬܩܢ. Af'el ܐܬܩܢ *to set straight, correct*, p. 37. 7; Infin. ܠܡܬܩܢܘ *to set up*, p. 146. 13; part. act. ܡܬܩܢ p. 226. 7; pass. ܡܬܩܢ p. 224. 14; plur. ܡܬܩܢܝܢ p. 171. 8; 182. 7; 200. 1; 238. 3; fem. ܡܬܩܢ̈ܢ p. 8. 14.

ܬܪܢܓܘܠܬܐ. Chald. תַּרְנְגוֹלָא, *hen*, p. 18. 7; plur. ܬܪ̈ܢܓܘܠܬܐ p. 56. 11.

ܬܪܣ. Ethpa'al part. plur. ܡܬܬܪܣܝܢ *to be fed upon*, p. 169. 6.

ܬܘܪܣܝܐ *food*, p. 75. 7, 15; 98. 7; 121. 17; 122. 2; 140. 15.

ܟܐܘܪܐܒ ܐܚܝ *to feed*, p. 39. 14.

ܬܪܥܐ ܬܪܥܐ plur. ܬܪܥܐ *gates*, p. 43. 7; *curtains*, 195. 11.

ܬܪܨ *to become straight* (of a bridge), p. 205. 14 ; *to march straight forward*, p. 190. 10 ; *to make a way straight*, p. 189. 15.

ܬܪܝܨܘܬܐ *what is right, straightness*, p. 54. 14 ; 83. 5 ; 140. 10 ; plur. ܬܪܝܨܘܬܐ *truths*, p. 83. 12.

ܬܪܝܨܐܝܬ *correctly, exactly, precisely*, p. 7. 2, 17; 9. 11; 50. 14 ; 95. 1 ; 121. 7 ; 122. 7 ; 178. 1 ; 197. 19 ; 203. 1 ; 220. 8; 239. 8.

## Note to page xxxiv.

Through the kindness of the Rev. Canon Maclean, M.A., the head of the Archbishop of Canterbury's Mission to the Nestorians at Urmia, I have obtained another MS. of the Syriac version of Pseudo-Callisthenes, which he caused to have copied for me during the present year. It measures 8¾ in. by 7 in., and consists of 217 leaves. The quires, unsigned, are 22 in number. Each page contains 16 lines. This manuscript is written in a fine, bold, modern Nestorian hand, with numerous vowel points, etc., and is dated A. Gr. 2200 = A.D. 1889. The faulty readings in it agree generally with those in D; occasionally however its readings are peculiar to itself, *e. g.*, ܡܕܘܕܝܠ ܕܩܝܠܟܘܡ for ܡܕܘܕܝܠ ܕܩܝܠܟܟܘܡ p. ܘ, l. 16. The collation of the difficult passages in ABCD and E with this manuscript has neither helped to amend the text nor to clear away any of the difficulties which exist in it. The following is the colophon :—

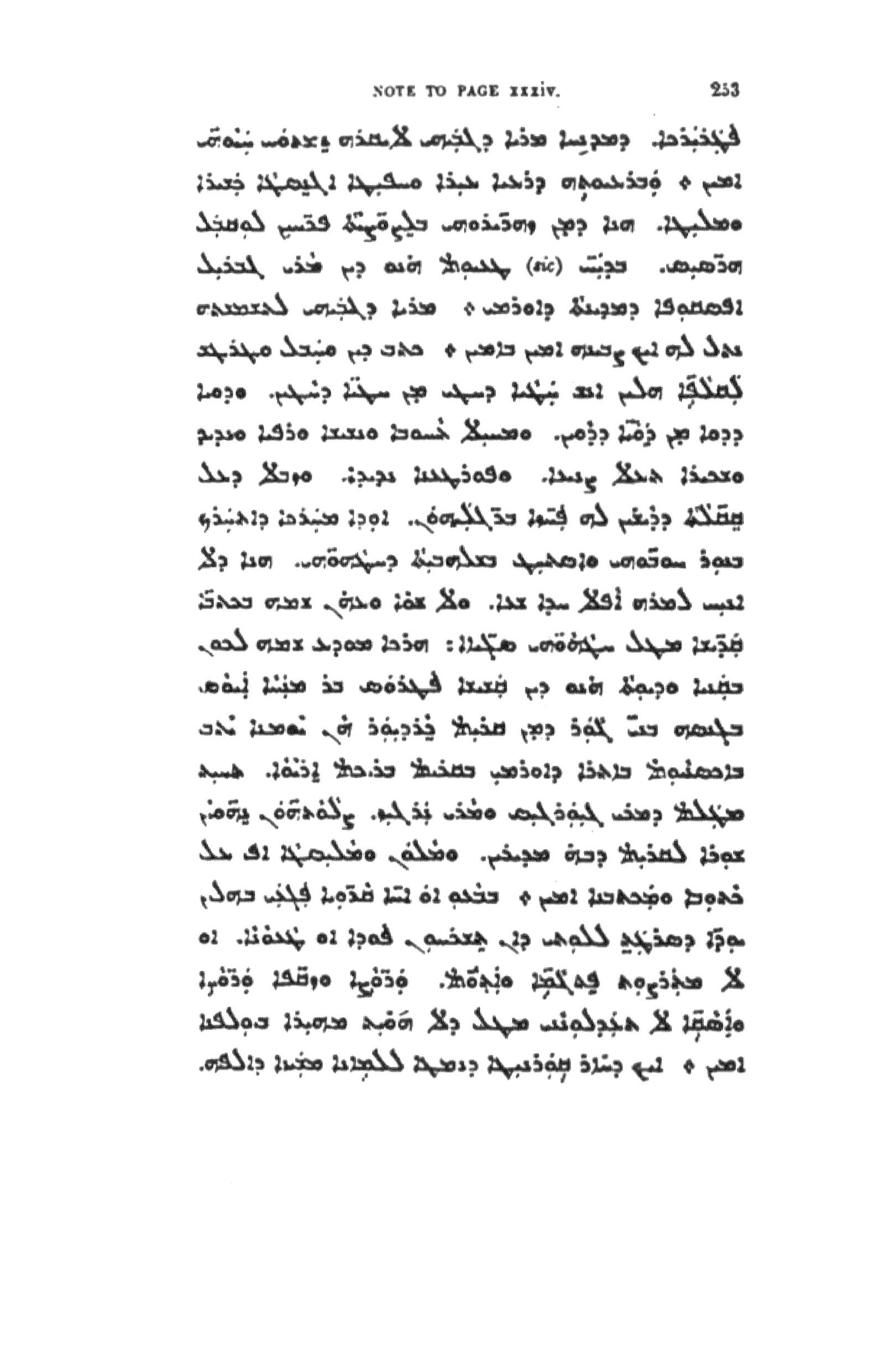

 (sic) 

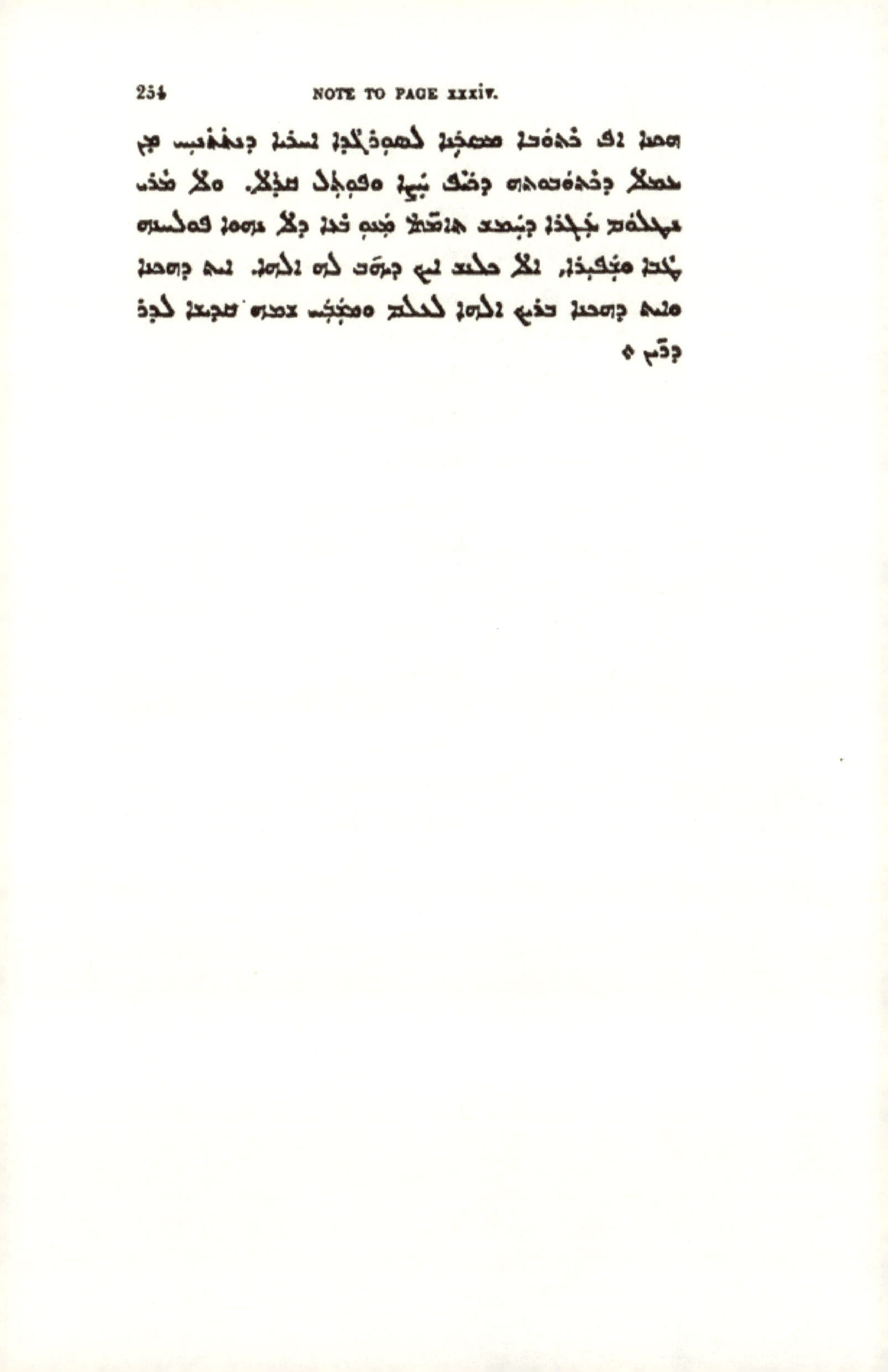

# CORRECTIONS.

Page 1, line 1. Read ܘܚܙ

„ 1, „ 5. „ ܕܘܝܢ

„ 2, „ 4. „ ܝܝ

„ 5, „ 10. „ ܗܠܢܒܚ

„ 8, „ 3. „ ܕܐܚܙ ܩܝܠ.

„ 13, „ 13. „ ܒܘܝܨܩ.

„ 22, note 8. CE omit ܝܚܕܐ.

„ 23, line 16. Read ܕܟܒܝܛܐ.

„ 26, „ 6. „ ܠܝܩܢ

„ 32, „ 2. „ ܠܕܘܚܐ.

„ 34, „ 15. „ ܢܙܘܕ.

„ 35, „ 15. „ ܕܨܚܣܘܙ.

„ 39, „ 2. „ ܕܟܡܛܐ

„ 40, „ 10; 41, line 12; 43, line 5; 45, lines 5, 7. Read ܕܘܚܛܐ

„ 47, „ 4. Read ܣܕܢܝܚܨܨܗ.

„ 50, „ 1. „ 21ܠܕܨܒܝܕܙܘܗܗ.

Page 69, line 9. Read ܗܡܙ.

  „   77,  „   8.  „   ܬܫܟܚ ܗܡ.

  „   79,  „  18. Should we not read ܟܟܘܣܟ ܕܟܠܡܕ ?

  „   87,  „   7. ܠܢܝ seems to be superfluous.

  „ 105, note 2. Read ܗܕܪܕ ܟܠܟܒ.

  „ 130,  „   6. D reads ܦܕܕܒܠ.

  „ 130, line 3. Place ܩ after ܕܣܠܟ.

  „ 137,  „  11. Read ܘܟܕܟܗ.

  „ 158,  „  13.  „   ܟܙܟ.

  „ 162,  „  10.  „   ܕܠܒܕܗ.

  „ 166,  „   3.  „   ܘܫܗܝ.

  „ 189,  „   8.  „   ܕܒܣܝ.

  „ 195,  „   7.  „   ܘܠܗܒܕܩܕ.

  „ 202,  „  17.  „   ܘܠܒܘܠܟܕܝ.

  „ 209,  „  12.  „   ܦܡܠܟܒܐ.

  „ 218,  „  12.  „   ܡܟܟܬܟ.

  „ 224,  „   9.  „   ܒܟܕܘܟ.

  „ 233,  „  12.  „   ܟܕܟܙܠܕ.

ܘ has been printed for ܩ on p. 31. 8, 12; 33. 1; 34. 12; 39. 17; 41. 17; 56. 20 and a few other places.

# ENGLISH INDEX.

R. A.

18

# INDEX

## OF SYRIAC FORMS OF PROPER NAMES.

* As this name occurs on almost every page of the Syriac text I have not thought it necessary to give many references to it.

/